D0675838

Keri Arthur won the *Romantic Times* Career Achievement Award for Urban Fantasy and has been nominated in the Best Contemporary Paranormal category of the *Romantic Times* Reviewers' Choice Awards. She's a dessert and function cook by trade, and lives with her daughter in Melbourne, Australia.

Visit her website at www.keriarthur.com

Darkness Unbound

A DARK ANGELS NOVEL

KERI ARTHUR

us

PIATKUS

First published in the US in 2011 by Dell,
an imprint of The Random House Publishing Group,
a division of Random House Inc., New York
First published in Great Britain as a paperback original in 2011 by Piatkus

A CIP catalogue record for this book
is available from the British Library.

ISBN 978-0-7499-5491-8

Printed in the UK by CPI Group (UK), Croydon, CR0 4YY

Papers used by Piatkus are from well-managed forests
and other responsible sources.

MIX
Paper from
responsible sources
FSC® C104740
www.fsc.org

Piatkus
An imprint of
Little, Brown Book Group
100 Victoria Embankment
London EC4Y 0DY

An Hachette UK Company
www.hachette.co.uk

www.piatkus.co.uk

ACKNOWLEDGMENTS

I'd like to thank everyone at Bantam who helped produce this book—especially my editor, Anne; assistant editor, David Pomerico; all the line and copy editors who make sense of my Aussie English; and finally, the cover artist, Juliana Kolesova.

I'd also like to thank my lovely agent, Miriam, and my mates—Robyn, Mel, Chris, Freya, and Carolyn. And finally, a special thanks to my daughter, Kasey.

You all rock, ladies.

Darkness Unbound

Chapter One

I'VE ALWAYS SEEN THE REAPERS.

Even as a toddler—with little understanding of spirits, death, or the horrors that lie in the shadows—I'd been aware of them. As I'd gotten older and my knowledge of the mystical had strengthened, I'd begun to call them Death, because the people I'd seen them following had always died within a day or so.

In my teenage years, I learned who and what they really were. They called themselves reapers, and they were collectors of souls. They took the essence—the spirit—of the dying and escorted them on to the next part of their journey, be that heaven or hell.

The reapers weren't flesh-and-blood beings, although they could attain that form if they wished. They were creatures of light and shadows—and an energy so fierce, their mere presence burned across my skin like flame.

Which is how I sensed the one now following me. He was keeping his distance, but the heat of him sang through the night, warming my skin and stirring the embers of fear. I swallowed heavily and tried to stay calm. After all, being the daughter of one of Melbourne's most powerful psychics had its benefits—and one of those was a knowledge of my own death.

It would come many years from now, in a stupid car accident.

Of course, it was totally possible that I'd gotten the timing of my death wrong. My visions weren't always as accurate as my mother's, so maybe the death I'd seen in my future was a whole lot closer than I'd presumed.

And it was also a fact that not all deaths actually happened when they were *supposed* to. That's why there were ghosts—they were the souls uncollected by reapers, either because their deaths had come *before* their allotted time, or because they'd refused the reapers' guidance. Either way, the end result was the same. The souls were left stranded between this world and the next.

I shoved my hands into the pockets of my leather jacket and walked a little faster. There was no outrunning the reapers—I knew that—but I still couldn't help the instinctive urge to try.

Around me, the day was only just dawning. Lygon Street gleamed wetly after the night's rain, and the air was fresh and smelled ever so faintly of spring. The heavy bass beat coming from the nearby wolf clubs overran what little traffic noise there was, and laughter rode the breeze—a happy sound that did little to chase the chill from my flesh.

It was a chill caused not by an icy morning, but rather by the ever-growing tide of fear.

Why was the reaper following *me*?

As I crossed over to Pelham Street, my gaze flicked to the nearby shop windows, searching again for the shadow of death.

Reapers came in all shapes and sizes, often taking

the form most likely to be accepted by those they'd come to collect. I'm not sure what it said about me that *my* reaper was shirtless, tattooed, and appeared to be wearing some sort of sword strapped across his back.

A reaper with a weapon? Now, *that* was something I'd never come across before. But maybe he knew I wasn't about to go lightly.

I turned onto Ormond Place and hurried toward the private parking lot my restaurant shared with several other nearby businesses. There was no sound of steps behind me, no scent of another, yet the reaper's presence burned all around me—a heat I could feel on my skin and within my mind.

Sometimes being psychic like my mom *really* sucked.

I wrapped my fingers around my keys and hit the automatic opener. As the old metal gate began to grind and screech its way to one side, I couldn't help looking over my shoulder.

My gaze met the reaper's. His face was chiseled, almost classical in its beauty, and yet possessing a hard edge that spoke of a man who'd won more than his fair share of battles. His eyes were blue—one a blue as vivid and as bright as a sapphire, the other almost a navy, and as dark and stormy as the sea.

Awareness flashed through those vivid, turbulent depths—an awareness that seemed to echo right through me. It was also an awareness that seemed to be accompanied, at least on his part, by surprise.

For several heartbeats neither of us moved, and then he simply disappeared. One second he was there, and the next he wasn't.

I blinked, wondering if it was some sort of trick. Reapers, like the Aedh, could become energy and smoke at will, but—for me, at least—it usually took longer than the blink of an eye to achieve. Of course, I was only half Aedh, so maybe that was the problem.

The reaper didn't reappear, and the heat of his presence no longer burned through the air or shivered through my mind. He'd gone. Which was totally out of character for a reaper, as far as I knew.

I mean, they were collectors of *souls*. It was their duty to hang about until said soul was collected. I'd never known of one to up and disappear the moment he'd been spotted—although given that the ability to actually spot them was a rare one, this probably wasn't an everyday occurrence.

Mom, despite her amazing abilities—abilities that had been sharpened during her creation in a madman's cloning lab—certainly couldn't see them. But then, she couldn't actually see *anything*. The sight she did have came via a psychic link she shared with a creature known as a Fravardin—a guardian spirit that had been gifted to her by a long-dead clone brother.

She was also a full Helki werewolf, not a half-Aedh like me. The Aedh were kin to the reapers, and it was their blood that gave me the ability to see the reapers.

But why did *this* reaper disappear like that? Had he realized he'd been following the wrong soul, or was something weirder going on?

Frowning, I walked across to my bike and climbed on. The leather seat wrapped around my butt like a glove, and I couldn't help smiling. The Ducati wasn't new, but she was sharp and clean and comfortable to ride, and even though the hydrogen engine was getting a little old by today's standards, she still put out a whole lot of power. Maybe not as much as the newer engines, but enough to give a mother gray hair. Or so *my* mom reckoned, anyway.

As the thought of her ran through my mind again, so did the sudden urge to call her. My frown deepening, I dug my phone out of my pocket and said, "Mom."

The voice-recognition software clicked into action and the call went through almost instantly.

"Risa," she said, her luminous blue eyes shining with warmth and amusement. "I was just thinking about you."

"I figured as much. What's up?"

She sighed, and I instantly knew what that meant. My stomach twisted and I closed my eyes, wishing away the words I knew were coming.

But it didn't work. It never worked.

"I have another client who wants your help." She said it softly, without inflection. She knew how much I hated hospitals.

"Mom—"

"It's a little girl, Ris. Otherwise I wouldn't ask you. Not so soon after the last time."

I took a deep breath and blew it out slowly. The last time had been a teenager whose bones had pretty much been pulverized in a car accident. He'd been on life support for weeks, with no sign of brain activity, and the doctors had finally advised his parents to turn off the machine and let him pass over. Naturally enough, his parents had been reluctant, clinging to the belief that he was still there, that there was still hope.

Mom couldn't tell them that. But I could.

Yet it had meant going into the hospital, immersing myself in the dying and the dead and the heat of the reapers. I hated it. It always seemed like I was losing a piece of myself.

But more than that, I hated facing the grief of the parents when—*if*—I had to tell them that their loved ones were long gone.

"What happened to her?"

If it was an accident, if it was a repeat of the teenager and the parents were looking for a miracle, then I could beg off. It wouldn't be easy, but neither was walking into that hospital.

"She went in with a fever, fell into a coma, and hasn't woken up. They have her on life support at the moment."

"Do they know why?" I asked the question almost desperately, torn between wanting to help a little girl caught in the twilight realms between life and death and the serious need *not* to go into that place.

"No. She had the flu and was dehydrated, which is why she was originally admitted. The doctors have run every test imaginable and have come up with nothing." Mom hesitated. "Please, Ris. Her mother is a longtime client."

My mom knew *precisely* which buttons to push. I loved her to death, but god, there were some days I wished I could simply ignore her.

"Which hospital is she in?"

"The Children's."

I blew out a breath. "I'll head there now."

"You can't. Not until eight," Mom said heavily. "They're not allowing anyone but family outside of visiting hours."

Great. Two hours to wait. Two hours to dread what I was being asked to do.

"Okay. But no more for a while after this. Please?"

"Deal." There was no pleasure in her voice. No victory. She might push my buttons to get what she wanted, but she also knew how much these trips took out of me. "Come back home afterward and I'll make you breakfast."

"I can't." I scrubbed my eyes and resisted the sudden impulse to yawn. "I've been working at the restaurant all night and I really need some sleep. Send me the details about her parents and the ward number, and I'll give you a buzz once I've been to see her."

"Good. Are you still up for our lunch on Thursday?"

I smiled. Thursday lunch had been something of a ritual for my entire life. My mom and Aunt Riley—who wasn't really an aunt, but a good friend of Mom's who'd taken me under her wing and basically spoiled me rotten since birth—had been meeting at the same restaurant for over twenty-five years. They had, in fact, recently purchased it to prevent it from being torn down to make way for apartments. Almost nothing got in the way of their ritual—and certainly not a multimillion-dollar investment company.

"I wouldn't miss it for the world."

"Good. See you then. Love you."

I smiled and said, "But not as much as I love you."

The words had become something of a ritual at the end of our phone calls, but I never took them for granted. I'd seen far too many people over the years trying to get in contact with the departed just so they could say the words they'd never said in life.

I hit the END button then shoved the phone back into my pocket. As I did so, it began to chime the song "Witchy Woman"—an indicator that Mom had already sent the requested information via text. Obviously, she'd had it ready to go. I shook my head and didn't bother looking at it. I needed to wash the grime of work away and get some sustenance in my belly before I faced dealing with that little girl in the hospital.

I shoved my helmet on then fired up the bike. The vibration through the metal told me she'd come to life, but there was little noise. Hydrogen bikes ran so silently that when they'd first become commercially viable, state laws had required manufacturers to add a fake-engine-noise device to warn people of their approach. That law was still in existence, but these days it was rarely enforced—mainly because people had a greater worry. Air bikes—or air blades, as they were officially called—were becoming more prevalent, but given the laws that restricted them to low-level airspace, pedestrians had more chance of losing their heads to a blade than being run over by a bike.

I wasn't a huge fan of the air blades, which in my opinion were little more than jet-powered skateboards. I preferred the feel of metal and the vibration of power between my thighs, and the exhilaration and sense of control that riding a bike gave. Blades were *all* about the danger. Riding them was akin to riding a wild horse that could buck you off at any moment.

Besides, I liked the option of being able to put my feet on the ground when I needed to.

I rolled out of the parking lot, and the old metal gates automatically closed behind me. The traffic on Pelham Street was already beginning to build, but I weaved in and out of the cars without effort, and was cruising down Punt Road toward Richmond in very little time.

I slowed as I neared my place. This part of Richmond was mostly pretty little Victorians, but scattered in among them were newer buildings and converted warehouses. My place was one of the latter—a big, square, two-story monstrosity whose bland gray exterior belied the beauty of its internal space. I'd bought and renovated it with two friends— the same two friends who co-owned RYT's (which stood for "rich young things") with me.

As I swung into Lennox Street, the sensor attached to the bike flashed, and the building's roller door began to open. I drove inside, seeing Ilianna's somewhat battered Jeep Wrangler but not Tao's vivid red Ferrari. I hoped it meant he was actually on his way to work rather than in someone's bed, having forgotten once again that it was his turn to work the morning shift. *Not* that the staff couldn't cope without him—mornings tended to be the slowest of the three shifts. Nights were the worst—or rather, the hours between one and five, when wolves hungry after a long night of loving at the clubs sought a different kind of sustenance. RYT's was one of a handful of Lygon Street restaurants licensed to be open twenty-four hours a day, and its gourmet hamburger and pizza menu was proving a huge success. Of course, it helped that Tao was a brilliant chef—when we could actually get him into the kitchen, that was.

I parked my bike next to my more mundane—and little used—Toyota SUV, then killed the engine and kicked the stand into place. I took off my helmet and dropped it onto a nearby hook, then shook out my hair to unscrunch my ponytail as I headed for the stairs. The door at the top was a thick metal alloy that was both fire- and bulletproof. Ilianna had insisted on both it and the accompanying eye-scanning security system. Despite the fact that between boarding school, university, and the restaurant, she'd now lived in the city for a good part of her life, she still didn't feel entirely safe here. I guess there was some truth to the old saying that you could take the mare out of the country, but not the country out of the mare.

I looked into the little scanner. Red light swept across my retina; a second later, the locks tumbled and the door slid silently open. The smell of roses hit almost immediately and my nose wrinkled. I might be half Aedh and half Helki werewolf—with little in the way of true wolf capabilities—but I *did* have a wolf's sensitive olfactory sense, which was why I didn't often wear perfume.

This wasn't perfume, however. It was far too strong.

I shrugged off my backpack and jacket, tossing both onto the nearest leather sofa as I walked across the huge, carpeted expanse that was our living room. The fans—big industrial things that went with the vaulted, metal-framed ceiling—were on full, creating a wind strong enough to tug the hair out of my ponytail. It said a lot about the strength of the rose scent that the fans weren't shifting it.

Gentle humming drifted from the kitchen, accompanied by the clink of metal against glass. I shook my head, knowing that sound—and that song—all too well. Ilianna was brewing potions in the kitchen again.

I stopped in the doorway, crossing my arms as I leaned a shoulder against the frame. Ilianna—a tall, strapping woman with a thick mane of pale hair and dark golden skin—stood near the stove, scooping out the contents of a bubbling pot and pouring it into long, thin, lilac-colored bottles.

"So what is it this time?" I asked, amusement in my voice. "A potion for the lovelorn, or the promise of passion?"

"Neither," she said, her voice low and sexy—the sort of voice that would make her a fortune if she ever decided to go into the phone-sex business. "We're off to the Healesville market this weekend. They love the harmony and peace potions up there, so I need to stock up."

They loved them because the damn things *worked*. I briefly touched the simple leather strap that held the charm currently nestled between my breasts. I'd been sixteen when she'd finally convinced me that I couldn't continue to walk the gray fields unaided. The charm she'd made me had been little more than a small piece of petrified wood, to connect me to the earth, and two small agate and serpentine stones for protection, but it had still saved my life when a spirit had attacked me on the gray fields. I'd been wearing it ever since.

"Is this the last of the lot?"

"Yes." She glanced at me then, her green eyes startling against the dark gold of her skin. "Sorry about the smell. I thought you'd be off to the hospital already."

I smiled. Not only was Ilianna a powerful witch, but she—like my mom, and sometimes like me—was clairvoyant. We'd all met at a school that had catered strictly to the offspring of rich nonhumans, and Ilianna, Tao, and I had been the misfits—the strange kids who could do things we shouldn't have been able to. Tao and I had the additional stigma of being half-breeds—although at least both he and Ilianna were able to take on their alternative forms. Alone we'd been vulnerable, but together we'd been safe. So the three of us had stayed together all through school and into our working lives. I couldn't actually imagine my life without Ilianna or Tao.

"Visiting hours don't start until eight. I thought I'd come home to shower and change first."

She nodded and returned her attention to her bottling. The rose scent sharpened every time she dipped the ladle into the bubbling mixture, perfuming the air with not only its scent but also an odd sense of tranquility.

"A parcel came for you last night," she said. "The delivery guy was a little weird."

My eyebrows rose. "Weird how?"

She glanced briefly at me, nose wrinkling. "He reminded me of a rat. You know, beady-eyed and furtive."

I laughed. "Maybe he *was* a rat." There *were* rat shifters, after all—even if they tended to keep to themselves rather than mix with other shifters and humans, like most nonhumans did.

"Yeah, I know, but he didn't feel like a shifter. He felt like something else. Something more." She shrugged, as if it didn't matter, but the mere fact that she'd mentioned it suggested otherwise.

"Was the security system on?"

She gave me a look, and I knew that was a dumb question. If Ilianna was home alone, then the security system was on.

"I'll check him out." Although I wasn't entirely sure what good it would do. Rat-faced or not, he'd come and gone. "Is the parcel that cookbook I ordered for Tao?"

"I didn't open it, but it looks like it. It's the right shape. I left it on your dresser." She dropped the ladle into the pot, then reached for the bag of corks on the shelf above her head. "I ordered the cake. It should be here for dinner tomorrow." She paused, then looked over her shoulder at me. "Make sure you are."

I frowned, an odd sense of tension tightening my limbs. "It's Tao's birthday. You know I wouldn't miss that."

And yet she was warning me not to. Which meant she'd sensed something on the wind. Something that meant trouble.

The image of the sword-carrying reaper rose like a ghost, and I shivered.

"I know. It's just—" She paused and shrugged.

"Ilianna, just spit it out. What are you seeing?"

"I'm not seeing anything, that's the trouble." She glanced at me again, her expression concerned. "I'm just sensing an unease in the air. Something is brewing, Ris, and it's going to hit us hard if we're not care-ful."

Then we'll be careful, I wanted to say, but I resisted the impulse. It was too flippant, and I'd known Ili-anna too long to treat her warnings *that* lightly.

"Then maybe you need to start working on some more protection charms," I said. "Better to be safe than sorry."

She nodded. "Next on the list. Not that Tao will want anything to do with them."

But only because Tao believed he was more than able to protect himself. And given that he—like his human mother—was a fire-starter of incredible strength, he was probably right. I pushed away from the door frame. "Is Mirri coming over tomorrow night?"

Mirri was Ilianna's lover, a mare she'd met at some creativity and love festival she'd gone to a year ago. She wasn't a witch in the sense that Ilianna was, but she *was* a pagan. And like many mares, she was bi-sexual, whereas Ilianna was desperately trying to keep the fact she was a lesbian under wraps. Espe-cially from her family.

"No. She's working night shifts at the moment."

I nodded. Mirri was a midwife, and was currently working in the Royal Women's natural birthing cen-ter. "Do you know that Tao is hoping to seduce her if you two ever break up?"

Ilianna laughed—a deep, throaty sound that tugged a smile across my lips. "I know. He's hopeless when it comes to women. I seriously doubt if there's been one he *hasn't* lusted after."

"He's not so hopeless when it comes to seduction,

let me tell you." The man, quite literally, was dynamite. In bed and out.

She quirked an eyebrow, her amusement evident. "I thought you'd stopped going down that path."

"I have. Sort of."

"Meaning that when your date book is empty and you're feeling horny, he's more than ready to float your boat?" She shook her head. "How can a woman who looks as hot as you *not* have a man around to cater to her more earthy needs? What is wrong with the men of this city?"

"This is a question I ask myself constantly." I grabbed a mandarin from the fruit basket and began peeling it. I actually wanted something more substantial than fruit, but given the task I'd soon be facing, I wasn't sure my stomach was up to it. "Have you got that meeting with Mike this afternoon?"

Mike was our accountant and a good friend of my mom's, having handled her considerable finances for well over twenty years. He was also, as far as I could tell, her lover—although that was a passion both of them kept well hidden. I was pretty sure the desire for secrecy was coming from Mike rather than Mom, because she never hid anything from me, not even her lovers. But I'd never questioned her about it, simply because it was her life and her decision. That *hadn't* stopped me from asking Aunt Riley, but she was as in the dark about it as I was.

"Yeah, Tao's going to cover the first part of my shift." She glanced at me again. "If you want a shower, you'd better go. The water will shut off in ten minutes."

My eyes widened as I popped a slice of mandarin

into my mouth, and she smiled. "A car's about to hit a hydrant and the water will have to be shut off temporarily. But don't worry, no one gets hurt."

"Damn, it's handy having a witch as a best friend. Thanks."

She nodded and started her humming again, happily corking her pretty bottles of harmony potion. I spun on my heel, eating the rest of the mandarin as I headed for my bathroom. We each had our own and, like all the other rooms in this place, they were oversized, with each one containing a massive spa bath, a double walk-in shower, and a big basin. In mine, the oversized white wall tiles contrasted sharply against the warm black slate under my feet. I stripped off, dumping my clothes into the chute that would suck them down into the auto washer-dryer system we'd installed a few months ago.

Mod cons are us, I thought with a smile as I stepped into the shower and the water automatically came on at just the right temperature. Sometimes, there *were* benefits to being obscenely rich, and one of those was never having to battle with the water temperature *or* do the laundry. I hated washing and ironing—something I'd picked up from my aunt, according to my mom. Of course, she also blamed Riley for my Coca-Cola addiction, but I honestly think I was *born* with that. I liked to joke that if I cut one of my veins open, it'd bleed fizzy brown liquid rather than blood.

Once I'd showered, dried, and brushed my hair, I padded into my bedroom. Again it was huge, but it didn't really look it, thanks to the rich violet on the walls. According to Ilianna, purple was a comforting and a spiritual color—one that generated mystery and tuned intuition. I'd picked it simply because I loved the color. It matched my eyes and contrasted wonderfully with my silver-blond hair.

I walked into the wardrobe and got dressed, donning faded, well-worn jeans and a wool sweater as well as grabbing spares to wear later, knowing I'd have to change once I left the hospital. The smell of the dead and the dying always seemed to cling to my clothing.

I slipped on my boots, then grabbed my watch from the bedside table and glanced at the time. It wasn't much after seven, but if I took the long way around to the Children's, I'd probably get there a little after seven thirty. I might be able to get in to see the little girl then.

Better to try to get it over with than to sit here and fret, anyway.

I spun around and grabbed my backpack, shoving my spare clothes inside. Once I'd pulled on my jacket, I slung the pack across my back, then yelled, "I'm off. I'll see you in a couple of hours."

"No, you won't," she said. "But I'll tell Tao to have a Coke and burger ready for you when you do get home."

Meaning she saw frustration in my future, because burgers were my food of choice when something was *really* pissing me off.

I grabbed my keys and headed back down to my bike. The morning traffic was rising toward its peak, so by taking the long way around the city, I actually arrived at the hospital close to eight. I parked in the nearby underground lot, then checked Mom's text, grabbing the ward number and the parents' names before heading inside.

It hit me in the foyer.

The dead, the dying, and the diseased created a veil of misery and pain that permeated not only the air but the very foundations of the building. It felt like a ton of bricks as it settled across my shoulders, and it was a weight that made my back hunch, my knees buckle, and my breath stutter to a momentary halt.

Not that I really *wanted* to breathe. I didn't want to take that scent—that wash of despair and loss—into myself. And most especially, I didn't want to see the reapers and the tiny souls they were carrying away.

I was gripped by the sudden urge to run, and it was so fierce and strong that my whole body shook. I had to clench my fists against it and force my feet onward. I'd promised Mom I'd do this, and I couldn't go back on my promise. No matter how much I might want to.

I walked into the elevator and punched the floor for intensive care, then watched as the doors closed and the floor numbers slowly rolled by. As they opened onto my floor, a reaper walked by. She had brown eyes and a face you couldn't help but trust, and her wings shone white, tipped with gold.

An angel—the sort depicted throughout religion, not those that inhabited the real world. Walking beside her, her tiny hand held within the angel's, was a child. I briefly closed my eyes against the sting of tears. When I opened them again, the reaper and her soul were gone.

I took the right-hand corridor. A nurse looked up as I approached the desk. "May I help you?"

"I'm here to see Hanna Kingston."

She hesitated, looking me up and down. "Are you family?"

"No, but her parents asked me to come. I'm Risa Jones."

"Oh," she said, then her eyes widened slightly as the name registered. "The daughter of Dia Jones?"

I nodded. People might not know me, but thanks to the fact that many of her clients were celebrities, they sure knew Mom. "Mrs. Kingston is a client. She asked for me specifically."

"I'm sorry, but I'll have to check."

I nodded again, watching as she rose and walked through the door that separated the reception area from the intensive care wards. Down that bright hall, a shrouded gray figure waited. Another reaper. Another soul about to pass.

I closed my eyes again and took a long, slow breath. I could do this.

I could.

The nurse came back with another woman. She was small and dark-haired, her sharp features and brown eyes drawn and tired looking.

"Risa," she said, offering me her hand. "Fay Kingston. I'm so glad you were able to come."

I shook her hand briefly. Her grief seemed to crawl from her flesh, and it made my heart ache. I pulled my hand gently from hers and flexed my fingers. The grief still clung to them, stinging lightly. "There's no guarantee I can help you. She might have already made her decision."

The woman licked her lips and nodded, but the

brightness in her eyes suggested she wasn't ready to believe it. Then again, what mother would?

"We just need to know—" She stopped, tears gathering in her eyes. She took a deep breath, then gave me a bright, false smile. "This way."

I washed my hands, then followed her through the secure door and down the bright hall, the echo of our footsteps like a strong, steady heartbeat. The shrouded reaper didn't look our way—his concentration was on his soul. I glanced into the room as we passed him. It was a boy about eight years old. There were machines and doctors clustered all around him, working frantically. *There's no hope,* I wanted to say. *Let him go in peace.*

But I'd been wrong before. Maybe I'd be wrong again.

Three doorways down from the reaper, Mrs. Kingston swung left into a room and walked across to a dark-haired man sitting near the bed. I stopped in the doorway, barely even registering his presence as my gaze was drawn to the small form on the bed.

She was a dark-haired bundle of bones that seemed lost in the stark whiteness of the hospital room. Machines surrounded her, doing the work of her body, keeping her alive. Her face was drawn, gaunt, and there were dark circles under her closed eyes.

I couldn't feel her. But I couldn't feel the presence of a reaper, either, and that surely had to be a good sign.

"Do you think you can help her?" a deep voice asked.

I jumped, and my gaze flew to the father. Before I could answer, Fay said, "This is my husband, Steven."

I nodded. I didn't need to know his name to understand he was Hanna's father. The utter despair in his eyes was enough. I swallowed heavily and somehow said, "I honestly don't know if I can help her, Mr. Kingston. But I can try."

He nodded, his gaze drifting back to his baby girl. "Then try. Either way, we need to know what to do next."

I took a deep, somewhat shuddering breath, and blinked away the tears stinging my eyes once more.

I could do this. For her sake—for *their* sake—I could do this. If she was in there, if she was trapped between this world and the next, then she needed someone to talk to. Someone who could help her make a decision. That someone had to be me. There *was* no one else.

I forced my feet forward. The closer I got, the more I could feel . . . well, the oddness.

Pain and fear and hunger swirled around her tiny body like a storm, but there was no spark, no glimmer of consciousness—nothing to indicate that life had ever existed within her flesh.

It shouldn't have felt like that. And if death was her destiny, then there would have been a reaper here waiting. But there wasn't, so either the time for her decision had not arrived or she was slated to live.

So why couldn't I *feel* her?

Frowning, I sat down on the edge of the bed and picked up her hand. Her flesh was warm, though why that surprised me I wasn't entirely sure.

I took a deep breath and slowly released it. As I did, I released the awareness of everything and everyone else, concentrating on little Hanna, reaching for her not physically, but psychically. The world around me faded until the only thing existing on this plane was me and her. Warmth throbbed at my neck—Ilianna's magic at work, protecting me as my psyche, my soul, or whatever else people liked to call it pulled away from the constraints of my flesh and stepped gently into the gray fields that were neither life nor death.

Only it felt like I'd stepped into the middle of a battleground.

And it was a battle that had gone very, *very* badly.

Fear and pain became physical things that battered at me with terrible force, tearing at my heart and ripping through my soul. My chest burned, breathing became painful, and all I could feel was fear. My fear, her fear, all twisted into one stinking mess that made my stomach roil and my flesh crawl.

And then there was the screaming. Unvoiced, unheard by anyone but me, it reverberated through the emptiness of her flesh—echoes of agony in the bloody, battered shell that had once held a little girl.

Her soul wasn't here, but it hadn't moved on.

Someone—*something*—had come into the hospital and ripped it from her flesh.

Chapter Two

THE REALIZATION HIT LIKE A HAMMER AND I began to shake.

Someone had stolen her *soul*.

Why would someone do that?

How could someone do that?

Surely it wasn't the reapers. They were charged with the protection and guidance of souls. They couldn't be capable of anything like this.

Could they?

Hands suddenly grabbed my shoulders and wrenched me away. My fingers were torn from the little girl's and it was as if a bucket of ice water had been thrown over my face. The darkness, the fear, the pain all sluiced away, and suddenly I could breathe again.

I took several gulps of air, then, with a shaky hand, swiped at the tears that were on my cheeks—tears I hadn't even felt until then.

When I opened my eyes, I met Fay Kingston's gaze. She *knew*. The knowledge of death was right there in her shadowed, tear-filled eyes and stricken expression.

I can't do this. I can't say the words that will destroy her world.

I clenched my fists again, my short nails digging

deep into my palms. The pain didn't help shore up my courage.

"It's too late, isn't it?" she said softly, her voice steady despite the grief in her expression.

Way, *way* too late. For her soul, for her future lives. I licked my lips and said, "I'm afraid she's already moved on." I hesitated, then added softly, "Her passing was peaceful. She was in no pain, and has moved on to a happier place."

The lie burned my tongue, but what good would it have done to tell the truth? Losing a child was bad enough. They didn't need to know that her last moments on earth had been a battle for the future of *all* her lives, not just this one.

A battle she'd lost.

Fear and horror rose up my throat like bile, and for a moment I couldn't breathe again. I needed to get out of here. I needed to get away from the horror.

I backed away a step, then stopped as Mrs. Kingston grabbed my arm. "Are you sure she's at peace?"

"Yes," I said, without hesitation. Then, when I saw her frown, I added, "Why?"

"Because—" She stopped, her grief making her hiccup. "Because I felt something last night. It was a darkness, a wrongness. It's why I rang your mother. I needed to know that Hanna was all right. That her soul—"

A chill ran through me. Whatever had been here, whatever had stolen that little girl's soul, her mother had been aware of it. I hesitated, fighting the instinctive need to grab her and make her tell me everything she'd felt, everything she'd sensed. If she was psychic—and her words suggested she at least had *some* ability—then she might hold some vital clue as to what this thing was. But doing that might give the game away. Might make her realize I hadn't been entirely truthful about her daughter's passing.

So I simply said, "Everyone who passes over does so with the assistance of a special guide. Sometimes we can sense them in the room—they are a warmth that seems to come out of nowhere, or a wrongness that often feels right."

She was shaking her head even before I'd finished. "This wasn't warm. It was cold. Evil, even." She rubbed her arms, her gaze searching mine. "Are you sure she's safe?"

"Yes, I'm sure." I hated myself for the lie, but I had little choice. Even if the truth came out, there was nothing any of us could do about it, and she didn't deserve to live with that. Neither of them did. "What makes you think it was evil?"

"My skin began to crawl the minute I sensed its presence." She hesitated. "I read from the Bible. That seemed to drive the sensation away."

But not before the battle had been fought and lost. "Maybe it was a ghost. There are enough of them haunting these halls, and some like to torment the souls of the dying."

It was a safe statement, mostly because it was true. Ghosts *did* haunt the hospital halls, and not all of them were happy about their state.

Her gaze searched mine again, then she nodded and gave me a somewhat tremulous smile. "That must be it." She reached out and touched my hand, steeping me in her grief. And in my own guilt. And once again I found myself resisting the impulse to pull away. "Thank you, Risa. Thank you."

"I'm just sorry I couldn't be the bearer of better news," I said honestly.

She lifted her shoulder—a half shrug that somehow seemed so sad. "We knew. We just needed—"

"I know." I squeezed her fingers, then stepped back. "I have to go."

"Thank your mother for me."

"I will." Then I turned and escaped. The shrouded reaper was still waiting in the hall. That surprised me, but also gave me hope. Maybe the matter of the child's passing wasn't as settled as it seemed.

Once free of the ward, I all but ran for the elevator, wanting, *needing,* to get out of this place—and away from its oppressive atmosphere—as quickly as possible.

Once on the ground floor, I headed with speed for the front doors. Outside, it was raining again, but I didn't give a damn. I just stood there on the top step and raised my face to the sky, letting the moisture soak my skin, washing away the scent of death and the feeling of wrongness.

It was only when I began to shiver that I opened my eyes and looked around me.

And saw my reaper.

He was standing at the bottom of the steps, staring up at me. He was still half naked, the rain beading on his warm, suntanned skin and running lightly down his six-pack abs. The leather holding his sword in place seemed to emphasize the width of his shoulders, and the wet denim of his faded jeans clung to his legs, hinting at their lean strength. Stylized black tatts that resembled the left half of a wing swept around his ribs from underneath his arm, the tips brushing across the left side of his neck. He stood like a fighter—lightly, warily, as if he expected trouble at any moment.

And if he was coming for me, he was certainly going to get it.

I continued to stare at him, unspeaking. Unmoving. For all I knew, this sword-carrying reaper might be responsible for the atrocity that had happened upstairs. And if he could do that, then God only knows what else he might be capable of.

"So," he said, after what seemed like an age. "You can see me."

His voice was mellow and rich—the total opposite of what I'd expected. On any other man it might have been sexy, but this *wasn't* a man. He merely held that form.

"I can." I kept my voice soft. I wasn't sure whether others could see him, and I didn't particularly want to be seen talking to thin air. Mom was a media star, and a daughter caught talking to imaginary people would certainly be great fodder for the gossip magazines. "And *I* know it's not my time to die. So if you try to take me, you'll have a goddamn fight on your hands. Sword or not."

Something akin to surprise ran through the bright depths of his oddly colored eyes. "Reapers do not steal souls. If you can see us, you should be aware of that fact."

"The only fact I'm aware of is the one lying in room six-eleven. Someone stole her soul. If not a reaper, then who?"

His gaze rose briefly, then met mine again. "Wait here," he said. "Do not run, because I will find you."

"If I'd wanted to run, I would have done so before now," I said. "But in case you haven't realized, it's raining and cold, and I need to warm up."

He obviously didn't. I could feel the heat of him even from where I stood. It didn't do a whole lot to warm the chill from *my* skin, but maybe that was due more to what I had just experienced.

"If the moisture bothered you so, you would have moved out of it before now."

Had any other man made that statement, I might have suspected he was being sarcastic. But he said it without inflection and without the slightest hint of amusement. Did reapers even feel amusement?

I had no idea. I might have been aware of them for most of my life, and I might be related to them by virtue of my Aedh blood, but that wasn't much help. Even Quinn—the half-Aedh vampire who'd taught me to control my Aedh gifts—hadn't been able to tell me a whole lot about the reapers.

I glanced down the street and spotted a McDonald's. "I'll be in there."

He glanced briefly at the building then back to me, his expression giving very little away. "Good."

And with that, he disappeared again.

I blew out a breath, then spun on my heels and splashed my way toward McDonald's. Once inside, I found the restroom and changed my clothing, dumping my wet things into my pack then dragging on my leather jacket in an effort to warm the chill from my flesh.

Once I'd paid for my burger and Coke, I made my way to a table in the corner, as far away from everyone else as possible.

He appeared seconds later, striding through the restaurant like an animal on the prowl. No one seemed to think it odd to see a half-naked man wearing a sword, yet he was obviously visible, if the man who apologized for getting in his way was any indication.

I picked up my burger and bit into it, but barely even tasted it. My attention was on the reaper. On this man who could destroy me with a single touch of his finger.

His gaze met mine again. Those bright depths burned, and if reapers were capable of anger, then this one was pissed.

He pulled out a chair and sat down opposite me, his movements economical and fluid. The heat of him rolled across the table, and it did warm me even as the psychic part of me shivered away from the power of that fiery caress.

And yet, if he was sitting down opposite me, surely that meant he didn't intend to take me.

Not yet, anyway.

"No reaper did that." The words were said flatly, without inflection, and yet his anger seemed to blaze all around me. "No reaper would ever do that."

"And yet you *are* capable of it."

He studied me for a moment, then nodded, the movement short and sharp. "As are you."

"The Aedh are not as adept at soul stealing as the reapers, and a half-Aedh even less so."

He acknowledged this with another nod, then said, "There are many other things capable of stealing souls in this world, but I've never seen one go after a child so young."

I took another bite of the burger, but the little girl's plight had really killed my taste buds and the burger tasted like ash. I dropped it back into its wrapper, brushed the crumbs off my fingers, then picked up my Coke instead. After taking a sip, I said, "So which of these other things is responsible for her destruction?"

"That I cannot tell you."

I raised an eyebrow—and felt somewhat surreal even as I did it. I mean, I was sitting here in the middle of McDonald's with a *reaper*. The day could *not* get any weirder if it tried. "Cannot, or will not?"

He studied me, and for the first time I noticed the hint of stubble around his chin. It made his face less perfect, and yet somehow more appealing.

I blinked. A reaper appealing? Someone obviously needed to knock some sense back into me.

"Cannot," he said, eventually, "because I do not know who or what is responsible. But we will endeavor to find out."

I paused. "We?"

"The Mijai."

"The what?"

"Mijai," he repeated. "We are the dark angels, the soldiers."

"Hence the sword." And the winged tattoo. "But

why would reapers need soldiers? Especially since reapers don't take unwilling souls?"

"Because, as I said, there are other things that do. The Mijai are responsible for stopping such thefts."

And for a whole lot more, I was betting. "Meaning someone screwed up big time when it came to that little girl." I paused, taking another sip of Coke. "So is that why you were following me? Was I a suspect?"

"How could I suspect you when I didn't even know the soul had been stolen?"

"Then why were you following me?"

He hesitated and leaned back in his chair. If the sword across his back was giving him any discomfort, he certainly wasn't showing it. In fact, it almost seemed an extension of his flesh—a metallic limb, of sorts.

"Where did you get that necklace?" he countered.

I blinked and automatically knew he wasn't talking about Ilianna's charm, but rather the gold filigree droplet I wore around my neck. It was shaped like two wings, and very much represented my heritage.

"It was my father's." Apparently, he'd given it to my mom the night of my conception, and Mom had passed it on to me when I was old enough to start asking questions.

"Indeed," he said, and I had the distinct feeling it was information he already knew. "When?"

"Twenty-eight years ago."

He raised an eyebrow. "That is your age, yes?"

"Why is my age important?"

"It isn't. I just want to talk to your father."

I nearly choked on my Coke. I coughed for several seconds—while he watched dispassionately—then somehow managed to say, "Well, I wish you luck with that."

"So you're saying you've had no contact with him recently?"

I swallowed a hiccup, then said, "I've had no contact with my father my entire *life*. He might have provided the seed that formed me, but that was his entire input."

"And yet he is apparently here in Melbourne."

"Well, if you know that, then you know a hell of a lot more about him than *I* do."

I didn't even know what he looked like, other than the fact that he had violet eyes and silvery blond hair, just like me. Of course, Mom's hair was also a silvery blond, but neither that nor the blue of her eyes was natural. As a Helki werewolf, she could subtly alter her appearance, and the silver and blue not only suited her psychic business better, but also enabled her to use her true form when she didn't want to be noticed.

Admittedly, she *had* tried to answer my questions about my dad, but the truth was, I was the result of a one-night stand, and Mom's entire time with him had totaled little more than six hours. Hardly long enough to form any lasting impressions.

I studied the reaper for a moment, wondering if he was telling the truth, then wondering what he'd have to gain by lying, and added, "Why do you think my father would even bother contacting me after all these years?"

"He has come to Melbourne for a reason. We believe you might be that reason." He shrugged—a small, economical movement.

"On the other hand, he might just have come home to die." After all, the Aedh only bred when they sensed their death was near, and while I was just over twenty-eight years old, that was merely a heartbeat in Aedh years.

"That is also possible."

I finished the last of my Coke, then pushed the empty cup away and crossed my arms on the table—an action that brought me closer to the heat of him. It trembled across my skin in waves, warm and disturbing. But oddly, he had no scent. He might wear the flesh of a man, but he didn't smell like one.

He didn't smell like anything, really. Not even the rain that still beaded his skin.

"Meaning there are others like you out there searching for him?"

He hesitated, then nodded—another brief but oddly lyrical movement.

"But why? What has he done to incite such interest from the reapers?"

"It's not what he has done, but what he *might* do."

Frustration rolled through me, but there wasn't much point in venting it. It wasn't exactly wise to get annoyed at someone who could steal your life away between one heartbeat and the next. And though it was obvious he wanted to use me to get to my father, that wasn't a comforting thought. Not when I knew so little about the reapers as a society or as individuals.

"So what is he up to that's causing you so much consternation?"

He crossed his arms, and I had to resist the urge to let my gaze linger over the lean, muscular goodness such an action revealed.

Damn it, I either needed to get to Franklin's—a discreet, upmarket wolf club—or break my vow to stop using Tao. *This* was getting ridiculous.

"To answer that," he said, after considering me for entirely too long, "I really need to know just how much you know about us."

I replied, "As much as any half-Aedh knows."

"Which is not helpful, as I am not aware of what a half-Aedh might know."

I swear his lips twitched as he said it—almost as if he was restraining a smile. I wondered again if reapers *were* capable of amusement, or whether it was simply a function of hormones that—for some damn indefinable reason—seemed to find him attractive.

But *that* could have been deliberate on his part. If he knew I was half Aedh, then he more than likely knew I was also half wolf, and the form he'd adopted could be an attempt to appeal to my more sensual nature. After all, the full moon was only a couple of days away, and for most werewolves this was the time of the moon heat.

But I wasn't a normal werewolf. My Aedh DNA had apparently curtailed much of my wolf heritage, and while I had werewolf sexual sensibilities and drive, the moon had no pull on me and didn't force a shape change during her full bloom. Hell, I couldn't take wolf shape *anytime,* no matter how hard I tried. And I'd certainly tried more than once.

And yet, weirdly enough, I *had* inherited Mom's

Helki skill for face-shifting. I didn't use it often, but I could, if I wanted to—and with a fair degree of effort—change basic things like hair, eyes, and facial structure. And like my mom, I could hold my altered shape for fairly long periods.

Which was handy for fancy-dress occasions, but not much else.

"Well," I said, "*this* half-Aedh knows that reapers are soul guides. You take them to heaven or hell, depending on what their allotted fate is."

"We do not call it heaven or hell. Those are human terms."

"Then what do you call them?"

"The light or dark path."

"Which is basically the same thing."

He merely shrugged, but something in the way he studied me suggested I was an idiot for believing that.

Irritating, to say the least.

"And is that the sum of your knowledge?" he asked.

"I know there are gates between this world and the next—one for your so-called dark path, and one for the light. I know that Aedh priests used to guard them, but the priests no longer exist." I eyed him for a moment. "Have the Mijai taken over that role?"

He hesitated. "Not really. We hunt what breaks through them, but we have no power over the gates themselves."

"But you're reapers," I said. "Reapers escort the souls from this world through the gray fields to the next. How can you *not* have power over the gates?"

"As you said, the Aedh were the gatekeepers. We are merely the guides."

"So how do the guides get the souls through the gates if they have no power to open them?"

Again his lips twitched. Part of me wished he'd smile for real. The other part was damn glad he didn't. This man—this being—was dangerous enough.

"The gates are attuned to souls and automatically open when one approaches. But the term *gates* is really a misnomer. Each gate is more a series of energy portals, not an actual structure."

"As you are not actual flesh?"

"I am flesh as of this moment. I am as real as you."

"So why isn't everyone in this place getting weirded out by the sword-carrying half-naked guy?"

"Because they do not see my true form. They see what they expect to see—whatever that might be."

"But this isn't your true form, is it? Reapers are energy beings, just as the Aedh are."

"It might be more accurate to call us shifters. We are all born with both an energy and a flesh form, whether Aedh or reaper. The reapers can take on other forms, however, to suit what their assigned souls expect. The Aedh cannot."

I nodded. The Aedh were also winged when they found flesh, which is why many people mistook them for angels. Thankfully, the wings were something we half-breeds missed out on. "As interesting as all this is, it's not explaining why you're so keen on tracking down my father."

He uncrossed his arms and leaned forward, resting his forearms comfortably on the table's edge. The sheer force of the heat and energy radiating off him had pinpricks of power crawling across my skin—a sensation that was uncomfortable but not exactly unpleasant.

And yet it scared the hell out of me. Uncle Quinn was the most powerful being I'd ever met, but I might as well compare a bonfire to the sun.

"Your father," he said slowly, "is on a very dangerous mission."

"Well, that certainly explains everything." Not.

He didn't seem to get the sarcasm, and continued in the same flat tone, "The portals, as I said, are set to open automatically for an approaching soul, but they can be temporarily opened via other means. Magic originating from this world has been the chief offender, but if enough power is gathered from the dark path, that gate can be opened by those on the other side."

I frowned. "How? I mean, hell is hell. You know, a place filled with suffering, pain, and all that. How would they even have time to gather such power?"

"As I've already said, *hell* is a human term and not truly accurate. The dark path is more a place where the sins of a soul's lifetime must be atoned for before he or she can move on, and that does not always involve suffering."

But sometimes did, obviously. "So all the souls who walk the dark path are redeemable?"

"Yes." He hesitated. "Those who are not are killed. That is another reason for the existence of the Mijai."

A chill crawled down my spine. It was a stark reminder that I was sitting in front of a man who could end not only *this* life, but every one of my lives, for all eternity. I rubbed my arms and said, "Once the souls are redeemed, are they reborn?" When he nodded, I added, "How?"

"There is only one way in and out of the dark path, and that is back through the portals."

"Meaning the gates are two-way?"

"Yes. Once souls are allowed back through the portal, we escort them across the fields to the light path."

"Are they instantly reborn there?"

"Sometimes. Sometimes not." He shrugged. "It depends on demand and how many souls are already waiting."

So what did the souls do if they weren't reborn instantly? Float around playing harps? The thought made me smile, even though I recognized the foolishness of it. "So how does this relate to my father?"

"Your father is a former priest. As such, he has some power over the gates and their locks."

My frown deepened. "I'm still not seeing the problem here."

"Your father," he said, slowly and somewhat heavily, "is thought to be working on a device to permanently close the gates to all things that come through."

Confusion swirled through me. "But that would be a good thing, wouldn't it? It would save you the hassle of hunting down the bad things that break through, at the very least."

He was giving me that look again—the one that suggested I was an idiot.

"The problem with shutting the gates permanently is the fact that it would not only stop things from breaking through, but also prevent things from *leav-*

ing." He paused, his oddly colored eyes searching mine and leaving a strange sensation of dread stirring in the pit of my stomach. "Which means no soul could move on. And *that* would be a disaster that could destroy us all."

Chapter Three

I STARED AT HIM FOR SEVERAL MINUTES, THE implications running through my mind.

The dead permanently caught in this world? A flood of ghosts who were both angry and confused, never able to move on and not understanding why? *That* would certainly be hell on earth for those of us able to see and feel them.

But a disaster that could destroy us all? Wasn't that overstating it a little?

"Your expression suggests you don't understand the true danger," he said. "But think on it. If souls cannot move on, they cannot be reborn into new flesh. Where would that leave the human—and nonhuman—races?"

"Up shit creek without a paddle, if your expression is anything to go by," I said. "But by saying that, you're suggesting no new souls are ever created. And yet the population of the world continues to grow, so that can't be true."

He nodded gravely and entwined his fingers, oddly reminding me of a professor I'd had—both as a teacher and as a lover—in college. They'd both had the same sort of grave, all-knowing air.

Although it has to be said that the professor had *never* been as hot as this reaper, in clothes or out.

"New lives—and new souls—are created daily, true, but that doesn't change the fact that the majority of these new beings contain old souls."

"Is there a finite number of new souls?" I asked curiously. "And is there a limit to the number of people the earth can carry? I can't imagine it's the master plan of whoever is in charge to keep adding souls until our world collapses under the weight of us all."

He smiled. Once again it was merely a quirk of the lips, but my pulse nevertheless tripped happily at the sight.

"There are always limits," he said, his deep voice low, creating nearly as much havoc as his almost-smile. "That is why there have been—and always will be—natural disasters. Once a limit has been reached, the clock is reset."

It was a hard statement to believe and yet, if you were inclined to believe in a higher power looking over us all, then it wasn't such a big leap.

"I still can't see how the gates shutting would be such a disaster. I mean, people would still be born."

"Yes, but if no souls could move on and be reborn, then the majority of the newborns would be little more than mindless flesh."

I stared at him for a moment, for the first time actually taking in the implication of his words. And I sure as hell didn't want to believe them. Surely if there *was* someone in charge upstairs, they wouldn't be that cruel. "Zombies?" I said incredulously. "You're saying they'd be *zombies*?"

He hesitated. "No. Zombies are flesh brought back

to life by the deadly desires of others. A body born without a soul is little more than a slab of meat. It is incapable of thought, emotion, or feeling. It has no needs or desires. It hasn't even got the will to live."

Vegetables, not zombies, something within whispered. I shuddered, and tried not to imagine the hundreds of babies lying in ICUs all over the world, their tiny bodies being kept alive by machines but never becoming capable of knowing love or life.

It made me want to throw up.

But bad situation or not, it really didn't make his following me any easier to swallow.

"Look, I hope like hell you track down my father and stop him, but I really think you're tackling it from the wrong angle. He's *never* had anything to do with me, so why on earth would he want to do so now, when he's about to embark on a course of action that could endanger all that I hold dear?"

He shrugged again, but I had a suspicion that the nonchalance was faked and he wasn't telling me all he knew. And that his reasons for following me were far more complicated than what he was saying. Though I wasn't entirely sure why I felt this. It wasn't as if his countenance or body language had changed in any way.

"As I said earlier, him contacting you is only a possibility, but one we must explore."

"So, you've explored it, and I've denied it. What happens next?"

He raised an eyebrow—another ever-so-elegant gesture. "Nothing. I will continue to watch you until we are sure there is no likelihood of him contacting you."

"I'm not really keen on the idea of a reaper shadowing me day and night."

Especially if he remained in *this* form. I might not have a werewolf's troublesome, moon-controlled hormones, but I was still female, and a good-looking male could affect me as easily as the next woman. Even if that good-looking male wasn't exactly flesh and blood.

"It is not by desire that I do this, trust me."

The edge in his voice had curiosity stirring again. "Then don't. It's not like I'm going to tell anyone."

"*That* is not the point or the problem. The duty has been assigned to me, and I must comply."

"Why?"

He looked at me like I was being a simpleton. "Because it is my duty."

"And duty is everything?"

"Without it, chaos reigns. Which is why we must stop your father. He threatens the true order of things."

Whose true order? I wanted to ask, but kept the question to myself. I very much suspected that it wasn't one he'd be willing to address.

Besides, did I really want to know the answer to a question like that?

"But what about the little girl? If you're following me about, how can you also track down whoever stole her soul?"

"You must sleep. I will use that time to hunt. And others will hunt when I'm unable to."

"And if you find the thing responsible?"

"I will kill it, of course."

"So sending it back through the gates is not an option?"

"For the Mijai, no. As I said, we are not gatekeepers. Whatever is doing this either broke through or was brought through the portals to get here. Besides, if it was powerful enough to break through one time, what makes you think it will not do so again?"

"The fact that you lot will be waiting?"

He didn't immediately answer, studying me for several seconds before asking, "Why would you worry about the fate of whatever stole that child's soul?"

"I'm not. You can chop it into little bits and serve it to the nearest rat for all I care. I just wasn't sure if that was your intention or not."

"As I said, the Mijai are not soul guides. We are hunters. Killers."

And I had one intending to follow me everywhere. Joy.

"So how are you going to stop this thing from killing again?"

He shrugged. "We may not. There were few clues left in the young girl's room and no trace to follow."

"Trace?"

He hesitated. "Dark energy has a certain resonance. Often it leaves a trace—a scent, if you will—that we can use to track the perpetrators down. But whatever is behind this theft left no such trace."

Fay Kingston's comments echoed briefly through my mind and I said, "There may not be any trace you can follow now, but the thing *did* have a presence. The mother mentioned it."

His gaze seemed to sharpen. "What did she say?"

"She felt something cold and evil in the room that

made her skin crawl." I hesitated. "She said that reading from the Bible made it flee, but personally I doubt that. The thing remained long enough to steal Hanna's soul."

Something akin to disappointment crossed his features, though the expression was so fleeting I might well have been imagining it. "The Bible would only affect those beings who were religious during their time here, and her description gives us no real clue to follow. Could you not question her further?"

I shook my head. "I didn't tell her Hanna's soul had been stolen. I told her she'd moved on peacefully."

That seemed to surprise him, though again, his expression didn't change. It was something I felt rather than saw. "Why would you lie?"

"Because the truth would only cause her more pain. Losing a child is enough to cope with."

"But it is the truth. That is always the correct choice, whether painful or not."

I smiled at the simplicity of such a statement. "It would be nice if things were that straightforward, but in this world, they rarely are."

"Hence the need for the dark path."

"So all of us liars go to hell?"

Again the ghost of a smile touched his lips. "To repeat your own words, it would be nice if things were that straightforward."

"It's just as well that they're not. Otherwise, hell would be one crowded place."

"The way this world of yours works, it certainly would." He pushed back his chair and rose, drawing my gaze up his long, magnificent length. "If by chance you are contacted by your father when I'm not on watch, will you contact me?"

"And how am I supposed to do that? I'm presuming reapers don't carry cell phones around."

"That would hardly be practical when we are not often of this world or flesh."

A smile touched my lips. Again he didn't seem to get the sarcasm, but I guess a being that was more energy than flesh—and who spent most of his time walking the twilight realm—didn't have much call or experience with emotion of *any* kind.

"Then how am I supposed to contact you?"

"Simply call my name. I have been tuned to your Chi, and will hear your summons."

So not only did I have a reaper following me about, but he'd been tuned to my Chi. Or life energy, as Ilianna preferred to call it. This day was going from bad to worse.

"And your name is . . . ?"

"Azriel."

I snorted softly. "Even *I* know that Azriel is the generic name all reapers go by."

"It may be generic, but when you say it, you will be summoning me."

"Because you've been tuned to me?"

"Yes."

Great. *Not.* "Do you have another name?"

He hesitated. "Yes, but that is private. No guide or Mijai will ever tell you his true name."

"Why?"

"Because names are things of power, and to give one freely would be placing yourself in another's control."

"So why even give yourselves a true name?"

"Having a family in which all are called Azriel would get a little confusing."

Meaning reapers had family units? Interesting, given that the Aedh *didn't*. "So where are you off to now, Azriel, if you've been assigned to follow me?"

"I will retreat to a viewing distance. It would be better for us both."

It would be better for us both if he wasn't following me at *all,* but that didn't seem to be an option right now. "So you're just going to sit back and watch? You're not going to do anything else?"

"I am not here to interfere with your life or anything that happens to you," he said softly. "I merely wait to see if your father will contact you."

For how long? I wondered, but didn't bother voicing the question simply because I doubted he would answer. "I'll talk to you later, then."

"Or not," he said, and disappeared.

No one in the restaurant seemed to notice or care. He may have been visible to everyone, but there was obviously some sort of magic at work, because it was simply impossible for anyone to disappear in the middle of a crowded room like that and *not* have anyone notice.

I rose and headed out of the restaurant. It was still raining, so I flicked the collar of my jacket up and ran for the underground parking garage. After finding the ticket machine and paying, I headed for the stairs and walked down to sublevel two, my footsteps echoing sharply in the silence.

I'd parked my bike in the slots near the elevators, which were on the opposite side of the garage from the stairs. I waited for a car to cruise past, then stepped out, but as I walked through the half shadows, the awareness that I was not alone hit. Which, given this was a multistory underground parking lot, wasn't exactly surprising. But the sense of wrongness that came with the realization *was*.

I glanced around. Cars were parked in silent rows and there was no one in immediate sight, walking either toward or away from them. The air was thick with the scents of dirt, oil, and exhaust fumes—aromas that seemed to be leaching from the concrete itself. There was nothing that suggested anything or anyone was near.

Yet someone *was*. The sensation of wrongness was getting stronger, crawling like flies across the back of my neck.

I'd lived with clairvoyance, warnings, and portents all my life. I wasn't about to start ignoring them now.

I slowed my steps a little and flared my nostrils, drawing in more of the air and sorting through the flavors.

And I found him.

Or rather, *them*—because there wasn't just one person nearby, but four. One ahead, one to the left, one to the right, and one attempting to sneak up behind me. Effectively, they had me boxed in, and you didn't do that unless you wanted to ensure your prey couldn't escape.

I flexed my fingers and wondered how I should play it. I could fight—years of sparring with Riley and Quinn had seen to that—but they'd also impressed upon me the need *not* to fight unless it was absolutely necessary.

I wasn't sure yet that it was necessary. It was possible my stalkers intended nothing more than to talk to me. They might even be intending to follow me. Hell, I already had a reaper playing tag, so why not four strange-smelling men?

But if these men had intended to do nothing more than talk, they wouldn't have bothered boxing me in so completely.

They were here to attack. Nothing more, nothing less.

I reached into my pocket as I neared the bike and wrapped shaking fingers around my keys. Doubt skittered through me, but these men left me with little in the way of options.

I couldn't see the man up ahead, but his scent suggested he was standing behind the cars to the left of the bike. The two to either side hadn't moved in closer, but the one behind *had*—although he still wasn't close enough to react to.

Obviously, though, none of them had any idea I was part wolf; otherwise they would have used a scent-erasing soap. Or, at the very least, eaten less garlic last night.

The back of my neck continued to crawl with the nearness of the man behind me. I resisted the growing need to turn around, and flipped my keys up between my fingers so that the sharper ends stuck out like little metal prongs. Just about anything could become a dangerous weapon if you had the know-how—and I certainly did. Then I shrugged off my backpack, holding it in my free hand as I walked on. The air was thick with the scent of garlic and the musk of the man behind me. He was human, not wolf. Not shifter.

I had no idea what the others were. I might be able to smell their body odor, but there was precious little else coming through. And *that* was weird. If I could smell them, I should have been able to tell what the hell they were.

Maybe the garlic was deliberate. Maybe they were using it the same way someone might use scent-erasing soap. And if that *was* the case, it was working.

Although if this was a chance robbery attempt, why would they reek of garlic? Even humans had noses good enough to catch a whiff.

And yet, despite my certainty otherwise, what else could it realistically be? Why would these men be sitting here waiting to ambush me when they couldn't have even guessed that I'd be here?

No one had followed me from home, I was pretty sure of that. Then again, I might not have noticed given I had no reason to look.

The garlic stink suddenly sharpened and the air stirred with movement. It was warning enough. I spun on my heel, letting the backpack fly, hoping to distract my attacker as I lashed out with a booted foot. He dodged the pack but saw the second blow too late, and my foot took him high in the chest. He staggered backward, arms flailing to keep his balance.

As the other three erupted from their hiding spots, I lunged forward, my right fist swinging upward, hitting the human as hard as I could under the chin. I might be only half werewolf, but that still gave me a whole lot of strength. The keys dug deep into his neck even as the force of the blow threw him off his feet.

Blood gushed, but I was already spinning around to meet the next man, and heard rather than saw the first hit the concrete.

The man who'd been hiding behind the car nearest my bike was in the air—literally in the air—his shape shifting, pulsating, becoming something less than human but not actually cat: a panther who retained human characteristics and height. He was grotesque—like something you saw in a bad horror movie—but that didn't make him any less dangerous.

I dropped under his leap, but as his body flew over mine he twisted, his arm sweeping down, his thick, cat-like claws slashing through the leather of my jacket and down into flesh. Blood gushed—and pain, unlike anything I'd ever felt before, rolled up my arm and through the rest of me in a heated wave.

All I wanted to do was curl up into a little ball and cry, but girlie reactions like *that* really weren't an option.

The other two were almost on me—and they were also changing, becoming something less than human but not quite animal.

I couldn't stay here.

I might be able to fight, but it was four against one and three of those four *weren't* human. Those were odds that would give Aunt Riley reason to pause, and *she'd* once been a guardian.

Fuck, where was Azriel when I needed him most? Why the hell wasn't he stepping in to help? Even as the thought crossed my mind, I swiped it aside. He'd warned me he wouldn't interfere, and I had no doubt he was a man—being—of his word.

But running wasn't really an option, either. I might

be part werewolf, but I couldn't attain that shape and I didn't have a wolf's speed. And two human feet wouldn't outrun these things, whatever they were. Which meant there was only one thing I could do if I wanted to escape.

Become Aedh.

It wasn't something I did very often—but then, it wasn't very often I found myself in a situation like this, either.

I reached into my pocket and wrapped my fingers around my phone and keys, then closed my eyes and reached into that place inside me that wasn't wolf— that was something far more—calling to the powers that were my Aedh heritage. Maybe it was the fear of the situation, because it surged to life immediately, flaring through me—a blaze of heat and energy that numbed pain and dulled sensation as it invaded every muscle, every cell, breaking them down and tearing them apart, until my flesh no longer existed and I became one with the air. Until I held no substance, no form, and could not be seen or heard or felt by anyone or anything.

Except, perhaps, by another Aedh, but none of these men belonged to that race.

I drifted toward the concrete ceiling, out of their way and yet close enough to hear everything they said.

The two who'd been coming in from either side skidded to a halt, and confusion crossed their half-animal features. One was lion-like, the other some sort of dog, and both of them had bodies that were deformed but powerful.

"What the fuck?" the lion one said, his voice a

growl and the words barely understandable. "Where's she gone?"

The dog-like one lifted his nose and sniffed the air. "Can't smell her," he said, his voice no clearer than the other man's. "She's gone."

The man whose neck I'd stabbed walked up at that point, wiping away the blood with one hand. "Well, she obviously has *some* form of shifting ability, despite what we were told."

"Doesn't matter either way," the panther-like one said. "She's gone, and the boss is going to be pissed."

The human glanced at him disdainfully. "Only if some meathead decides to tell him. She has to come back for the bike eventually. All we have to do is wait."

"She'll come back with help."

The human glanced at the lion. "Obviously, but it won't matter. We'll just follow her again and wait for another opportunity. And this time, it'll be less caution and more speed."

"A gun might be useful," the panther commented.

"We need to question her about her father first, remember?"

The panther gave him a disdainful look, then lowered his head, sniffing the droplets of blood briefly before his tongue flicked out. He licked it.

Eeeewwww.

"Graham, Mario, keep an eye on the exits in case she comes through before we can grab our car." He glanced down at the cat. "Frankie, you lick that one more time and I'll put a boot in your fucking face. Go get the car."

The cat snarled in reply, but otherwise did what he

was told, his skin rippling as he moved until what reached the stairs was human once more—albeit a human with somewhat torn and shredded clothing. The other two did the same as they walked up the ramp toward the exit level.

The human studied my bike long enough to make me uneasy, then spun on his heel and walked after the panther. I followed, an unseen force of energy that crept along the roofline, flinching at the dust that rained through the pieces of me and hoping like hell they didn't stick to the particles. Re-forming when grimy was never a pleasant experience, and it usually took days for the muck to work its way out of my system.

The human ran up the stairs and out into the street. Frankie—the cat—was half a block away, climbing into a black Toyota SUV. It wasn't exactly a nondescript car, but I guess that wouldn't have mattered, because under normal circumstances I wouldn't have paid it much attention. And at least now that I knew who was driving it, it made an easier target to spot.

I glanced down at the plate, rolling the numbers through my mind to memorize them, then headed for the rear exit. The other two men were standing near an old gray Ute, one casually smoking, the other drinking a can of Pepsi. Like they had all the time in the world and hadn't just tried to attack me.

I noted their plate number, then made my way back up to my bike. After making sure no one was on the level, I reached for the Aedh again, re-forming and re-building my body particle by particle, until I was once more flesh and blood.

I released my grip on my phone and keys, and

dropped to the concrete on my hands and knees, my body shaking and my breath wheezing past my throat. For several seconds it was all I could do to stay upright, and if those men had chosen that moment to come back, I would have been theirs.

Becoming Aedh had its price for those of us who weren't full blood—and, for me, it was a complete inability to do anything other than breathe for several minutes after re-formation.

When the debilitation finally started to ease, I cautiously rocked back on my heels. And that was when the headache hit like a knife through my brain and I closed my eyes, fighting not to cry out. I had no idea just how keen my attackers' hearing was, and the last thing I wanted to do was give them warning I was back.

At least my arm had stopped bleeding, even if the wound was still raw and it hurt like hell.

Several more minutes passed, and the stabbing pain settled to a more durable ache behind my left eye. I took a deep, shuddering breath, then climbed carefully to my feet. The pain remained, constant yet bearable.

The other bad thing about becoming Aedh was its effect on my clothes. They disintegrated just fine, but re-forming them was trickier, as the magic didn't always delineate bits of me from other particles. And like the dirt that clung to my atoms when in Aedh form, I often ended up with a dust-like sheen covering my skin rather than fully formed pieces of clothing.

This time, the leather jacket had come back almost complete—aside from the hole under my right elbow and the slashes caused by the cat's claws—but the dust from the missing elbow clung like second skin to my arm, and the sweater underneath all but fell around me in shredded bits. My jeans were also a mess, peppered with holes. My boots, like my leather jacket, had basically come through unscathed, although the Kevlar lining showed through in patches. Once I hit any sort of speed on my bike, I was going to end up half naked. And wouldn't *that* thrill the passing motorists. I guess it was just as well I had a change of clothes with me.

Of course, before I went anywhere I needed to check my bike. Those men were intent on following me, and I was pretty damn sure they would have ensured they had a means of tracking me if they lost sight.

There had to be a bug on my bike. *Had* to be.

And the thought that those bastards had dared to put their grubby little hands on her had anger rolling though me.

A pretty useless reaction, really, but I still couldn't help it. I might be rich enough to buy anything I liked, but this bike had been earned through sheer hard work. She was my present to myself the first year our restaurant made a profit.

I retrieved my backpack, then walked back to my bike and double-checked the area before I stripped off and changed into the clothes I'd worn into the hospital. They were cold and damp, and smelled of antiseptic and death, but I guess they were better than rags.

I retrieved my keys and phone from the remnants of my jeans, then tossed them away. I shoved my phone into the pack and my keys went into my jacket pocket. Metal and plastic weren't affected by the shift into—or back out of—particle form, but unless they were touching skin, they wouldn't actually change. Which was why I'd wrapped my hand around them before I shifted. I knew from experience that there was nothing worse than metal and plastic bits stuck in the middle of your particle form.

Maybe they needed to find a way to make bras and panties out of soft, breathable plastic. At least then when I came back out of an Aedh shift, I'd be wearing lingerie. Right now, there were just annoying bits caught in unmentionable places.

I flicked off the alarm, then bent and studied the bike. There was nothing out of place—nothing that jumped out and screamed *Bug*. But I knew enough from hanging around Riley and her brother Rhoan to realize that bugs and trackers could be wafer-thin and virtually invisible.

And the only way to find them was to feel them.

I knelt and carefully ran my hands over the bike's sleek silver frame. I found one on the front suspension, and another on the inside of the left turn signal. Both were little bigger than a toenail, and thinner than a piece of hair. If I hadn't known every inch of the bike as well as I did, they would have been easy to miss.

I carefully peeled them both off, then jerked around—my heart going a million miles a minute—as the elevator dinged and the doors swept open. An elderly couple stepped out and headed left, not even glancing my way.

I looked at the sliver-fine pieces of plastic in my hand, then smiled and rose, quietly following the old couple. They stopped at a small brown Toyota about halfway down the ramp, the woman glancing at me as I strolled past. Her gaze swept me and her face pinched with disapproval. Clearly, she thought I was up to no good—and in that, she was right. I gave her a smile as I continued on, my hand brushing against the rear of the car and sticking the two trackers to the paintwork. Then I loped down to the next level and took the stairs back up to my bike. The knife inside my head swung back into action and I blinked away tears as I shoved on my helmet, then jumped on my bike and gunned the engine to life.

I was behind the Toyota in an instant, following it up the ramps and out the gate. The two shifters leaning against the gray Ute didn't react when they saw me—although one touched his ear and began speaking. If they had in-ear communication units installed, then someone with money was behind all this. Those damn things cost a fortune.

I kept behind the Toyota, not wanting the men to realize that the tracker wasn't on my bike. Only when I was absolutely sure neither car was in sight did I veer off and get the hell out of there.

But I didn't head home.

I needed to talk to someone about what might be going on—someone who knew all about trackers, weird shifters, and would-be mugging attempts. Someone who also had a steady supply of chocolate and Coke on hand for drop-ins like myself.

My aunt Riley, former guardian and one of the most dangerous, kick-ass women I knew.

If she couldn't help me sort out this big pile of shit I'd apparently landed in, no one could.

*   *   *

Riley and Quinn shared a big old warehouse in Abbotsford near the banks of the Yarra River with her brother Rhoan and his lover, Liander. Three of their five children still lived with them, but the oldest two—and the ones I was closest to—were currently undergoing training at the police academy in Glen Waverley. Riley hadn't wanted them to become cops, but Liana and Ronan were very much their mother's offspring. When they had their minds set on something, neither hell nor high water could convince them to do otherwise.

I drove up to the metal gates at the back of the building, then pulled off a glove and pressed my hand against the scanner. Red light swept it, then the gates swung open. I parked beside Riley's somewhat battered Mercedes SUV and kicked the side stand out. After pulling off my helmet and dropping it onto the seat, I ran up the metal stairs and leaned on the back doorbell.

Footsteps echoed, then the door opened and Aunt Riley was standing there, her hair a blaze of red and gold in the weak sun struggling through the still-threatening clouds. Her gaze swept me, then her gray eyes narrowed, glinting dangerously. "I hope like hell you made them pay for what they did to you."

I grimaced. "The odds were a little in their favor."

She grunted, then stood aside and motioned me in. "Let's get you cleaned up. You can explain what happened and who we have to chase after."

I grinned. I might not have come here for *that* sort of help, but it was always nice to know she was ready to kick some ass for me. Then again, she'd always treated me like one of her own.

She slammed the door shut and fell into step beside me, her gait long and easy. She was dressed in her usual jeans and T-shirt, but her feet were bare and half her toenails were painted an iridescent orange that clashed wildly with the vivid red of her hair.

"I'm gathering Uncle Liander has found a new nail color?"

She rolled her eyes, her smile warm and amused. I'd known her all my life, and she looked as young now as she had when I was a kid. So did Uncle Rhoan. Liander was the only one who'd aged, and even then you could only see it in the fine lines around his eyes and near his mouth.

"He never wears it himself, you know. I think he just enjoys painting my toenails."

"Well, Uncle Rhoan never sits still long enough, so I guess you're the next best option."

She laughed and pushed open the door that led to the huge expanse that was their main living area. It was actually very similar in design to my own place, with the metal and brick of the old warehouse in plain view, and enhanced with lots of chrome and glass. But unlike ours, this place was filled with a riot of colors, from the green and rust of the huge sofas dominating the center of the room to the cherrywood and black of the kitchen. Huge paintings were dotted around the old walls—family portraits intermingled with light frames containing rolling images of forests and beaches. Aunt Riley had become so proficient at photography that she'd recently had her first exhibition. If the success of that was anything to go by, she was going to make a name for herself in the art world.

Not that *that* was her aim. Shoes were her true passion, and she'd been designing her own for years now. I had prototypes of the latest line in my wardrobe, and I have to say, they rocked.

Liander was sitting on the huge glass-and-chrome coffee table in the middle of the U-shaped line of sofas, but his welcoming smile faded as he looked at me. "What the hell happened to you?"

"Some shifters decided it would be a nice day for an ambush," I said, then changed direction as Riley nudged me toward the bathroom. "Although they weren't *actually* shifters."

"Strip and shower," Riley ordered. "And I'll get you some clean clothes. You," she added, as Liander made to follow us in, "go make me a coffee and grab Ris a Coke. The explanations can wait until we get her cleaned up. Or do you want to explain to Dia why we let her little girl stand around and bleed to death?"

"I'm hardly bleeding to death," I commented.

"That is not the point," she said. "I've seen your mother annoyed. And trust me, it isn't pretty. Go shower. I'll be back with antiseptic."

I stripped as she hustled Liander out the door, then stepped into the shower—which was even bigger than mine—and washed the grime and blood from my skin. It took a while, thanks to the fact that there were remnants of my discarded jeans and sweater stuck like glue to my skin.

Riley appeared as I began to towel off, clothing

over one arm and a medical kit in her other hand. She dropped the clothes on the chair, then opened the kit.

"Those look like wounds from a large cat's claws." She grabbed the antiseptic and twisted the cap open.

I held up my arm. Though the slashes had stopped bleeding, the wounds still looked raw and bloody. I might be a crossbreed shifter, but quick healing was another of those things I didn't quite get enough of. "They are. But the thing responsible could only take on half-cat form."

"No explanations until I'm there to hear," Liander called from the kitchen. "The coffee and Coke are waiting on the table."

Riley touched my hand lightly, holding it steady as she began to spray my arm with antiseptic. The cool liquid formed a protective coating across my skin as it killed off whatever germs might be left. "It doesn't look like it'll scar," she said. "You're lucky."

Unlike you, I thought, my gaze drifting down her left arm. Not only did she have lots of scars and a missing pinkie, but she'd partially lost feeling in her fingers—all thanks to her years as a guardian.

It was part of the reason she'd objected to Liana and Ronan becoming cops—because she hadn't wanted them to face the hurt and scarring that she had. Of course, being a cop was far different from being a guardian, but I think she feared *that* might be the next step for them. They certainly had the skills for it—physically and psychically.

So did I—and it was a fact that hadn't gone unnoticed by the Directorate. If Riley ever discovered they'd approached me some time ago, I think she'd blow a fuse.

And I'd be dead if she knew that I'd actually considered the idea, ever so briefly.

But in the end, it had been a mix of vanity, self-preservation, and more than a little fear of what I might be getting into that had made me walk away. I might be able to fight, and I might have talents that could be more than a little dangerous, but there was no way I was ever going to end up like Riley—scarred, battle-worn, and, worse still, never able to fully escape the claws of the Directorate.

"There," she said, squeezing my hand before releasing it. "Get dressed, then come outside and explain, before Liander bursts."

I grinned and got dressed. The faint scent of vanilla and musk clung to the clothing, meaning the jeans and the beautiful pale blue cashmere sweater I was borrowing belonged to Darci, Riley and Liander's middle daughter—the only non-twin in their brood, and the only one who'd inherited Liander's silver coloring. She also happened to be the only one who was close to my size. I was several inches taller than Riley or any of Darci's siblings, and was more traditionally wolf-like in form as opposed to the lovely curves they possessed. Although at least I wasn't completely flat-chested, like most wolves—and Darci—were.

Once I'd pulled my own boots back on, I dumped the damp hospital clothes back into my pack, then grabbed my jacket and headed out. Liander and Riley were already at the table consuming cake, but there was a bottle of Coke and another slab of thick, gooey chocolate sponge waiting for me. I grinned and sat down, feeling like a kid in a candy store and not sure what to tackle first. In the end, the need for caffeine won out.

"So," Riley said, cradling her coffee cup between her hands as she studied me over the rim, "explain."

I did, eating as I went, telling them everything from the reaper and his quest for my father to the attack.

"I've never heard of a shifter being able to partially shift," Liander said with a frown.

Riley nodded in agreement. "It's usually impossible to stop mid-shift and retain characteristics of both forms."

I leaned back in the chair and lightly spun the empty Coke bottle. "I don't think these things partially shifted. I simply think they weren't able to take full form."

Her frown deepened. "Did they smell like shifters?"

I shook my head. "But they didn't smell human, either. Although the man in charge *did*."

"Why would a human be interested in your father's whereabouts?" Liander asked. "It's not like humans can see or use the gates."

"They can if they're sorcerers," Riley commented. "Although I can't imagine a sorcerer powerful enough to see or use the gates doing his own dirty work. Did you get the license plate numbers?"

I grinned. "If I hadn't, my teacher would have clipped me over the ear."

"Too right." She grabbed a pen and notepad from the counter behind her, then slid them across the table at me. "Write them down. I'll get Rhoan to chase them down for us."

I scrawled the numbers on the notepad, then pushed it back. "I don't get why they'd attack me, though. Given they had my bike bugged, why wouldn't they have just followed me, like the reaper is?"

"Is that reaper here?" Liander asked suddenly, looking around with a frown.

"He said he was keeping his distance." Though given how much I actually knew about the reapers, he might very well be in this room, just invisible to sight and senses.

"Good," Liander muttered, then leaned back in his chair and scrubbed a hand through his thick silver hair. It was streaked with a deep purple today, which would clash horribly with the orange nail polish if he actually decided to use it. "These people obviously bugged your bike when you were at work, so it might be best to get dropped off and picked up for the next couple of days. Especially given the hours you work."

I wrinkled my nose at the thought of having to rely on someone else but, at the same time, I could see the sense in what he was saying. I wasn't stupid. Nor was I looking to meet those men again soon.

"Is there any way we can find out who they might be working for?"

"I'll get Rhoan to nose around and see if there's any word about shifters who can't fully shift," Riley said. "In the meantime, you'd better head to your mom's and talk to her about your dad."

"But Mom's told me everything she knows about my father."

Riley gave me a tolerant sort of smile. "Trust me, a mother *never* tells her child everything about their father. There are *always* secrets."

I could feel the smile teasing my lips. "So you're

saying there's stuff about Liander that none of your children know?"

"Of course," she said, voice solemn but gray eyes dancing. "I'm sure if they ever found out what terrible taste in nail polish he has, they'd be mortified."

Liander scooped up a bit of chocolate cake and tossed it at her. I laughed as she ducked, her movements vampire-fast. The cake splattered across the counter behind her.

"I was testing it for an upcoming movie," he said. "The heroine has red hair."

"Yeah, believing that," Riley said drily, then glanced at me. "As to why those men would attack you rather than follow, we really won't know until we track down the people behind the attack and talk to them."

"What about talking to the thugs themselves?"

"If we find them, we will. But given their propensity to attack rather than talk, I suggest you keep out of their way—at least until we know who they are and what they're up to."

It might be the sensible option, but it wasn't one that was likely to get me any answers. I whirled the Coke bottle around again, watching the reflections dance in a dozen different directions. Sort of like my thoughts.

"Risa," Riley said sternly, "don't even consider going after them. It's far too dangerous."

My gaze jumped to hers. "I wasn't—"

"Not believing that, either," she commented, voice wry but a smile on her lips. "Wait until Rhoan tracks down the car registrations. Then we can plot our next course of action."

"As long as you promise to let me in on it."

"I will."

"Good." I pushed to my feet. "In the meantime, I'll talk to Mom."

Though personally, I doubted it would help. Mom had never kept many secrets from me, and I'd certainly never sensed that she was holding back when it came to my father.

"Will you be at lunch on Thursday? We should know more by then, so we can plot over cake."

And wouldn't *that* please Mom. She might be best friends with Riley, but she'd be horrified to find me in any way involved in her more nefarious activities. Riley was retired as a guardian, but she was still a consultant for the Directorate, and she still got herself into some dangerous situations. Of course, this was me getting Riley involved rather than the other way around, but that wouldn't stop Mom from worrying.

The sensible thing to do was not tell her at all, but it was almost impossible to keep secrets from a clairvoyant as strong as she was. I'd learned long ago it was simply easier to be up front about these things.

"Tell Darci I'll clean her clothes and return them then."

Riley waved a hand dismissively. "That child has more clothes than she knows what to do with. I'm betting she won't even miss them."

And I was betting she would. Cashmere was expensive, and this sweater didn't look old. "If anything else happens, I'll let you know."

"Good." She walked around the table and dropped a kiss on my cheek. "In the meantime, be careful."

"I will." I waved a good-bye to Liander, then headed out.

The fickle Melbourne weather was playing its usual tricks, and the rain had returned. I slipped on my jacket and gloves, then raced down the stairs and jumped on my bike. I didn't get much farther because the phone chose that moment to ring.

The ring tone said it was Mom. "Hey," I said. "I was just about to drive over—"

"Ris," she cut in, her voice harried and more than a little stressed, "you need to get to Coppin Street as soon as possible."

"Why the hell—"

"Just go," she said, "or Ilianna will die."

Chapter Four

Ilianna? Die?

I didn't ask for details—the urgency in Mom's voice was enough to convince me. I hung up and rang Ilianna, hoping like hell she'd answer, that it wasn't already too late. Mom might have told me to go, but I'd be stupid not to at least try the easy option.

But her phone was either off or out of range—which was no doubt why Mom had told me to go.

Swearing softly, I shoved on my helmet and fired up the bike. The gates were barely open before I was through them. I rocketed up the streets, weaving in and out of traffic, pushing both the bike and my skills to their limits as I ignored traffic signals and left more than a few angry drivers in my wake.

Ilianna was the sister I'd never had. I wouldn't lose her. I *couldn't.*

Fear twisted through my gut but I tried to ignore it, concentrating on the road, on finding the best way through the traffic, on not stopping for anyone or anything.

The gods must have been on my side, because not one cop made an appearance, though I had no doubt—given the number of red-light cameras I ran—that a raft of fines would soon be making their way to my mailbox.

I turned left onto Abinger Street, my knee so close to the tarmac that it scraped a hole in Darci's jeans and took off a layer of skin. One replacement pair to be ordered, I thought absently, gunning the engine and speeding down the street. It seemed to take forever to reach the next street. I took a right, the tires all but screaming as they left a layer of rubber behind. I didn't slow until I neared the small single-fronted terrace that served as Mike's office.

I couldn't see Ilianna's car parked anywhere near, so she was either inside already or still on her way. We lived close enough to Mike's to walk, and the frequent bouts of rain wouldn't have deterred Ilianna. She liked getting wet—it soothed the wildness in her soul, apparently.

I glanced at my watch. Mike never ran anywhere close to his appointment times, so we'd fallen into the habit of arriving ten minutes later than he told us. The appointment was at two, and it was barely that now. Ilianna wouldn't be in there yet.

If she was walking, then she'd more than likely be cutting through the Mary Street lane and strolling across the park.

I spun the bike around, leaving another trail of rubber behind me, and gunned up to the park. I jumped up the curb and rode into the park itself, scattering pigeons and chewing up the lovely green grass.

But there was no one here.

I swore, dropped the bike, and ran for the lane at the back of the park.

And I smelled them—two of the shifters who'd attacked me earlier.

I slid to a stop, my heart going a million miles a minute as I scanned the laneway. Neither Ilianna nor the shifters were in sight, but the wind brought me the scent of both.

I clenched my fists but resisted the urge to charge in. I was downwind of the shifters, so although I was aware of them, they wouldn't have yet realized I was near.

If I could take out at least one, the odds would be more even. And if it came down to us against them, Ilianna was a mare, and more than capable of using her teeth and feet to protect herself.

But even a mare can't outrace a bullet.

Fear rose, sharper and harder, but I shoved it aside. Mom hadn't said how she would die—just that she would if I didn't get here. Well, I was here.

And Ilianna *wasn't* going to die.

I reached to my left and grabbed the top of the fence, hauling myself onto it and balancing somewhat precariously.

And found the first shifter.

He was crouched on the roof of one of the buildings that backed up against the lane, his attention on the top end of the lane. The rich gold of his hair said it was the lion shifter, and the glint of silver in his hand told me he was armed.

Just like that inner voice had feared.

God, there were days I cursed being clairvoyant. It only added to the fear, and this situation was bad enough without intuition heaping more shit on top of it.

I scanned the rest of the rooftops and trees, but couldn't spot the other shifter. His scent was coming from the left—the opposite side of the lane from the lion shifter—but that was about as defined as the location got.

I glanced at the ground, looking for a weapon. The small backyard was concrete and basically held nothing but rotting leaves from the nearby gum trees and a stack of bricks.

But they were better than nothing.

I jumped down lightly, took off my helmet, then picked up three. Spiders crawled out of the middle holes and I had to resist my instinctive urge to drop them. They were mainly daddy longlegs and harmless, but my skin still crawled as one of them scampered across my hand. I blew it off, resisted another instinctive urge to jump up and down on the thing, and made my way back to the fence instead.

But as I hit the top of it, Ilianna appeared down at the far end of the lane. The lion shifter raised his gun.

"Ilianna, run!" I screamed.

A gunshot rang out. Ilianna twisted sharply and I couldn't see if she'd been hit or not. Fear churned my insides, but I raised the brick and threw it as hard as I could—just as the shifter spun around to face me. The brick missed, but so did his second shot—this one aimed at me.

Ilianna's footsteps disappeared down the street—she was running, as mares were wont to do when faced with danger—and relief surged. Running meant she was alive—and just then, that was all I cared about.

A third shot ripped the air. The bullet burned past so close to my shoulder I felt the heat of it, but before he could fire again, I threw another brick. This one hit him full in the face. Blood spurted and he howled, his voice thick with pain and fury.

The second shifter appeared, leaping over the fence of the house a few properties down. He raced toward me rather than Ilianna, but any relief I might have felt disappeared as I stared at him.

His eyes were filled with destruction.

My destruction.

They might need to talk to me, but it wasn't going to be pleasant, and I wasn't going to live for very long afterward.

Would Azriel step in to save me if things got that bad? I didn't know and, to be honest, I really didn't want the situation to even *reach* that point.

I flexed my fingers and watched the shifter, ignoring the ever-increasing urge to run. Running was useless. His legs were already elongating—thickening—until they were almost twice the length of mine. He had speed in droves—more than I could muster up, even as a half-wolf.

His face was also changing as he ran, until it resembled something more canine than human. But his torso and his hands remained fully human. I guess a dog's paws weren't as dangerous as a human's fists.

I waited, my knuckles almost white with my grip on the remaining brick, watching his eyes, waiting for his leap. I saw the fury deep in those brown depths and once again tried to ignore the inner voice that said I couldn't do this, that it was better to run.

I'd been *trained* to fight. Now it was time to put

that training to the full test. There were only two of them—it was probably the only opportunity I was going to get at these sort of odds *and* at getting any answers as to why these people were after me.

He leapt, teeth bared and a low growl rolling up his throat. I jumped from the fence and swiped sideways with the brick. He twisted in midair and the blow swooshed past his side, overbalancing me as I landed. He hit the top of the fence and leapt again, coming straight at me. I brushed my fingers against the concrete to steady myself then twisted around, flinging my arm up and using the brick as a ram. It smashed into his arm and bone snapped, the sound clearly audible above the steady growl of traffic coming from the nearby streets.

He howled—a furious, angry sound—and swung sideways with his other fist. I leaned back, but the blow still caught the edge of my chin, the power of it snapping my head back and dropping me onto my butt. He was on me in an instant, all teeth and hands and ferocity. I blocked several blows with my right arm, tried to ignore the pain of the ones that got through, and smashed the brick into his ribs. He howled again and jerked sideways. I bucked with my body, flinging him off me, then quickly scrambled to my feet. His hands caught the edge of my borrowed sweater and jerked me backward, into his arms.

"Now, my pretty, you are going to tell me what we need to know, or I'm going to enjoy tearing sweet chunks of flesh from your neck."

"Sorry," I muttered, "but I don't talk very well under duress."

I lashed back with a foot, but he jumped out of the way, his grip tightening against my neck and just about choking me.

"Nasty, nasty," he whispered, his breath putrid as his lips brushed my neck. "For that, I might just have to provide a little taste of what happens to naughty little girls who attempt to castrate their betters."

"As interesting as that sounds," a deep, somewhat amused voice said behind us, "from where I'm standing, her neck actually looks rather fine just as it is. It would be a shame to mar it, don't you think?"

The dog shifter spun, dragging me around with him, his chunky gold watchband tearing into my neck. The man who'd spoken was tall, broad-shouldered, and golden-haired. And his face . . . well, *beautiful* was the only way to describe it. Angels would surely have wept to achieve the same sort of perfection.

And that's very much what he was—an angel.

Or at least he was the flesh-and-blood counterpart of a myth that ran through time and religion.

He was Aedh.

With that face, and with eyes such a vivid jade green and so filled with power it was almost impossible to stare at them without wincing, he could be nothing else.

Jade eyes, I thought. *Not lilac like mine. Not my father.*

He could also handle himself. The lion shifter was lying at his feet, his neck twisted at an odd angle. Such casual destruction sent a chill through my soul, but then, if this man *was* full Aedh, he probably didn't hold human—or nonhuman—life with any sort of regard.

Not that these two deserved *anyone's* regard.

"Who the fuck are you?" the dog shifter spat.

"I'm the man who's going to kick your ass if you don't release the lovely lady's neck."

His grip tightened, his watch cutting deeper into my skin. Blood began to trickle down my neck, and if I'd had the breath to curse, I would have.

The shifter backed up a step, dragging me with him. His attention was on the stranger more than me, and I knew there was never going to be a better time to break free.

I reached back, grabbed his gonads, and twisted—as hard as I could. He screamed, and his grip around my neck loosened reflexively. I broke free but didn't release him, spinning around and punching him as hard as I could instead.

I released him then, and he dropped like a stone to the concrete. I blew out a relieved breath and glanced up at the Aedh. He was a good six inches taller than me and solidly built. And he didn't have wings, which was decidedly odd. Given he was in flesh form, he should have.

"Thank you for the timely intervention."

He gave me a slight bow, but the grin that teased his full lips was both sensual and amused. "I could hardly walk past and let those men accost such a beautiful woman, now, could I?" He glanced down at the shifter. "Would you like me to finish him off?"

Again that frisson of fear rolled through me, but I swiped it away. These men—as shifters who'd attacked another shifter with the clear intent to harm—would be lucky to last through the night once I called Uncle Rhoan. The Directorate had gotten harsher over recent years, and while death had once applied only to nonhumans who'd murdered, the increase in street violence had meant those boundaries had been eased in recent years. The trouble was, it hadn't done a whole lot to reduce the aggressive tendencies of those on the streets.

"Thanks, but I need to question him."

"Then permit me to at least break his leg. That way, you'll be in no danger from him." He hesitated, his gaze briefly sweeping me before rising to meet mine again. Amusement, and something else—something heated and primal—began to burn bright in those jade depths. The warmth of it flooded my senses, and the embers of need and desire stirred. He added, in tones that suddenly seemed a whole lot lower and sexier, "You can obviously handle yourself, but I'd hate to see you with bruises—or worse—when we go on our date."

I raised an eyebrow. "I can't remember hearing—or accepting—such an invitation."

His smile grew, and mirth crinkled the corners of his bright eyes. It marred the perfection of his face, yet made him all the more appealing. "But is it not the human way to thank your savior by sharing a drink or a meal?"

"Ah, but I'm not human."

"Neither am I," he conceded, his warm and seductive tones nothing like I'd expected of an Aedh. At least, not a full Aedh. All the stories Uncle Quinn had told me about the full bloods had made me believe them to be cold and distant beings, but this man seemed about as far from an iceberg as you could get. "Yet it is a custom that—in this case—I'm eager to embrace."

Something in the way he said that suggested he wanted to embrace a whole lot more than just a custom.

"You may have saved my life, but I can hardly go out with someone when I don't even know his name."

The shifter moaned and his fingers twitched. I stepped out of range and the stranger stepped forward, but I raised a hand to stop him. I could do my own dirty work.

Even if the thought made my stomach churn.

I raised a booted foot and—after taking a deep breath and thinking of Ilianna and what they might have done to her—stomped down on the bottom half of his leg. The force of the blow reverberated up *my* leg, but the snap of bone was clearly audible. The shifter twitched, but didn't react any more than that. Hopefully, the break would keep him in the depths of unconsciousness a little bit longer.

I stepped back and met the stranger's gaze again. Desire was sharper in his eyes, as was something else—something I couldn't quite define. But seeing it made my nerves quiver, and I couldn't decide whether it was a good sensation or bad.

"My name, lovely lady, is Lucian Dupont." His gaze burned into mine, scorching every part of me. "And yours?"

"Risa." My breath was caught somewhere deep in my throat and the word came out low and breathy. "Risa Jones."

"Then, Risa Jones, there is a lovely little restaurant called Wintergreen in Carlton. Shall we say tonight, at eight?"

I licked my suddenly dry lips and managed to nod.

He smiled and gave me another bow. It was an oddly old-fashioned movement, and yet extremely sexy. "Until tonight then."

He walked away. I watched him, enjoying the economical and yet oddly powerful way he moved. It was only once he'd disappeared around the corner that I remembered how to breathe properly again.

And suddenly I had to wonder how much of what I'd felt was real, and how much of it might have been enhanced by the Aedh. They might be cold and clinical beings, but I'd gotten the impression from Mom that they could—when they wanted—be as sexually alluring as any wolf.

Although from what I understood, that only happened when the Aedh was nearing the end of his long life span and needed to breed. Lucian certainly hadn't looked ready to die. Far from it.

But I hadn't *felt* anything untoward caressing my senses, and surely I would have. I *had* felt the sexual energy—the need and desire burning off him—but that had in no way been designed to seduce or coerce.

Besides, he'd invited me to dinner, not a roll in the sack. Although part of me was totally hoping a roll in the sack ensued at some point in the near future.

And maybe satisfying my more basic need—as Ilianna would call it—would stop my stupid hormones from hungering after the reaper the next time he showed up.

The thought of him had me looking over my shoulder, but there was nothing and no one there. Or at least visible.

Part of me wished he was.

I dug my phone out of the pocket and called Uncle Rhoan.

"Risa," he said, his gray eyes—the image of Riley's—showing surprise even on the phone's small vid-screen. "What's happened?"

"Two shifters attacked me. One's dead and the other is—"

"I've got your location," he cut in instantly. "I'm not far away. Hang tough."

He disconnected and I had to smile. I might never have had a dad, but I had Rhoan and Liander and Quinn, and I really didn't need any other fathers in my life. Especially not one who was planning to wreck the very fabric of life here on earth.

The shifter groaned again. I put my phone away then walked across to pick up the brick I'd dropped. As my fingers wrapped around it, the shifter jerked and tried to get to his feet. Either he hadn't felt the break or he was still partially out of it, but the sudden movement ripped a scream from his throat.

Almost instantly his flesh began to ripple and pulsate as his body fought to heal his bones. I raised the brick and said, "Stop that now, or I'll break more than your fucking leg."

He stopped the shift and glared up at me balefully,

anger mingling with pain in his eyes. Then he lunged sideways at me, his hand grasping for my ankle. I leapt backward, a gasp surging up my throat but not quite reaching my lips, then brought the brick down, smashing it against his hand, trapping it between the brick and the concrete. He howled a second time.

"Move again, and I'll break every bone in your hand."

Sweat trickled down his twisted face. "What do you want?"

"I want your name and the name of your boss. I want to know why you're after me." They might have said my father was the reason I was being hunted, but it never hurt to be certain.

"My name is Graham Turner." He hesitated, and something flickered in his eyes. "I can't tell you who my boss is."

I pressed all my weight down onto the brick, and he screamed again. I eased up, then said, "I don't believe you."

"It's true," he all but spat. Pain and fury were etched deep into his expression. Maybe it was just as well the Directorate had a kill policy, because otherwise my life would not have been worth much. "Marcus is the only one who knows how to contact him. I've only ever heard his voice over the phone."

"Marcus is the human who was with you at the parking lot?"

"Yes."

"His last name?"

He hesitated, and I leaned a little on the brick. "For fuck's sake," he said, licking the sweat from his lips. "It's Handberry. Marcus Handberry."

I eased up again. "And where might I find this Marcus Handberry?"

"He's at the club most nights after eleven."

"What club?"

"The Phoenix. He owns it. Has an office out the back. Jesus, woman, let me go. I've given you everything you want."

"You haven't told me why you were assigned to me in the first place."

"Marc had to get some information out of you, that's all."

"What sort of information?"

"About your father. I don't know any more than that—honest."

I didn't believe him. Or maybe I didn't *want* to believe him. "And then you intended to kill me afterward."

"No—"

I didn't let him finish the lie, just rammed the brick down a little harder. The part of me that wasn't comfortable with violence didn't seem to be making an appearance right now.

"Okay, okay, yes," he yelled. "We were to determine your father's whereabouts, then get rid of you. I don't know why and I don't really care. It was just part of the job."

How come everyone seemed to be aware of what he was doing but me? And if they were so aware of his actions, why the hell where they even after me? Surely they'd know he hadn't contacted me.

"Why go after Ilianna?"

The dog shifter stared at me with wild eyes. "Who?"

"Ilianna. The mare."

"Oh, she was just bait. To get you, like."

Bait they were going to shoot. Bait they were going to kill. *Bastards,* I thought, and resisted the urge to crush his hand once again.

"How did you know she'd be here, at this time?"

He snorted. "How do you think? Decent scanners are a dime a dozen these days."

Great. They were monitoring our phone calls. Which meant that until we found the person behind all this, we were going to have to be very careful about what plans we made over the phone.

Footsteps echoed behind us and I glanced around sharply. Uncle Rhoan was running toward me, his red hair glowing like a fire in the wan afternoon light. When our gazes met, he slowed, obviously realizing I was in little danger.

He looked from me to the shifter then back again to me, and a slow grin stretched his lips. "It appears we've trained you well."

I nodded and rose. "Have you talked to Riley yet?"

He nodded. "I was on the way to talk to the owners of the black Toyota when I got your call." He nudged the shifter with his foot, his expression hard and cold. What Aunt Riley called his guardian face. Seeing it for the first time had chills running down my spine. "I'll take care of these two. You get yourself home."

I hesitated, but I knew that tone well enough to realize there was no arguing with him. "You'll let me know if you get anything else out of him?"

He glanced at me, gray eyes hard. "Yes, but let us

take care of this, Ris. This is our area of expertise, not yours. Okay?"

I nodded.

But if he thought I was about to drop it, he had another thing coming.

Chapter Five

BOTH ILIANNA AND TAO WERE WAITING FOR ME when I got home.

As the door slid open, Ilianna collapsed into my arms and hugged me fiercely. "Thank the earth," she whispered. "You're all right."

I returned her hug briefly, then pulled away and held her at arm's length. "Are you okay? The bullet didn't get you, did it?"

She shook her head, her gaze searching my face then dropping, coming to rest on the scratches around my throat. "You need some ointment on those."

She spun and strode toward her bathroom, a woman on a mission. I threw off my coat and bag and walked across the room. Tao handed me a coffee and a burger.

I took the coffee—my stomach still churned far too much to eat anything solid right now—and wrapped my fingers around the mug in an effort to warm the chill from them. A chill that came from shock more than the cold.

Tao leaned his jean-clad butt against the glass dining table and crossed his arms. Like most werewolves, he was slender in build, but he worked out daily and it showed in the way his T-shirt strained across his muscular shoulders and forearms.

"So," he said, his warm brown eyes studying me intently. "What happened? Ilianna wasn't exactly in a state to give proper explanations."

"You wouldn't have been, either, if you'd just been shot at." She came out of the bathroom and strode toward us, a potion bottle and cloth in hand. "And don't you be giving us any of that hero bullshit, either. You wouldn't have hung about to help any more than I did."

He glanced at her, a flicker of pain showing in his expressive eyes. "That happened a long time ago, Ilianna," he said softly. "If you think I'd abandon either of you now, you are seriously mistaken."

I touched his arm, squeezing gently. He glanced at me, the dimples in his cheeks barely showing thanks to the tightness of his smile. He knew that despite our closeness, despite the fact that the three of us would do anything for one another, Ilianna had never entirely forgiven him for what had happened to her sister.

And she never would.

Not when her sister still bore the scars of that night.

In truth, what had happened to Kandra wasn't really Tao's fault. He'd been little more than sixteen and besotted with the older shifter. She should have known better than to tease a kid five years younger, but even then he'd had that special something—the twinkle in his eyes, the promise of sensuality on his lips. A way of walking that was loose-limbed and yet seductive.

They'd gone to a bar and Kandra, being a mare in

her prime, had flirted with a few too many men. Men who had followed them when they'd left. Tao had done his best to protect them both, but at that age his fire-starting skills had been raw. When his fire failed, he'd run.

But not very far, and not for very long.

Still, by the time he'd come back, the damage had been done. Kandra had fought them, forcing them to reach for weapons. The knife that gutted her had been silver, and they'd left it in her as they'd faced Tao's onslaught. The silver had damaged several internal organs beyond repair.

Tao was still paying for her medical expenses. Because of the guilt, because of the self-loathing he felt about his actions, he always would.

Ilianna stopped in front of me and undid the bottle's cap. Sage and a peculiar sweetish smell that vaguely reminded me of licorice stung the air.

"Why was Ilianna attacked?" Tao asked as she dabbed some of the antiseptic onto the cloth and began to wipe my throat. It stung like a bitch and I had to resist the urge to jerk away. "And if you were aware of the impending attack, why didn't you just call and tell her not to leave the house?"

"I tried, but I couldn't get through."

Ilianna grimaced, her gaze on my neck as she continued to wipe it with the cream. "I turned the phone off. Mom's been hassling me to have dinner with them again."

Tao snorted. "Another prospective stallion in the offering, I gather?"

"I guess." She shrugged—like it wasn't the huge hassle we all knew it was.

"You should tell them, Ilianna," he said gently. "They love you. They'll understand."

It was Ilianna's turn to snort. "All my life I've heard my father go on and on about how he looks forward to having lots of little foals under his feet once we come of age. And now that Kandra can't—"

She stopped, but not before a flash of guilt ran across Tao's expression.

"I can't disappoint them," Ilianna said eventually.

She couldn't give them children, either. Not the way they expected her to—by allowing herself to be claimed and branded by a stallion and producing his offspring. And with Mirri beginning to make noises about meeting her family, the secret would be out sooner rather than later.

I shared a glance with Tao. He shrugged and grimaced. We'd both tried convincing her to out herself to her parents for years, but to little avail. Obviously, the status quo wasn't going to change anytime soon.

Ilianna finished wiping my neck, then stepped back. "You'll need to use this after every shower, just to ensure it doesn't get infected. You never know what sort of germs men like that are carrying."

A smile curved Tao's lips, bringing his dimples to full bloom. "I think the germs they were carrying would have been the last thing on her mind at the time."

"I guess." She put the lotion on the table, then propped her butt besides Tao's. "So, explain."

I sipped some coffee and winced a little. After all these years, you'd think Tao would remember I liked my coffee sweet. The sweeter the better.

He must have seen my grimace, because he pushed

away from the table with a grin and loped over to the kitchen, fetching the sugar bowl and bringing it back. He held it while I scooped three spoonfuls in, then shoved it on the table.

"It's a long story," I said as I stirred in the sugar.

"It's not going to get any shorter unless you start talking," Tao commented, the dimples flashing again.

So once again I repeated the tale of the day, from the reaper's appearance to the attack in the parking lot, then my discussion with Riley, and finally my mad dash through traffic to get to Ilianna.

She frowned once I'd finished. "But how did they even know I'd be heading toward Mike's office?"

"Scanner, no doubt," Tao said. "I'll contact Stane and see if he can grab us some scramblers. Until then, we'd better stay off our phones."

Stane Neale was Tao's cousin, a wolf who ran a small electronics business down in Clifton Hill. He was also something of a wiz when it came to computers—which just might come in handy if I needed information. Uncle Rhoan, as much as I loved him, obviously wasn't about to let me investigate this, but it wasn't in me to sit back and let others solve my problems.

Although that would obviously be the wise thing to do.

"They also placed a tracker on my bike, so it'll be worth checking your cars before going anywhere."

Ilianna snorted. "Like me checking is going to do any good. I wouldn't know a tracking device if it slapped me in the face."

I grinned. "I'll do it. In the meantime, you'd better

start preparing some repelling potions. You just might need them."

"I always carry a bottle or two when I'm out. I just didn't get the chance to use them this time, because you were screaming at me to run." She crossed her arms and studied me with concern. "What are you going to do?"

"Well, first off I have a date—"

"Date?" Tao said, surprise evident in his expression. "Wasn't it yesterday you were moaning about the dearth of eligible men in your life?"

"It was," I agreed, "but this one stepped in to help me against the shifters who attacked Ilianna."

"I do believe you skipped that little detail," she said, her voice cross but a twinkle in her eyes. "What have I told you about skipping the important bits?"

"He's tall, broad-shouldered, golden-haired, and handsome enough to tempt even you." My grin grew as she snorted. "He's also an Aedh."

"Aedh? I didn't think there were any left in the city." Tao hesitated. "That's a bit of a coincidence, isn't it? I mean, all these men after your father, and you getting rescued by an Aedh."

"I hadn't really thought about that." It wasn't like I'd actually had a whole lot of time to think during the attack. And afterward, my hormones had well and truly been in control.

Damn it, I wanted the date to be real, wanted it to be based on mutual attraction, not some subversive desire to mine information about a father I'd neither seen nor met.

But now that the seed had been planted, I couldn't

ignore it. Tonight's date suddenly lost some of its shine, and that was a shame.

"I could be wrong," Tao said, touching my arm lightly.

I smiled and squeezed his fingers. "You might, but you might not. It's better that I'm alert and aware rather than lost in attraction."

"Wolves," Ilianna commented drily. "All hormones and no common sense."

Tao laughed and threw an arm around her shoulder. "And you mares are positively virginal by comparison, aren't you?"

"Hey, I never said it was a *bad* thing." She pressed into his embrace a little, but her gaze was sober when it met mine. "What do you plan to do about these men?"

"Well, as it happens, I managed to get the name of the man in charge. He owns a club called the Phoenix—"

"The Phoenix?" Disgust ran across Tao's face. "That place is a cesspool."

I raised my eyebrows. "And you know this because?"

"Because the premises are a few doors down from Stane's, and there are all sorts of drunken misfits coming in and out. Stane had to put grilles on the windows because the bastards kept smashing them."

"So, it's not the sort of place someone like me—"

"Certainly *not* as you are," he said, voice stern. "And certainly *not* alone. I'll come with you."

I hesitated, then nodded. Tao knew the place, and I didn't. And although I didn't want to drag him any deeper into the situation, I also wasn't stupid enough to go alone. If I called either Rhoan or Riley, they'd simply forbid it.

I wanted—needed—to do this. To do *something*.

"Okay. The dog shifter told me he usually gets there after eleven, so we'll head there tonight."

Ilianna said, "What about your date?"

I looked at her. "What about it?"

"Well, weren't you the one going on and on about the lack of shaggable men in this city? And now that you actually have a date, you're ditching him early to go hunt bad men with Tao? That makes no sense." She nudged Tao with her shoulder, then added with a grin, "Not that you're bad company or anything less than shaggable, but you're not Mr. Long Term. Not for Risa, anyway."

"Oh yeah? Meaning you've seen Mr. Long Term?"

Her eyes twinkled. "You know I can't divulge secrets like that."

"In other words, she's just yanking your chain." Tao's voice was dry as he pushed away from the table and glanced at his watch. "I'm off to the Blue Moon tonight. What time do I need to pick you up?"

"Eleven, at a restaurant called Wintergreen." I hesitated. "Just how amenable would Stane be to a little detective work?"

"It would make his little hacker's heart sing with glee," Tao answered with a smile. "Especially if the request came with a bottle of chilled Bollinger. What do you need?"

"Anything and everything he can find on Marcus Handberry, the owner of the Phoenix."

"I'll contact him and ask. We can drop by tonight before we head to the club."

"Doesn't he ever close down?"

"Nope. He lives and breathes that shop, and only sleeps when he has to. You want to inspect the cars now, or later?"

"Now." I drained the coffee and dropped it onto the table. "I need plenty of time to sleep so I'm fresh for tonight."

He snorted softly. "Darling girl, all you have to do is suggestively bat those gorgeous eyes his way, and the man won't care if you have monstrous bags underneath them."

I rose on tippy-toes and dropped a kiss on his cheek. "You do say the nicest things."

"That's what best buds do." He grinned and hooked his arm through mine. "Now, shall we go find bugs?"

We did—and we did.

Three, to be exact.

One on Tao's Ferrari, one on my Toyota, and the final one on Ilianna's battered Jeep. Obviously, they'd had no intention of losing any of us—which made me inspect my bike again, but we didn't find any more. Maybe they'd run out of time. Or bugs.

"I'll replant these later," Tao said, placing them carefully into separate plastic bags. "But they're obviously going to be watching us, so we'll need to think of a way to stop them from following us tonight."

We headed back up the stairs. "Can I just note here that your friend Rocky, and his mate Kiera, are about our heights and builds? Why don't you invite them around for a movie night?"

He grinned and dropped a kiss on my cheek. "You're so clever sometimes, it's scary."

Face-shifting wasn't as easy as shifting into an alternate form. From what Mom said, donning your wolf form—or whatever other form of animal you might be—involved little more than reaching into that place inside where the beast roamed and releasing the shackles that bound her. This was a little more complicated. Not only did you have to fully imagine all the minute details of the face you wanted to copy, but you had to hold it firm in your thoughts while the magic swirled around and through your body. Easier said than done when the magic was designed to sweep away sensation *and* thought.

What made it even harder was the fact that I very rarely did it.

I took several deep breaths, slowly releasing each in an effort to calm the tension running through my limbs. Then I closed my eyes and pictured Kiera's face in my mind. The sharpness of her nose, the smattering of freckles across her cheeks, the slightly upward tilt on the edge of her golden eyes, the curl in her brown hair.

Then, freezing that image in my mind, I reached for the magic. It exploded around me, thick and fierce, as if it had been contained for far too long. It swept through me like a gale, making my muscles tremble and Kiera's image waver. I frowned, holding fiercely to her likeness. The energy began to pulsate, burn, and change me. My skin rippled; bones restructured; hair shortened, curled, and changed color.

When the magic faded, I opened my eyes. Kiera

stood before me. It was a strange sensation, staring into the mirror and not seeing me. I didn't like it, but it was better than having those men following us again.

I wiped the sweat from my forehead and ignored my wobbly legs as I headed into my walk-in wardrobe. Like everything else in this warehouse, it was oversized—but then, it had to be. Another thing I'd learned from Riley was an appreciation of really fine shoes and the clothes that matched them.

I stood in the middle of the room and studied the long line of dresses. A first date required something sexy, but not too revealing—especially given that sex *wasn't* going to be on the menu tonight. I'd learned the hard way that discretion was a must when it came to catering to my earthier needs.

Everyone knew who Mom was. A lot of people also knew I was her daughter. And there were men out there—and a lot of reporters—who where willing to do or say anything to get their story.

Tears pricked my eyes, but I blinked them away furiously. My encounter with Jak Talbott had happened a long time ago. The hurt was gone. I was *over* it. Over him.

And if I kept telling myself that, maybe one day I would believe it.

But as a result, I was a werewolf who no longer visited the popular wolf clubs, who didn't often have casual sex except in the safety of places like Franklin's—where they catered to people who could pay for discretion—and who went on at least one date before giving in to base need.

Aunt Riley called it unnatural. I preferred to call it cautious. One broken heart was more than enough for one lifetime.

After several more minutes of indecision, I pulled out a simple, dark purple silk dress that skimmed my curves and floated gently to my knees. The stilettos were the same color, but had three-inch silver heels—a Riley Jenson specialty. My purse was also silver. When I shifted back to the real me, the effect would be sexy, but not overtly so.

I spun and headed into the main room. Ilianna had already darkened the electrochromic windows, so there was no chance of any of watchers seeing us. Tao was waiting, his brown hair temporarily dyed to match Rocky's outlandish blue—the same blue as his eyes, thanks to contacts.

His gaze skimmed me then rose to my hair. "I really do prefer you silver."

I grinned. "And you look far sexier as a brown wolf. Did you contact Stane?"

"I told him to expect us about eleven thirty. I'll buy the Bollinger before I pick you up at eleven." He hesitated. "What happens if the date goes badly?"

"Tao," Ilianna said, voice sarcastic, "she's meeting a sexy man. How can the date go badly?"

Tao shrugged and glanced at me. I smiled at the concern in his eyes. "I'll grab a cab and meet you outside the club."

He nodded, then glanced at his watch as the doorbell rang. "Right on time," he said as he headed for the door.

Ilianna looked at me. "I actually think this is all

overkill. I really don't think they're watching us anymore."

"It's better to be safe than sorry."

"I guess. It's just—" She frowned, then shrugged. "I have this feeling they're smart enough to realize we're on to them, and change their plan of attack."

"Well, until we know what the new plan is, we're better off playing it safe."

I glanced around as Rocky and Kiera entered. Both of them did something of a double take, Kiera's mouth dropping in an O as her gaze skimmed me. "It's like looking in a mirror," she said, shrugging off her coat and kicking off her shoes. "How weird is that?"

"Totally," I agreed. "Thanks for doing this."

Rocky tossed Tao his car keys and coat, then strolled across the room to kiss my cheek. "It's really no hardship when the basketball finals are on, you have the biggest TV screen ever made, and there's a fridge filled with beer."

"God, *basketball*," Ilianna groaned, her gaze meeting mine as she crossed her arms. "The things I suffer for you two."

I grinned. "I promise I'll bring back ice cream."

"Then I shall suffer in silence." Her quick grin faded a little. "Be careful out there, won't you?"

I raised an eyebrow. "Is that a general be careful, or an I-see-nasty-stuff-ahead be careful?"

"General." She frowned. "I think."

Tao rolled his eyes. "Ris, let's move, or she'll be here all night deciding."

I pulled on Kiera's coat and swapped shoes, then

shoved mine into a large bag that also held my purse and a change of clothes for when we investigated the Phoenix club. Then, with Tao's hand warming my back and lightly guiding me, we headed out.

As we drove off in Rocky's beat-up SUV, I flipped down the vanity mirror and checked the road behind us. No cars discreetly pulled out to follow us from a distance. The ruse had apparently worked.

Even so, I didn't change my features until we were five minutes away from Wintergreen. This change was always the easier one. The burn of energy filled the car with heat as it reshaped my features.

"God, that is a stomach-churning sight," Tao commented, glancing at me once I was done.

"You don't have to look." My arms trembled as I shucked off Keira's coat and changed into my own shoes. Then I pulled some lipstick out of my purse and tilted the mirror so I could quickly redo my lips.

"It's sort of hard not to." He shuddered. "At least our shift magic has the decency to hide the process."

"Just as well, considering it's a whole-body change, not just a facial one." My stomach fluttered as he began to slow down, and I took a deep breath to calm my nerves. It had been a while since I'd had a proper date, and I really did hope this was just that. That it was nothing more than a coincidence that he happened to walk past as those men attacked us.

I undid the seat belt, then leaned across and kissed Tao's cheek. "Have fun at the club. I'll meet you around the corner at eleven."

He touched my cheek lightly. "To echo Ilianna, be careful."

I smiled and climbed out. Once he'd pulled away, I took another deep breath that didn't do a damn thing to settle the butterflies in my stomach, then turned and walked into Wintergreen. The restaurant was small and intimate in feel. A big open fire dominated one wall, and the exposed bricks on either side were lined with aging photographs of Melbourne. Old wooden tables and plush leather chairs were scattered throughout the rest of the room, with plenty of space between each setting. Candles flickered warmly in the middle of the tables; the only other light came from the low glow of the electric wall sconces.

My gaze swept the shadows, then halted as I saw him. He was at a table in the far corner sipping a glass of wine, but suddenly looked up, as if he'd felt the weight of my gaze. The slow smile that stretched his lips sent the butterflies flopping.

I didn't even notice the maître d' approaching, and jumped a little as he said, "May I help you?"

"I'm with that gentlemen over there," I said softly, nodding in Lucian's direction.

"Of course, ma'am. This way, please."

I followed him through the maze of tables and diners, my gaze on Lucian's, watching the warmth of his smile stretch to the jade of his eyes, then become something a whole lot more as his gaze flowed down my body.

He rose as the maître d' pulled out my chair, then caught my hand and brushed the lightest of kisses across my fingertips. My whole body quivered—and not just from that kiss, but from the heated closeness of him. I licked my lips, wondering again if he was enhancing my reaction to him.

"I'm so glad you were able to make it," he said, his voice low but powerful. "I was worried you might have had second thoughts."

He waited until I was seated before sitting back down himself. His scent flowed around me—an enticing mix of lemongrass, suede, and musky, powerful male.

I smiled as I placed my purse to one side. "If I was going to say no, I would have done so when you first asked me out."

Mischief gleamed in his eyes, but he didn't say anything as a waiter approached. "Wine, madam?"

"It's a very fine Riesling," Lucian commented. "Not too sweet, not too dry."

"Sounds good." The waiter filled the glass. I took a sip, savoring the delicate fruity flavors and lingering acidity as I studied Lucian over the rim of the glass. "Thank you again for coming to my rescue this afternoon."

"As I said at the time, I could hardly let those men assault such a lovely lady." Amusement flared in his eyes. "Of course, it turned out the lovely young lady was more than capable of taking care of herself."

"She is," I agreed. "But it was fortunate you happened to walk by anyway. I hadn't realized the second shifter was up and awake."

"I noticed." His fingers were toying with the rim of the glass, and though I'd never been turned on by mere fingers before, his had my breath catching. Or maybe it was the way he played so gently with the glass. It was all too easy to imagine him toying with me like that. I gulped and tried to concentrate on what he was saying as he added, "I'm not normally in that area, but I had a business meeting just down the road."

I only had his word to go on, but I really didn't want to believe he was lying, either then or now. And that instinctive bit inside me *was* relaxing, so it didn't sense anything untoward, either. "What business are you in?"

"I'm an investment adviser. Boring stuff, really."

This man was about as boring as a tiger snake. And probably twice as deadly—in more ways than one. "An investor who handles himself like a soldier is a rare commodity."

He chuckled softly. "As a race, we Aedh are rather long-lived. I've been many things over my lifetime so far, including a soldier. Believe me, the boredom of my current job is a welcome change."

He was still playing with the glass, and I watched the reflections dance across the shadows—the ones that surrounded us and the ones that seemed to lurk in his jade eyes. "Then you've always lived in Melbourne?"

He shook his head and leaned forward, crossing his arms against the table. His skin was a pale shade of gold, and almost seemed to glow against the dark wood. "I've just moved down here from Brisbane. I'm currently sharing a house with a friend in Carlton until I can find somewhere of my own."

"A male friend or a female friend?"

He raised an eyebrow. "Would it matter?"

Amusement touched my lips. There was enough wolf in me for the answer to *that* particular question to be a decided "No."

He smiled, and I felt the heat of it right down to my toes. "My friend is a he."

"An Aedh, like you?"

"No. Which is why, when I saw you, I knew I had to see more of you. It is rare to find another Aedh—even in a city this size—let alone one who wears such beautiful skin."

"I'm not full Aedh." And though such an obvious compliment didn't usually faze me, this had the butterflies stirring again. Or maybe it was just the warmth in the words, the lack of artifice in his expression. The sheer force of desire in his eyes.

Surprise flickered in his eyes. "You feel it?"

Oh yeah, I thought wryly. I not only felt it, but I wanted it. Wanted him. "What happened to your wings?"

"Ah." He leaned back in his chair. "They were torn off."

"Torn *off*?" I stared at him in horror, desire briefly forgotten. "Why?"

"I'm afraid I committed the grave mistake of caring for my half sister. When she was murdered, I hunted down and killed the man responsible. For that, I was punished."

"By having your wings torn off? Fucking hell."

"I believe I said words to that effect at the time."

Despite the horror that still swirled through me, I couldn't help laughing. "I think you would have said a bit more than that."

"You could be right." Again, that delicious smile teased his lips. "In fact, I believe I got rather physical. Not that it did me a lot of good in the end."

"So who . . . ?" I didn't finish the sentence, simply because I didn't need to.

"The priests," he said, "they're the only ones who can."

"But why didn't they understand your reaction? It's a normal response, after all."

"For humans—or people like yourself—maybe. But Aedh cannot be judged by human standards, and the priests are the least human of us all. They are cold, clinical creatures who believe in duty, logic, and the power of clear, concise thought. According to them, emotion is an aberration that should not exist."

I frowned. "But there are no priests left. They died out a long time ago."

"If that were true, I would dance through the streets."

"So there *are* Aedh priests left?" And if there were, how come Uncle Quinn didn't know about them? He'd once trained to be a priest, after all.

"There are no working priests left, but there are Aedh still living today who undertook but never completed the training."

Of which Uncle Quinn was one. I half wondered if he'd know Lucian, then shoved the thought away. It wasn't important right now.

"So if the priests tore off your wings, that would mean you're—" I hesitated, trying to do the calculations from what Uncle Quinn had told me about the time span of Aedh priests. All I got was *old*.

"It means I have seen many centuries on this earth." He leaned forward again. The heat and scent of him washed over me once more—a siren song calling to the baser parts of my soul. "Does the thought of me being old enough to be your grandfather—many times removed—appall you?"

I grinned and let my gaze sweep the length of him. Or the bits that were visible, anyway. "When it comes in such an admirable package, most certainly not."

He reached across the table and caught my right hand, turning it over in his. My skin looked pale against his, my hand small.

"When they took my wings, they robbed me of many things."

He touched a finger to my palm and began to trace gentle circles. My heart slammed into my chest and desire crashed through me. It was all I could do to say, "Like what?"

"I can no longer fully become one with the breeze, nor will I ever be able to walk the worlds between this one and the next."

"Why? Are wings the source of an Aedh's power?"

He grimaced. "Not really. But the process that strips us of our wings also limits our skills."

The skill of seduction obviously *wasn't* one of them. His gaze rose to meet mine, and something within me stilled. It was the weirdest sensation, as if I were standing in the eye of a storm that no one could see and no one but me could feel. And it was so peaceful, so right, that it scared the hell out of me. Without even thinking about it, I tugged my hand free from his and picked up my glass with fingers that were still trembling. The cool wine did little to ease the tumult inside, or the sudden feeling that I'd been right before. This man was dangerous in ways I couldn't even begin to understand.

"What skills were you left with?"

He shrugged like it didn't matter, but I could feel the tension in him, sense the lingering, ever-burning fury. He hadn't forgiven them, but I guess that was understandable if he'd been left half the man—half the being—that he once was.

"It leaves me pieces of everything, but not the whole." He smiled, and it was both beautiful and poignant. "I am trapped in this flesh—and this world—until my time is nigh or the world ends."

"Well, it could have been worse," I said teasingly. "You could have been trapped in ugly flesh."

He laughed softly, and some of the fury in him seemed to ease. "There is that."

The waiter chose that moment to approach. "Would you like to order now?"

Lucian glanced at me. I nodded and picked up the menu. "I'll have the char-grilled eye fillet with vegetables, thanks. Medium rare."

"I love a woman who appreciates a good bit of meat," Lucian said, amusement dancing around his lips as he handed the waiter the menu. "I'll have the same."

The waiter left. Lucian leaned his arms on the table again. "Okay, your turn. Tell me about yourself."

So I did, though I omitted lots of important stuff, like my mom and the fact we were obscenely rich. While I no longer thought it was anything more than a coincidence that he'd been in the right place at the right time to come to my rescue, I still preferred to keep my secrets until I knew him a little better.

We continued to chat over the meal, talking about

everything from movies to politics. He was easy to talk to, easy to be with, and it was with some surprise that I glanced at my watch and saw it was nearly eleven.

"I have to go," I said, pulling my hand from his regretfully.

"And here I was hoping this night would last into morning," he teased.

I smiled. "It almost has."

"You know what I mean."

"I do, and I'm sorry, but I've already arranged for a friend to pick me up." I hesitated, and gave him a slow, sexy smile. The furnace in his eyes flamed even brighter, burning me with the scent of his desire. "But I'd love to see you again."

"Then call me," he said, pulling his wallet out of his pocket. He dumped a wad of notes onto the table to pay for the meal, then handed me a business card. All it had on it were his name and a cell phone number. "This friend who's picking you up—male or female?"

My smile grew. "Male. Is that a problem?"

"To repeat your rather emphatic statement, no." The heat still burned in his eyes, but there was something else—something that made me quiver in anticipation and perhaps a little fear as he added, "Although I do prefer to know whether I have competition or not."

"Tao's not competition. As I said, he's just a friend." I smiled and picked up my purse. "Thank you for the lovely evening."

"Indeed." He waved a hand to the front door. "Allow me to escort you out."

He did so, his fingers pressed lightly against my spine, causing all sorts of havoc to my pulse rate. The maître d' opened the door as we approached, and a blast of wintry air hit my skin. I shivered and crossed my arms as we left the restaurant, half wishing I'd brought Kiera's coat with me. But that was a risk given that, at the time, I'd had no idea if this man was safe or not.

I still wasn't sure, but for entirely different reasons.

"Here," he said, stripping off his jacket and resting it over my shoulders. My nostrils flared, taking in the scent of him, feeling it wrap all around me as securely as his jacket. "Take this. You can return it on our next date."

I smiled. "Thereby ensuring I *do* have to see you again."

"Of course."

He was still holding the lapels of the coat and he tugged on them lightly, pulling me closer. My chest brushed the silk of his shirt, and my already erect nipples reacted as if we were both naked.

"Call me tomorrow," he added, voice little more than a murmur. Then he kissed me.

It was like no kiss I'd ever felt before. It was heat and passion and desire, but it also transcended all that, becoming as tumultuous as the fiercest storm. Electricity surged between us, swirling around our flesh, *through* our flesh, until it felt as if we were nothing more than night and air and energy.

When we finally parted, I could barely breathe and my legs felt like water.

"Is it always like *that*?" I muttered, touching his forearm to hold myself upright.

He smiled and ran his finger lightly from my cheek to my kiss-swollen lips. "Kissing another Aedh is like flirting with the sun. There isn't another sensation quite like it."

He could say *that* again. And what the hell would making love to the man be like if a mere kiss had this effect?

Part of me wasn't entirely sure I was up for it, but the long frustrated rest of me howled those doubts down.

"So why have you guys got the reputation for being such cold and clinical beings?"

"Because it is true. It is only the brief breeding urge that hits near the end of our life span that causes such a dramatic turnaround."

I said, "Meaning you're near the end of your life span?"

And if so, maybe I'd better rethink the whole sex thing. I might be chipped to prevent conception—all wolves of breeding age were—but that didn't mean accidents couldn't happen. Especially around someone who'd been born energy rather than flesh.

He smiled and shook his head. "I am nowhere near the end of my span, but I have been in this form for a long time now, and have come to appreciate its more—shall we say—earthy peculiarities?"

"Peculiarities?" I said, releasing his arm and stepping away on still-unsteady legs. "I've never heard sex described *that* way before. I'll call you tomorrow."

"Do," he said, shoving his hands into his pockets—as if to stop himself from reaching for me again.

I turned and walked away. His gaze followed me,

burning into my spine long after I'd turned the corner and he was no longer in sight.

Rocky's beat-up SUV was parked three cars down. Tao leaned across the passenger seat and opened the door for me. His nostrils flared as he retreated, and a wry smile touched his lips.

"Don't you smell unbearably frustrated."

"And you smell unbelievably satisfied." I tossed my purse into the back and climbed in. "If you say one more word about my condition, I shall beat you to a living pulp."

He laughed, threw the car into gear, and took off. "I'm always available for a little light relief. All you have to do is say the word and I'm there."

"We agreed six months ago we were not going to cross that line anymore." Because it was easy, because it was safe. Because it wasn't forcing me to step out into the dating scene and risk my heart again.

"Yeah, but that was before your current level of frustration." He gave me an amused glance. "You're going to cause a riot at the Phoenix."

"Only if there are other werewolves in the club. And if there are and they try to hit on me, you can beat them up."

He laughed again. "So, are you meeting with the man who got you into this state again?"

"Tomorrow." The sooner the better.

"Then he checked out?"

"As much as anyone can check out on a first date, yes."

"Good." He glanced in the mirror, then said, "The road is fairly empty, so it's safe to face-shift."

I did, imagining a face that was broader than either

mine or Kiera's, with fuller lips, blue eyes, and jet-black hair. Once the magic had done its work, I waited for the trembling to ease, then stripped off, changing into the jeans, baggy sweater, and boots I'd brought along.

"You do realize," Tao commented, "that you smelling like you do, and stripping so blatantly like that, would test the control of any other wolf?"

I leaned across the car and kissed his cheek. "That's why I love you."

He snorted softly. "Love teasing me, that is."

"That too." I gathered my belongings and threw them all into the big bag. I'd need them later to change back into—I couldn't go home wearing jeans, just in case Ilianna was wrong and those men were still watching.

We arrived at Stane's fifteen minutes later. Tao parked several doors down from the shop—away from the club, not closer to it. The heavy beat of music vibrated through the car even from this distance, and underneath it ran the sound of raucous voices. Men *and* women.

I reached around and grabbed Kiera's coat from the backseat then climbed out of the car, trying to ignore the noise emanating from the club as I dragged on the coat and studied the shop. As on every other building nearby, the brickwork was grimy and graffiti-covered. Thick grates barred the windows, but a lot of the bars were bent. Given the thickness of the metal, it had to be the work of drunken nonhumans. Short of using power tools, humans wouldn't have been able to do that sort of damage.

I glanced at Tao as he walked around the rear of the car, a bottle of Bollinger in one hand. "Did you warn Stane that we won't be looking like ourselves?"

"Yep."

I grunted, and glanced down the street at the sound of more laughter. A man in blue jeans had fallen into the gutter, and his friends seemed to find it hysterical. "Why doesn't he shift his shop? This area has to be bad for business."

"He's somewhat stubborn, and refuses to be driven out." He touched a hand to my back, guiding me toward the front door.

"Meaning others have?"

He nodded. "Most of the shops between here and the club have been empty for a while. Apparently someone is in the process of buying them out."

"That someone being the club?"

"Actually, no. Stane reckons it's some corporation intent on re-energizing the area."

I snorted. *Re-energizing* was another way of saying building heaps of tiny apartments, adding a small shopping precinct, and charging a fortune to live there.

"So who else is holding out?"

He shrugged and pushed the front door open. A tiny bell rang cheerily and a camera buzzed into action, tracking our movements into the shop. Light shimmered briefly around the small entrance then flickered out, and I realized Stane had a containment field around his doorway. People might be able to walk freely into the shop, but they couldn't get any farther unless he let them.

"Besides the club?" Tao said, catching my hand and tugging me forward. "A milliner and a general store."

The shop was small and smelled of dust and mold, which was weird considering neither was good for computers. There were shelves everywhere, all packed with boxes, old and new computer parts, and ancient-looking monitors of varying sizes. Organized it wasn't.

I shook my head, wondering how he found anything as I said, "Why the hell would a milliner want to work in an area like *this*?"

"Because," a voice said as a figure appeared out of the gloom, "we are all fools. And you have the Bollinger. Well done, you."

I smiled. Stane, like his shop, was an unholy mess. Given the cobwebbed brown hair, thick gray cardigan, and wrinkled, ill-fitting jeans, he resembled something the cat had coughed up and forgotten. He certainly didn't look like someone who'd put up any sort of fight—until you actually gazed into his honey-colored eyes. Stane, like Tao, was smarter and harder than he looked.

Tao handed him the champagne. Stane thanked him, but his gaze was on me. "You know, if Tao was any sort of friend, he'd help you out with that ache."

"The whole friends-with-benefits deal is off," Tao said, before I could answer. "It's heartbreaking, I tell you."

I slapped his arm, then gave Stane a steely look. "One more smart remark about my state and I really *am* going to hit someone. Hard."

He grinned. "Warning heeded."

"Good. Did you manage to find anything out about Marcus Handberry?"

"Yeah. He's a nastier piece of work than even *I* realized." His grin grew, but the amusement that had been crinkling the corners of his eyes faded as he added, "And he apparently didn't exist until a year ago."

Chapter Six

"No one can just pop up out of nowhere fully formed," I commented. "He had to exist *somewhere,* even if it wasn't in this incarnation."

He smiled and glanced at Tao. "She's smarter than she looks."

"I keep telling you to look deeper than the skin," Tao said drily.

"But the skin is so pretty—even when it's not her usual one. This way, my friends."

We followed Stane as he weaved through the shelves and dust, then climbed the set of stairs at the back of the store and entered another world. A world that was clean, dust-free, and bristling with all sorts of shiny electronic equipment.

"God, it looks like the bridge of the *Enterprise,*" I commented.

Stane spun around. "*You* know about *Star Trek?*"

"Watched every series, old and new."

"Favorite?"

"The latest incarnation." I grinned. Tao and I had this argument all the time. "Better beefcake."

Stane groaned. "And I had such hope for you, too."

"I like my men less cobwebbed, I'm afraid."

He snorted softly, but didn't bother removing said

webs as he parked his butt in the plush chair of his "bridge." There were several light screens to the left that were showing images of the building, both outside and inside, and others to the right running everything from games to websites. He touched the nearest screen, and on one of the others a blue shimmer flared up around the entrance downstairs. The containment field was once again active.

"Marcus Handberry, as we know and love him today," he said, touching another screen.

A picture of a pockmarked, thin-framed, dark-haired man came into view, and something within me shivered. The picture had been taken from a side angle, but he was looking at the camera and there was nothing resembling humanity in the muddy depths of his eyes. Even if Marcus Handberry was human, he'd left any semblance of it behind long ago.

"According to his driver's license," Stane continued, "he was born in Ireland and came here ten years ago. He holds dual citizenship, but travels on an Australian passport."

"How can he have all that if he only popped into existence a year ago?" Tao asked.

I glanced at him. "It's easy enough to do if you know the right people and have enough money."

He gave me a long look. "And you know this because . . . ?"

I smiled. "I have an aunt and uncle who were or are guardians."

Stane glanced at me. "Then why are you the one investigating this creep and not them?"

"Oh, they are. I just refuse to sit back and twiddle my thumbs."

"It would undoubtedly be safer."

"Undoubtedly." I flicked a hand toward the screen, and he took the hint.

"I did a search using his photo as a reference, but I can't find anything so far. Either he's had work done, or he really did pop up fully formed a year ago." He glanced at us. "If you could get a fingerprint, that might help."

"Unless he's been re-fingerprinted as well."

"That would be a costly procedure, would it not?" Tao asked. "And surely if he had that sort of money, he wouldn't own a dump like the Phoenix."

"Unless the Phoenix is a cover for something else."

Stane smiled. "That was my thought as well, but I can't find anything that suggests he's involved in anything nefarious. Nor does the club seem to be anything more than a rowdy bar catering to less-than-savory types."

If he wasn't involved in anything nefarious, he wouldn't have taken on the job of kidnapping and killing me. "Any idea what Handberry actually is?"

"According to his records, human, but I've walked past the man and whatever he is, it *isn't* human."

"But you couldn't tell what else he might be?" The men who'd attacked me hadn't smelled of any race, either—even though several of them had half changed. And I suppose it shouldn't have come as a surprise that Handberry had the same no-species scent, given that he was apparently the man in charge. But why would he put a human in charge of his nonhuman thugs? Unless that so-called human *was* something else, and I just hadn't picked up on it.

"He smelled vaguely of cat," Stane said, "but the

scent of a cat shifter is usually far stronger and more acidic. If I hadn't almost run into the man, I wouldn't have even smelled it."

"And why would you be running into him if you're always on the bridge?"

He grinned. "Even I am forced to obey the needs of my body during the full-moon phase."

I raised an eyebrow. "So why are you here rather than at a club?"

"Because the moon heat has been temporarily sated, and besides, my baby misses me if I'm away too long."

He patted his bridge affectionately, and I snorted softly. "Have you found anything else?"

Stane shook his head. "But," he said, rising to walk across to the neatly stacked shelving unit lining the rear wall of his main room, "if you'd like to plant this little electronic gadget, I'll be able to hack into their security system and keep an eye on him for you."

He came back with something that looked like a little black beetle. It even moved like one.

"What is it?" I asked, leaning closer but not actually touching it. Bugs, like spiders, weren't really my favorite things to play with.

"This, my friends, is a semi-intelligent spybot, and the latest in nanotechnology."

"It's a robot?" I said, touching it lightly. What looked like bug-skin was actually cold metal. "How does it work?"

"I give it basic commands from here, and it goes to work. In this case, you drop it inside the Phoenix, and I'll program it to go into the office area and hide in some corner. It'll then send through everything that goes on in that office."

"And what if someone spots it?" Tao asked. "You couldn't afford to get something like this squashed by a well-placed boot."

"That's where the intelligence comes in. If it senses a threat, it scuttles."

"Amazing," I murmured. And scary. No one would ever suspect that an everyday-looking bug could be a spy camera. It made me wonder just what else was out there. I glanced at him. "How the hell did you get hold of it?"

"Ask no secrets and you'll be told no lies." He grinned and dropped it into my palm. "I'll program it as you're heading to the bar. Just be sure to place it near the office. Otherwise the walk will drain it and it won't be able to transmit immediately."

"So it recharges itself?"

He nodded. "With whatever is the closest power source—in this case it'll be either body heat or heat from the lights."

I wrapped my fingers around it. Its little legs made my skin itch, and it felt for all the world like I was holding a real bug. I shuddered and carefully dropped it into the unused coin section of my purse. At least it wouldn't get lost there.

Tao glanced at his watch, then said, "We'd better get going. You've got the morning shift tomorrow, remember?" When I groaned, he slapped me lightly on the back, adding with a smile, "It's Wednesday. Wednesdays are always slow."

For him maybe. I was the one who did all the paperwork, and Wednesday was paperwork day. But I was betting that all the little numbers were not going to make sense after tonight.

"Thanks for all this, Stane. I really appreciate it."

"Thank *you* for the Bollinger. I shall enjoy it at my leisure. Or swap it for something shiny." He nodded toward the screen. "I'll switch off the shield when you get down there."

Tao touched a hand to my back and guided me down the stairs. The night air seemed fresher after the mustiness of the shop, but it was no less noisy. The heavy beat of music seemed to vibrate through my body, and the sheer loudness hurt my ears. It was going to be hell inside but if it helped get some answers, then it'd be worth it.

Two heavyset men were standing on either side of the iron gates that served as an entrance. One was a bird shifter of some kind, and the other smelled of cat. They looked us up and down, then the grimier of the two flashed some teeth and opened the door.

"Enjoy your night," cat boy said, his voice sounding as if it were coming from the vicinity of his toes.

Tao grunted. It seemed to fit the atmosphere.

Surprisingly, the noise inside wasn't actually any worse than outside, but the overwhelming scent of humanity and alcohol had me wishing for nose plugs. The Phoenix was an old-fashioned bar—meaning people basically stood around drinking. There was a three-piece band huddled in one corner pumping out noise, and at the rear there seemed to be half a dozen billiard tables, most of them occupied. The bar dominated the left-hand side of the room, and the crowd before it was three deep. If there was an office, I couldn't immediately see it.

"Let's see what's at the rear," Tao said, his lips close to my ear. Wolf hearing or not, I probably wouldn't have heard him otherwise.

We weaved our way through the crowded shadows and billiards tables to the small, tabled area at the back of the bar. The smell of alcohol was thicker here, but this seemed to be more a "couples" area, if the pairings at the tables were anything to go by. There were three tables free, and one of them was nice and close to both the back wall and a somewhat battered-looking door. It had to be the office, given it had a burly, bronzed beefcake type standing watchfully next to it. Either that, or it was a storeroom. In this noisy, boozy crowd, there was probably good reason to keep an eye on the supplies.

"I'll go get us a beer," Tao said as I sat down. "Try not to cause too many problems."

I snorted softly. "I'm not the one who enjoys a fight, boyo."

"Oh yeah, that's right." He grinned and cracked his knuckles, then spun around, whistling softly as he made his way back to the bar.

I shook my head and hoped like hell people stayed out of his way. These days, Tao never backed away from a fight—in fact, he often went looking for them. It was almost as if he needed to keep proving him-self—and not to anyone else, but to himself.

I leaned back in the chair and tried not to breathe too deeply. Even so, it was hard to ignore the scents that swam around me. Everyone in here was human—even the burly guard at the door. My gaze flicked down. Light crept out from the crack between the door and the floor. Somebody was obviously in.

I drew the bug out of my purse and carefully placed it near the wall. Its little feelers twitched for several seconds, then it scuttled away, getting temporarily lost in the shadows before something small and black ran between the guard's feet and under the door. The bug was in.

With nothing else to do, I tapped my fingers against the somewhat grimy tabletop and tried not to think about how badly I wanted to get out of this place. Or the fact that I'd given up an undoubtedly amazing night of sex to come here.

Tao returned with two glasses of beer, handing me one as he sat down. "At least it's cold," I said, licking the froth from my lips. In a place like this, that had to be a bonus. I nodded toward the doorway. "Looks like Handberry is in."

"Well, the light is on," Tao said. "That doesn't mean Handberry is home."

"True."

"Did you deliver the package?"

I nodded. "It scuttled in about five minutes ago."

"Then hopefully Stane is picking up the feed okay."

"With what that thing is probably worth, he'd be pissed off if he didn't."

Tao snorted. "Trust me, Stane wouldn't have paid for it. He would have done some sort of nefarious deal. He's got a nice sideline of black-market electronics."

I wasn't entirely surprised. "So the mess in the shop is a cover?"

"Would you think of looking for illegal components in all that grime?"

"Not when there are probably hundreds of spiders just waiting to pounce."

"The webs are fake. Stane hates spiders as much—" He paused, glancing toward the front of the bar as a commotion started up. Two men were going at it, the smack of flesh against flesh audible even above the rest of the noise. It didn't last for long—security moved in quickly and escorted them out of the venue.

But a reaper followed them out.

I shivered and took a quick sip of beer. It didn't help much. Nothing did—not when I knew death was so close.

"They don't muck around," Tao commented.

"I suppose they can't afford to in this sort of crowd." I scanned the room, looking for another reaper. Looking for mine. I couldn't see either, and something within me relaxed a little.

The guarded door was suddenly flung open and Handberry stalked out. His weaselly, pockmarked features were stained a dark shade of red, and the stink of anger poured off him.

"Matt," he snapped, barely even glancing at the guard, "I'm off home. If anyone is looking for me, tell them to fuck off until tomorrow."

"Yes, boss," the guard said, relief crossing his features before settling back into bored disinterest. Maybe Handberry was as unpleasant to work for as he looked.

Handberry strode past our table and pushed his way through the crowd. Not that it was hard—this place might be filled with humans, but even they were feeling the fury radiating off him, and they parted like the Red Sea.

Tao finished his beer in one long gulp, but I didn't bother. With my wolf constitution, drinking *any* alcohol that fast tended to make my head spin, even if I didn't actually get drunk often. I had enough wolf in me to prevent that, at least.

Tao caught my hand and led me back through the crowd. He was big enough that people tended to move for us, so we weren't that far behind Handberry when he exited.

"Leaving so soon?" the toothy guard asked.

"The band is too fucking loud," Tao commented, glancing after Handberry but turning right toward to his car.

"Fucking werewolves," the guard muttered. "There's no pleasing the bastards."

"Werewolves just have higher standards." Though Tao's comment was soft, we both knew that the cat shifter, at least, would hear it.

Anger swirled through the night after us, but the two men remained at their posts. Maybe if Handberry hadn't still been visible, it would have been a different matter.

Tao opened the passenger door for me, then ran around to the driver's side and climbed in. On the opposite side of the street, just up from the club, Handberry was getting into a red pickup. After several seconds, he pulled out into the street, tires smoking as he hit the gas.

"Moron," Tao muttered as he followed at a more sedate pace.

"Wonder what's made him so angry?"

He glanced at me. "Maybe he just found out that the two thugs he sent after a certain werewolf failed in their task."

"I'd call it more than a failure," I mused. "One is dead, and the other is in the hands of the Directorate."

"Which is enough to make any madman intent on evil *extremely* pissed."

"I guess." But why would he be reacting now to events that had happened this afternoon? If Handberry was a good thug-master—and we had no reason to believe he wasn't—then he would have known almost immediately that something had gone wrong. The lack of communication from his men would have told him that.

No, this was caused by something else.

We continued to follow Handberry from a safe distance—a task aided by the fact there were few cars on the road. He slowed down once he hit Hoddle Street and headed away from the city, taking the Heidelberg Road turn-off then scooting along that until he reached Dan Murphy's. He swung into the parking lot behind the liquor store, then climbed out and walked across to the house next to it.

Tao turned right onto a side street, then came to a halt several cars up from Handberry's house. It was a small, single-fronted brick and—like the man who lived in it—rather ugly.

"What do you want to do now?" Tao asked as he killed the lights but kept the engine running.

"I don't know." I twisted around in the seat so I

could see the house better. "I guess it depends on whether Handberry actually lives here or not."

"Well, that's a question that can be solved by a simple phone call." He dug his phone out of his pocket and said, "Stane." A few seconds later, I heard the answering rumble of Stane's voice. "I need another favor if you've got the time."

I tuned out their conversation, watching as lights went on inside the house. We were too far away to hear any noise or conversation from the house, and only Handberry's silhouette appeared in any of the windows. But one thing I *could* sense was that there was an odd feeling in the night. A wrongness that made my skin crawl.

And it was different from the feeling I got when I looked at Handberry.

"Okay," Tao said, his voice breaking into my thoughts and making me jump. "According to Stane, this is the address listed on Handberry's license, meaning it's probably his place."

"Did Stane manage to pick up anything from the bug?"

"A telephone conversation. He's enhancing the audio now, and running a search on a couple of names mentioned. He'll let us know if he comes across anything."

More lights went on at the back of the house, and the feeling of wrongness suddenly sharpened. I rubbed my arms and fought the urge to tell Tao to just get out of here.

"Looks like he might be settling in for the night," Tao commented. "I really can't see—"

The rest of his sentence was cut off by the sudden sound of screaming. Horrible, high-pitched, about-to-die screaming.

And it was coming from the house Handberry had entered.

Chapter Seven

"Fuck," Tao said. "What the hell is going on?"

"I don't know." I quickly stripped out of Kiera's coat so it wouldn't be destroyed when I re-formed, then wrenched the car door open. Tao grabbed my arm before I could scramble out.

"Are you crazy? There's no way I'm letting you go in there. Especially alone."

"Tao," I said, voice sharp with impatience, "I can go in as an Aedh. No one will see or hear me, and neither the cops nor the Directorate will know I've been there. You breaking in is a completely different story. Ring Uncle Rhoan for me," I added, and gave him the number.

Tao made a low growling sound that spoke of frustration, but released my arm. "Go. But promise you'll let me know if you need help."

"I will."

I scrambled out and ran for the front door, calling to my Aedh form as I did so. By the time I hit the front steps I was little more than a stream of fast-moving smoke, and I slipped easily under the gap between the door and the porch.

The screaming had stopped, but the silence was even more terrifying. I flowed through the house cautiously, looking for Handberry and whoever else was in here with him.

Because, given those screams, someone—or some*thing*—had to be.

The front section of the house was dark, and consisted of bedrooms and a bathroom, all of which were empty. The rear—which turned out to be a massive kitchen and living area that ran the entire width of the premises—was ablaze with lights.

Handberry lay sprawled in the middle of the kitchen, a knife clutched in one hand. His body was twisted, broken, suggesting that someone—something—had battered him to death. And yet there were no bruises and very little in the way of marks on his flesh to suggest this had actually happened. My gaze rose to his face—it was locked in an expression of terror, as if death had frozen the muscles into that position even though his flesh would still be warm.

I flowed past him and inspected the remaining rooms. I couldn't see anyone, couldn't feel anyone. But that didn't mean there wasn't someone here.

I went back to the kitchen and hovered over the body for several more seconds. Waiting to see if it was safe, wanting to delay the moment of change a little bit longer. Deep down, I already knew what I would confront once I found flesh again.

I pulled back, then called to my human form, dropping to the ground in a half crouch and staying there for several seconds as the room spun and my limbs trembled.

The scent of evil was so thick and strong, it made me gag. The charm resting against my chest flared into life, heating my skin fiercely but not burning.

Even if the scent of evil hadn't been so strong, that would have been warning enough that something had gone *very* wrong here.

I reached out psychically and it hit like an express train—the emptiness, the same terrible agony that the little girl in the hospital had gone through. Only Handberry had screamed from within *and* without—screamed and fought and struggled to survive.

To no avail.

His soul had been ripped free as fiercely and as efficiently as little Hanna's.

I closed my eyes for a moment, furious at both the thing that was doing this and myself for not getting here earlier to try to save Handberry's life. He might have been an evil weasel, but even *he* hadn't deserved to die like this. Besides, his death destroyed the only real lead I'd had—unless Uncle Rhoan decided to share whatever he came up with. And I doubted he would—especially now, when I'd been following Handberry against his orders.

I pushed to my feet, hauling the threadbare remnants of my sweater back onto my shoulder as I dug my phone out of my pocket. Tao answered almost immediately.

"Risa?" he said quickly. "You okay?"

"Yeah. Handberry's dead. Something has stolen his soul." Tao swore rather colorfully, and I smiled grimly. "You want to give me a call when you spot Uncle Rhoan? He's going to be pissed enough that we're here. I don't want him to catch me in the house."

"Ris, he needs to know about the soul stealer—"

"They have highly trained witches and clairvoyants

of all sorts at the Directorate. They'll uncover it soon enough. Trust me, in this case, discretion is the better part of valor."

He grunted, clearly not happy but not about to argue. "Okay."

I hung up, then glanced down at the body again, feeling the tendrils of pain still emanating from his flesh. After taking a deep breath to steady my nerves, I said softly, "Azriel."

I felt him before I saw him. He was heat and energy and perhaps a hint of anger. I turned and saw him snap into being near the windows at the far end of the living room. His gaze met mine, one eyebrow lifted in query; then he straightened abruptly. Obviously, the scent and feel of evil had just hit him.

"The soul stealer has been here." His words were clipped as he strode forward. I stepped sideways, giving him room, not really wanting to touch him even though every sense I had screamed with awareness of his presence.

"Yes. It happened about three minutes ago. I came straight in, but whatever did this was already gone."

"You should have called me straightaway."

"I had no idea Handberry's soul was in danger until I re-formed."

He grunted and stepped over Handberry's twisted legs, squatting next to him and touching his fingers to either temple. The edges of the silver sword strapped across his back ran with blue fire, and I noticed that the wing tattoo that was so noticeable across the left side of his chest and neck was actually part of a stylized dragon image that dominated the left side of his spine. The right-side wing seemed to fade into his flesh before it could sweep under his armpit. But there were other tattoos running up the back of his neck and disappearing into his hairline—a mix of patterns that sometimes resembled the known (one looked vaguely rose-like, another like an eye with a comet tail) and at other times looked nothing more than random swirls. But I very much doubted *random* was a word known or spoken in the reaper culture.

Energy suddenly surged, and in the small space between his hands pictures began to flow—flickering images that moved too fast for me to clearly see. But I got the gist of them. They were Handberry's last moments.

I bit my lip against the urge to ask Azriel what he saw and waited until the images died. He removed his hands but didn't immediately get up. He bowed his head for a moment and spoke, the words musical and oddly captivating, but no language I knew or had ever heard before.

It was a prayer, I realized, and wondered what good it would do when Handberry's soul would never be reborn, never know life again.

When Azriel finished, he rose and glanced at me. Fury burned in the depths of his eyes. "The thing that did this is not something I've seen before. It appears to be little more than a shapeless gray shroud."

"Will that hinder you tracking the thing down?"

"Yes. It was brought here by magic, so there's no scent trail to follow."

"It won't be a witch." Despite what Hollywood would have us believe, witches would never, ever be capable of something like this. The Wiccan Rede

banned them from harming anyone—and that included themselves—except in cases of self-defense.

And then there was the whole threefold law—one
that said all the good a person does for another re-
turns threefold, as does all the harm. No true Wiccan
would risk hurting another, let alone killing them.

Those who *did* cast dark spells weren't witches.
They might be sorcerers, they might be Satanists, or
they might even be Charna—a name given to those
who followed the darker paths of magic.

Azriel nodded. "The person behind this is someone
who follows darkness. The magic is powered by
blood. *That* is never a good sign."

A shudder ran through me. Blood magic. The worst
kind. "What about the soul stealer? I know you said
you couldn't see it, but were you able to see anything
that might provide a clue in Handberry's memories?"

He shook his head. "No. All this man saw was a
twisted, smoky essence."

I frowned. "That could describe the Aedh."

"This wasn't Aedh. They can free souls without the
need for this." He indicated Handberry with a short,
sharp movement of his hand that was all anger and
frustration.

My frown deepened. "I was under the impression
that it was tough for Aedh to take souls from flesh."

"It is, but that doesn't mean they have to resort to
such force. It drains them, that is all."

Great. So we'd eliminated a possibility, but it didn't
leave us a whole lot closer to the who.

"Blood magic has an individual taint, so did you
sense it in Hanna's room?"

He shook his head. "But that death was older.

Within an hour, the scent of this will be long gone, too."

"Then why can't you follow it back to its source now?"

"Because it begins and ends in this room."

Which more than likely meant some sort of transport spell had been involved. Great. Just great.

"So basically, we're no closer to solving the riddle of these deaths than we were before."

"No." He glanced at me, and there was something almost annoyed in his otherwise impassive features. "It would be useful, though, if you slept like a regular person. I would have more time to hunt."

I said, "Hunt away, reaper. It's not like I want you to follow me around."

"As I said before, that is not an option." Though his tone suggested he wished it was. Either reapers were more capable of emotion than I'd originally thought, or I was reading *way* more into the brief changes in his expression than was warranted.

"So if you're stuck following me around, why didn't you help me when I was attacked?"

"As I've already said, I only follow. I do not interfere."

"Well, your quest would have been up shit creek if those men had succeeded in killing me."

"*That* I would have stopped. You are no good to any of us dead."

"Gee, that's *such* a comfort." I glanced at my watch then said, "I hate to break this to you, but I'm not going to get a whole lot of sleep tonight. So you're stuck with following me around for a while yet."

He didn't say anything, but displeasure seemed to

swirl through the heated air. The phone rang into the silence, making me jump a little. It was Tao.

"A car with Directorate plates just pulled into the parking lot behind Dan Murphy's," he said quickly. "Get your ass into gear if you don't want to be caught in there."

"Wind down the car window for me." I hung up and met Azriel's gaze. "I need to go."

"Call if you discover anything else." He crossed his arms, watching as I flowed into my other form, his expression as unreadable as ever. Then he simply winked out of existence.

I turned and sped for the door, sweeping underneath it, then surging toward the car. I couldn't see Uncle Rhoan—the old wooden fence stood between me and the parking lot, and I very much preferred to keep it that way. He was half vampire, after all, and his infrared sight was sensitive. I might be invisible in this form, but I had no idea how much body heat I was emitting. Uncle Quinn had never really mentioned it.

The car window was only open an inch or so, but it was enough. I swept through it, then changed to human form, landing with some inelegance—and a whole lot of pain—in the passenger seat. Two shifts in a short space of time had not only left me weak and shaky, but basically destroyed my sweater. My jeans had disintegrated, too, the cotton plastered to my skin.

"He's coming," Tao murmured, reaching back to grab another sweater from the backseat and thrusting it at me. "Put that on."

With some difficulty, I hauled it over my head,

struggling to thrust my hands through the sleeves then pushing them up because they were way too long for me. The wool smelled of Tao—the musk of wolf combined with exotic wood and Oriental spices—and for some reason it made me feel safe. The world might be going to hell, but I had my friends—and that was all that mattered.

Soft footsteps echoed across the night. I blew out a breath that flicked the sweaty strands of hair away from my forehead, then pressed the button and lowered the window the rest of the way, watching Uncle Rhoan's approach through the side mirror.

"Have either of you been in there?" he said, his silvery gaze sweeping us both as he leaned down. His expression was dark, to say the least.

"I went in there briefly as an Aedh," I admitted, knowing it wasn't the time for all-out lies. "I wasn't in time to help and there was no one else in there, so I came back out."

"And you didn't touch anything?"

"Other than the floor briefly when I shifted shape to see what scents haunted the room, no."

"Good. Now, would you like to explain just what the fuck you're doing here?"

I retreated from the anger that was practically boiling from him, even though his voice was calm. "We were just following him."

"Risa, I said we'd deal with it. You haven't got the training to handle this sort of stuff."

I might not be trained, but I sure as hell was more capable than *him* when it came to sensing soul stealers. I wisely kept the words inside, though. Taking *that* particular tack wouldn't gain me anything more than his fury. And he was angry enough as it was.

"Go home, Ris," he said, slapping the car with his palms. "I'll contact you when we have any news."

He stepped back. I glanced at Tao, who grimaced but shoved the car into gear and left.

"Well, that went surprisingly well," I commented once we were out of earshot.

Tao gave me an incredulous look. "The man was barely resisting the urge to rip you out of the car and spank you!"

"Ah, but he didn't, so I consider that a win for our side."

"It's hardly us and them. You're on the same side, remember?"

"Yeah, but they won't let me help."

"With good reason, I'd say. They're the professionals, not us."

"I promised Mom I'd investigate this." Which wasn't exactly the truth. All I'd really promised was to see the little girl and advise the parents as to her state. But after seeing her, after feeling what she'd gone through, I couldn't let the matter drop. Her death haunted me, and her pain wouldn't ease until I knew who—or what—had caused it.

And stopped them.

"Then what's our next course of action?"

I smiled at his use of *our*. Whether I liked it or not, he was going to help, and that was both scary and comforting. "We need to stop and get Ilianna her ice cream."

He waved a hand dismissively. "I know *that*."

I smiled. "Azriel said—"

"Azriel?" Tao interrupted. "As in the reaper? You spoke to him in there?"

"I called him. Apparently he's tuned to my Chi or something."

"Oh, that has to be fun," he muttered darkly. "You have a reaper at your beck and call."

"Trust me, this is one reaper you would *not* want to play with."

He snorted softly. "I can't see a good reason to be playing with *any* of them."

"It's not like I actually have a choice in this." And to be fair, neither did he, apparently.

"I guess." He half shrugged. "Go on."

"He said there was blood magic involved—that it was used to transport the thing that did this into the house, and to also hide its form. Handberry's last memories showed little more than a vague, smoky mass."

"So we have a dark practitioner at large." He flicked on the turn signal and turned onto Hoddle Street. "Do you think Ilianna will know if there's one active in Melbourne?"

"It's worth asking." Neither Ilianna nor Mirri was a member of a coven, preferring to practice individually, but both had some serious contacts in the witch world. If there was a Charna active, those contacts might have heard whispers. Or at least felt the wisps of his or her evil.

"And if she hasn't heard anything?"

I scrubbed a hand across my eyes. "I don't know."

Tao was silent for a moment, then said, "What about looking for the connection between the little girl and Handberry? If blood magic was involved, then it surely couldn't be a random attack."

"That would involve running a complete background check on both victims. Neither you nor I have the skills for that sort of hacking." And I couldn't ask Uncle Rhoan. He'd kill me. Or lecture me, which was usually worse.

"But Stane *has*. And he loves a challenge."

I frowned. "I don't know. This situation could get very dangerous. It's bad enough that I've involved you and Ilianna."

"Stane is more than able to take care of himself—"

"Not against something that is transported by magic and can steal souls."

He made a frustrated growl, then said, "Do you want this solved or not?"

"Yes, but—"

"Then you need outside help. Stane will do it. And surely Ilianna can magic up something that will repel evil?"

I nodded reluctantly. "She can do wards—that might help protect him if he gets a little too close to the source."

"Then that's what we do." He glanced at me, blue contacts catching the passing lights and gleaming brightly in the darkness. "You are not doing this alone, Ris. End of story."

I knew that tone. He would not be dissuaded. I drew in a deep breath and blew it out slowly. But it didn't do much to ease the frustration flowing through me.

"Contact him tomorrow," I said. "Right now we all need to get some sleep."

Or the damn paperwork was not going to make *any* sense.

"You'd better shift shape and clothes," he said. "Just in case those men are still watching the house."

I face-shifted back to Kiera's image—I was so tired, it seemed to take even more effort than usual—then stripped off Tao's sweater and put my dress and Kiera's coat back on. After changing shoes, I closed my eyes and leaned against the window, letting the rhythm lull me into a half sleep. It didn't last very long—all too soon we were pulling up outside our apartment.

"Wakey, wakey, sleeping beauty," Tao said, altogether too cheerfully. "We're home."

I grumbled something unintelligible even to me and pushed away from the window, stretching my arms above my head in an attempt to wake up. He was already out the door and, a second later, my door was opened. He clasped my fingers and helped me out, his skin a furnace compared with mine.

He frowned. "You need to eat. You've obviously shifted too much."

"What I need," I murmured, keeping my voice low because we had no idea where those men might be or if they had listening devices with them, "is sleep. And lots of it."

He grunted and looked into the scanner. It was only then that I realized he was holding a tub of ice cream in his other hand. He must have stopped when I was asleep. "I'll make you a burger before you go to bed."

I shuddered. "At this hour? I'll never sleep."

"Then grab some cake, at least." He gave me a sideways look, a wry smile touching his lips. "Don't try to tell me you can't do chocolate cake, because I know for a fact that would be a lie."

I grinned. "Chocolate cake can and should be eaten whatever the hour."

The door opened. Ilianna was standing on the other side. Her glance ran from him to me and back again, then she sighed. "I'm so glad you're both safe. I had a really bad feeling things had gone wrong."

"They did," I said grimly, walking past her as she stepped aside. "Just not for us."

The door slammed closed behind us. I made my way to my bedroom and shifted back to own face. I felt even shittier as I stripped off my clothes and grabbed a T-shirt and jeans from my wardrobe. Tao was right—I needed to eat. Three seconds later I was heading for the kitchen.

"Where are Kiera and Rocky?" I asked over my shoulder, opening the fridge and pulling out the cake. It was six inches high and chock-full of cream, ganache, and strawberries.

"Asleep in the guest room," Ilianna replied. "We weren't sure what time you'd get back."

"Don't wake them." Tao walked across to the coffee machine and pulled out three cups.

"I won't." Ilianna shoved her tub of ice cream away, then added, "So, what happened?"

"Handberry was killed by the soul stealer, meaning our two different cases might have collided." I glanced at Tao. "You want a piece?"

He shook his head and started making coffee. I looked back at Ilianna. "I don't suppose you've heard if there are any Charna active in the city?"

She raised her eyebrows. "And why would you be asking a question like that?"

"Because according to Azriel—"

"Hang on," she said. "Who is Azriel?"

"The reaper who's following me. According to him, the soul stealer is being transported and protected by blood magic. To me, that indicates either a Charna or possibly a Satanist."

"If blood magic is involved, you're more than likely right." She frowned. "I haven't heard anything, but I'm not a member of a coven, so that's not unusual. I can ask around, if you'd like."

"I'd like." I dropped a big slab of cake onto a plate and headed into the living room. Tao followed with the coffees, handing them out once we'd sat down. "But be careful. We don't want the wrong people aware that we're asking any questions. That could get dangerous."

And things were dangerous enough as it was.

She lightly blew on her coffee, then asked, "So have you any idea why Handberry was killed?"

"None whatsoever," I said as the doorbell rang.

"Who the hell could that be at this hour?" Tao said, frowning as his gaze met mine.

"Well, I'm sure not expecting anybody—are you?"

He shook his head. Flames danced briefly across his fingertips, then were extinguished. "I'll watch your back."

I regretfully dumped my cake onto the table, then walked across to the door. A quick look at the monitor revealed a small, slender woman with dark hair and the most amazing green eyes. It wasn't anyone I knew.

I pressed the intercom and said, "Can I help you?"

"I need to speak to Risa Jones rather urgently."

"And who can I say is calling?"

"Madeline Hunter."

I knew that name. It was a name that had been spoken in whispers by both Riley and Rhoan. This woman—this tiny presence standing outside my door—was one of the most powerful and feared vampires in Melbourne. And if it *was* her, she was rarely seen outside the halls of the Directorate.

So what the hell was she doing standing on my doorstep?

"Prove it."

A smile flickered across her lips, but never made it to her eyes. The green depths remained cold and calculating. She pulled a small wallet out of her purse and opened it up. The ID inside said MADELINE HUNTER.

The woman in charge of the whole damn Directorate.

Chapter Eight

"Now may I come in?" she drawled, putting the ID away.

"Not on your fucking life," I muttered. I hit the MUTE button then, swung around, meeting Tao's and Ilianna's curious gazes. "Say nothing. Do *not* invite her in."

"Why?" Ilianna asked, confusion crossing her features. "I saw her badge—she's Directorate. She's not about to hurt us."

I snorted softly. "You need to listen to some of the stories Rhoan and Riley tell about the Directorate. Besides, she's a vampire. If we invite her across the threshold, she can waltz in anytime she likes."

"So what's to stop her using her vamp mojo on us and forcing an invitation that way?" Tao asked.

"Because the invitation has to be freely given." But that didn't mean she couldn't use her vamp telepathy skills to create other sorts of orders. I walked across the room, retrieved my phone from my purse, flicked it across to vid-screen, and said "Quinn." I knew he'd be up. He might be half Aedh, but he was also a vamp and he rarely slept nights—even if he spent half of them in bed with Riley.

"Risa," he said, the Irish lilt in his voice holding a

hint of surprise. "Why are you calling at this hour? Is anything wrong?"

"I'm not entirely sure. Hang on." I walked across to the door and pressed the control screen. As the door slid aside, I said into the phone, "There's a woman outside my door claiming to be Director Hunter. Is this really her?"

I turned the phone around so he could see. Again, amusement flirted with Hunter's lips—and again, the look in her eyes suggested she was anything but amused.

"Madeline," Quinn said immediately, his voice cool and the soft lilt gone. "Do not try anything on her. Do not tamper with her mind. I'll know."

She snorted softly—almost elegantly—as her gaze moved to me. "You have some mighty powerful allies, Risa, but I'm no threat to you."

Not yet.

The unspoken words hung in the air between us. I turned the phone back around. Uncle Quinn's dark eyes glittered like black diamonds in the small screen. "If you don't call back within the hour, I'm coming after you."

"Thanks." I hung up, then slipped the phone into my jeans pocket. Uncle Quinn might be one step down the ladder from this woman in the vampire hierarchy, but he was something the older ones weren't. He was part Aedh, and he'd once been an assassin for the vampire council. And they feared him. I knew that tidbit from Riley herself.

I looked Madeline Hunter square in the eyes. "What do you want?"

With a long, slender hand, she motioned past me to

the apartment's interior. "A bit of common courtesy would be a nice start."

"If you want to talk to me, we can go elsewhere. McDonald's is around the corner and open twenty-four hours." I smiled tightly. "I'm sorry, but you're not getting permission to waltz into my house."

Her lip curled ever so slightly. Obviously, Director Hunter and McDonald's were not compatible. Or maybe it was my attitude she wasn't compatible with. After all, she'd been running the Directorate since its inception, and I doubted she'd heard the word *no* very often.

"If you insist," she said flatly. "Let us go there now."

"Just let me grab my coat." I didn't wait for her answer, just jogged to my bedroom to fetch my leather coat and shove on some shoes. "Azriel," I said softly, "You might want to listen in on this conversation."

There was no answer, but then I didn't really expect any.

"Are you sure this is safe?" Ilianna whispered as she and Tao came into my bedroom. "I mean, why the hell would the Director be visiting you at this hour?"

I snorted softly. "Who's betting it has something to do with my father?"

After all, almost everything else that had gone wrong so far did.

"You want me to come along?" Tao asked, flexing fingers that danced with little jets of flames.

"No." I squeezed his arm in appreciation of the offer, then added, "But it might be handy to see if

Stane can get us the latest in nanowires. If the Directorate is getting involved, we might just need them."

He frowned. "Will they stop someone as powerful as Hunter?"

"Probably not—but they sure as hell will make reading or controlling our minds a bit more difficult."

He nodded. "I'll get on it right away."

"Get three."

"Ris—" Ilianna said.

I cut her off with a sharp movement of my hand. "You're wearing one, Ilianna. I don't care if it goes against some witch rule. I want you protected."

She didn't look happy, but she didn't argue, either. I squeezed Tao's arm again and headed out. Hunter was still standing where I'd left her. I guess it had been too much to hope that she'd given up and left.

I waved her forward. She turned around and walked down the stairs, her black stilettos making little sound the metal stairs. A woman who walked so lightly in heels that high was, in my estimation, extremely dangerous. But then, the mere fact that she was the head of the Directorate suggested that. You couldn't maintain control for as long as she had by being anything but.

"McDonald's is one street over," I said as we hit the pavement. "On the corner of Swan and Botherambo streets."

She glanced at me. "Botherambo?"

"Yeah. Odd name." I shrugged. "They do good coffee."

Or rather, it was far better than the stuff the old bar they'd ripped down and replaced used to produce. The older folk in the area were still boycotting

McDonald's to protest losing their local watering hole, but I couldn't see the point. Especially since those of us who liked to party late could get something to eat at all hours.

Hunter didn't say anything else and neither did I. Her scent rolled across the night—a faint mix of jasmine, bergamot, and sandalwood that was surprisingly pleasant, even for a nose as sensitive as a werewolf's. Or a half-were's, as was the case.

The chrome-and-glass building that housed McDonald's soon came into sight. The big golden M dominated the rooftop and spread warmth through the darkness. Nearby, Swan Street was surprisingly busy, especially considering the early hour and the fact it was a weekday morning. The constant rumble of noise was regularly punctuated by the clatter of trains scooting across the old brick bridge, the bright light coming from the carriage interiors creating crazed patterns on the streets below.

Hunter held the side door open by her fingertips until I was through.

"What would you like?" I asked.

She somehow managed to look down her nose at me, even though she was several inches shorter. "I'd like not to be here, but I suppose a skinny latte will do."

A skinny latte? Since when did a vampire have to worry about her weight? I ordered—and got—both a skinny and a full-cream latte, then walked across to the table she'd selected in the corner.

I placed her cup in front of her then sat down opposite. After peeling off the plastic lid, I dumped three packets of sugar in and gave it a quick stir.

Hunter took hers as is—although the brief flicker of distaste that crossed her face once she'd taken a sip more than backed up her statement that she liked neither this place nor this coffee.

Tough.

I took a drink, tried not to think about the thick, gooey cake I'd left sitting at home, and said, "So why am I the lucky recipient of a personal visit from the woman in charge of the Directorate?"

She interlaced her fingers and stared at me blandly. "I'm here about your father."

"Isn't everyone," I muttered, and wished I'd brought some alcohol with me. I had a feeling I was going to need it.

She raised a sculpted black eyebrow. "There have been others inquiring about your father's whereabouts?"

"Yeah, but you already know that. Uncle Rhoan took one of the thugs in for questioning yesterday afternoon."

"Ah yes," she said, as if she'd forgotten, though we both knew she hadn't. "Unfortunately, that man couldn't tell us anything we didn't already know."

"And what do you already know?" I didn't think she'd answer, but it was worth a shot.

She simply gave me one of those cool vampire smiles they all seemed to do so well. "Have you heard from your father?"

"No. And I don't expect to, either." I raised the cup, took another drink, then reached for another sugar packet. "Why is the Directorate suddenly so interested in whatever my father is up to? You hunt down bad vamps, not Aedh up to no good."

She took another sip of coffee, and it wasn't a case of second time lucky. She took a handkerchief from her purse and gently patted her lips, as if to wipe away the flavor. I snorted softly. Okay, so it wasn't top-shelf, but it wasn't *that* bad, either.

"We are responsible for tracking down anything that is guilty of destroying human lives," she said eventually. "And if the rumors about what your father is attempting are true, then he could potentially destroy millions. That makes it our business."

"Only if he's doing what everyone thinks he's doing." Not that I particularly wanted to defend the man, but hey, I owed him my existence. No one had actually brought me any proof that he was up to no good. "And you could have sent any of your subordinates here to ask about my absent parent, so why are you really here?"

Again the sculpted eyebrow rose, but the green eyes underneath gave nothing away. Then again, this was a woman who'd seen over fifteen hundred years. She'd be more than a little practiced at containing her emotions.

"I merely wish to ask you to contact me the moment you hear from your father."

Contact *her*. Not the Directorate. Did that mean this wasn't an official Directorate meeting? Was she here for reasons of her own?

My heart skipped a beat. Madeline Hunter wasn't just the woman in charge of the Directorate, but also a top-ranking member of the vampire high council. And it was a scary thought that *they* might be getting involved in this.

I swallowed to ease the sudden dryness in my throat, and said, "Why?"

"Because I wish to speak to him."

Again, *I* rather than *we*. "The Directorate doesn't usually talk to people intent on destroying millions."

"Unless," she drawled softly, "they are involved in research that has interesting possibilities."

Dread rippled through me. I stared at her for a moment, then leaned back in my chair. "What sort of interesting possibilities?"

"It occurs to us that a device designed to permanently close the gates could be re-engineered and used to open or close them at will." She tapped a purple-painted nail against the plastic tabletop. "The ability to do that would be useful, and it would also provide us an interesting alternative."

Something cold settled into the pit of my stomach. I took a long drink of coffee, but it didn't do much to dislodge the ice. I licked my lips, then said, somewhat incredulously, "You want to use *hell* as your own private jail?"

Yet again that eyebrow rose. "You sound surprised."

"It's *hell*. You know, the place where all manner of demons, devils, and bad souls hang out. Playing around with the gates that protect us all is not a good idea."

And I could just imagine what the reapers would make of it. They certainly wouldn't be thrilled about the prospect of someone *else* gaining control over the light or dark pathways.

"Demons and devils enter this world all the time,"

Hunter said, "so the gates are an insufficient means of protection."

"The gates are not the problem. The magic that forces them open temporarily *is*. Stop the Charna, sorcerers, or Satanists responsible, and you'll stop the dark ones from entering."

She leaned forward a little, as if to convince me of her earnestness. All it did was make me suspect there was more to this than what she was saying. "But if we could learn what makes them work, then perhaps we can also make them stronger."

"If it were possible for them to be strengthened, then I think the reapers would have done it by now." I took another sip of coffee and tried to ignore the chills running down my spine. Tried to ignore the little voice in the back of my mind suggesting that Hunter's plans involved me a whole lot more than she was admitting.

"Reapers?" A brief glimmer in her eyes suggested interest. Or maybe that was me reading far too much into the flicker of movement in her otherwise well-controlled features. "You can see them?"

"Whether I can or not is irrelevant to this conversation."

"I disagree. If you can see the reapers, you can see the gates. And that is a talent we sorely lack."

We as in the Directorate, or the high council? I wasn't entirely certain which one she meant. "I've never seen the gates," I said. "I've never walked the gray fields."

Of course, the latter part of that statement was a total fabrication, but I was betting she really didn't know what I was capable of. Mom certainly wouldn't have told her, and the only other people who knew were those who'd been in the hospital room when I'd pulled Aunt Riley from those fields so long ago.

But one of those people had been Jack Parnell—Hunter's brother and the man in charge of the guardian division. It was totally possible that he'd mentioned it in passing in his report.

And that could also explain why she hadn't sent a lackey to talk to me. She'd wanted to examine me in person.

I finished my latte in one long gulp, then stood. "How do I contact you if I hear from my father?"

She drew a business card from her wallet and slid it across the table. "This conversation is not finished—"

"Yeah, it is," I said. "I have to work today, and I really do *not* want to sit here listening to half-truths. When you feel like telling me what you're actually planning, contact me. Until then, don't bother."

I expected the cold rush of anger, but instead she merely leaned back in her chair and gave me a small smile. "You really *are* your mother's daughter."

"No, I'm not," I bit back, barely managing to control the anger that flared deep inside. "I won't let you use me like you do her."

Her smile grew, warm on the outside, calculating within. I had a bad, bad feeling that I'd managed to intrigue her further.

"Your mother helps us because we saved your life. Which means, technically, you owe us *your* existence."

"The only person I owe existence to is my father. If he ever bothers to contact me, I'll let you know. Until then, good-bye."

I walked away. Her gaze burned into my spine, the sensation like a knife, cold and sharp.

"We'll meet again soon, Risa," she said, her voice soft and yet carrying through the noise as clearly as a shout. "That I promise you."

Goose bumps ran across my skin. I slammed open the door and walked out into the night, taking several deep breaths to ease the hammering of my heart.

Damn, she was scary. And yet she'd been the epitome of politeness. I ran a hand through my hair, then called Uncle Quinn to let him know I was safe before heading home. Not surprisingly, Tao and Ilianna were waiting for me.

I flopped down onto the sofa and blew out a relieved breath. "Well, that was exciting."

Tao handed me a large glass of Coke, then parked his butt on the coffee table in front of me. "Were you right about what she wanted?"

I nodded, then scooped up my abandoned cake and began munching my way through the thick, gooey mess, filling them in on events in between mouthfuls.

Ilianna grimaced when I'd finished. "It's a damn shame no one seems to believe that he hasn't contacted you yet."

"Yeah." I dumped the empty plate beside Tao. "I wish there was some way we could find him. I'd love to know what he's really up to."

Ilianna said, "You don't believe either the reaper or the Director?"

I met her gaze. "Right now, I'm not sure what to believe. But I find it curious that everyone seems to know what he is up to, and yet no one seems to know where he is. I get the feeling there's a whole lot of information we're not being told."

"You could always ask your Aedh if he's heard anything," Tao said.

"His name is Lucian, and he's not my anything." Not yet, anyway. "And all I really know about my father is his first name—Hieu. That's probably not helpful."

"But you can describe him," Ilianna said. "And you have his necklace. Your mom gave you that much, at least."

"True." I drank my Coke in several long gulps, then placed the empty glass on the table and glanced at the clock. "I need to go to bed, or I'll screw up the accounts tomorrow."

Tao rose, then offered me a hand and hauled me up with ease. He dropped a kiss on my cheek and said, "Stane's hunting up the nanowires. He said they'll be expensive, but I told him cost was no object. We just need the best."

"You really think Hunter would try to invade our thoughts?" Ilianna said, doubt in her voice and expression. "She's Directorate. They have all sorts of checks and balances in place—"

"The trouble," I cut in, "is not the fact that she's Directorate, but that she's also vampire high council. Those bastards are a law unto themselves, no matter what appearances suggest. And I got the distinct feeling she was here just as much as *their* representative as the Directorate's."

"Meaning the vampire council wants to get control of the gates?" Tao said, voice incredulous. "Why on earth would they want a power like that?"

"I don't know," I said grimly. "But Hunter said the Directorate was interested in using the gates—and hell—as an alternative to killing. Maybe the council is thinking along the same lines."

After all, the council didn't exactly sit on their hands and let the Directorate catch all the bad guys. They had the Cazadors—their very own, highly specialized squad of hit men. But the little of them I knew from Uncle Quinn suggested they were an extremely small unit. I guess hell provided an easier option—as long as you weren't worried about the whole human-race-becoming-vegetables scenario.

Ilianna snorted. "Yeah, like them controlling the gates wouldn't end up spewing trouble over the rest of us."

I glanced at her. "I *did* point out that playing with hell wasn't really a good idea, but I don't think she believed me."

"She's a vampire," Tao muttered. "They always think they know better than the rest of us."

He had a point. Ilianna frowned and said, "But why come to you? They'd have to know your dad hasn't contacted you."

"I think my father was merely an excuse." My voice was grim. "No one on the council or in the Directorate can walk the gray fields. If you can't walk the fields, you can't see the gates."

"And that punches a mighty big hole in their plans." Ilianna thrust a hand through her mane of hair. "Meaning, the bastards want to use you, just like they're using your mom."

"Yeah," I said grimly. "Only this time, the situation

they want to drag me into could very well result in the end of the world as we know it."

And *that* was a pretty scary thought to go to bed with.

After managing only a couple of hours of sleep, I dragged my butt into the office and tried to make sense of the accounts. Thankfully, the system was all but automatic, and I only had to double-check that all the input data was correct—a hard enough task given the overtired state of my brain.

By twelve, I'd double-checked, then rechecked the figures, and had basically had enough for the day. I finished the dregs of my fourth glass of Coke and listened to the rattle of cooking pans and dishes rolling up from the kitchen below. My stomach rumbled a reminder that it hadn't eaten anything since my rather rushed breakfast, and I half reached for the intercom to ask Tina—the chef currently running the afternoon shift—if she could fry me up something.

Then I remembered there was a better option and reached into my purse instead, drawing out the business card Lucian had given me last night.

Call anytime, he'd said. I needed food, and I also needed to ask him some questions. So why not combine the two needs?

And if a third, more basic need was also satisfied over lunch, then that would be a definite bonus.

Grinning in anticipation and suddenly feeling a whole lot more energetic than I had in hours, I touched the vid-phone's screen and read out his number.

He answered on the second ring, his expression distant and somewhat formal. The Aedh, rather than the warm man I'd come to know. "Lucian speaking."

His voice was a low rumble that seemed to vibrate pleasurably through my entire body. "Lucian, it's Risa."

"Risa." The cold distance in his eyes fled, replaced by a lovely warmth. "It's wonderful to hear from you again so soon."

I smiled. I couldn't help it—he had that sort of effect on me. "I was just wondering if you're free for lunch."

"As it happens," he said, his green eyes sparkling with warmth and amusement, "a previous appointment just canceled, so I'm all yours. You can do with me what you will."

"You might regret saying that," I teased. "We half-weres have a very healthy list of wants."

He chuckled softly, the sound whispering across my skin as sensually as a caress. "No healthier than mine, let me assure you."

Oh yeah, this was going to be a *good* lunch. "Have you any particular preferences when it comes to food?"

"Not really." He paused. "Not Italian. The garlic could prove problematic."

"Not if we both have it," I countered.

He laughed. "Italian, then. There's a lovely little place called Alimento in Carlton. We could meet there at"—he paused, glancing down briefly—"one."

My pulse rate increased. He lived in Carlton. What was the betting Alimento also happened to be very close to his house?

"That sounds perfect."

"I'll see you soon then, lovely Risa."

He signed off. I sighed, and barely resisted the urge to fan myself. *Hot and bothered* really didn't go far enough to explain just what I was feeling right now—and yet, he'd done little more than flirt with me. I'd never met anyone who could affect me like this—but I guess I'd never met a full Aedh before now, either.

I glanced at the time and realized I wasn't going to make it home to Richmond to change and then get back to Carlton before one. I'd have to go dressed as I was. Thankfully, I'd had enough brain cells functioning this morning to pull on decent jeans and a cotton-mesh sweater that was see-through enough to tease the imagination of any hot-blooded male. But just in case his imagination needed a little more teasing, I reached underneath my sweater and unhooked my bra, pulling it off then dumping it into my desk drawer. If there was one good thing about being smaller in the breast department, it was the fact that they didn't sag a whole lot when unsupported.

Which meant I was ready to go, but I still had a good twenty minutes to kill. I glanced briefly at the accounts, half thought about making a start on next week's payroll, and decided to ring Mom instead. I pressed the vid-screen again, said her name, and watched the psychedelic colors swirl as the phones connected.

"Risa," she said, a warm smile touching her lips. Her eyes—the same almost-almond shape as mine, but electric blue rather than violet—showed a touch of surprise. "I wasn't expecting you to call so soon."

I smiled, too. "Nice to know I can still surprise you."

She chuckled softly. "Oh, trust me, you are more than capable of that, even now. What can I do for you?"

Straight down to business. Which meant she had clients waiting. "Have you heard from, or seen, my father since the night of my conception?"

Again surprise flickered across her almost ageless features. Werewolves tended to be a long-lived race, but Mom was also a clone—lab-created and enhanced—and, by rights, she should have been dead by now. Every clone who'd been created at the same time as her had died, most of them taken by a defective gene that either accelerated aging or caused their organs to fail inexplicably. In Mom, that gene had—for some reason—flipped. It rejuvenated rather than destroyed. No one was sure if I'd inherited that gene, and Mom had never allowed such tests—as much as the Directorate had pressed her for them.

"No," she said slowly, "I've never seen him since that night. Why?"

"Because I've had a barrage of people insisting that he's going to contact me. I was just wondering if maybe he'd contacted you instead."

"No, and I wouldn't expect him to. We both got what we wanted out of that night."

And what they'd both wanted was me—the daughter she'd longed for, and a continuation of his genes.

"Is there anything at all about him that you haven't mentioned?"

She frowned. "I think I've told you everything I could about that night, Ris."

"So you never really talked about what he was or what he did for a living?"

"Not really. I knew he would give me you; that's all that really mattered to me."

"You knew he was Aedh, though."

"Yes, but that was not something he mentioned. It was more an information leak from our merging."

I blinked. "Merging? That's an odd way of putting it."

"Having sex with an Aedh is an interesting experience, Ris. The first meeting—the first kiss—is very explosive, and designed, I think, to ensnare completely. After that, it's pure functionality. But"—she paused, as if searching for the right words—"while the actual sex is mundane, for those of us who are psychic there can also be a melding of minds. It's not a very deep connection, but it's a connection nevertheless—and I suspect it goes both ways."

I frowned. "So when this connection happened— did you happen to catch whether he was a priest or not?"

"No." Something flickered across her eyes. Uneasiness, perhaps. "But there was something about being a member of the Raziq. I have no idea what that was, but I got the distinct feeling he was troubled by something involving them."

"Maybe the trouble he sensed was his approaching death." Aedh only bred when their end was nigh, after all.

"Possibly." Her gaze was still pensive. "Has this anything to do with what almost happened to Ilianna?"

"Yes." There was no use lying to her—she'd sense it, even over the vid-phone. Mom might be blind, but she didn't need her eyes to be able to see stuff like that. Of course, most of the time she wasn't exactly blind, either. She was psychically linked to several spirit creatures known as the Fravardin, and they took turns being her eyes and her guards whenever she ventured outside the walls of her home. I added, "But Riley and Rhoan are hunting down those behind the attack, so I'm not expecting any more trouble."

She didn't look convinced. But then, neither was I.

"Just be careful, Ris. That's all I ask."

"I will."

I glanced at my watch again. I really needed to get going because cabs were always damn hard to get along this section of Lygon Street, thanks to the proximity of two of the most popular wolf clubs and the fact that street parking was almost impossible to find these days.

And of course, Tao had insisted I take a cab this morning rather than risk the possibility of my bike being bugged again. I *could* walk, because Carlton wasn't actually that far, but I'd be rushed for time now and the last thing I wanted was to arrive all hot and bothered. But there was still one question that needed answering. "Mom, what can you tell me about Mr. and Mrs. Kingston?"

"Fay's been coming to me for years, but I don't really know a lot about her family. Why?"

"Because the thing that stole Hanna's soul took someone else's last night, and I don't think it's a random event. I need to find out what connects them."

"God," she said, rubbing her temple wearily. "If only I'd foreseen this—"

"Mom," I interrupted gently, "even you can't predict everything bad that is about to happen to your clients."

And even if she did, sometimes warning them didn't alter events, because there was no way to stop the reapers when a death was inevitable. I could only intervene when the matter was undecided.

"I know, but—"

"Mom, let it go. What we need to concentrate on is finding the connection between little Hanna and the second victim, and then stop this thing before it can attack anyone else."

She took a deep breath and released it slowly. "I'll talk to Fay and see what I can uncover."

"I didn't tell Mrs. Kingston how she died, so you'll need to be careful."

"I will." She hesitated. "Will you be joining us for lunch tomorrow?"

Unease swirled through me. "I've already told you I would be, so why are you asking again?"

She waved my concern away, her gaze suddenly vague. "I'm meeting Fay tonight, that's all. I should have information tomorrow."

Which was the truth and yet, not all of it. That swirling sense of dread increased. "Mom, what aren't you telling me?"

"Nothing, Ris. All is well." She hesitated. "You know I'm keeping stuff in the safe for you, don't you? I mean, if anything should ever happen to me?"

"Mom!" Alarm shot through me and for a moment, I couldn't breathe. "Fuck it, tell me—"

"Ris, it's *nothing*," she said quickly, as if sensing my distress. "I promise. I just wanted to make sure you remembered, that's all."

It was more than that—I felt it as deeply as I feared for her safety. And yet I knew she wouldn't tell me anything. Not yet. "Is something going to happen between now and tomorrow, Mom?"

If there was, Aunt Riley was going to get a call. If not, I was talking to her after lunch tomorrow.

Mom's gaze snapped back. "No. I'll meet you tomorrow, love. Be careful with your Aedh—they are more than you can ever imagine, and they do not play by human rules."

"Because they're not—" The rest of the sentence died on my lips. Mom had already hung up.

I opened my mouth to say her name and reconnect, then stopped. If there was any immediate danger—either to me *or* to her—she would have said something. Whatever she was worried about, it would happen *after* our get-together tomorrow. Which meant I could confront her about it then.

I switched off the computer, grabbed my purse, and headed downstairs. It took me ten minutes to catch a cab, which meant it was exactly one o'clock by the time I got to Alimento. Only to discover the place was closed.

I frowned and peered in the front window. The restaurant was dark and the tables unset. There was no noise emanating from the place, but light seeped out from under a door at the back. I stepped away, checked that I did indeed have the right place, then got out my phone and rang Lucian.

"Don't tell me you can't make it," he said, by way of answering. "Not when I've gone to the trouble of preparing a rather amazing Italian beef stew for you."

"A proper Italian beef stew needs to be simmered for at least an hour and a half," I said, smiling. "Did I not mention the fact that I own a restaurant and know a little about cooking myself?"

"Oh blast, caught out." His smile was wide and not in the least repentant. "I shall have to admit that I merely reheat it, but that makes it no less amazing. And the bread is fresh and hot."

"None of which will do me any good if you don't tell me where you actually are. I'm at the door, the restaurant is closed, and you're nowhere in sight."

He laughed. "In my eagerness to impress you, I forgot to open the door. Forgive me."

He hung up, and a moment later he appeared, sauntering toward the door, the grace and economy of his movements only emphasizing the dangerous power that seemed to reside within him. A power I could feel, even from out on the street.

Again that odd mix of excitement and fear swirled through me, and for a brief moment the itch to flee arose. Then I thrust the fear away and walked across to the door as he opened it.

His gaze swept me, then rose to meet mine, alive with desire and approval. The force of it vibrated through me, making my senses hum in pleasure. "You look lovely," he said, kissing each cheek then stepping aside and motioning me in. "Perhaps we should skip the main meal and go straight to dessert."

Yes, please, I thought. Because if that smile was any indication, dessert was *me.*

But all I said was, "Do you own Alimento?"

"No." He locked the door behind us then touched his hand lightly against my spine. The heat of it traveled all the way down to my toes. "But the friend I'm staying with does. His apartment is upstairs."

So I'd been right. He did live close. *Really* close. I licked lips suddenly dry with excitement and said, "And he allows you to cook in his kitchen when they're preparing for the evening sitting?"

He pushed open the metal swing door, guiding me into a kitchen that was small, neat, and extremely clean. Even the huge exhaust hood sparkled, and I knew from experience how hard those were to keep spotless.

It was also very empty.

"The restaurant is closed Monday through Wednesday, so as long as I clean my mess, Robert has no problems with me using his kitchen. Would you like a drink of some kind?"

"Just a Coke would be fine."

He peered at me. "You wouldn't prefer something alcoholic? There are some very drinkable whites in the cooler."

"I prefer not to drink during the day." I shrugged. "A habit left over from the days when our restaurant was new and we often had to fill in at a moment's notice."

"So what is the name of your restaurant?"

He walked across the kitchen, and I found my gaze drawn by the way his faded jeans fit his butt. *Nice* didn't even begin to do it justice.

"RYT's," I said, suddenly remembering he'd asked a question.

He opened the door of the huge commercial fridge and cold air rushed out, swirling around his boots. He glanced at me before he stepped inside, and the amusement so evident in his bright eyes suggested he knew *exactly* what had been distracting me.

"Your restaurant has been creating some buzz recently," he commented as he reemerged. He kicked the door closed, then strode back, two bottles of Coke in his hand. "Glass or bottle?"

"Why create more dishes?"

"A girl after my own heart." He opened the Cokes, then handed one to me, his fingers brushing mine then pulling away. But the heat of that all-too-brief caress lingered and burned.

"We've been lucky," I commented. "We hit the market at the right time, and we managed to employ some great staff."

"Timing and staff are both very important, but management also plays its part. A restaurant is only ever as good as the people who run her."

He stopped in front of me, filling my senses with his intoxicating presence. It wasn't just the scent of him, wasn't just the heat of him, but rather an overwhelming sensation of danger and desire and man. As if the three had combined in this one being, creating something that was far beyond the norm.

Which he was. He was an Aedh, after all—and from what Mom had said, this burn was designed purely to get me into bed.

And I wasn't about to fight it.

But that meant I had better ask my questions now, because I had a suspicion my brain wouldn't be capable of thinking in another few minutes. Not if the look in his eyes was anything to go by.

"You told me last night that your friend wasn't Aedh," I commented, leaning my butt against the steel of a counter. The coolness of the under-counter refrigerator played across the backs of my legs, but did little to ease the fire burning through my body. "Does that mean you don't actually know any Aedh in Melbourne?"

He reached out, catching the stray strand of hair resting against my cheek and gently tucking it back behind my ear. His fingers lingered against my neck, sending a delighted shiver through my limbs.

"Not many," he said, his green eyes slightly distracted as his fingertips traveled from the base of my ear down to my collarbone. "Aedh are solitary beings as a rule. Few of them even live fully in the flesh."

My gaze involuntarily dropped, and the anticipation of getting *his* flesh inside me sizzled. I licked my lips and tried to control the urge to tell him to just get on with it as fingers slid over the collar of my cotton sweater and continued their slow, sweet journey toward my breasts.

"Then what do they do?"

He shrugged, his gaze following the progress of his fingers. When he brushed—ever so slightly—the edge of my areola, a groan of pleasure rolled up my throat. I held it in check, wanting to delay the moment of complete surrender a little longer.

"I have not been capable of attaining my full shape for eons. I have forgotten what it is like to be truly Aedh."

I reached out, resting my hand against his chest, feeling the heat of his skin through the cotton shirt. Feeling the pounding of his heart, as rapid as my own. "It must be hard for you, existing only on this plane."

"At times like this," he murmured, his fingers sliding up under my chin and drawing it forward, until his lips were a hairbreadth away from mine and our breaths mingled, "it does not seem so bad."

Then his lips met mine, barely touching, kissing my top lip, then the bottom, before claiming them fully. His hand slid to the back of my neck, holding me still as the kiss deepened, becoming an exploration that was intense and passionate and explosive. Once again electricity surged, filling the air, filling my flesh, until all that was left was this kiss and the power that surged between our bodies.

After a while, he pulled back, his breathing as quick as mine. "It seems we have two choices here," he said softly, stepping closer and placing his hands on either side of my body. Not touching me, simply stopping me from moving—even though I had no desire to. "We could enjoy our meal first and delay this moment, or we could go upstairs and finish what the kiss has started."

I smiled and trailed my hands up his body, enjoying the way his muscles reacted to even that lightest of touches. When I reached the top button of his shirt, I flicked it open, then did the same to the next one.

"Something to eat would be good," I murmured, my gaze following the progress of my fingers as I undid more buttons, revealing the defined, muscular lines of his chest and stomach. "But you forgot to mention the third option."

My gaze rose to his, and he said, almost lazily, "And that would be?"

"We could continue our discussion."

He laughed softly and let his hand trail from the

back of my neck and down my arm until his hand wrapped around mine. With one quick and gentle tug, I found myself pressed against the hardness of his body and then trapped in the prison of his arms. Not that I was complaining—not when every inch of me tingled with awareness of his closeness. And of the rampant readiness pressed so neatly against my stomach. Even through jeans, he was pretty damn impressive.

"And what, exactly, were we talking about?" he murmured, dropping a kiss on my forehead, then trailing them down either side of my face.

My breathing just about stopped when his mouth brushed mine again, but he didn't linger, his butterfly kisses moving back up again.

"I wanted to know about the Aedh," I somehow managed to say. "I wanted to know if perhaps you knew my father."

"It is always possible," he said, his gaze meeting mine as he pulled back a little. My skin mourned the loss of his lips, but the heated, sexual look in his eyes suggested it wouldn't be mourning for long. "Although as I said, we tend to be singular rather than a community."

"Except for the priests."

"Except for the priests," he agreed, then his lips came down on mine again and, for the longest time, there was no talking, no thinking, just enjoyment of this man and the incredible electricity of his kiss.

"Let's resume this conversation upstairs," he murmured eventually.

"What about the stew?" I glanced across to the stove as his fingers entwined mine and he tugged me forward. The jet was on low, so it was doubtful any-thing would burn. And even if it did, I really couldn't have cared. Right now, my hunger for him was far greater than my need to eat.

"Right now," he said, as he weaved through the kitchen then out into the rear of the dining room, "I couldn't give a damn about the stew."

The door at the back of the restaurant had hand-print security. He pressed his free hand against it and, after a moment, the door clicked open. He stepped back and ushered me through, pressing his hand lightly against my spine as we began to climb the stairs side by side. The heat and rawness of him swirled around me, almost overriding the sweetness of jasmine drifting down.

"So what is your father's name?" he asked as he opened the door at the top.

"Hieu." I glanced around the room. It was an open kitchen, dining, and living area, the wall sparsely dec-orated and the furniture expensive but well used. A large vase of jasmine and roses dominated the dining table.

He guided me left, toward a small hall. "It's not a name I know, but then, I haven't been in Melbourne long. Is the filigree around your neck his?"

I nodded. "Why?"

"Because it is the type of filigree worn by priests, and they don't exist anymore."

"Well, he was alive twenty-eight years ago, and the priests died out long before then."

"That's true. I shall ask around, if you like."

I flashed him an appreciative smile. "That would be great."

He half shrugged. "You are aware, of course, that an Aedh only breeds when his death is near. He might well have gone from this world."

Not likely, given the number of people who suddenly wanted to talk to him. But I held the comment back and simply nodded. "I know. I was just curious, that's all."

His bedroom was the last door on the right. The room was simply decorated in creams and brown, and there was little in the way of furniture—mainly because the bed was so large, it dominated the room.

"Aedh rarely choose to meet their offspring." He closed the door behind him, then turned to face me. My mouth went dry with the sheer force of his desire. "Even if I find him, he may wish to have nothing to do with you."

"I know." I brushed my fingers underneath his shirt and slid them upward, pushing the material from his shoulders. He let it slip to the floor, then raised his hands, catching the end of my sweater and pulling it gently over my head. He tossed it to one side as his gaze slipped down my body, the heat of it making my nipples pucker even more fiercely.

"Lovely," he murmured as his hands continued their journey downward. He tugged lightly at the button on my jeans, then undid the zip.

His touch slid erotically down the outside of my panties and my breath hitched. God, how I ached to be touched. No, not just touched, but filled. I needed him, needed the hardness of him, inside me, thrusting deep. I licked my lips and undid his jean button fly. His cock sprang free of its restriction, engorged with blood and quivering with readiness. I caressed it lightly, saw the bead of pre-cum on its tip, and felt the shudder that went through his body.

"I have to warn you," he said as I hooked the edges of his jeans and underpants and thrust them down his hips, "that it has been a while since I've shared this experience with another. I'm afraid that I may not last very long."

"Then let's make the first time all about satisfying basic urges," I said with a grin, as my jeans joined his on the floor. "And the second all about passion."

"And what about the third time?" he growled, as he pressed his fingers against my shoulder and lightly pushed me backward.

"Will you be able to manage a third time?" I teased.

Something flared in his eyes and my heart skipped several beats. A challenge had been given and accepted. I was in for one *hell* of an afternoon.

The backs of my knees hit the base of the bed, and I let myself fall backward, bouncing lightly and grinning in anticipation. He smiled and crawled onto the bed, his body straddling mine but not touching.

"I am Aedh," he murmured, his face so close to mine that it felt like I was breathing in the very essence of him. "And I intend to make love to you until your body is weak and you beg me to stop."

I chuckled and cupped his cheek with my hand. "I'm half werewolf, so it'll take a whole lot of loving before *that* happens."

His lips twitched. "Don't say I didn't warn you."

Then his mouth met mine and he kissed me fiercely. I wrapped my legs around his, desperately trying to pull him down on top of me, aching with the need to feel skin on skin, skin inside skin. He resisted, his mouth moving from mine, trailing kisses over my chin and down my neck. But it was teeth that grazed my nipples, and I gasped in pleasure, my body arching in response.

He chuckled softly. "I think you like that."

He didn't give me the chance to reply, simply nipped again, teasing each hard nub lightly between his teeth then sucking gently. I shuddered and groaned under the pleasurable assault, and wrapped my legs higher around his body, drawing my hips upward until his penis teased my clitoris. I rubbed gently, back and forth, gradually sliding him farther and farther into my slickness until he pushed lightly inside. I kept the contact shallow, allowing only the tip of him to enter before quickly pulling back and repeating the whole process. His body began to shake with the force of his desire and the smell of lust and sex was thick in the air, mingling with the aroma of man and power, creating a heady mixture that had all my senses reeling.

Or maybe that was the magic of his mouth, the kisses he rained all over my body, the clever way he seemed to know just when to bite and when to caress.

And then, just when I thought I could take no more, he leaned close, his lips brushing my ear as he said, "I think I need to fuck you now."

"Do it," I said, my voice so breathless with longing that I barely recognized it. "Please, just do it."

And with those words, he plunged inside me, going as deep as it was possible to go. Pleasure, pure and basic, rammed through me as forcefully as his flesh, and I gasped, my body arching up against his, my hands on the scarred planes of his back, holding him tight.

He began to move, not slowly, not gently, but fiercely. My own movements were just as urgent, just as demanding. It had been far too long—if ever— since I'd experienced pleasure this damn good.

Then he tangled his hand in my hair, holding me still as he kissed me. But this was no ordinary kiss, because it was more than just a meeting of lips, a tangle of tongues. It was energy and power and heat, flesh and spirit, as if our joining was on this plane *and* the other.

Then thought was swept away, becoming pure bliss on all levels. His movements became more frantic, and my body shook under the assault. The tightness built up inside me, radiating out to the very tips of my toes and fingers, until it felt as if my body was ready to explode and my mind about to fracture.

Then everything *did* explode, and I was shuddering, shaking, not only with the force of my orgasm but the sheer intensity of sensation rolling through me on that other plane. A heartbeat later, an animal roar was torn from his throat as he came so very deep inside me.

For several minutes neither of us moved. He kept his weight off me, but his forehead rested against mine and his breath washed my face. It was a pleasant sensation that did little to cool the heat still lingering in my flesh.

Mom was right. The sex *didn't* live up to the promise of the kiss, but it was still as far away from functional as you could get.

He sighed and moved enough to claim my lips, our

kiss soft and sweet. Then he shifted to one side and gathered me close.

"I should go down and turn the stew off," he said, running his finger lightly down my cheek. His eyes still burned with unchecked desire. "But that would involve moving from this bed and, right now, I have no desire to do so."

I said teasingly, "Don't tell me you're tired already. What happened to that legendary Aedh stamina I heard so much about?"

He chuckled softly and kissed my nose, then tucked his leg over my hip and pressed me closer. He was already rampant, and my pulse rate skipped then raced.

"There's nothing wrong with my stamina, young lady, and I shall prove it to you if you wish."

"Please do," I murmured and shifted a little, allowing him to slip inside again.

He chuckled softly. "I think we are in for a very long, very delightful afternoon."

"Only if you stop talking and get down to business," I said, voice husky as desire began to flare again.

He did stop talking at that point.

And it *was* a very long, very delightful afternoon.

"Hey, sleepy-head."

The soft voice squirreled its way into my slumber. I mumbled something unintelligible and turned away from the sound, burying my head deeper into the cloud of pillows.

"Ris," the intruder said again. "You wanted to be woken at five."

"It can't be five yet," I mumbled, and swiped lazily

at the thing suddenly tickling my ear. I brushed away air. "I only just went to sleep."

"You went to sleep at three thirty," that all-too-cheerful voice informed me. "That was an hour and a half ago."

I gave up on trying to hang on to sleep and opened a bleary eye, gazing up at him balefully. "You're lying. It *can't* be five already."

His jade eyes danced with mirth, but rather than replying, he simply showed me his watch. He was right. It was five.

"Goddamn it," I muttered, rubbing at eyes that felt gritty with sleep. "I need to sleep some more. Then eat. And shower. Maybe not in that order, either."

He laughed and dropped a kiss onto my cheek. He smelled fresh and his hair was damp. "What about you go have a shower, and I'll go see how the stew has fared in our absence."

"I really haven't got time to eat." I pushed myself upright. My body felt languid and my mind still hummed from the afternoon of loving. It almost felt as if we were still connected in some metaphysical way, though our only contact was the press of his knee against my thigh, and even then a sheet lay between us. "They'll kill me if I miss the party."

"You won't miss the party because I'll drive you there. And you can eat in the car."

His expression dared me to challenge the offer, but I had absolutely no intention of doing so. Being chauffeured was a far better option than trying to find a taxi at peak hour. "You just want to see where I live."

"Too right," he murmured as his palm cupped my

cheek, holding me steady as his lips came down on mine. The kiss was passionate, hinting at hunger that had yet to be satisfied.

And I thought werewolves had stamina. This man was a goddamn machine.

"It is too bad I have an evening appointment," he continued after a while. "Otherwise I'd be angling for an invite to the party, as well."

"You wouldn't have been successful, because it's just close friends." But it *was* a case of bad timing on both our parts, I thought, casually running my fingertips down his well-defined abs. Right now, I could think of nothing more pleasant than spending several more hours in bed with him.

"Given the afternoon we just shared, I dare anyone not to call us close." He placed a hand over mine, stopping my playful progress downward. "And if you don't move, my resolve to let you go will weaken and you'll end up being *extremely* late for your friend's party."

I sighed regretfully, but tossed the sheet off me and rose. His gaze skimmed my body and the scent of his desire sharpened. "I'll be in the kitchen," he said abruptly. "Everything you need for a shower is in the bathroom."

I watched him leave, my smile dying a little as I saw the puckered, ruined skin on his back. The remnants of what once were wings. *Bastards.*

I gathered my scattered clothes, then headed for the bathroom, quickly washing the scent of sex, sweat, and him from my skin before drying and getting dressed.

The smell of burned meat filled the stairwell as I

headed down the stairs. He'd obviously set the heat under the pot too high. "Is the pot salvageable?" I said as I entered the kitchen.

"Yeah," he said, dumping it upside down on a tray before pushing it into the dishwasher. "It probably only started to burn in the last hour or so. I'll leave the fans on, and that should clear the smell out quickly enough."

He washed his hands in the sanitizing sink, then walked toward me, catching a quick kiss before presenting me with several sandwiches on a plate. The beef inside was thicker than my thumb.

"Best I could do on short notice," he said, sweeping his keys off the countertop. "Shall we go?"

"Yes. And thank you."

He smiled as he motioned me toward the front of the restaurant. "Next time, you can pay for the meal."

I snorted. "It's not like you paid for the sandwiches."

"No, but I paid for the stew in the sweat and tears it took to clean the damn pot."

I laughed, but having cleaned a few burned pots in my time, I knew exactly what he meant. Even in this day and age of machines capable of doing anything, they failed to as good a job as good old-fashioned elbow grease. "Okay, my treat next time."

"Excellent," he said as he guided me left down the street. "If only because that means there will *be* a next time."

I gave him a teasing grin. "Only if you promise to up your performance in the bedroom. It seemed a bit lacking when compared with our kiss."

He raised his eyebrows. "And does that imply the sex wasn't satisfactory, my dear?"

"No." Far, far from it. "It simply means the kisses of an Aedh are fucking amazing."

He laughed, the sound like rain on a tin roof after a long hot day. "Then I shall endeavor to ensure that next time, the sex is its equal."

I didn't honestly care one way or another, and actually doubted it *could* get any better. But anticipation still hummed through my body and I wondered if tomorrow was too soon.

His car was parked several houses away and wasn't what I'd expected. Given he was an investment adviser, I'd thought his mode of transport would be something sleek, sporty, and fast. Instead it was a Ford Ute—brand new and shiny and fire-engine red, granted, but still not the sort of car you expected a man dealing with millions to drive. And it suggested there was a whole lot more to this man than a great body and unbelievable sexual prowess.

He opened the door and ushered me inside. The cabin still had that fresh-leather smell and I flared my nostrils, drawing in the scent and enjoying the richness of it. Especially when the aroma of lemongrass, suede, and musky, powerful male rode underneath it.

He climbed into the car and started it up, the throaty roar of the engine making the whole car rumble and vibrate. "Good grief," I said, glancing at him in surprise. "What's in this thing? A V-8?"

"It's better than that—it's a revved-up V-12."

"I thought they stopped making those things when the climate crisis hit and the environmentalists got all hostile?"

"They did, except for a few specialized places. But this baby runs on synthetic gas."

That widened my eyes. "I didn't think they had full pump coverage for synthetic yet."

He pulled out into the traffic, the big engine roaring like a mad cat on the prowl. "They haven't. Which is why, when I drive beyond city limits, I have to plot my course extremely carefully." He cast an amused glance my way. "Not only is running out of gas embarrassing, but the tow fees are damn high."

I laughed. "If you can afford a hand-tooled engine, you can afford tow fees."

"I'm not rich," he said, smiling. "Just moderately well off. Where do you live and when are we meeting again?"

Any near-immortal possessing an average amount of smarts when it came to investments would *have* to be enormously wealthy, but I could certainly understand his reluctance to admit it. I bit into my sandwich, munching for several seconds and making him wait. I gave him my address, then added, "You sound anxious for our next date."

"I am. I've been asked to up my game, remember?"

I laughed again. "I've already got a lunch date tomorrow, and I'm working the evening shift. But you can meet me at RYT's at midnight, and we can go from there."

"Isn't the Blue Moon just down the road from you?"

I had another mouthful of sandwich, so I simply nodded. But I was half hoping he didn't want to go there. After the mess with Jak, I really preferred to avoid the club. Going there just wasn't worth the risk—if only because Jak still went there on occasion, and I really didn't want to meet up with him. If I did, I'd no doubt punch him—and that would only give him something else to write about.

"I've never been there," he commented, glancing at the rearview mirror, "but I've heard it's the best of the big clubs."

Damn. He wanted to go. "How could someone as old as you not have visited the Blue Moon? It's been around *forever.*"

He snorted softly. "Hardly. Even white settlement hasn't been here *that* long. Besides, I haven't been in town long enough yet to visit all the local hot spots."

He glanced in the rearview mirror again, and something in his expression had the hairs along the back of my neck rising.

"What's wrong?" I resisted the urge to look around and flicked the sun visor down instead, looking into the vanity mirror. The traffic behind us looked normal. Certainly there wasn't anything I could see that jumped out and screamed *Problem.*

"See that green Toyota on the right two cars back?"

I frowned. "Yeah. What of it?"

"I noticed it pulling out of a parking space several cars back from us when we left the restaurant. It's been shadowing us very carefully ever since."

"He could be just going the same way as us."

"He could." His gaze met mine. "But do you really want to take that chance, given what happened yesterday?"

I drew in a breath and released it slowly. "No."

"Then we'll question them."

"How? The minute they have any idea we're on to them, they'll fuck off."

His sudden grin was fierce. "I've been a soldier and a cop several times over in my long lifetime. Trust me when I say I know a little about dealing with tails."

"Then deal away."

I grabbed the other half of my sandwich and bolted it down. I had a feeling I was going to need the sustenance.

He flicked on the left-hand blinker and turned, keeping his speed even and giving our tail no reason to suspect we were aware of them. After several minutes of cruising, he turned right.

"Okay," he said, as I brushed the crumbs off my shirt and lap. "We're going to do another left up ahead. It's a through-road, but when I traveled down here yesterday they were doing road work and there was only one passing lane. They'll make us stop."

"What if there's no traffic and we're just waved through?"

"Then we think of something else." He gave me a smile, his bright eyes alight with anticipation. "I must warn you, I do like a good chase. It makes me hungry."

And the look in his eyes suggested he didn't mean food. "I've satisfied your hunger enough for one day," I said, voice dry. "You'll just have to find someone else, or wait until tomorrow."

He laughed again and swung left onto a street. Up ahead was the promised road work, and a little man in an orange vest was leaning casually against a stop sign. Lucian slowed, his gaze flicking to the rearview mirror. "Okay, we've struck the jackpot. There's another car stopping behind them. You ready?"

I licked my lips, clenched my fingers around the door handle, and nodded. The car came to a stop. He pulled on the handbrake, slid the gear into neutral, then said, "Go."

He was out his door before I even had mine open, but the men in the car were faster still. They were out and running in an instant, going separate ways, forcing us to do the same.

The guy on my side was thin and angular, with legs as long as a giraffe's but possessing none of their ungainly gait. He was over the front fence of the nearest house with an impossibly high leap and quickly disappeared from sight. I leapt, grabbed the top of the fence, and hauled my ass over it—far less elegant, but effective nonetheless.

He was already disappearing around the side of the small brick house. I gave chase, hurdling the trash cans and other bits and pieces he tossed into my path, trying to keep up with him—or at least not let him out of my sight.

He leapt another fence, ran into another yard. I followed, catching my jeans on a nail, the sharp edge tearing the material and my calf. I cursed and dropped down, my fingers brushing the ground to steady myself before I ran on. He was already out into the next street. This one was busier—several cars screeched to a stop, their tires smoking as he leapt over their hoods. I followed, leaving dents in the metal, unable to leap the entire width of the vehicle as he had. Abuse followed me down the street.

A small shopping center came into view. He swung

into it, no doubt hoping to lose me in the crowd. I sucked in air, sorting through the flavors running within it, picking out his scent—fear, sweat, and shifter. A mammal of some sort.

He bolted through the doors and into the bright, wide walkway. People scattered, and those who didn't were knocked aside. A old woman was sent flying, her arms flailing as she teetered toward an escalator. I slowed and grabbed her fingers to prevent her falling, but it cost me. The distance between me and the shifter had suddenly doubled.

I swore and ran on. He crashed through a stairwell door and disappeared from sight. I leapt over a prone teenager and three seconds later hit the door myself, my heart racing and sweat beginning to dribble down my spine. Steps echoed in the concrete well—some going up, some coming down. None of them were running. I flared my nostrils to catch his scent and stepped forward, looking up. I couldn't see him, but the stairs curled upward for a good five or six floors.

If I ran, he'd hear me. And if I walked, I'd risk losing him.

I took a deep breath, then reached down inside myself to the place where the Aedh resided. She came in a tide of fierce energy that swept across my body, brushing away the pain of my torn skin even as she dissolved my flesh and made me little more than smoke.

I swirled upward through the center of the stairwell. Several people were using them, but none of them was the man I was after. I continued to rise.

I found him near the top floor. He'd paused by the exit into the parking area, his head tilted slightly to one side, expression intent. I waited, hovering near the ceiling, itching to attack but not wanting to run the risk of someone coming through the door and perhaps getting hurt in the fight.

After several minutes, he pushed the door open and walked through. I swirled after him. There were few cars on this level, and no sign or sound that there was anyone else but us here.

Which was perfect.

He paused, his gaze sweeping the area, then he strode across the empty space, heading for several cars in the far corner. After a moment, I realized why—the rotating security cameras didn't quite make it into this corner. It was a dead spot for them.

He pulled something out of his pocket and pressed several buttons as he aimed the device at the three of cars parked in the corner. The third one beeped, the taillights flashing to indicate a response. A lock pick, I realized. *Shit*. I'd just run out of time.

I surged forward and formed a mass over his head. As he reached for the driver's door, I found flesh and dropped right down on top of him.

He grunted and collapsed to the floor on his hands and knees, winded but not knocked out. I remedied that by knocking his head sideways into the car. He collapsed and didn't move.

I pushed into a sitting position, my legs on either side of his body and my weight resting firmly on his butt, doing nothing more than breathing deeply for several minutes. When the tide of weakness began to fade, I wiped the sweat from my forehead and looked down at my captive.

Now what did I do with him?

It wasn't practical to drag him back to the car with me—not only because some do-gooder was bound to intervene, but because he was a good foot taller than me. And despite his thin frame, his body felt like steel. The minute he came to, he'd have me beat in reach *and* strength.

Which meant I'd have to question him here. I glanced around, checking that we were still alone and that the cameras definitely *didn't* scan this particular corner, then rose and looked inside the car he'd opened. There wasn't anything useful in the backseat, so I popped the trunk and checked that out. And discovered the owner was obviously into hiking, because there was not only a backpack filled with gear, but also hiking boots.

I pulled the laces free, then slammed the trunk closed and grabbed my prisoner's arms, hauling them behind his back. I tied one lace around his wrists, and the other around his thumbs. They might not hold him for long, but I didn't really need much time.

I rolled him onto his back, then dropped down onto his stomach and slapped his face. "Hey! Wake up."

His eyelids flickered. I slapped him again, harder this time, the sound echoing.

Brown eyes were suddenly glaring at me balefully. "Get off me, bitch."

"Tell me why you were following us, and I might consider it."

"We weren't following anyone. You're fucking crazy."

The words were barely out of his mouth, and he was bucking like a mad thing, trying to dislodge me.

I rode the first few attempts, then punched him in the diaphragm. Hard. He gasped, and for several seconds made like a fish out of water as he struggled to suck in air. I felt a little sorry for him—until I remembered that he might just be involved with the people who had tried to kill Ilianna.

"Why were you following me?" I repeated.

"Fuck you, lady!"

I hit him again. He swore—fluently and creatively—when he was able, but otherwise he remained tight-lipped. I sighed. I had two choices. Either I could call Rhoan and let him deal with the man—and in the process lose any hope of gaining additional information on the who and why behind all this—or I could play hardball.

"Tell me," I said quietly, praying—hoping—that he did talk, "why were you following us, and who put you on to us."

It couldn't have been Handberry, because he was dead. But he'd been talking to *someone* prior to his exit from the club—someone who'd made him so mad, he'd stormed out. Maybe that someone was the next person up the tree of command—and the person behind the current tail.

"Call the cops if you think I did anything wrong, lady," he spat. "Otherwise get off me or I'll start screaming for help."

"Yeah, you do that," I said, and reached for the Aedh again. But this time, I controlled the surge of power, channeling its fury, containing its strength, focusing it on just my hand. Making it transparent, but not entirely smoke. There, and yet not.

His gaze widened. "What the hell—"

"You *will* tell me," I said softly, resting my hand against his chest, just above his heart. Only my fingers held no substance and slipped easily through his flesh, into his body, until they were positioned near his frantically beating heart. "Or I will wrap my fingers around your heart and squeeze every bit of life out of it."

Chapter Nine

I RE-FORMED JUST ENOUGH FLESH AROUND MY fingertips to carry out the threat. Though I only squeezed gently, because I really didn't want to kill him. And I could—so easily—if I wanted to. Uncle Quinn had made that abundantly clear when he'd shown me—somewhat reluctantly—how to do this.

The shifter screamed, and it was a high-pitched sound of pain. Sweat broke out across his forehead and fear filled his eyes. I let my fingers become smoke again.

"Tell me," I said, voice harsh.

"What the fuck *are* you?" he said, eyes wide as he stared at me in horror.

"I'm nothing you've ever come across before." I kept my voice abrasive, even though weariness was beginning to pulse through my body. I couldn't keep this up much longer. Going from barely ever using my Aedh skills to using them several times over several days had taken more from me than I'd imagined. And the lack of sleep wasn't helping, either.

"Look, I don't know much." His words tumbled over one another in his haste to get them out. "We got the job offer and took it. Nothing more, nothing less."

"So you're thugs for hire?"

"Not thugs," he said. "We're private investigators. Of sorts."

They weren't particular in the sorts of cases they took, in other words. "So you were asked to follow us? Then what?"

"Nothing. I swear, we were just asked to follow you and report back."

"To whom?"

"He gave us a phone number. That's all I know, honestly."

I believed him. The stink of his fear rode the air, and there was too much horror in his eyes for there to be any room for lies.

"So how were you supposed to be paid?"

"He's already deposited the money into our account."

"What phone number did he give you?"

"I don't know it by heart," he said, seemingly unaware of the irony, "but grab my phone out of my right pocket. It's there."

I shifted my leg slightly and then, with my free hand, dragged his phone out of his pocket. I opened it up, brought up the contacts list, and glanced at him. "Which one?"

"It's under Jones Job."

I snorted softly. How original. I scrolled down, found the contact and the number, then closed his phone and shoved it into my pocket.

"Hey, that's—"

"Mine," I finished for him. "The price you pay for following the wrong people. Is the number they gave you to contact the same number the caller used?"

His lips twisted. "No. It came up as unlisted, but we ran a cracker program and got it, just in case."

"Then give me that number, too."

He did. I withdrew my hand from his chest and re-formed my flesh, then patted his cheek with cold, somewhat shaky fingers. "Consider yourself lucky that I'm not taking anything more vital than a phone."

With that, I rose. My limbs trembled and my head felt ready to explode, but I ignored both as I looked down at him. "If I catch you following me again, I won't just threaten to squeeze your heart. I'll rip it out of your fucking chest." I paused, watching him. Watching the threat sink in. "Okay?"

"Okay, okay," he said. "I get it."

I turned around and walked away, my footsteps echoing softly in the concrete emptiness surrounding us. I kept my head down, letting my hair swing over my face, and avoided looking at any of the cameras. I hit the stairwell but didn't stop, scrambling down the stairs two at a time even though every step made the ache in my head and the turmoil in my stomach worse. As I neared the ground floor, the door was flung open and two laughing teenagers all but fell into the stairwell. They looked me up and down and snorted softly, distaste evident in their expressions. Which said a lot for the state of my clothes if a couple of kids barely wearing rags were giving *me* disgusted looks.

I headed out into the mall and quickly found a bathroom. A quick glimpse at the pale face in the mirror proved the teenagers were right to laugh, but I tore my gaze away and all but bolted for a stall—where I lost everything I'd eaten over the last day.

God, I'd put my hand in that man's *chest*.

I'd felt his fucking *heart* beating.

My stomach heaved and I spent the next few minutes unable to think as my empty stomach kept trying to jump up my throat.

The reality of it was much more terrifying than the knowledge.

I *hated* that I could do it. Hated that I'd *had* to do it.

And yet I knew neither of those would stop me from doing it again if it meant getting answers to stop this madness and protect my friends.

I closed my eyes and breathed deep, and after a few minutes the trembling in my limbs eased and my stomach seemed less intent on reaching my throat. I flushed the toilet then opened the door. The face in the mirror was still pale, the violet eyes frightened.

But I had every right to be.

I splashed cold water over my face, then rinsed my mouth until the bitter taste had gone. I straightened my clothing as best I could, but there was little I could do about the frayed remains of my jeans or the holes shredding the bottom half of my sweater. I guess I had to be thankful that I even had something resembling clothing left.

I ran my fingers through my hair a final time, shook my head at how little difference it made, then left the bathroom and headed back to the car.

Lucian had moved the Ute, because it was now parked several houses up from the road work. He was leaning against the side, his arms crossed and his expression concerned. When his jade gaze met mine, the concern deepened. He uncrossed his arms and strode toward me.

"Fuck," he said, stopping in front of me and placing his hands on my arms, as if to hold me upright. I wasn't *that* weak. Not really. "Are you all right? You look as pale as a ghost."

I forced a smile. "I'm fine."

He snorted. "You don't look it."

I placed a hand on his arm, letting the heat of him wash through me, warming the chill from my bones. "I had to take Aedh form to keep up with my felon. I don't do it much, and I'm afraid this is the result."

Which was the truth, but not the whole truth. I might have taken him as a lover, but that didn't mean I trusted him completely. I'd made that mistake once before. I wasn't about to repeat it.

"So you did get him?"

"Yeah, but he couldn't tell me much. Apparently he just had to follow me and report back to a number his client gave him. He didn't even know the client's name."

Lucian snorted and slid his touch to my elbow, lightly guiding me across to the Ute. "My felon said much the same. It doesn't sound like a practical way to run a business, if you ask me."

"They got paid. I guess that's all that matters to them."

He opened the door and I climbed in, closing my eyes in relief as the warm leather seats wrapped around me. Lucian slammed my door shut then walked around to the driver's side and got in.

The big engine rumbled to life. Once he was back on the road, Lucian said, "Are you going to follow up the phone number?"

I kept my eyes closed. Though the day wasn't bright, the sunlight made my headache worse. "Yeah, but I doubt it'll come to anything. Whoever is behind all this is clever, and would no doubt have considered the possibility of me noticing the tail. I'm betting the phone number will lead to some sort of message service."

"Message services don't take anonymous clients."

"No," I said, "but it's easy enough to grab fake IDs these days."

He glanced at me and smiled—a heat I felt rather than saw. It shimmered through me like sunshine, warm and inviting. "And you know this because . . . ?"

"Because I was once a teenager who used fake IDs to get into places I wasn't supposed to be."

He laughed, and something within me wanted to sigh in pleasure. "They could be using a prepaid cell."

"I doubt it—if only because the number can still be traced."

"Not if they dump it."

"Which they can't do if they want regular reports."

"It seems you have an answer for everything."

I smiled. "Only most of the time."

He laughed again, and this time I did sigh. "Do you want help tracking down the number?" he asked. "I'm sure I could dig up a nefarious friend or two."

"The boring investment adviser has nefarious friends?"

"No, but this incarnation of me has only been

around for the last eight or nine years. I was something far less savory before this."

I opened an eye and peered at him. "Like what?"

A grin teased his lips and crinkled the corners of his bright eyes. "A politician."

"No!" I stared at him for a minute. "Seriously?"

He nodded. "Of course, having to kiss babies got old *really* quickly. So I lost the election and retired gracefully from the scene."

"I don't believe you."

"It's true." He looked at me, eyes wide. "Google news reports for the Shire of Merredan. You'll find several mentions of me."

"And why would you be mentioned?"

"Because there was a severe lack of lovely half-Aedh up there, which meant I had no choice but to assuage my more earthy needs with local lasses."

Lasses, plural. I smiled. "Just how many lasses are we talking about?"

"More than two. Less than ten."

I laughed. It hurt my head, but I didn't really care. "So that's what lost you the election."

"It wasn't so much my lascivious tendencies, but rather the fact they included several married women." He slowed the car and pulled into a parking spot, and I realized with surprise we'd arrived at my warehouse. He looked up at it for several seconds, then said, "It's a lovely old building."

"It's lovely inside, but no one with any taste in architecture would call the outside lovely." I undid my seat belt, then leaned across and dropped a kiss on his cheek. "Thank you for an interesting afternoon."

He smiled and ran his thumb down the side of my

cheek. "My pleasure. In more ways than one." His lips met mine, the kiss brief and yet intense. "Until midnight tomorrow."

"Until then," I said, and forced myself out of the car.

He left with a squeal of tires, the rumble of the big engine shaking the windows in the houses opposite. I smiled and headed up the stairs, typing in the key code, then peering into the scanner. The door clicked open, and Ilianna said from the kitchen, "About time!"

"Sorry," I said, dumping my handbag on the couch, then making my way toward the bathroom. "And you were wrong about us being followed. They haven't given up."

Her head appeared around the kitchen doorway. "You all right?" Her gaze swept me, and she frowned. "God, you look like shit. Did they attack you?"

"No." Quite the opposite. I waved a hand—the same hand that had been in that man's chest. "I'm fine. I just need a shower."

"Grab one, but fast. I need you to plate up the desserts ASAP. Everything else is ready to go."

"Be there soon."

I stripped off the remnants of my clothes and tossed them in the trash rather than the laundry chute, simply because there wasn't enough left to wash. It took a good twenty minutes to get rid of the fibers stuck to my skin, but I was betting I'd still be pulling out bits over the next couple of days.

Once dressed, I helped Ilianna with the desserts, then grabbed some tape and wrapping paper from the cupboard we used to store such things and headed into my room to wrap Tao's present. Only to discover two parcels sitting on the dresser rather than the expected one.

I frowned and picked them both up, looking at the postmarks. One was from England, which meant it was the rare cookbook I'd ordered. But the other had no identifying marks, no stamp, and no return address.

"When did this other parcel come in?" I shouted.

"Yesterday," Ilianna replied.

"Did the same rat-faced courier deliver it?"

"No—why?"

"Because I wasn't expecting a second parcel."

"Maybe it's from your Aedh lover."

"Doubtful." Aedh weren't the sentimental type. From everything both Mom and Uncle Quinn had said, they basically just fucked and left. And while Lucian might have been earthbound long enough to have the harsh edges rubbed off, I very much doubted he was the gift-giving type. Highly sexed, maybe, but not sentimental.

I placed the parcel containing Tao's cookbook down on the dresser, then raised the other one. It smelled of cardboard and old leather. Frown deepening, I gave the parcel a quick shake. Nothing rattled. Whatever it was, it was well packed and heavy. I'd have to open it if I wanted to know what it was.

Carefully, I flipped it over and slid my nails under the tape holding it together, tearing it away from the cardboard. The end came apart, revealing bubble wrap and what looked to be the edges of a very old book. Maybe someone overseas had goofed and sent me two copies of the cookbook rather than one.

I undid the wrap. The book wasn't a cookbook, and it was far older than the one I'd ordered. The binding was spiderwebbed with cracks, and the brown leather was so worn the color had faded in patches. The edges of the pages were yellow and frayed looking, and the scent rising from it was one of age and mustiness. There was no writing on the cover, and nothing on the spine.

Which was damn weird.

I opened it carefully. The leather binding creaked and dust puffed up, making my nose crinkle. The first two pages were blank, but the third had several sentences written on it. I didn't recognize the language, and there was only one word that seemed to make sense—*Dušan*. The writing itself was scroll-like and beautiful, but the rest of it reminded me of the tattoos decorating Azriel's neck.

Several more empty pages followed; then came a picture of what looked like a wingless, serpent-like dragon. Unlike anything else in this old book so far, the colors were vibrant and colorful, the serpentine form drawn with such skill that the tiny violet scales almost appeared to glow in the half-light of the room.

I touched it lightly, running my fingers down the jeweled spine and spiraled tail. It almost seemed warm, as if life really did pulse underneath the luminous paint.

"Fuck, Risa," Ilianna yelled from the other kitchen. "Whatever you're doing—"

The rest of her warning was lost in an explosion of

power that knocked me backward and tore the dragon from the book.

It was no picture. It was *alive*.

The violet dragon was real and whole and powerful, and it swirled toward me—a glinting, arcane force I could feel through every fiber of my being.

I screamed and scrambled backward as fast as I could, but the creature was faster. It hit my fingertips, curled up my left wrist and arm, then seemed to settle, its little claws sinking into my skin, drawing blood but not really hurting. Its scaly hide felt like ice, and the bright violet of its scales glittered jewel-like against my skin.

"Risa, what the hell . . . ?" Ilianna skidded to a halt in the doorway, her gaze widening as it fastened up my arm. "What on *earth* is that thing?"

"I don't fucking know." I shook my arm, trying to loosen the dragon's serpentine grip, but to no avail. "It sort of exploded from the book and attached itself to me."

And it *was* attaching itself. Even as I watched, it flattened out, seeming to sink into my skin, until it looked more like a vivid tattoo that curled from my wrist to my shoulder rather than a creature that had exploded to life from a book.

Ilianna knelt beside me and carefully touched the beast. "My God," she said, awe in her voice. "It's alive. I can feel the beat of its heart."

"So can I." And that beat was tuning itself to mine. A tremor ran through me, and fire flared briefly in the creature's obsidian eyes. It was almost as if it was responding to my fear. I swallowed heavily. "What the hell is it?"

"I don't know." She skimmed my arm with her fingertips, not quite touching the dragon, but close enough to rustle the fine hairs on my arm. "It's powerful. *Extremely* powerful. But I've never felt anything like this before."

"That'll teach me to open strange fucking parcels," I muttered, then blew out a breath. It didn't do much to calm the trembling. "So it's powerful, and it's attached itself to my arm. I'm thinking this can't be a good thing."

"The charm hasn't reacted to it." Her green eyes rose to mine. "And it doesn't feel evil. Whatever it is, I don't think it was sent here to harm you."

"Well, that's a relief." *Not.* I mean, the thing had *attached* itself to me. How could that be good? "There was some weird sort of writing in the book, but the only word I could make out was *Dušan*. Does that mean anything to you?"

She shook her head and sat back on her heels. "I can ask around, but I've never seen anything like this. Not even in the old texts at the Brindle."

The Brindle was the witch repository, and few outside the covens even knew of its existence. Ilianna's mother was one of the custodians—a fact I knew only because they'd once needed my help to evict a ghost who'd taken up residence.

"Do you think your mom would be able to look it up for us?"

She wrinkled her nose. "That would no doubt involve accepting that goddamn dinner invitation she's been on about."

"The one with the potential mate in tow?"

"Yeah." Amusement touched her lips as her gaze

met mine again. "Apparently his name is Carwyn, and he's a prime from the Western Districts."

"Which doesn't mean a lot to me."

She sighed. "The Western Districts are a key agricultural area. His family owns one of the larger farms, but he's keen to start his own herd."

"So he's a catch, in other words."

"Yes. And it's not the first time Mom's tried to foist him onto me. But despite my repeated refusals to go anywhere near him, he's quite persistent." She snorted softly and half shrugged. "But for you, I shall walk into the den of pressure and useless hope."

I smiled. "If you were just honest with your parents—"

"Don't," she said, her voice sharp as she pushed to her feet. "You don't know what they're like."

After fifteen years of being friends with Ilianna, I *did* know what they were like. They weren't the ogres she was depicting them to be. She was underestimating them. Or at least, underestimating her mom. Her dad *was* a stallion, and they did tend to have one-track minds when it came to mares and their uses.

But this battle wasn't one I could help her with. I reached out and squeezed her hand. "I'm sorry. And thank you."

She smiled. "The things I do for you two—first basketball, now dinner. You owe me big time, girl."

"Meaning you want me to take your place at the dinner?" I waggled my eyebrows at her. "I certainly wouldn't mind getting to know a prime bit of stallion."

She laughed and swatted at my shoulder. "Wrap Tao's present. His mom will be here any minute."

Tao's mom was human, not wolf, but it was from her he'd inherited his fire-starting skills. His dad had been from the wealthy Neale brown pack, and Tao the result of a one-night stand. All wolves—even the half-breeds like me—were electronically chipped at puberty to prevent conception, but something had gone wrong—or right, depending on which way you looked at it—with the device that night. Tao's dad had supported both him and his mother, but he'd died when Tao was nine. Tao had inherited his wealth on turning eighteen, and had been supporting his mom ever since.

Ilianna walked out, closing the door behind her. I contemplated the serpent-like dragon now decorating my arm, and wondered who the hell would send me such a thing . . .

My thoughts froze. Oh *God*.

Not my father.

Surely not.

And yet, everyone was so convinced he *would* contact me.

What if this was some kind of message?

How it *could* be, I had no idea. But then, I didn't know my father. I didn't know where he was, or what he was really involved in. For all I knew, this could be some important key in the research meant to bring an end to the gates.

I closed my eyes and gingerly rubbed my temple for several seconds. My head was suddenly aching even more fiercely than before, and it had nothing to do with the strain of the last few hours.

I didn't need this extra bit of shit in my life. I really

didn't. And there was no one who could help me understand what this dragon—this Dušan—was.

Or was there?

Those symbols in the front of the book *had* resembled the tattoos on the back of my reaper's neck. It was a long shot, but it was worth a chance. I took a deep breath, then said softly, "Azriel."

He appeared in an instant, the heat of him filling the room. He was standing behind me, not touching, but near enough that the small hairs at the back of my neck rose in awareness. And with it came an awareness of an entirely *different* kind.

"*Now* what's happening?" Ilianna yelled from the other room.

"Nothing," I said. Although altogether too much was. Why did this man—this being—affect me so much? He was a reaper, damn it! Not what I'd call prospective lover material in *any* way, shape, or form. Even if the form was rather nice. "I just called Azriel."

"The reaper?" Ilianna was suddenly standing back in the doorway. Her gaze flew past me and her mouth formed an O of surprise. "That is *so* not what I was expecting."

"And just what were you expecting?" he said, his voice a low, almost amused rumble that vibrated through every part of me.

"I don't know." She waved a hand in his direction. "Something not quite this . . . dangerous looking."

"You see the real me, not the projection. Like Risa. That is odd."

What was odd was how sweetly my name seemed to roll off his tongue. Damn it, *no*. He was a reaper. I *wasn't* attracted. No way, no how. I scrambled to my feet and put some distance between us before turning around.

"You have a reaper at your beck and call, and a goddamn dragon attached to your arm," Ilianna muttered. "The day cannot get any weirder."

With that, she left, closing the door behind her.

Azriel's gaze met mine, his expression as unreadable as ever. "I believe you called?"

I nodded and shoved my arm toward him. "Do you know anything about this?"

He muttered something under his breath—the words musical despite my suspicion he was actually swearing—then stalked forward and grabbed my hand, his touch light but his flesh hot against mine. He studied the dragon for several seconds, giving little away despite the tension practically humming through his body.

"Where did you get this?" His mismatched blue gaze jumped to mine. "Tell me, immediately."

"It was sent to me."

"Where is the book it came in?"

I raised an eyebrow. "On the dresser."

He walked around me and picked up the book, quickly flipping to the inscription page.

"You can read that?" I asked.

He glanced at me briefly. "Yes."

"What does it say?"

He hesitated. "It is an incantation, set to release the Dušan the moment you touched the inking."

"Does it say why I was given this thing?"

"No." He snapped the book closed and dropped it back onto the dresser. "But their usual purpose is to protect the wearer when they are walking the gray fields or commuting the portals."

"Given I don't do one very often and the other never, what's the point of giving one to me?"

"That I do not know." He frowned and walked back. He touched my fingers again, lifting my arm gently. Violet fire rippled down the Dušan's bright scales, and the obsidian eyes gleamed with awareness. Reacting to the touch, or the power of the man behind it? "It is an extremely strong one, though. Whoever made this for you knew what they were doing."

I stared at him for a moment, my mouth suddenly dry. "This was made for me? *Specifically* for me?"

"Yes. There are few left capable of making a Dušan such as this." His gaze met mine again. "I suspect your father might be one of them."

"But if the Dušan was made for me, how come that book is so old?"

He shrugged. "Modern paper does not hold magic as well."

"So why in the hell would he even make one for me?" I ripped my fingers from his and stalked across the room, stopping at the window and crossing my arms. The traffic on the street below was a blur, muted by the electrochromic windows, but it didn't matter. I wasn't really looking at it, anyway. "Damn it, tell me what's really going on, Azriel! Why would he contact me—in any way—after all this time?"

"Because you are his daughter."

He said it like that was a complete and obvious answer. I swung around to face him. "A daughter he hasn't bothered seeing for twenty-eight and a half years."

He made a short, elegant movement with his hand. His fingers were long, I noticed absently. Long and strong. "That is but a heartbeat in the life span of an Aedh."

"But if I'm so important in his quest to destroy the world, then why leave it until now to contact me?"

He hesitated briefly. Though there was as little emotion as ever in his face, I felt the conflict in him. Which was as odd as the awareness that throbbed between us.

"Twenty-eight and a half years ago, the first of the dark path portal locks was partially opened. It wasn't forced, and there was no magic involved. Someone used a key." He hesitated, then added, "Three weeks ago, all three were briefly opened."

I blinked. Locks? Key? What the fuck? "I thought the gates were just gates. Ethereal and powerful, granted, but functioning the way all gates function. You know, they open to let a soul in, then slam shut behind."

He crossed his arms and shook his head. The room's half-light flickered across his dark hair, making it shimmer a rich black-blue. "No. There have always been security measures in place to stop those on the dark path from retreating. Every portal contains three interconnected gates, each possessing a stronger lock. One must close behind the soul before the next one opens."

"But demons and things like this soul stealer we're hunting do get out."

"Because enough magic has been gathered—either on this plane or across the other side—to temporarily link the portals and cause a rift."

"So what made the rift three weeks ago different?"

"The fact that it was no rift, and the portals sent out no warning."

I rubbed my head. All this information was making the ache worse. "The gates send out warnings?"

"Once the warning of a rift would have been sent to the priests, but since they no longer exist, we have managed to subvert the magic enough so that we are warned instead. We may not be able to control the gates, but we *can* eliminate what comes through."

Sometimes, I wanted to snap, but that would have been petty. He'd already explained that there were too few Mijai to stop whatever did come through. "None of this explains why my father would have sent me the Dušan."

"It does if he expects you to be a part of his plans."

"How?" I half yelled. "I can't work magic and I've never even seen the portals! How the hell am I going to be any assistance in a plot to destroy them?"

"Hey," Ilianna said from the other room. "Everything all right in there?"

I blew out a breath and tried to calm the anger boiling though me. It was due more to fear than frustration, but that didn't make it any easier to deal with. Neither did Azriel's impassive expression.

"Yes," I replied, then walked across the room, stopping when only a few feet remained between me and the reaper. His heat surrounded me, a caress of warmth that did little to ease the chill deep within. "If there are keys to the gates, how did this person get hold of them? I would have thought they'd be well guarded."

"They would be, had there been such things. But there are not."

I frowned. "But you said—"

"What I said was true. Someone has *created* keys. We believe the brief openings we sensed—both the most recent and the one twenty-eight years ago—were merely a test."

"If it was, and it worked, why aren't the gates now permanently closed?"

"We do not know. Which is why we need to hunt down your father. He can help to further our knowledge of what is going on."

I snorted. *Help to further our knowledge* was no doubt a polite way of saying he was going to give up the information or die. Possibly both.

"That suggests you're not even entirely sure he's involved in whatever nefarious plot is currently under way."

His gaze dropped briefly to my arm. "The Dušan proves his involvement."

"How?"

Again he hesitated. "The priests could traverse the gates and travel either path if required. The Dušan were their protection when the final portal was opened and the dark path revealed. We thought the knowledge of their creation had died with the priests, but we discovered the hard way that that's not entirely true."

"You're big on explaining things without really explaining, aren't you?" I said, exasperation in my voice.

A smile briefly tried to escape his solemn countenance. "We discovered the existence of the Dušan when I was sent one. It attached itself to my back rather than my arm."

My eyes widened. "The tattoos on your back are a Dušan?"

"The tattoos, no. They're my tribal signature. The winged dragon *is*."

"I wouldn't have thought a dragon with one and a bit wings would be of any use." I crossed my arms and rubbed them lightly. The serpentine flesh felt cool under my fingertips, but I could feel the beat of life and power within it. It wasn't a comforting sensation. Far from it.

This time, the smile escaped. And it was breathtaking. "The creature is fully winged when whole. It saved me recently on the gray fields."

Surely if my father was behind the creature that had saved Azriel's life, then that meant he had to be on the side of the angels? Or, in Azriel's case, on the side of the dark angel? "Why would someone send you a Dušan? How would they even know where to send it? You're a reaper, for fuck's sake. You float around saving souls and whatnot."

"That is not all I do. I have an existence outside my Mijai duties."

And I was betting his definition of *existence* was far different from mine. "Which doesn't answer the question."

"No. And that is another reason we need to talk to your father."

"What if you're wrong? What if he's not involved in this whole plot?"

"He was once Raziq. He will know of this plot, even if he is not involved."

I frowned. "Mom mentioned that word. What is it?"

"The Raziq were a minority group of priests dedicated to preventing demons from being summoned, and they believed the only way to do this was to permanently close the portals between this world and the next. They also believed this world would be better for it."

"Meaning they didn't care about the whole human-race-becoming-vegetables scenario?"

"No." He briefly looked surprised. "Why would they? The Aedh are not human—they aren't even nonhuman as you define the word. Nor are they reborn. They welcome the eternity of their death when it finally comes."

"But they interact with us. Hell, they beget children on us when they can't find an Aedh female. Surely there'd be a little self-interest in preserving us?"

"There are enough new souls born in this world to satisfy their need. They would not care about everyone else."

I stared at him for a moment, wishing I could read him, but in some ways glad I couldn't. "Would *you* care?"

One eyebrow rose fractionally. "Of course. It is our duty to guide souls. Without humans—or nonhumans—we have no purpose."

"And yet you said you have an existence outside of duty."

"I do. But that doesn't alter our purpose in life."

I shook my head. I didn't understand him at all, but I guess that wasn't really surprising. He *was* a reaper. "You said your Dušan saved you—from what? I would have thought the gray fields would be safe for reapers."

"For those of us who hunt, less so."

"Meaning the attack happened during a hunt?"

"No. Afterward. Someone tried to destroy me."

I frowned. "Why would someone want to do that?" *How* would someone do that?

"I can no more answer that than I can the question of why either of us was sent a Dušan. Now, if that is all—"

He hesitated as my phone rang, a brief expression of displeasure crossing his features.

Though I wondered why, I didn't bother asking. He wasn't likely to answer given he wasn't telling me all he knew about this whole situation.

An intuition as odd as the man himself.

I drew my phone out of my pocket, saw it was Tao, and walked across to the window to answer it. "What's up?"

"You need to get over to Stane's right away."

I frowned at the edge in his voice. "Why? What's wrong?"

"Ilianna set up the wards this afternoon. I just got a call from him. Something's trying to get past them. Something that resembles a gray shroud."

Chapter Ten

MY STOMACH CLENCHED.

God, it was the soul stealer. It *had* to be.

But why in hell would it be attacking Stane?

"Risa?" Tao said. "You need to get over there. *Now.* Both you and that reaper of yours. You need to stop this thing before it gets Stane."

"We'll try. You stay away—"

"Ris, he's my cousin—"

"And that fucking soul stealer can take you just as easily as him. Fire won't stop it, Tao. Just wait for my call. Please."

He didn't look happy, but his grunt told me he'd do as I asked. I hung up and swung around. Azriel had drawn his sword. The blade was ethereal, alive with flickers of blue fire. It was the same sort of blue fire that now burned in his mismatched eyes.

"Where do we go?"

"Follow me," I said, and called to the Aedh.

"No, wait—" he said, but it was already too late. I was out of that room and speeding toward Stane's.

Outside, darkness was already falling, and the city's blanket of lights was beginning to twinkle into the shadows. The wind was sharp, buffeting my fleshless body, freezing even though there was nothing real and whole to freeze. I arrowed on, reaching for as much speed as I could, trying to ignore the wind and the cold and the fear that burned deep in the pit of my stomach.

I recognized Stane's street and flew down it. Music began to ride the air, loud and heavy. The outside of the Phoenix was lit up like a Christmas tree, but it didn't make the façade or the club any more inviting. Not that it seemed to stop anyone, because from the look of it, the place was packed. Maybe they were there mourning Handberry's loss. Or maybe they were celebrating it. He certainly hadn't appeared the most popular of bosses in the brief time we'd seen him last night.

I swept on. Stane's grubby, steel-barred building came into sight. I swept around it, seeing little out of place, then realized I probably wouldn't. Ilianna would have set her wards inside, not outside, where there was a greater chance of them being disturbed.

I slipped under the gap between the front door and the floor, then swirled to a stop as the containment field shimmered its warning. I reached for the Aedh again, re-forming and rebuilding my body particle by particle, until I was once more flesh and blood.

As I dropped to the concrete on my hands and knees, my body shaking and my breath wheezing past my throat, I felt it.

Evil.

An evil so thick and ripe bile rose up my throat and my soul shivered away from the awareness of it. The charm at my neck burned to life, its light ablaze with a fierceness I'd never felt before, smoldering against my skin and warming the air.

"Stane," I said, my throat tightening against the urge to be sick and the words coming out little more than a harsh whisper, "lower the containment shield. I need to get in."

The slight buzz of electricity died, and all that filled the silence was the rapid beating of my heart. Then I saw it—a shadow, a wisp, a trick of the light—hovering near the steps that led up to Stane's command center.

But as I saw it, it saw me.

And suddenly it was right in front of me, its evil filling every breath, every fiber, until I couldn't think, I couldn't breathe, and all I wanted to do was run.

But I couldn't.

My limbs were shaking, my muscles weak with exhaustion, and they just wouldn't do what I wanted.

And that thing was reaching for me, its ghostly shroud forming hands that pierced my flesh and reached inside me. For the briefest of moments, I felt the power of the woman who had summoned and now drove it. I felt the depth of evil in her soul—a darkness that stained the very heart of me.

She was going to kill me—just as she'd killed little Hanna and Marcus Handberry. Not because she hated me, but because that was her task—to kill all those who stood in the way. Right now, the one standing in the way was me. And her creature was going to rip my soul from my flesh and consume it.

I screamed then. Screamed and ran.

Not physically, but psychically.

I ran into the gray fields, where the tenuous link between this evil and that woman would fade, as all things that stepped into the gray realm faded unless they had the skill and the power to traverse them.

I did.

This creature—no matter how powerful—didn't.

But on the gray fields, the invisible became visible. The real world might fade to little more than shadows, but those things not sighted on the living plane gained substance when viewed from here. The soul stealer was a dark and twisted thing, its body mutilated and limbs malformed. Its skin was black and leathery, its face all teeth and snout, and two long horns extended from the top of its head. The claws reaching into my flesh were viciously curved. It was like nothing I'd ever seen before, and it wasn't something I wanted to see again.

It shoved its claws deeper into my flesh, still seeking that energy, that spark, that gave me life and made me *me*. I was safe as long as it didn't find the delicate thread that connected my soul to my flesh. If it did . . .

As I battled to breathe, battled against the rising tide of panic, power surged from my flesh. The Dušan came to life, her lilac body exploding from my arm. Her energy flowed through me, around me, as her body grew and became so solid and real that I wanted to reach out and touch her warmth. She screamed as she whipped around me—a sound filled with fury and frustration.

Because the thing that was attacking me wasn't on the fields and the Dušan couldn't get at it. I needed help. *We* needed help.

Azriel!

The scream was silent, but it echoed across the fields like a call to war.

I saw him before I felt him—he was a blaze of sunlight in this ghostly otherworld, and the sword clenched in his right hand was pure blue and wraith-like, throbbing with a life of its own.

He was half on the gray fields and half in the real world—a ghostly fierceness that was suddenly standing between my body and my soul.

He swung the sword. A scream rent the air—a scream that was pure energy and coming from the sword itself—and the blade cut through the creature and then me, severing the shroud-like contact between me and the soul stealer. The sword swung again, straight down this time, rending the creature in two. It fragmented, its ethereal remains becoming just another ghostly remnant of the gray fields.

I closed my eyes and willed myself back to my flesh, careening into my body with enough force to knock me sideways. My head hit something hard, but I barely even felt it. As the Dušan crawled back onto my arm, I hugged my knees close to my chest. For several seconds I did nothing more than simply lie there, shaking and crying at the horror of the evil that had so briefly stained my soul.

Heat warmed the air. But I kept my eyes closed and didn't acknowledge him.

"Risa," he said softly. "You are all right."

It was a statement, not a question. I curled up into a tighter ball and wished he'd go away. Wished they'd all go away and leave us all in peace.

But that train had long since left the station, and there was no catching it now.

"Risa," he said, his voice still soft and even. And God, that irritated me. Right now, I *wanted* emotion. Wanted to be held and hugged and told that he understood, not just that it was all right. I knew he was a reaper, I knew he confronted this sort of evil on a regular basis, but I *didn't*. "There is no remnant of evil left inside of you. Valdis severed the connection and ensured that no scraps remain."

Despite myself, I looked up. "Valdis?"

He moved his sword lightly. Fire shimmered up its side and the blade hummed. "That is her name."

His sword was a *she*? Weird. I released my knees and pushed up into a sitting position. But the movement was too sharp and my stomach rebelled. I managed to scramble to a nearby trash can before whatever was left in my stomach rose yet again.

Azriel didn't say anything, simply stood and watched.

"What was that thing?" I said, when I could.

"An oni."

I blinked. "A what?"

"Oni. They are not usually soul stealers. Flesh is more to their liking."

Well, at least it hadn't tried *that*. Stuck as I had been on the gray fields, I couldn't have done much to stop it.

"Why wasn't the Dušan able to attack it?" I'd already guessed the answer, but I knew so little about the creature who now shared my flesh that I wanted it confirmed.

"Because they can only protect on the gray fields. The oni remained on this plane, so the Dušan could do nothing."

"Fuck, Risa, are you all right?"

Stane came down the stairs two at a time. From behind me came a fierce half cry—Azriel moving his sword into attack position.

"Whoa!" Stane said, skidding to a halt at the base of the stairs and throwing up his hands. "Ris, tell the man-mountain I mean you no harm."

Man-mountain? Azriel wasn't small, but it was obvious Stane was seeing something far different from what both Ilianna and I did.

"Azriel, he's the one we came here to rescue." I sat back on my heels and wiped a hand across my mouth. What I really needed was a drink to wash the sour taste away. "Stane, why the hell would a soul stealer be attacking you?"

"Was that what that thing was?"

"Yeah. It killed a little girl two days ago, and Handberry last night. Now it's come after you. There's obviously a link we're not seeing."

"Well, I can't think of a goddamn thing Handberry and I have in common." He knelt down beside me and touched my arm lightly. "Are you all right? Do you need to come upstairs and freshen up?"

"That would be wonderful." I glanced back at Azriel. "You'd better come, too."

He nodded, his gaze on Stane, his expression intent. Assessing. I briefly wished I was telepathic. Right then, I really would have loved to know just what was going on behind those bright eyes of his.

Stane's grip slipped underneath my elbow; then he all but lifted me to my feet. The room did several giddy turns before settling down, as did my stomach.

I swallowed heavily, then said, "Okay, ready to move."

It was slow progress, but by the time we reached the top of the stairs, I was actually feeling a little better.

"The bathroom is the second door on your left," Stane said, releasing my arm but keeping rather close—no doubt ready to catch me should I suddenly drop.

"Thanks." I took a tentative step forward. A slight tremor ran in my limbs and my head was aching even fiercer than before, but it didn't immediately seem like I was going to collapse again. I gave him a reassuring smile and added, "You'd better call Tao and give him the all-clear."

He nodded. I walked across to the bathroom. Azriel followed me in and closed the door behind him.

"You know," I said, exasperated, "it is polite to let a lady go to the bathroom in peace."

"There is nothing you can do in here that I haven't seen before."

"Maybe," I said, "but that doesn't mean there aren't certain things that a girl desires privacy for."

"But you wish to speak to me privately, do you not?"

"I do." But how the hell did he know that? Did the fact that he was connected to my Chi give him a far deeper connection than I'd figured?

"Then talk." He crossed his arms and leaned a shoulder against the wall, his expression once again dispassionate.

Annoyance flickered through me, but I thrust it down and turned on the tap, wetting my face and rinsing out my mouth before asking, "What took you so long to get here?"

"The fact that I cannot follow you in Aedh form. I tried to tell you, but you'd already left."

I frowned. "Why wouldn't you be able to follow me when you're supposedly connected to my Chi?"

"The Chi is a complex form of energy that manifests itself in the form of your human vitality, spirit, and flesh. But when you become Aedh, you become an entirely different form of life—one that I am *not* attuned to."

"But I'm still me. No matter which form I take, it's my spirit, my soul, inhabiting that form. So I can't see why that would make any difference."

"The soul may be the same, but the energy force changes greatly. I cannot track that force, nor can I attune myself to it."

"Why not?"

He shrugged. "I do not know the whys, I only know the fact."

Huh. Helpful—*not*. "And yet you heard me when I was on the gray fields."

"Because I am a reaper, and the gray fields are our domain."

I frowned, splashed some more water over my face and neck, then turned off the tap and sat down on the edge of the bath. "Were you able to get a sense of the soul stealer's creator before you destroyed it?"

"Unfortunately, no. I thought it more important this time to rescue you. As I have said, your death would be inconvenient right now."

Meaning that in the future, my death might not be so inconvenient? Irritation flared brighter, but I

wasn't entirely sure why. I really didn't expect anything else from a reaper.

"Well, I sensed her—she's evil, through and
through. Unfortunately, I wasn't able to get much
more than that."

Or had I?

I frowned, thinking back over the impressions that
had swamped me a heartbeat before I'd fled my flesh.
The soul stealer had been at the base of the stairs
when I arrived, looking up but not moving . . .

"But you would know her if you saw her?"

I jumped at Azriel's question, then nodded and
rubbed my arms. The stain of her still lingered in the
dark recesses of my mind.

"Good," he said. "That is at least a starting point."

"We may have more than that." I pulled out my
phone and said, "Ilianna." When her somewhat
exasperated-looking features appeared on-screen, I
added quickly, "I know, I know, we'll hurry. I just
need to ask a question."

"Ask. Then you and Tao better get your asses into
gear and get over here. The roast is spoiling."

And given she was a vegetarian and only cooking
the roast for Tao, she'd be totally pissed off for the
next several days if that actually happened. "We'll be
there in twenty-five minutes. Tell me, those wards you
set up—just how strong were they?"

"Strong enough to hold up for several minutes
against a concerted attack. Why?"

"So enough time for Stane to escape, but not
enough to completely stop a major magical attack?"

"Yes." She frowned. "I didn't have enough time to
create those sorts of wards. You know that."

I knew, but I needed to check. "Thanks. I'll see you soon."

"But why—"

I cut the connection and looked at Azriel. "The stealer wasn't actually trying to kill Stane."

"This is the name of one you came here to rescue?"

"Yeah." I carefully stood up. My stomach behaved itself, but it felt like there were a hundred tiny drummers going mad inside my head.

"Why would you believe the oni wasn't sent here to kill?" He turned around and opened the door, stepping back so I could precede him.

"Because Ilianna's wards weren't strong enough to physically stop it, yet when I arrived, it was simply hovering at the bottom of the stairs." I hesitated, glancing at Azriel as I walked past. "Why does Stane see you as a man-mountain?"

"I merely present a form he feels inclined to trust."

"Most male wolves would feel threatened by someone fairly sizable."

"But your friend was once rescued by a man similar to the form he sees."

I paused. "And how would you know that?"

"Because I may be a Mijai, but I am still a reaper. We can reach into the minds of humanity and see their desires and fears."

Fuck, I hoped he wasn't seeing *my* desires and fears. That might get a tad embarrassing! "Then why do both Ilianna and I see your true form?"

"Because there are a rare few in this world who can see past the glamour."

"Feeling better?" Stane swung around in his chair and gave me the once-over. He frowned slightly. "You still look a little peaked. Maybe a coffee would pick you up—"

"Not coffee," Tao said, as he galloped up the last couple of steps. "In times like this, only a Coke will do."

He handed me several cans, then his gaze fell on the dragon glittering fiercely on my arm. "What the fuck is that?"

"Long story. I'll explain on the way home."

He grunted, and his gaze slid past me. "Then who's that?"

"Azriel." I popped a can open and gulped down some fizzy brown life-giver. I immediately felt better—although by rights, given I'd only just finished chucking my heart out, it should have had the opposite effect.

"The reaper?" Tao said, surprise in his voice. "Why the hell does he look like Marat Neale, then?"

Marat Neale was the youngest of the brothers who co-ran the Neale wolf pack. Kellen—who'd once been one of Aunt Riley's lovers—was Stane's father and the oldest. Sian—the middle brother—had been Tao's. I looked over my shoulder. Azriel's gaze met mine, a small smile touching his lips and briefly warming his eyes. "The man-mountain previously mentioned."

"Ah," I said, then reached out and squeezed Tao's shoulder. "Long story. Right now, we need to concentrate on finding the people behind the attack on Stane."

"And we need to do it quickly," he said. "Ilianna's stuck at home with Mom, and she's *not* happy."

"Yeah, already spoke to her." I glanced at my

watch. "We've got fifteen minutes. I told her we'd be back in twenty-five."

"Ris, this is far more urgent than a goddamn birth—"

I pressed a fingernail against his chest and tapped lightly to emphasize my point. "You tell that to Ilianna after she's spent weeks organizing it, because I have no intention of having a clumsiness spell—or something far worse—flung my way."

Which she probably wouldn't actually do given the threefold rule, but when Ilianna was pissed off enough, you never knew.

He obviously saw my point, because he said, "Okay, what did we learn?"

"We learned that the people behind this didn't want Stane dead. They were merely trying to scare the shit out of him."

"Well, they succeeded." Stane leaned forward, caught a nearby chair with his fingertips, then rolled it in my direction. "But why would they spare me and not the others?"

I gratefully spun the chair around and collapsed more than sat down. The day had been a long one, and it was starting to tell. I felt like something the cat had regurgitated. Worse still, I thought with a sliver of amusement, I probably looked like it.

I met Stane's gaze. "Maybe the other attacks were either a final warning or a last resort. Maybe there *had* been previous warnings that had been ignored. Or maybe they simply need you alive for the moment."

"There are simpler ways to send a warning," Tao commented. "Why in hell would anyone want to wreck a person's very existence? Especially when it's a little girl?"

"Humanity is often more monstrous than the monsters they endeavor to emulate or control," Azriel said softly. "And many times the cause is nothing more than money."

I spun the chair to look at him. His mismatched eyes were as unreadable as his expression, but the wash of his contempt ran across my senses, stinging like flame. He might be a reaper, he might be a warrior who protected us from the things that came through the portals, but that obviously didn't translate to any respect for those of us who populated the real world.

"Not all of us are like that, Azriel."

One dark eyebrow rose slightly. "Did I say they were?"

"No. But you implied it." I spun around again. "When the soul stealer attacked me, I got an impression of the witch behind it. She's powerful, she's mean, and she's borderline insane. But while she might be part of whatever is going on, in the end, this is just a job for her."

"Could the link between me and Handberry," Stane said slowly, "be something as simple as the fact that we both work on this street?"

"A street someone is trying to buy up," Tao said, catching on. "Although I still can't see why they'd go to *this* extreme for a housing development."

"Interestingly enough," Stane commented, "this area is classified as commercial, but no approaches have been made to the council about rezoning the land."

I frowned. "Why would they make an approach if they don't own the land?"

Stane snorted. "Why would they waste millions without at least investigating whether a rezoning application would go through?"

Unless they were idiots, they wouldn't. "So I guess that begs the question: What else is here that they're willing to go to such extremes for?"

"An intersection of several major ley lines," Azriel said softly.

I swung around to face him. "What?"

"Ley lines are powerful sources of magical energy—"

"I know what ley lines are," I interrupted testily.

Azriel gazed at me. "Then you are aware that their intersections can used be to manipulate time, reality, and fate?"

No, I wasn't. "Are all intersections that powerful?"

He shook his head. "But this is one of the strongest in Melbourne."

"So it makes sense," I said softly, "that a practitioner after power would want to control the area in which such an intersection sat."

"Wouldn't the Brindle witches be aware of something like that happening?" Tao asked, confused. "I mean, they'd have to know that there was an intersection sitting here."

"That's a question for Ilianna, not me." I rubbed my aching head wearily. "I'm guessing that Hanna Kingston's parents own either the milliner's or the general store. If they did refuse an offer on their property, then maybe Hanna's death was the hammer blow to budge them."

"Now, *that* is something I can check. Their names?"

"Her name is Fay, his Steven."

"I don't recognize either, but I'll run a quick search." Stane turned around, his fingers speeding over light screens and sliver-thin keyboards. After a minute or so, he said, "No Steven or Fay Kingston listed with either the Australian Business Register or the local land office, but there is a Fay Bruner listed as the owner of the milliner's building."

"If you check the marriage certificate, I'm betting that was her maiden name."

He didn't answer for a moment, then said, "Yep, you're right." He faced us again. "So if they're going after relations or employees to scare owners into sign-ing over the properties, why haven't mine been at-tacked?"

"Possibly because most of them are interstate," Tao commented. "And few people here in Melbourne ac-tually know we're related. They just think we're friends from the same pack."

"Then why kill Handberry?" I asked, confused. "He can't sign anything over if he's dead."

"No, but if he has no heirs or kin, the government will take his assets and sell them off," Tao said.

Note to self, I thought. *Do a will.* I glanced at Stane. "Have you actually received any purchase of-fers yet?"

"One," Stane admitted. "I haven't gotten around to reading it in detail yet, and told them as much when they called. And if they kill me off, then everything I own goes to my pack."

"Meaning this attack was probably nothing more

than a hurry-up," Tao commented. "These people are truly twisted."

"Totally," I muttered.

"Is it possible to uncover the names of the people behind the land purchases?" Azriel asked. "We'll need to interrogate them in order to ascertain the witch's location."

I wondered what passed as interrogation in the world of the Mijai. And whether it involved the sword that screamed.

"I've been trying to uncover that for a while," Stane said heavily, "but there's a mountain of misinformation and government tape to wade through."

"So how long?" I asked.

He looked at me and shrugged. "The program is running. It could be minutes, it could be days."

"Either way," I said, "you can't stay here. Gather some clothes and whatever bits of computer wizardry you need, because you won't be back here until it's over."

"But—"

"It's sensible," Tao cut in, then glanced at his watch. "And you have two minutes. Any later and Ilianna is going to start throwing curses our way. I'll go down and start the car."

As the two men disappeared, I pushed to my feet. The room spun a little and I grabbed blindly for the chair—and got Azriel's arm instead. He'd obviously moved without me even hearing him. But as my fingers touched his flesh, the heat of him leapt up my arm and fanned through my body—a warmth and strength that chased away much of the weakness from my limbs.

"Fuck," I said, jagging my hand away. "What was that?"

He shrugged, like it was nothing of consequence. Yet there was a fierceness about him that belied his otherwise impassive expression. "As I've mentioned, I'm attuned to your Chi. A consequence of that is the ability to inhibit or enhance your life energy."

"Meaning the link is a whole lot more than what you're admitting."

"No." The denial sounded genuine, but I wasn't believing it. He added, "You will call me when you get more information?"

"If it means breaking this link and getting you out of my life," I muttered, "most definitely."

"As I have said, I want this no more than you do." He winked out of existence, but wasn't gone, because the heat of him still swirled around me. Then he added softly, "And you do not look like something a cat has regurgitated. I'd put it more on the level of a dog's effort."

Then the heat of him did fade and I was left smiling—despite the confirmation that he *could* read my thoughts.

The reaper had a sense of humor. Fancy that.

It was a close-run thing, but we made it home in time to stop both the roast being ruined and Ilianna from throwing curses our way. Although—given the scent in the air—she'd been in the process of preparing some nasty little potions as we walked in the door.

It seemed she *had* been pissed off enough to risk the threefold rule.

After the food was eaten, the wine consumed, and

Tao's birthday appropriately celebrated, I went to bed and slept the sleep of the dead.

It was well after ten by the time I crawled out from underneath the blankets and staggered into the bathroom, but the shower did little to wash the fuzziness from my mind. I dragged on clothes with little thought, then headed out into the main living area.

"Well," Stane said, amusement evident as he studied me from the dining room table, "I take it you're planning to cause a riot in the near future."

I frowned in confusion, then glanced down. The shirt I'd grabbed was a striped black-and-white tee. The only trouble was, the white bits were actually sheer, revealing my flesh in teasing flashes. And I hadn't bothered putting on a bra.

I struck a pose. "I'm thinking diversionary tactics here."

"Well, it's diverting me. But I think it'll only work on the witch bitch if she's into women."

"Don't let Ilianna hear you call the bitch a witch," Tao said, coming out of the kitchen. "You won't be getting the old boy up for a year if she does."

Stane laughed, but Tao was actually serious. Ilianna *could* do something like that if she wished. I walked across to the table and studied the light screen. "Anything?"

He shook his head. "The company buying the land is the first in a long series of business fronts. As I've already said, backtracking through all the paperwork is taking time. But I think we're close."

I glanced at Tao. "Has Ilianna had a chance to create stronger wards?"

"She did it this morning, and they're active as we

speak." He hesitated, then added, "I talked to her about the whole ley line thing, too. She said she'd mention it to her mother."

And hopefully, her mother would mention it to the powers-that-be at the Brindle and they'd start investigating. They might even be able to track down and stop the Charna from raising any more soul stealers—although I doubted Azriel would be happy with such an outcome. He seemed to think the Charna's fate was his responsibility.

I moved on into the kitchen and toasted some crumpets. Once I'd added Vegemite and cheese, I grabbed a Coke, then headed back out.

"I'm lunching with Mom and Riley, so I'll ask if Rhoan's found anything." I very much suspected Riley would be under orders not to tell if he had, but it wouldn't hurt to ask. You never knew just what my aunt might or might not decide to do.

Tao nodded. "It might also be worth getting the Kingstons' contact details. Asking them if they'd received any prior threats might save time."

I frowned. "But I talked to them at the hospital, and they made no mention of threats. And Stane's letter didn't threaten him"—I paused and glanced at him—"did it?"

"No, but maybe the threats came *after* Hanna's death. You know the type—*this is what we can do. If you don't want your husband to die as well, sign the papers.*"

Maybe. I glanced at Stane. "Anything else?"

He shook his head. "The Directorate is handling Handberry's case, but I can't find much information on it."

Stane probably couldn't find anything because Uncle Rhoan was the guardian in charge, and he only ever wrote reports when he had something to report. "What about Handberry's true identity?"

"Ah, now that *is* interesting." He scrolled the screen over. "A month after his appearance in his current—and last—identity, Handberry was involved in an altercation and was arrested. He was never charged, but they did take print and iris scans."

"And you found a matching print in the system?"

"Not in the police system, and not in Australia."

"Really," I said. "Then where?"

"In England, in the cached files at the Criminal Records Bureau."

"Meaning it's an extremely old record? As in, several hundred years?" Tao asked.

Stane nodded. "There's no iris scan, and they've been around for a very long time now. The matching print belonged to Gordon March."

"Who is obviously more than just a criminal if your sudden smugness is anything to go by."

Amusement crinkled the corners of his honey-colored eyes. "I did a background check on him, and discovered his father wasn't listed on the birth certificate. Which wasn't an unusual thing for unwed mothers at the time. So I checked his mom's background, and discovered she was placed in a sanitarium by her parents not long after Gordon's conception."

Sanitarium being a polite term for "loony bin" back then. "Did the records say why?"

The little crinkles at the corners of his eyes grew. "Now, this is where it gets really interesting. It seems our unwed mother claimed to have been visited by an angel, and that Gordon was the result."

I blinked as the information hit me. Gordon March—the man we knew as Handberry—was a half-Aedh.

One I hadn't sensed, even though I'd been close enough to touch him.

It was a fact that might be unrelated to anything else that was going on, but I had a strangely bad feeling that things had suddenly gotten ten times worse.

Chapter Eleven

"THAT'S IMPOSSIBLE," I SAID, EVEN THOUGH I HAD no doubt it was *very* possible. After all, I only knew one half-Aedh, and Uncle Quinn had an energy force as fierce as any full blood. But that didn't mean all of us half-breeds did.

And Lucian *had* thought I was a full blood, which in itself implied that half-breeds didn't always get the Aedh powers.

"They've recorded her statements," Stane said. "You can read them if you want, but it's the same type of story I've found recounted hundreds and hundreds of times."

Meaning he'd been doing some research on the Aedh. Interesting. "So why the hell would a half-Aedh disguise his identity, come to Australia, then buy a dump like the Phoenix?"

"If we find the answer to that, we might just have our first real clue as to what the hell is going on," Stane commented.

I knew what was going on—if Azriel and Madeline Hunter were to be believed, that is. And right now, I wasn't exactly trusting either of them. There was more running under this than what they were saying, and until I discovered just what that was, the only people I was going to trust were the people I'd trusted all my life.

But by the same token, I couldn't tell them too much or ask any more than I already had. It was just too dangerous.

"I'll ask Lucian if all half-Aedh inherited the Aedh gifts, or whether it was just a few." Which wouldn't tell us much more than whether Handberry had been disguising his powers or not, but at least it was a start. I hesitated, then added, "I don't suppose Tao asked you to run a search on an investment adviser named Lucian, did he?"

Stane snorted and glanced up at his cousin. "I told you she'd ask. You owe me a fiver."

Tao glanced at me, expression sorrowful but eyes amused. "And here I thought you knew me better than to think I'd do something like that."

"If something happened to me, Ilianna would insist on taking over the accounts, and we both know what a disaster that would be. So, naturally, you're protecting your investment by looking after me."

"Something like that." He half shrugged, and I knew without asking he was thinking about Jak Talbott, the reporter who'd hurt me so badly.

"There's a Lucian Dupont registered with the Australian Securities and Investment Commission," Stane said, "and his address has recently been changed from Brisbane to Melbourne. Everything I can find about him seems to indicate he is who he says he is."

Which didn't mean that he actually was. After all, he'd been earthbound long enough to be good at deception. Not that I actually thought he was deceiving anyone; every instinct insisted he was one of the good guys. And this was one time I'd be right royally pissed off if instinct proved to be wrong.

I glanced at my watch and stood up. I needed to go if I was to be at the café on time. "Given he told me he was a politician before he was an investment adviser, I'm guessing his registration records don't go back too far."

"No. He only registered five years ago."

"Then keep looking, and let me know if you find anything."

"I certainly will. Oh, Ilianna said to mention that another parcel arrived for you last night."

Trepidation ran through me. I forced a smile and headed back to my bedroom—and wasn't surprised to hear Tao following. He knew the first parcel had resulted in the Dušan. Besides, he would have smelled the rush of my fear.

The box was sitting on my dresser like before, but this time it was far smaller—the size of a folded letter rather than a book. I picked it up gingerly. It was heavier than a letter should be, and there was a slight bump in the middle of the envelope. And, like before, there was little in the way of postmarks on the outside.

"You want me to open it?" Tao said. "Whatever magic is aimed at you isn't likely to affect me."

I was shaking my head even before he'd finished. "We can't take that risk. Stand back."

He didn't. I didn't argue, but simply slid my nail under the tape and sliced it open. Nothing jumped out at me. No magic, no creatures, nothing.

Inside was a piece of paper wrapped around something small and heavy. I slid it out onto my palm and waited a heartbeat to see if anything happened. When nothing did, I carefully unwrapped the paper.

It turned out to be a key. A small silver key—the type that came with post office boxes or gym lockers.

"Well, that doesn't look too dangerous," Tao commented, peering over my shoulder. The warmth of his body seeped into my back but did little to erase the chills still rolling down my spine. He added, "There's something written on the letter."

I glanced at it. Unlike before, the writing was plain English. "Locker ninety-seven, Southern Cross Station."

"Well, that's a pain," Tao commented.

"Totally." I glanced at my watch. "And it's going to make me late for my lunch date."

"You want company?"

I shook my head. The last thing I wanted was to put Tao in front of anyone who might be keeping an eye on the locker—especially given I had no idea who this key was really from. Certainly there was no evidence that any of it had come from my father, even if Azriel's suspicions pointed that way.

I shoved the key into my pocket then turned around and dropped a quick kiss on his lips. "Thanks for the offer, but they're hardly going to try anything in the middle of a busy train station."

Tao snorted, his expression concerned. "Until we know who is behind either parcel, I think you need to expect the unexpected."

That might be true, but it still didn't alter the fact that he wasn't coming with me. "You *could* do me a favor, if you've got the time."

He half smiled. "That depends on what it is."

"Go through the security tapes and get a picture of the delivery guy. We might be able to trace him back to the company. If we get that, Stane might be able to raid their system and hopefully get the sender's name."

"I'll do it before I head to the Blue Moon." He hesitated, then added with a grin, "You do realize that if you keep giving him stuff like this to do, he's going to become a permanent fixture in your life? I don't think he's ever enjoyed himself as much as he has in the last few days."

I smiled. "Just tell him my life isn't always this exciting. And don't forget you're working tonight. If you don't show, I'm walking down to the Blue Moon to drag your ass back."

He grinned. "Jackie's in the kitchen. She's more than capable."

"Jackie is, but the Lisbornes come in tonight, and they want your special burgers. And don't say Jackie's capable of making them, because you're Mrs. Lisborne's favorite chef—and if she wants you, she gets you. She's bringing in a lot of customers."

He rolled his eyes. "The old dear gets very touchy-feely. You know that, don't you?"

"Most of our other customers do, too. We cater to werewolves—it goes with the territory." I dropped another kiss on his lips, then added with a grin, "And you can thank your lucky stars you're such a good chef, or we'd have you out there charming the customers at every shift."

"Thanks, but no thanks." He half spun around, then waved me forward. "You'd better get going, or your mom is going to be calling to see what the delay is."

He had *that* right. I grabbed a cardigan to put over my semi-transparent shirt, then headed out.

After doing a quick check for bugs, I climbed onto my bike and started her up. It didn't take me long to get into the city, but parking was hell. Ever since they'd made the inner-city area a car-free zone, the outer streets had become more clogged than ever, which meant parking had been banned twenty-four/seven. So parking lots were like gold. I ended up in one outside the central-city area—past Jeff's Shed, in fact—then jogging back.

Southern Cross Station, with its undulating roofline that always reminded me of mounds of snow, came into view. I found the information desk and, through them, the locker area. But I didn't go over there immediately, instead hanging around the station to see if there was anybody—other than me—lurking about suspiciously.

No one seemed to be, and I couldn't sense or smell anyone who set off internal alarms. After taking a deep, somewhat shaky breath, I headed in.

There were several other people present, either retrieving or depositing goods. I ignored them, though my nose registered their scents and I was hyper-aware of every move they made. Locker 97 was easy enough to find, and there was nothing outwardly suspicious about it.

I shoved the key into the lock and opened it. Inside sat a folded piece of paper. I opened it. *Explanation at one A.M.*, it said, *Sandpiper's Inn, Charles Street, Sed-*

don. The back door will be unlocked. Come alone, or I won't appear.

And that was it. No name and no clue as to who had sent it. But it was in the same bold writing as the letter that had held the key, so I guess that was something.

I closed the locker, pocketed the note and the key, and headed out. If I wanted an explanation as to what was really going on, then I had no option but to do as the note asked. But it was risky given I had no idea just who might be behind it.

And the whole come-alone thing only emphasized the danger.

It also meant I'd have to rebook my date with Lucian, and that was something I was sorry about. And not just because I hungered for his touch, but because I actually enjoyed his company.

I blew out a frustrated breath, then got out my phone and called him.

"Risa," he said, his bright eyes crinkling with warmth. "I wasn't expecting to hear from you so soon. Anything wrong?"

"I'm afraid I can't make our date tonight. Something's come up that I can't get out of."

He tsked. "That, my girl, is completely unacceptable. Especially given the challenge you threw out only yesterday."

"Yeah, I know, and I'm sorry—"

"What about this afternoon?" he cut in.

I blinked. Talk about eager! "I have a lunch date, and I start work at five."

"Which, presuming lunch will be finished by two,

gives me at least two and a half hours for my sexual performance to match our kisses."

I laughed. I couldn't help it. "With a promise like that, how can I resist? When and where?"

"Well, the restaurant is open today, so my place won't be very private."

"And mine is *never* private." Which was a lie, because all the bedrooms were soundproofed. But there was still the possibility of the building being watched, so the fewer people I brought there, the better. Stane was risky enough. "We could go to Franklin's, which is a very discreet, very exclusive wolf club on Lonsdale Street. It offers both private dining and privacy booths in the main dance area."

"I take it *exclusive* means it requires membership?"

"Which I have, so no problem."

"Oh yeah?" Lucian said idly, a smile teasing his lips and a dangerous light in his eyes. "And do you have a regular partner there?"

"And what if I did?" I said archly. I did, of course, because that was what Franklin's specialized in—providing partners for those who didn't have them, or for those who wanted nothing more than unemotional, mind-blowing sex. And Zane had certainly provided that. Although right now, he was off visiting his pack. Hence my frustrated state pre-Lucian.

"Meaning you do," Lucian said. "I'll have to size up the competition."

I laughed. "Franklin's is a service club. No one employed there is going to get emotionally involved with customers. It's against the rules." I glanced at my watch and saw it was nearly twelve. I really needed to get moving. "Shall we say two, then, out front?"

"Done. Eat well at lunch, dear Risa. You're going to need the energy."

I laughed again and hung up, my body humming with expectation as I jogged back to my bike. I sped through the traffic and quickly reached Brunswick Street, but by the time I found parking, I was still twenty minutes late.

"About time," Mom said, her expression critical as I walked through the tables to one they'd marked as their own. She was, as always, dressed simply but elegantly, and her dark blue suit made the blue of her eyes seem even brighter. Her silvery white hair was pulled back into a ponytail, and it oddly gave her face a sharpness that I hadn't noticed before. "Where have you been?"

"I got delayed by a hot man with an even hotter body," I said with a grin, and gave her a hug and quick kiss.

"About time," Riley said. "I was beginning to think I'd have to drag you down to one of the clubs myself."

I laughed as I perched beside her. She smelled of soap and sunshine, and the vivid orange nail polish had been replaced by a more subtle red. "I always have other options. I just don't always take them," I said.

"Franklin's isn't really an option when it comes to a relationship." Mom crossed her arms on the table—a none-too-subtle warning I was about to get interrogated. "So, is this hot man the Aedh I warned you about?"

"Yes." I reached past Riley, swiped my credit card, ordered a Coke, a burger, and a piece of banana cake, then glanced at Mom again. There were shadows under her bright eyes, and concern slithered through me. She obviously wasn't getting much sleep, but I bit back the need to ask why. She'd just wave away my concern, like she had the other few times I'd asked what was worrying her. "What did you see about Lucian?"

"Nothing. He may exist, but the universe is giving me very little about him."

I couldn't help feeling a little more secure about the fledgling relationship. Although Mom wasn't infallible. She'd never seen the havoc Jak could cause, although she *had* warned me that the relationship wouldn't last. "Maybe you're getting zip simply because there's nothing much to tell. Maybe he *is* what he says he is, nothing more."

"Maybe." She shrugged and gave me a rueful smile. "I'm too used to grabbing bits of information about people from the cosmos. It always disturbs me when nothing is forthcoming."

"Well, the cosmos might not be forthcoming," Riley said, "but I'll bet the Directorate's computers could cough up something. Give me the juicy details, and we'll run a check."

I doubted she'd get much more than Stane, but just in case I filled them both in on how'd we'd met and what he'd told me about himself.

My cake, burger, and Coke arrived, so I ate that while they fired yet more questions my way—some of Riley's explicit enough to have me choking. She laughed and thumped me on the back.

"A man can be as hot as he likes out of the bedroom," she said philosophically, "but if he can't perform in it, he's not worth keeping."

"Trust me," I wheezed, "he can perform."

"Good," she said. "Now on to more serious stuff. Rhoan's been questioning the dog shifter who attacked you, and he hasn't given us much at all. Interestingly, DNA tests show he *is* fully human. Whatever has given him the skill to partially change, it's not nature or science."

I wrinkled my nose and glanced at my mom. "Is magic capable of something like that?"

She shrugged—an elegant movement, like everything else she did. "I'm no expert, but I doubt whoever is bringing the soul stealer into this world would be powerful enough to alter the basic nature of life. It would have to be someone far more powerful."

"But this Charna is practicing blood magic—"

"I doubt even that would be enough," she commented, "but as I said, I am no expert."

Meaning I'd have to ask Ilianna to ask her mom. Again. At this rate, she'd be meeting stallions over dinner at her mom's for the next month. I met Riley's gaze again. "Rhoan ran a background check on him."

It wasn't a question—running a background check was pretty much standard procedure, even for the police.

Riley nodded. "It didn't come up with much. Apparently Graham Turner popped into existence a year ago. As yet, we haven't tracked down who he was before that."

"Might be worth trying the cached files at the Criminal Records Bureau in Britain. That's where we found Handberry—or rather, Gordon March, as he was born."

Amusement wrinkled the corners of Riley's gray eyes. "I told Rhoan you were more resourceful than he thought. Although he's going to be miffed you got the information before him."

"God, he's mad enough at me as it is."

She laughed and patted my hand. "Let me handle Rhoan. You just promise me to keep calling one of us if things start getting hairy."

"Deal."

"Good." Her gaze flickered to Mom for a moment, and I knew then that Mom had asked her to plead for caution. And again it made me wonder just what she'd seen—and wouldn't admit to.

"What else do you know?" Riley asked.

"Well, we know Handberry appeared a year ago, too, when he turned up as owner of the Phoenix club. He's apparently a half-Aedh rather than human— although I didn't sense that when I was close to him." I paused to order another Coke, then added, "Did they run a DNA test on Handberry?"

She nodded. "His profile confirmed his Aedh-human origins."

"What about his background check? Or autopsy? Did either of those reveal anything?"

"Nothing. He is—was—perfectly healthy. No known cause for death, other than your witness report that his soul had been stolen."

I blinked. "Do I actually have to write up a witness report?"

She nodded. "Rhoan will help you once he gets around to the paperwork. There was one interesting connection between Handberry and Turner, though. Each man had the same tattoo on his left shoulder."

"Really," I said. "What sort of tattoo?"

She glanced down at my arm. "A similar but smaller version of the one you're almost hiding with the cardigan and long-sleeved T-shirt, only theirs have two swords crossed at the center."

"You have a tattoo?" Mom said, and again there was something in her voice that snagged at my concern. "Where?"

I pushed the sleeves up and revealed the bottom half of the dragon. In the half-light of the restaurant, she glowed fiercely, fanning violet light through the shadows. Mom might be blind, but she'd see it thanks to the Fravardin giving her sight. I could feel its presence hovering behind her.

Mom closed her eyes for a moment and breathed deep. "He had one of those."

He being my father, obviously. "I'm told it's a Dušan, and that they protected the Aedh priests when they were guiding souls through either the light or dark path."

Something sparked in her eyes. Maybe hope, maybe something else. "So it's a good thing that you have one?"

"So Azriel tells me. He also has one."

"So who is sending out these Dušan, and where can I get one?" Riley commented, lightly touching my arm. Fire rippled across the dragon's scales, and if her eyes had been visible, I'm sure they would have gleamed.

"*That* is the million-dollar question," I said grimly.

Riley's gaze jumped back to mine. "Your reaper can't tell you?"

"Not when it comes to why we both got sent one. Did Rhoan run a check on the tattoo?"

She nodded. "Nothing came up, and it wasn't something Jack had seen before."

Jack being the vampire who ran the guardian division, and the man who happened to be Director Hunter's brother. On a hunch, I asked, "Did anyone happen to show the tattoo to Director Hunter?"

Riley smiled and patted my arm. "You know, you would have made a damn fine guardian—although I'd kick your butt to hell and back if you ever decided to take that path."

"Only if I couldn't get to her first," Mom said, voice grim but amusement tugging her lips.

"Both of you know I've seen too many of Riley's scars to ever want to go down that path myself," I said drily, and once again thanked the intuition that had told me to keep the Directorate's approach a secret. She really *would* kill me if she ever realized I'd actually gone as far as doing some entry tests before I'd come to my senses. "So what did Hunter say about the tattoo?"

"That the tatt used to be the marker for the Razan—human serfs who tended to the day-to-day running of the temples that the Aedh priests lived in."

I blinked. Aedh priests lived in temples? "But Handberry wasn't fully human. And why hasn't Uncle Quinn ever mentioned them? Didn't he undergo priest training?"

"Yes, but from what he said, the priests were in decline by the time he began training, and the Razan were only kept by the older ones."

"So these two Razan are either far older than they look, or the priests did not die out as everyone was led to believe, and we have an Aedh temple here in the city that no one knows about."

"According to Quinn, there's no temple here. But I suspect Hunter will be investigating that option regardless."

Yeah, by following me, and hoping I'd lead her to my father, who apparently *did* know something about the priestly ways of the Aedh. I glanced at my watch and was startled to find that it was nearly one thirty. I needed to get going if I was going to meet Lucian on time.

"If the sudden buzz of excitement radiating from you is any indication," Riley commented wryly, "I'd say you have a hot date planned for this afternoon."

"Very hot, and hopefully very sweaty." I shared a grin with her, then glanced at Mom. "Did you talk to Fay Kingston?"

She nodded. "From what I can gather, a company that has been trying to buy an old building she owns threatened to harm Hanna if they didn't sell. They reported it to the police, but without physical evidence the police had their hands tied."

"Did you get a contact name off her?"

"Not directly." Which meant that—in this instance— the cosmos had been talking to her, not Fay. She reached into her purse, drew out a pink Post-it note, and handed it to me. On it was a name—Joseph Hardy—and a phone number. "That's the man who

contacted her with the original offers—the ones before the threats were made."

Riley plucked the note from my fingers and pocketed it without a word. Which didn't matter, because
while she might get Rhoan to chase it up, I now had
Stane. "Has she heard anything else from the company now that Hanna is dead?"

Her expression was grim. "She didn't say anything
else, but I think she knows Hanna's death was not as
peaceful as we told her. She also mentioned that she'd
decided to sell the property for the lower-than-market
price they offered, so I think the threats have moved
to encompass Steven. She certainly fears for his life."

Damn. If Handberry didn't have heirs, that meant
everything he owned would go to auction and these
people—whoever the hell they were—were possibly
only two properties away from gaining control over
the ley line intersection. Which meant something else
Stane would have to check for us.

"And what about you?" I asked, reaching across
the table to take her hand in mine. "What do you
fear?"

I felt the sudden sharpening of Riley's interest—it
was an intensity that seemed to electrify the air. I ignored it as best I could, concentrating on Mom, trying to read her reactions. She could be a great actress
when she wanted to, but, over the years, I'd learned a
few telltale signs.

I saw them now.

The slight flaring of her nostrils. The twitch of the
little finger on her left hand. Things just about anyone
else would miss, but ones that told me things were
more wrong than even I'd guessed.

"Mom—"

She squeezed my hand. "Risa, you are my daughter and I love you more than anything, but sometimes you read far too much into things. I'm simply tired, that's all."

She was simply lying, and that was a fact.

"Then why don't you go away for a while? Just pack up this afternoon and go somewhere exotic?" Get out, I wanted to add, before whatever it was she feared could catch up with her.

She smiled. Warmth mingled with sadness, and it made the fear in me rise. "Ris, it's nothing." She hesitated briefly, then added, almost reluctantly, "A decision I made a long time ago—a decision I could never regret—is about to catch up with me, that's all. And that's okay."

"Dia, if there's anything I can do—"

"No," Mom said, cutting Riley off. "I don't want anyone else dragged into this mess."

"But—" I got no further than Riley.

"No," she repeated, with a touch of anger. "This has to be. Trust me on this."

I glanced at Riley and saw the determination in her expression. She'd work on Mom, and hopefully get something more out of her. But she couldn't do it while I was here—Mom obviously wasn't going to tell me *anything*.

Which was frustrating, but I guess she simply didn't want me involved in whatever the problem was. We might have a very close and loving relationship, but there were lots of things I really didn't know about my mom. Still, I guess all children could say that about their parents.

"Ris," she added, squeezing my hand a final time before withdrawing it, "if you need to go, then go. There's nothing you or anything else can do about my problem. Some things are simply meant to be."

Which didn't make the twisting sense of wrongness ease any.

Riley's gaze met mine and there was a strength in her, a belief that everything would be all right. I wished I could believe it. I gathered my bag and stood. "If you need me, call. I can be there within minutes, you know that."

She smiled. "I know. Have fun with your Aedh."

"Oh, that was never in doubt." I leaned forward and kissed her. "You'd tell me if anything was seriously wrong, wouldn't you?"

She smiled, and while I saw no lie in her eyes, I still heard it leave her lips. "Yes, I'd tell you. Now go. And I love you heaps, my darling child."

I smiled. "Not as much as I love you."

I glanced at Riley again. She nodded briefly, as if in acknowledgment of my unspoken plea. While it didn't ease the tension sitting in my stomach, it did at least give me the comfort of knowing she was there, and that she would do her utmost to figure out what was wrong.

I turned and headed out. As I walked back to where I'd parked my bike, I rang Stane and asked him to do a search on the name Mom had given me. Then I tried to ignore the urge to run back and shake my mother until all the answers came out—although I would have done it in an instant if I thought it would actually do any good.

The ride back into the city was pleasant, thanks to

the fact that there wasn't much in the way of traffic and I could cruise at the speed limit without having to duck and weave past idiots in cars. Although I did almost head-butt an idiot on an air bike. His laughter overran my curses as he sped away.

I parked in the members-only area around the rear of Franklin's, secured my helmet, then took off my cardigan and shoved it in the underseat storage area. Excitement drummed through me as I walked around to the front of the building.

Lucian leaned against the far end of the small building, looking divine in dark gray suit pants and a white shirt. The sleeves were roughly rolled up, revealing the perfection of his muscular arms, and his tie was loose, lending him a casual yet elegant air. Several buttons on his shirt had been undone, revealing tantalizing glimpses of golden chest hair. My fingers itched with the sudden need to run through it.

He turned, his gaze meeting mine briefly before sweeping down and then stopping at chest level. A slow smile stretched his lips. "Now, that is the sort of shirt every woman should wear," he said, voice low and vibrating with desire. "Although if you intend to wear it to work, I expect I'll see news reports about werewolves rioting in a certain restaurant."

I laughed and rose on my toes to kiss him hello before saying, "Why do you think RYT's is so popular? It's not just the food, baby."

He grinned. "Then it's a custom more restaurants should follow—but only if their staff have breasts as shapely as yours."

I laughed again, then caught his hand and tugged him toward Franklin's. The building itself was a

pretty, two-story structure with lots of lovely fret-
work and arched windows. The glass was mirrored
and one-way, and there was very little signage out
front. If you didn't know it was a wolf club, then
you'd never guess. And that was deliberate.

I got my member card out of my purse, swiped it
through the slot, then pressed my palm against the
reader. After a moment, the door clicked open.

We walked into a foyer that was all dark marble
and gold fittings. A small desk sat to the right, and a
plush gold sofa and several potted plants to the left.
Harriet—a petite and very human blonde—manned
the desk, and she gave me a warm smile as we entered.

"It's a pleasure to see you again, Ms. Jones," she
said, before her gaze moved to Lucian. "And your
guest is?"

"Lucian Dupont."

She glanced at the light screen to her left, where his
name had suddenly appeared. "Would you prefer a
short-term or longer-term visitor pass?"

"That very much depends," he said, a wicked
gleam in his eye as he glanced at me, "on the lady
standing beside me."

"Short-term," I said, trying to keep a straight face
but not really succeeding. "I'm not sure if he's worth
keeping just yet."

He laughed. The sound echoed around the room,
warm and inviting. "Oh trust me, I do intend to
prove my worth."

Harriet ordered a short-term pass, then said, "He'll
have to register his print with us, as per the rules."

"No problem," Lucian said, giving her a smile with

enough wattage to short-circuit half the city. "Just show me where."

Her cheeks turned a lovely shade of pink and the scent of arousal swirled—the first overtly sexual reaction I'd seen out of her in all the time I'd been coming here.

She pointed to the small screen to her right. "Just place your hand here please, Mr. Dupont."

"My pleasure," he murmured, voice low and seductive.

I rolled my eyes—an action he caught, because he rewarded me with another of those high-wattage smiles. Only this time, it was accompanied by a sparkle in his eyes that somehow suggested his pleasure would soon be mine.

The scent of arousal surged, and this time it was mine.

"Thank you, Mr. Dupont," she said once his prints had been scanned and recorded, then waved an elegant hand to another door. "Now, if you'll both just go through the next door, Katie will escort you upstairs."

The door silently slid open as we approached and, beyond it, another blonde waited.

"Ms. Jones," she said. "Lovely to see you back again. And Mr. Dupont, welcome. I hope you enjoy your time here."

"Oh, I'm sure I will," he said, glancing at me with a smile.

"If you'll follow me, I'll take you up to the main dance area."

She turned and led the way up the long hallway that was all cream-and-gold elegance. It wasn't trying to be sexy, just warm and sophisticated, and in that it succeeded. There were doors to the left and the right, and they all led into private dining rooms. I'd never used them myself, but I knew there was a mix of styles, from bohemian and medieval to ordinary, six-star dining.

"No cameras," Lucian murmured. "Isn't that a little unusual in an establishment that caters to a certain type of clientele?"

"Oh, the cameras are there," Katie answered, before I could. "We have the latest systems installed, be it infrared, heat-activated, or motion, and everything that happens in this establishment is recorded."

"Everything?" he said.

"Of course." She glanced at him over her shoulder. "It protects both our clients and ourselves. But the recordings are scrambled on multiple levels. Without the proper code, they would be useless to anyone."

A gold-and-glass staircase came into view, sweeping up toward two heavily carved oak doors. A grand entrance to a discreet but beautiful dance floor.

We climbed the stairs. At the top, Katie swiped her pass through the slot, then leaned toward the iris scanner. Once that had been checked, one of the massive doors clicked open. She grabbed the handle and opened it wider.

"Have a good time, Ms. Jones and Mr. Dupont."

We walked through the doors. The room was bright, lit by the sunshine filtering in through the glass-and-steel ceiling that soared high above us. Like the glass in our warehouse, the ceiling was electrochromic, so it could be darkened to cut much of the heat, and it was also one-way. The many build-

ings that looked down on us couldn't actually see
anything. The room itself was large, and had kept the
industrial feel of its origins. The old brick walls were
a feature, and industrial artwork and old bits of ma-
chinery decorated the walls. The dance floor dominated, but the old cobblestones were covered by a
clear plastic mix that smoothed the stones and provided a nonslip surface. Private rooms lined the west
wall, and a large bar dominated the rear of the room.
The changing rooms were located on the right.

Music swirled around us, heavy and melodic, filling
the room with its sensual and erotic beat. The dance
floor was packed, the lunchtime crowd obviously
staying late today. My nostrils flared, taking in the
rich aroma of lust and sex as I allowed the ambience
of the room to soak through my pores, into my very
bones. An answering tremor of excitement coursed
through me. I loved this place. It had always been
something of a refuge for me—a safe retreat in a
world that seemed intermittently to go mad.

"This is very civilized," Lucian said, his green eyes
holding an unearthly glitter in the brightness of the
room. "And totally different in feel from the other
clubs I've been to."

"It feels the same once you're on the dance floor," I
said, then pointed. "Your changing room is over
there. I'll meet you out on the dance floor."

"Don't start without me."

I grinned. "If you're not there on time, I most certainly *will*."

He laughed and strolled casually toward the men's
changing room. I headed for the ladies', storing my

clothes, keys, and purse in a locker before scanning in my prints to lock it and then heading back out.

I paused on the steps heading down to the main floor, looking for any sign of Lucian. There was a sea of brown and black hair out there, interspersed with red, but no gold. He hadn't come out of the changing rooms yet.

Grinning, I headed down. Closer to the dance floor, the sensual beat of the music was accompanied by grunts of pleasure and the slap of flesh against flesh. Desire quickened and my breath caught. I should have come here sooner. Zane might be a safe and passionate partner, but there were plenty of others here willing—and more than able—to fulfill my need.

I began making my way into the crowd. The press of flesh made my skin tingle with excitement, and my already erratic heart raced that much harder. I danced, I flirted, and I quickly caught the attention of a brown wolf—a big-shouldered, hard-bodied man a few inches taller than myself.

We danced, and while it was both playful and sensual, it was also very much an erotic foreplay. We teased each other, sharing caresses, kisses, pressing our bodies close and enjoying the slide of flesh against flesh.

I sensed Lucian before I saw him. The heat of him wrapped around me—a touch more electric than the caresses of the brown wolf. Then his hands slid around my waist and he cupped my breasts, his touch teasing, playful. He pressed me back against him, his body like steel against my spine, his erection pressing teasingly between the cheeks of my rear. Little flash fires of desire skittered across my already overheated skin, and I half expected him to herd me away from the wolf. Instead, he pressed me closer, until I was the meat inside a sandwich of two sexy, hard-muscled men.

And oh, it was *good*.

We continued to dance, the wolf's touch roaming across my hips and down between my legs, teasing my clit and sending waves of pleasure spiraling through my body. Lucian's clever fingers teased and pinched my nipples, his breath warm against my neck and ear, the kisses he dropped across my shoulders and neck as sensual as his touch. And his touch had me melting.

All around us people danced and made love, and the smell of sex was so fierce it was almost liquid. We danced some more, played some more, teasing and tasting, nipping and kissing one another, until the need that pulsed among the three of us became all-consuming.

Just when I thought I could stand no more, Lucian's hands slid from my breasts to my hips, forcing me to bend forward, then holding me steady as he entered from behind. It felt so damn good I groaned.

In this position, I took the wolf's rigid shaft in my mouth, teasing his head with my tongue, then moving down his shaft, exploring his length before my lips touched him, drawing him deeper into my mouth. I timed my movements with Lucian's, and savored the sensations flowing through me—the growing fierceness of hunger and need coming from the two men to either side of me. Waves of pleasure rippled my skin, their power increasing as our movements became fiercer, harder, until pleasure was a molten force that would not be denied. Then my orgasm ripped through me, temporarily stilling my movements as it spun me over the abyss and into that space of pure and utter bliss. A heartbeat later the two men came, Lucian inside me and the wolf in my mouth, until all three of us were replete and satisfied.

I rose, kissed the wolf, then stepped back into Lucian's embrace.

"Not a bad opener," he murmured, kissing my shoulder softly before adding, "Thanks, friend."

The wolf nodded and spun away, pressing himself thicker into the throng of flesh and desire. Lucian's fingers slid down to mine, then he tugged me forward, away from the press of flesh and toward one of the privacy rooms.

"Do they have private showers in this place?" He looked over his shoulder at me, the hunger in his expression making my pulse skip several beats.

"No showers—other than those in the changing rooms—but there's a spa room down at the end."

"That'll do nicely."

His pace quickened as if he couldn't get there fast enough. I trotted along after him, anticipation swirling.

The room itself was on the small side, meaning the kidney-shaped spa dominated the space, filling the air with its aromatic scent. They didn't chlorinate the water here, as the smell tended to be too strong for many wolves. Instead, they'd installed huge rainwater-collection tanks under the building, and the spa was fully flushed and the water replaced every time the room was vacated.

He locked the door behind us, and the spa automatically came on, bubbling away merrily.

"I have to say," I said, rinsing my mouth out with the thoughtfully provided mouthwash before stepping into the spa, "I was a little surprised that you allowed that wolf to dance with us. I had you figured for the jealous type."

"Hardly." He slid into the spa, his skin a gleaming gold in the soft lighting. He swam over to me, grabbed my hands, and pulled me toward him. "You forget how old I am. Let's just say that I've indulged in more than my fair share of threesomes and orgies. They can be quite an erotic experience."

I smiled and wrapped my legs around his waist, pulling myself onto his lap as he sat down. The thick hardness of him settled between my legs but didn't enter. I rocked back and forth, teasing him, teasing myself, as I placed gentle kisses on his chest and neck, then worked my way up to his lips and claimed them.

"It was hardly a threesome," I said after a few minutes. "The poor fellow never actually fucked me."

"But your mouth can do amazing things. I know this for a fact."

I said, "Do you want me to work magic with my mouth right at this moment? Because it's a little hard in the water."

He slid his hands down to my hips and lifted me slightly, shifting on the seat so that, when I came back down, his cock speared me. "It most certainly is," he said, a devilish smile teasing his lips and crinkling the corners of his eyes. "But I'd much prefer you to work magic with your body."

So I did. And then he returned the favor tenfold. It

still didn't match the power of his kiss, but it blew away every other lover I'd ever had, and that was more than enough for me.

All in all, it was a lovely way to spend an afternoon.

"God," I said, looking at the clock discreetly placed near the door. The one that said it was four forty-five. "I'm going to be horribly late if I don't get moving."

"Hmmmm," he said, his concentration obviously more on the foot he was kneading than what I was actually saying.

Not that I was objecting, mind.

Although it *was* just as well we'd moved from the spa room to the jungle room an hour ago, because my foot—and the rest of me—would have resembled a prune by now.

But as much as I knew I had to go, I still had a reason to stay—a reason beyond the teasing, erotic sensations being caused by the light caress of his fingers.

"Do you know why a couple of Razan would be living in the city?"

He looked at me. "*Are* there Razan living in Melbourne?"

"Two of the men who attacked me wore the Razan tattoo, and one of them was apparently a half-Aedh."

"Half-Aedh rarely become Razan."

"Even if they don't have Aedh powers?"

"Many half-breeds don't get Aedh powers." He began kneading my foot again. "And few of them ever have such depth of power that they feel fully Aedh, like you do."

"Which doesn't preclude the possibility that a half-breed could become Razan."

"That is true." His touch moved up my leg, his fingers light against my skin.

I licked my lips, the need to ask my questions warring with the need to just lie back and enjoy. "So, to repeat the question, why would there be Razan in the city?"

He shrugged. "Their master could be here. I have met no other full Aedh as yet, but that doesn't mean there aren't any."

"So if these Razan are coming after me," I said, my breath hitching a little as his fingers caressed the inside of my thigh, "then it's because their master has ordered them to?"

"They never do anything without their master's consent," he agreed, his expression distracted as his fingers brushed the junction between my legs.

"Is there any way you could perhaps trace them back to their master?"

He shrugged. "It's possible. As I said, I have met no other full Aedh as yet, but there are ways and means of finding them. If you give me their descriptions, I'll try to find who owns them. No promises of success, though."

"But you've more chance of succeeding than I do. And I really need to know who these people are, because they keep—"

He moved with lightning speed, straddling my body and kissing me fiercely.

"Darling girl," he said, after a long and glorious kiss, "you talk entirely too much."

"But I need answers," I said, resisting his attempts to lay me back on the lush green grass that carpeted the jungle room. "And I'm going to be late for work."

"Oh, you're going to be *very* late," he murmured, and kissed me again.

The fight in me quickly fled, as did all thoughts of work.

And he was right. I was *very* late for work.

The place was packed by the time I got there. Thursday nights were always busy, with wolves getting into party mode and gearing up for a weekend of fun and games at the nearby clubs. After dumping my stuff in the upstairs locker room, I began pitching in, going wherever I was needed, be it helping to serve at the bar, clearing tables, or carting food out to patrons.

The time slipped by quickly and, before I knew it, it was after midnight. As the girls on the next shift came in, I tugged off my apron and headed into the kitchen. Tao was scraping the grill clean, getting it ready for the next chef.

He looked up as I entered, his eyes tired but his smile wide. "That was a great night."

"Yeah. I think you made Mrs. Lisborne's week by giving her that peck on the cheek. It was all she could talk about for the next half hour."

He chuckled softly. "And next week, she'll bring in more of her friends to show off her pet chef."

I grinned, even though she probably would do just that. The old dear had a crush a mile high on our brown wolf—and if she'd been any younger, she would have made a serious play for him. "I've got to go to my meeting. If I'm not back—or don't ring—by three, come looking for me."

The laughter faded from his expression. "Where is the meeting happening?"

"Sandpiper's Inn, Charles Street, Seddon. I was warned to come alone, so don't even think of following me. We need answers, Tao, and this may be the best way of getting them."

"If it *is* your father who left the message, and not the idiots who have been hassling you . . ."

I didn't answer that, simply because there was no answer. The reality was, it *could* be a trap. There was no saying that the notes and the Dušan had come from the same person, even if the packaging was similar.

"Did you manage to find out who delivered the packages?"

He screwed up his nose. "Yes and no. The same man delivered the parcel and the letter, but we checked the name listed on his ID tag with the company, and they've never heard of him. Stane's using his image to run a license check through the Vic Roads computers and see if he can grab a match. But again, it could take a while."

I sighed. "No surprise there. It seems to be the pattern with this case."

"Yeah." He hesitated. "Ilianna said to be careful. She reckons the shit surrounding us is on the rise, and it'll splatter all over you if you're not extra cautious."

I laughed softly. She did have a wonderful way with words. "Did she manage to get hold of her mom?"

"Dinner is arranged for tomorrow night. Carwyn is on the menu." He grinned. "She's forwarded a copy of the writing in the Dušan's book, and has asked her mom if it's possible to translate it."

I hoped it could be, because I really needed to know what it said. Not that I didn't trust Azriel; it was just that I had a suspicion he wasn't telling me everything. About the book, about the Dušan, and about this whole situation.

I glanced at the clock and sighed again. "I'd better go, or else I'll be late." I leaned forward and kissed his cheek. "See you at three."

He touched my cheek lightly, his warm chocolate eyes filled with concern. "Make sure that you do."

I smiled and headed up the back stairs to the locker area, grabbing my things before heading out. I'd parked in the Blue Moon's underground lot rather than our restaurant's parking area, not only because there'd be more people about but because security patrolled twenty-four/seven. Most of the Moon's patrons were well behaved, but in any crowd there was always that one small group of folk who got their kicks out of causing trouble or destroying other people's property. Or, in my case, putting bugs on vehicles.

By the time I got over to Seddon it was beginning to rain, making the streets slick and the night even more miserable. The Sandpiper's Inn was situated in the center strip of shops, and there was a FOR LEASE sign out front. The bricks had been painted a dark red, the door and window frames were a gaudy faded gold, and the tattered remains of a swag valence decorated the inside of one of them. It reminded me more of a brothel than a restaurant.

There were no lights on, and no indication that anyone had been near the place for months. I drove on past, found a side street, then cruised into the lane behind the restaurant. I parked, then turned to study the rear of the building.

It wasn't any more attractive from this angle. There were several windows, but each one was covered by rusting security bars and the glass behind them was smashed. Water poured from the corroded spouting and the wind tugged at the loose sheeting on the roof, filling the night with an eerie creaking.

I shivered, shoved my hands into my pockets, and tried to ignore the whisper that said I should have taken Tao up on his offer. I would have felt safer with him at my back.

I studied the back door. Like the windows, it was barred, but the metal around the lock was twisted and the door was slightly ajar. Another shiver stole across my body. Whoever had done that to the security door had been extremely strong. I just had to hope he or she wasn't still in there.

But the night was clear of any scent other than the rain and the nearby trash cans. If there were shifters—or worse—nearby, then they'd used something to erase their smell.

I licked my lips and forced my feet forward. I paused at the door, one hand on the metal as I flared my nostrils, searching for any hint that something— or someone—was inside.

Again, there was nothing.

I released a shuddering breath, then carefully opened the door. The room beyond was small and dark, and smelled of piss and decay. I stepped inside, my nose wrinkling as I waited for my eyes to adjust to the deeper darkness of the room.

There was dirt and garbage everywhere. Boxes of trash were piled up in one corner, while in the other was an old industrial washing machine that obviously held laundry long forgotten, if the smell was anything to go by.

I stepped through another door and found myself in a kitchen. The trash was thicker here, and the scent of decaying food matter was interspersed with rancid oil and urine. I had a suspicion the cause was either cats or possums. It had more of an animal tang than a human one.

I walked carefully through the mess and found a set of swinging doors at the far end. I had no sense that there was anyone waiting beyond these doors, and the only sound to be heard was the howl of the wind and the creak of loose roofing.

I flexed my fingers, then carefully pushed through into the next room. The light from the street filtered in through the dusty windows, creating two strips of brightness beyond which the shadows gathered. A few chairs and tables were stacked up along one wall, and along the other were a small reception desk and bar area. Beyond that, the room was empty. It also smelled a whole lot better.

I glanced at my watch. It was five past one, so whoever was supposed to meet me here was either delayed or not coming. The latter wouldn't actually surprise me, given everything else that had gone wrong of late.

I walked around the room, keeping to the shadows and away from the squares of light. I stopped near one of the windows, which gave me a good view of both the kitchen door and the front door, and also gave me an exit—the window—if I needed it.

After another five minutes, an odd sense of awareness stole over me. I'd heard no one approach—no one beyond the occasional pedestrian on the pavement outside—and the air remained clear of any scent other than the overripe smells drifting out from the other rooms. But in the midst of all that came a wash of heat. Not body heat, but rather the heat of a powerful presence. There was an Aedh close by, and he was in spirit form rather than physical.

I licked my lips, then said softly, "I know you're here. Show yourself."

"That is not possible," came the measured, cultured reply. It whispered around me, familiar in a weird sort of way.

Because it sounded like me. A male version of me.

My pulse quickened. "Who are you?"

"You know who I am. You can feel it."

"I can feel an Aedh. Of more than that, I can't be certain." I paused, then added, "After all, it's not like I've ever had any interaction with the man whose seed gave me life."

"Under normal circumstances, you would not be interacting with me now. But these are far from normal circumstances."

"Yeah, you're trying to permanently close the gates between the light and the dark path, and thereby bring about the destruction of life as we know it."

He paused, and a sense of surprise rolled across the darkness. I wished he'd show himself, because I really did want to see the man who was my father. But I guess I could also understand caution. He had no more idea of whether he could trust me than I did of him.

"That is not entirely true," he said. "Yes, I am a Raziq, and yes, we were working on keys that could be used to close the portals, but that is not my purpose now."

"Then what *is* your purpose?" I crossed my arms and leaned back against the wall. Although the pose appeared casual, every muscle quivered, ready to launch into fight mode should the need arise.

Not that I really expected to be able to prevail against a full Aedh.

"I plan to stop them."

"So you spent all that time with the Raziq making the keys, and now you're hell-bent on stopping them? That doesn't sound very logical to me."

The heat of him was closer now. It spun around me—a warm, nonthreatening presence that nevertheless made my skin crawl because of the power behind it. Because there was no underlying sense of humanity. This was a being who wore flesh rarely and who had no love or understanding for those who possessed it full-time.

Which made me wonder why he was now trying to stop the Raziq.

"Magic alone works the portals, and it is *because* that magic can be corrupted that the keys were made. If magic wasn't as intrinsic in the opening of the portals, then neither those on this plane nor anyone on the other could affect them."

Which made basic sense, but it also meant the power of the gates lay in those keys rather than magic. And that seemed ultimately more dangerous to me.

"So why not simply destroy the keys yourself? If you helped make them, then you must know how to unmake them."

"I do. The trouble is, the keys are on this plane, and I no longer can interact with this world."

My eyes widened. "But aren't you interacting with it now?"

"Not on a flesh level. That ability was torn from me when they discovered the part I played in the keys' disappearance."

"Meaning there's more than one of you trying to destroy these keys?"

"No, but all Raziq have Razan, and mine hid the keys while I created a diversion."

"So why not just ask *them* where they put the keys?"

"Because they are dead. They were under orders to destroy themselves should I not return by a certain time."

Charming. But then, why would an Aedh care whether one of his servants lived or died? He could undoubtedly create more as needed. "And you couldn't return because you were captive?"

"Precisely."

"This plan of yours wasn't really that well thought out, was it?" I said, slightly sarcastically.

"In any venture of worth, there is always an element of risk."

The jury was still out on whether *this* venture was worth the risk. I wasn't about to trust that he was telling the truth rather than twisting facts.

"So did all your Razan die?"

"No, I still have some who *aid* me, but they have no knowledge of the theft or the location of the keys."

The odd emphasis on the word *aid* had my intuition

tingling. "I hope it isn't your Razan who have been attacking me and my friends."

"No. I would not order that when I need your assistance."

Which didn't actually imply he would *never* do it. I contemplated the shadows for a moment, wishing he was visible, yet half glad he wasn't. If I couldn't see, I couldn't be disappointed. And I couldn't read the lies.

Why did I think there were lies?

Maybe it was just the whisper inside my head telling me it couldn't be so simple. That there was more to his quest than what he was saying.

"Then why didn't they destroy you when they discovered your part in the theft?"

"Because without me, they have no hope of finding the keys. So they imprisoned me, but not quite as successfully as they thought. I am free, but powerless to do anything more than conduct events."

"Then why pull me into it if you have the Razan?"

"Because I used my blood to alter the form of the keys, and only one of my blood can find and destroy them. You are my only offspring, so the task must fall to you."

"What happens if the keys are destroyed?"

He didn't answer straightaway, and I had a sudden inkling that this was the crux. That he didn't *know* what would happen.

"The Dušan's book will tell you what form the keys are now in and where I sent each of the Razan," he said, eventually. "You will know when you are near them. You—and you alone—will feel it."

"I tried reading the book. It was gibberish."

"That is because you were not reading it as you should."

Which made a whole lot of sense. *Not.* "Never mind finding them. How about telling me what will happen if I destroy them? And how the hell am I supposed to do that anyway?"

Again he didn't answer, and frustration skidded through me. Why couldn't someone just be fucking honest for a change?

Then the sense of him changed. The warmth fled, becoming a hostile iciness that scorched my skin and made my soul quiver.

"I told you to come alone," he said, the words low and vibrating with fury.

I frowned, my nose twitching, searching for any hint that someone was approaching. The air remained free and there was little in the way of sound other than the wind and the loose roofing. "I did come alone. Why?"

Again he was silent, then, "It is them. Run. *Now.*"

And with that, he disappeared.

For a heartbeat I was too shocked to react, then I shifted my butt into gear and ran for the kitchen door. Only to slide to a halt as the warm rush of another presence hit me.

I'd expected more half-Aedh. What was coming at me was full Aedh.

Fuck, fuck, *fuck*!

I ran for the windows. But as I launched myself into the air, something wound around my legs and yanked me backward. I hit the floor with a grunt, but reached for the Aedh within me. Felt her surge, felt the power rush through my body, eager to fling me from one form to another.

Then another force hit me and suddenly the power was gone, leaving me fully fleshed and gasping in pain. And all too aware of the danger I was in.

I twisted, grabbed at the bolas wrapped around my legs, and quickly untangled them. Even as I did, the kitchen doors crashed open and two men entered. Both of them smelled human, and both of them obviously weren't. Their eyes held the luminosity of the Aedh.

So much for Lucian saying it was rare for half-Aedh to become Razan.

I jumped to my feet and twisted around, kicking the first hard in the gut and knocking him back into the second. Then I bolted for the window again.

I was midair when it hit me. I have no idea what it actually was, but it was hot and it was heavy and it crushed me back to the floor, all but smothering me with its fierce, blanketing heat.

Aedh, I thought.

It was the last thing I *did* think for a very long time.

Chapter Twelve

WAKING WAS AN EXPERIENCE IN PAIN.

Everything hurt. My head, my body, my soul.

Even groaning hurt—and I was aware enough to realize the sound seemed oddly flat, as if something was stifling it. I forced my eyes open.

To be greeted by darkness. Complete and utter blackness.

The air was warm but slightly stale, and it smelled of damp earth. There was little in the way of noise—no rain, no creak of roofing, no wind. I was lying on what felt like ice but was more than likely concrete, and my feet were bare. Which was odd given they'd left the rest of my clothes on.

I pushed upright, but the movement was too quick and my stomach and head rebelled in unison, leaving me dry-retching and dizzy.

I sat there for several minutes, breathing deep and waiting for everything to settle down. Eventually it did, and I took stock of what I actually had on me. Although they'd taken my shoes, they'd left both my keys and my phone in my pockets. I swept my hands across the surrounding concrete but failed to find my jacket—although given its somewhat tattered state, it wasn't a huge loss. The boots, however, had been new.

I reached into my pocket and drew out my phone. Not surprisingly, there was no reception, but it did at least give me some usable light.

I flipped it open and discovered I was in a cell. The floor might have been concrete, but the walls had been hewn out of the earth and were full of rocks and old tree roots. To the left was a rusting metal door, and while it didn't appear to have much in the way of locks, I resisted the urge to jump up and attempt an escape. I very much doubted it would be as easy as it looked. After all, they'd dragged me here for a reason, and it was unlikely they'd be so careless in making sure I was secure.

I shifted my legs and slowly stood up. The dizziness threatened to drop me again, but my stomach remained steady. I continued to breathe deep and, after a moment, felt a little steadier. In the cell phone's light, I saw the reason for the lack of boots and socks.

I was standing in a sea of broken glass.

My little square of concrete was about three feet wide. The rest—and there was a good eight feet between me and the walls—had the jagged remains of bottles and glasses cemented into it.

Any wolf—even us half-breeds—could jump eight feet without a decent run-up, and it showed both arrogance and overconfidence to make *this* the only barrier. But then, they didn't actually *think* like the rest of us.

Unless, of course, there was something else here and I just couldn't see it.

I frowned, my gaze sweeping the darkness again before coming back to the door. It might be unlocked, but it was sturdily built. If I didn't hit it with enough force to crash it open, I'd risk dropping down onto the glass.

But I didn't actually have to *use* my flesh form. I had another option.

I reached for the Aedh, but the minute I did, there was a sudden buzzing and the air above the glass shimmered briefly—a rainbow of color that was oddly threatening. Then the pain hit—pain so deep and dark it felt as if the jagged edge of a heated blade had been shoved into my flesh, spearing my soul and burning her alive.

I dropped to my knees, doubled over in agony, sweat breaking out over my body as I struggled to breathe. The buzzing continued, burning into my brain, intensifying the pain and rendering me all but helpless.

Then it stopped. Suddenly and without reason, leaving me shaking in shock and agony.

For several minutes I couldn't do anything more than sit there, my arms crossed over my stomach as I rocked back and forth. Sweat dripped from my nose, staining the concrete beneath me and oddly resembling blood. I hoped like hell it wasn't an omen.

Gradually, the pain ebbed enough to allow me to take a deep, shuddering breath. As I did so, an oddly dark surge of electricity ran my skin, making the little hairs at the back of my neck stand on end and my soul shiver away in fear.

There was another Aedh near.

"Why don't you show yourself," I said, "or are all Aedh cowards?"

"I have no desire and no need to show myself," the disembodied voice whispered out of the darkness from near the door. "And I do not understand this term *cowards*."

I shifted the phone, pointing it toward the corner where the voice seemed to be coming from, but its light failed to pick up anything in the shadows.

"It means you're spineless." Which was pretty much a given when I was talking to a being who was little more than energy. "Afraid."

"It is not I who needs to be afraid," he said.

As if to prove the point, the sense of him briefly amplified, burning my skin and making my head hurt again. My breath hissed between clenched teeth, but I resisted the urge to curl up into a defensive ball. I had a vague feeling that any sign of weakness would just make the situation worse. That these people—these beings—would respect courage more than fear.

Whether that would actually save me remained to be seen.

"Why have you dragged me here?" I hesitated, trying to keep the sarcasm out of my voice and not entirely succeeding as I added, "Or is that a stupid question?"

"You are here because you need to answer questions. Whether you do that willingly or unwillingly is your choice."

He obviously hadn't caught the sarcasm. No surprise there, given Azriel apparently didn't, either, and they were basically two sides of the same coin.

I blinked. *Azriel.* Maybe *he* could get me out of this hellhole. I closed my eyes and ran his name through my mind. He'd stated he would hear me, anywhere, anytime, and although he apparently couldn't follow me while I was Aedh, I wasn't wearing that form now.

But there was magic here, and a powerful Aedh. I didn't know if he could—or would—get through, either.

"Look, as I keep telling everyone else who is hunting down my father, I have no fucking idea where the bastard is."

"And yet you were talking to him in that building. We felt his presence."

"Then you'll know he disappeared long before you got there. And he didn't tell me squat."

"You lie," the presence said. "That is unwise."

"*That* is the truth," I bit back. "You bastards turned up before he could tell me anything useful."

"Another lie," he said. "It would appear you prefer not to cooperate. We shall try other means."

"Wait!" I said, almost frantically.

But he didn't.

This time the pain came as a sledgehammer rather than a knife, and it knocked me not only sideways but damn near senseless. I lay on the concrete and battled to breathe as my body quivered under the assault and my brain felt like it was on fire.

But this wasn't *just* a psychic attack. It went far deeper than that. It felt like they were pulling me apart, atom by atom. It felt like every part of me was screaming—every part except my mouth, because the sound seemed to be stuck somewhere inside my throat.

I have no idea how long I lay there, writhing and twisting and silently—endlessly—screaming, but it seemed like hours. Days even.

Eventually, it stopped, leaving me tenuously holding on to consciousness as my whole body ached with a ferocity I couldn't even begin to describe.

"She is very resistant," a distant voice said.

Or maybe it wasn't distant. Maybe it just seemed that way.

"Unusually so," the original voice said. "But she has been in contact with Hieu. There is a text we must seek—it may aid our search."

Oh God, some distant, still-functioning part of my brain thought. I had to warn Ilianna. I had to warn her mom. They might only have a copy of the text, but I'd put both of them in danger by asking them to translate it.

Yet I couldn't move. I could barely even manage to breathe.

"Anything else?"

"No. But you may wish to try yourself while her defenses are weak."

No, no, NO!

But again, no one was listening. The pain this time was razor-sharp, and it flayed me inside and out, tearing me apart as they looked for answers. I quivered and shook and pleaded for them to stop, but no one heard my words—voiced or unvoiced.

It went on and on, until I felt raw and battered and bruised, and my skin ran with rivers of blood that pooled underneath my body—a warm halo that gradually grew bigger. Just as instinct had seen earlier.

Eventually—mercifully—I blacked out.

When I came to, I was alone. My muscles had stopped quivering, but just about everything else felt like it still burned—my head, my body, my soul.

I carefully rolled onto my back. It was sticky with dried blood, but, oddly enough, the pain I felt came from the energy that had lashed the inner me, not the outer. If my flesh *had* been cut, then it had healed.

The cell was still wrapped in darkness, and I couldn't see the rough-cut ceiling high above me. But the rainbow shimmer was still present, which meant the magical barrier was still in place. No surprise there, I guess.

I tilted my head back a little and looked at the door. It, too, was closed. I had no sense of any other presence in the room. I was alone. At least for the time being.

I scrubbed a shaking hand across my face, and wondered just how successful they'd been in getting the information they wanted. Surely the fact that I was still alive meant I'd managed to hold on to at least *some* secrets. Not that I had a great many, because I really didn't know much.

Maybe that was the reason I still lived. Maybe they simply didn't believe I knew so little.

But they would be back. I had to get out before then, because I very much doubted I'd survive another onslaught.

I forced myself up onto my hands and knees. The room spun around me and my stomach leapt up my throat. I swallowed the bitter taste and closed my eyes, pushing the pain and the sickness away. I couldn't acknowledge it—couldn't deal with it—until I was out of here.

After a few more minutes, I crawled to the edge of my safe circle and studied the door. The catch was old and heavy, and looked like something you'd find in a medieval castle rather than anything made in recent—or not so recent—years. And there was definitely no lock.

Which meant I could get out—*if* I could get past the glass.

I gently placed my hand on the nearest peaks. The jagged edges sat against my palm, ready to pierce it should I exert the slightest bit of pressure. I looked across the width of it. Eight feet had never seemed so far.

But I really didn't have much in the way of options. It was either walk across this barrier or take another round of Aedh questioning. At least with the first option, it was only my feet that would be cut up.

And I *could* do something about that.

I sat back on my heels and undid my jeans, slipping them down my hips before shifting onto my butt and pulling them off my legs. Tearing them in half wasn't so easy—not when my whole body felt as if *it* had been torn apart. Hell, right now I wasn't entirely sure that parts of me weren't going to start unraveling.

Eventually the seams gave way, tearing in half along the crotch. I carefully wrapped each foot in one jean leg, tucking in the ends to stop them unraveling as I walked.

I grabbed my phone, then stood and eyed the expanse of embedded, broken glass between me and that door. There was no obvious path where the glass wasn't quite as sharp.

I breathed deep, my nostrils flaring and filling my lungs with the scent of my own fear, then gingerly stepped onto the glass. The jeans helped a little, as long as I didn't put too much weight on my feet for too long. I took another quick step, then another, concentrating on that door and the freedom it represented. The metallic tang of blood began to taint the air. Sweat trickled down my hairline, and my breathing became short and sharp. The jeans grew heavier and my feet felt like they were on fire. I kept my gaze on my target, and punched the bolt across when I was near enough, then thrust the door open.

I was dead meat if there were guards. But I knew that, and I didn't care. I just had to get off the glass.

Thankfully, there were no guards.

I caught the door before it could slam back against the wall, then leaned a shoulder against the brickwork, hopping gently from one foot to the other, trying to ease the pain. It didn't help much.

But my head felt clearer, and the aching buzz that had become such an underlying presence in my mind had gone. Still, I didn't reach for the Aedh. Not only because I was so weak, but because they might just sense the surge of power. Even us half-breeds could sense the presence of another Aedh, and I had no doubt that a full blood would have sharper senses than us. Besides, Lucian had commented that I felt full Aedh even in human form, which might just mean that if anyone did notice me out here, they'd maybe dismiss me as one of their brethren.

Maybe.

I unwound the bloody remnants of my jeans and tossed them back into the cell. If I was caught and put back, maybe I could use them again. *If* they didn't take them away, and *if* I managed to survive another bout of questioning, that was.

I shut the door, then looked around. The corridor was long and filled with shadows. Though the air was rich with the earth and humus, the corridor itself was lined with red bricks that looked to have seen more than a few hundred years of wear and tear. It made me wonder if it had been a part of the sewerage system that had serviced Melbourne from settlement to the twenty-first century. If it was, then there had to be a way out—service entry points or whatever the hell they were called. The system might not be in official use, but there'd been recent newspaper reports of the "mousers" who spent every available free hour down here, and there were undoubtedly a ton of homeless folk who'd made themselves at home, too.

I padded forward. The cold bricks soothed the fire in my feet, but I had no doubt I was leaving bloody footprints behind. The taint of it curled through the air.

The silence was unnerving. I couldn't sense anyone nearby, but there were at least two Aedh here somewhere, and undoubtedly some form of human guards as well. After all, the Aedh who'd attacked me at the restaurant hadn't come alone.

So where was everybody?

There *had* to be guards here. Even the youngest Aedh couldn't be *that* oblivious to the instinct of survival—and neither of the two who'd questioned me had felt young. Surely it would make sense to post one or two of their servants at strategic points along the corridor.

Not that I was complaining about the oversight, but I couldn't quite believe that luck was going my way, either. There would be checkpoints somewhere, and if they weren't staffed by humans, then they would be some kind of physical or magical barriers. I had to hope for the former, because I was all but useless against the latter.

I walked on, keeping to the shadows and trailing one hand against the coolness of the bricks, more to keep my still-quivering limbs steady than from any actual need to maintain something solid by my side.

The bricks began to curve gently to the left—something I sensed more than felt. Sound began to invade the rich, damp air—two men talking over what sounded like some sort of sports commentary.

I'd found my guards.

I edged closer to the wall and slowed even further. As the bricks continued to curve away, light began to shimmer up ahead. It was a stark, almost fierce white that pooled brightness across the floor and walls. The minute I tried to cross it, they'd see me.

"Azriel, where the hell are you?" I murmured.

He didn't pop into existence—which was typical, I thought sourly. The one time in my life I would actually welcome the arrival of a reaper was the one time I couldn't find one.

As I crept closer to the two men, it became obvious they were watching football. Which meant it was either Friday evening and I'd lost a whole lot of time, or they were watching a replay.

I drew in the air, sorting through the scents, trying to discover just what I was dealing with. They smelled human, but the last couple of days had proven I couldn't exactly rely on my olfactory sense when it came to these people.

My gaze went from the large pool of light in front of me to the doorway. I couldn't actually see the men, which meant they had to be sitting in the rear section of the room and would have a good view of the corridor beyond the pool of light.

Leaving me with two options—turn around and try to find another exit up the other end of the corridor, or risk trying to get past the guards.

I looked over my shoulder, contemplating the darkness. If there was an exit at the other end, then it would more than likely be guarded as well. My father had said all Raziq had Razan, and while I'd only felt two, I had no doubt there would be more.

Besides, the longer I remained in this hall, the greater the chance I'd be discovered. It was better to risk this patch of brightness than backtrack and risk the unknown.

I closed my eyes and gathered the remnants of my strength. I could do this. I *had* to do this. There was no way I was going back to that cell.

I sprinted forward as lightly as I could. The TV was loud, but even so, the sound of my footsteps seemed to echo above it.

My body hit the light. I kept my gaze on the darkness beyond it, my heart in my throat and determination in my limbs.

I could do this. I *would*.

But just as I hit the shadows, one of the men in the room swore and scrambled to his feet.

They were coming.

The realization sent a surge of fresh energy through my limbs. I kept running, following the wall, hoping against hope to find some sort of vent or shaft that would offer a way out of this tunnel.

But there was nothing.

Still, the air seemed fresher and came with a tantalizing hint of rain. Freedom was out there somewhere. I just had to find it.

Awareness shimmered across my battered body. Though I heard no sound, the men were behind me. I could feel the heat of them, smell their anger.

Somehow, I ran faster, but it wasn't enough. It was never going to be enough. Before I knew it, one of them grabbed a handful of shirt and yanked me backward. I didn't fight it, allowing myself to pulled back into a body that was well muscled and lean. But before his grip could shift and secure me more tightly, I lifted my elbow and jabbed it—as hard as I could— into his midriff. He hissed in pain and his hold loosened. I spun around, raised my other elbow, and smashed it into his face. His nose shattered even as the force of the blow sent him sprawling backward into the other man. Then I turned and ran.

They were after me all too quickly. But the smell of rain was growing, and in the distance came the steady trickle of water. If the rain was getting in, then surely that meant there was some sort of storm water opening ahead. I hoped so.

Hoped that I could get out *through* it.

But the men were once again closing in fast and time wasn't on my side. Panic surged, but this time, there was no answering rush of energy to accompany it. My body had nothing more to give.

Azriel, I thought again, *where the hell are you?*

Fingers reached for me—something I felt rather than saw. But this time, it came from the front rather than behind. I slid to a halt, but to no avail. A hand grabbed me and yanked me forward—not into capturing arms but behind a body that blazed with heat.

Azriel.

He took shape, his sword dripping blue fire as it arced over his head, slicing the air with a scream. Slicing the throats of the two men as easily as a hot knife through butter.

As their bodies and severed heads dropped to the floor, Azriel turned, his blue eyes as bright as the blaze of his sword.

"We must go. The Raziq will have felt the death of their creatures. There are far too many of them here for me to battle."

I nodded, unable to speak, my breath rasping and body shaking with fatigue and reaction.

"Risa," he said, my name sounding oddly sweet on his lips. "We must go."

"I can't," I said, the words forced and hoarse. "No energy to change."

He said something I didn't understand, the words musical but oddly vehement. "Wrap your arms around my neck," he added, then glanced over his shoulder. His sword seemed to blaze brighter and began emitting a soft hum. "Hurry. They come."

I didn't argue. I wasn't in any state to face the Aedh, and I sure wasn't about to argue if Azriel felt no inclination to do so, either.

I pressed my body against his and hugged him close. Though he had no identifiable scent of his own, he smelled of rain and freshness, and the heat of his skin burned into mine, chasing away the chill and lending me strength.

His arm came around my waist, holding me steady as his gaze met mine. "Ready?"

I nodded, my eyes searching his, wondering at the slight flicker in those bright depths. It was almost as if he were fighting a reaction—although maybe that was just wishful thinking.

Or rather, *stupid* thinking. I had no real desire to get involved with a reaper, no matter how pretty or sexy the packaging. And he'd certainly given no indication that he wanted anything to do with me. Quite the opposite, in fact.

Power surged through the darkness. His energy enveloped me, running through every muscle, every fiber, until my whole body sang in tune with it. Until it felt like there was no me and no him, just the sum of the two of us—energy beings with no flesh to hold us in place.

And then the darkness was gone, the brick tunnel was gone, and we were in a place that was bright and vast and beautiful. The gray fields, but not as I saw them.

Then it, too, was gone, and suddenly I was surrounded by the familiar walls and scents of my apartment.

"I found her," Azriel said, rather unnecessarily, because both Tao and Ilianna were bolting out of the kitchen and heading toward us at full speed.

And Ilianna at full speed was a fearsome sight. Even Azriel took a step back as she all but threw herself at us.

I disentangled my arms from Azriel's neck, grunting as her weight hit and barely holding us both up. In fact, I think it was only the steadying hand Azriel placed on my back that kept me upright.

"You're safe, you're safe," she whispered, smelling of fear and relief and tangerines. "God, I've been having such weird visions—"

"Ilianna," Tao said gently, his gaze meeting mine briefly over the top of her head before moving on. He nodded an acknowledgment at the man who stood behind me. "She's battered and bleeding. Right now she needs medical attention, not your weight."

"Oh God, sorry." She jumped away, her gaze sweeping the length of me. "You look like crap. And where are your jeans?"

"I used them to escape." Her gaze jumped back to mine, but I waved the unasked question away. "Long story. Right now, I need Coke, something to eat, and to get off my bloody feet. Oh, and I need to get my bike back before someone decides to steal her."

"I retrieved the bike once it became obvious you were missing. I knew you'd worry about her." Tao stepped forward and swung me into his arms. "Ilianna, grab the med kit. I'll handle the rest."

He walked me across to the table, kicking a chair to the side and placing me on it. My feet he propped up on a second chair. "Stay," he said, and disappeared into the kitchen.

I glanced across to Azriel. He was still standing where we'd appeared, but his sword was sheathed and his arms were crossed. It was a defensive stance, a watchful one. It had me suddenly wondering if the Aedh could track us here.

"Yes," he said softly. "And the scent of them lingers. They have been here already."

"Oh God—"

He disappeared before I'd even finished the sentence, then reappeared a heartbeat later. He did not look happy. "The book has gone."

I closed my eyes briefly, relieved and yet not. Because while they'd at least taken it without harming Tao or Ilianna, they couldn't read it or find the keys without me—if my father was to be believed, anyway.

Would they come back here the instant they realized that?

"Yes," Azriel said.

I glanced up at him. "So you really *can* read my thoughts?"

"Sometimes," he admitted, a glimmer that could have been amusement flaring briefly in his eyes. "But I have discovered over the years that human thoughts are often not worth listening to, so I usually don't bother."

"I'm not human."

"No, you are not."

And again that glimmer rose. *Damn,* I thought, a hint of heat touching my cheeks. He'd heard *those* thoughts.

I cleared my throat and said, "What took you so long to find me? I must have called your name a hundred times when I was being questioned."

"There were impediments—barriers that prevented me getting any lock on your location."

I remembered the rainbow shimmer. "The cell had some sort of magical halo around it. It almost killed me when I tried becoming Aedh."

He nodded. "What restricts your shift would also restrain my connection with you. Until you were clear of that halo, I could not answer your call. The earth is restrictive as well."

"Why?" I asked. "And if that's the case, how do people involved in accidents underground ever get moved on?"

"A reaper's sense of death is more attuned than the connection I share with you." He hesitated, as if to say something else, then glanced past me as Tao came into the room. "I think it would be better if we left this place."

"We're as safe here as anywhere else." Tao dumped a large glass of Coke and a sinfully large burger in front of me. It had obviously been microwaved, but I wasn't about to complain. Food was food, and I needed it badly. He turned to face the reaper. "We have Ilianna's wards, cameras, and motion detectors activated. No one is getting in here without us knowing."

"The Aedh have already retrieved the Dušan's book from this building," Azriel said. "And my sword is no match if they come in a group."

"He's right." Ilianna walked back into the room,

med kit in hand. "The wards are designed to work against evil, but the Aedh—as far as I know—are not intrinsically evil. And the sensors can only detect flesh, not those who are fundamentally energy." She nodded Azriel's way. "They didn't go off when our not-so-grim reaper appeared, and if the Aedh have already stolen the book, they're obviously not impeded in any way by my magic."

"I guess not," Tao said. "But that leaves the problem of finding a place where the four of us are going to be safe."

"Speaking of that," I said, looking around, "where's Stane?"

"Catching some sleep," Ilianna said. "He was practically dead on his feet, so I frog-marched him to bed."

Tao snorted. "He took his laptop with him, so I'm betting he's just retreated to quieter quarters."

"Has he had any luck finding out who Joseph Hardy is, or uncovering the names of the people behind the consortium?" I asked.

"Not yet." Ilianna placed the kit on the table, then carefully picked up one of my feet. Her nose screwed up. "Damn, girl, your feet are a mess."

"They'll heal soon enough." And we had bigger problems. "Ilianna, you need to warn your mom about the copies of the book pages you gave her. The Aedh may not go after them, but just in case—"

"She'll be fine." Ilianna began wiping down my feet with a lotion that was cool and soothing, and smelled faintly of lavender. "Both she and those copies are at the Brindle, and not even the devil himself could get into that place uninvited."

"What copies?" Azriel asked.

I glanced at him. "We made copies of the Dušan's book."

"An excellent move, but why would you give that copy to the witch repository?"

"Because I need the contents translated."

"But I told you—"

"No," I interrupted. "You told me what you thought I needed to know. But there was more than just an incantation in there, wasn't there?"

He merely lifted an eyebrow. I snorted softly. The reaper, like everyone else, was looking after his own interests first and foremost.

"So what *is* in there?" Tao said, propping his butt on the table and pushing my burger forward.

I took the hint and picked it up, taking several delicious mouthfuls before answering, "According to my father, it'll tell me what the keys are."

Ilianna's gaze jumped to mine. "You talked to your *dad*? What's he like?"

"Ghostly."

"As in dead and just a spirit?" Tao asked with a frown.

"No. He's alive, but the ability to take on flesh has been taken from him."

"Oh." Ilianna began slathering a thicker, smellier cream over my feet. "Why don't you just ask the reaper what the keys are?"

"Azriel is my name," he said, voice holding a slight edge. "Not reaper. And you *can* ask me questions directly."

She glanced at him in surprise. "Fair enough. So tell us, Azriel, what do the keys look like?"

"I do not know, because there is no such description in the book. Maybe Hieu lies."

"He said I was reading it wrong, so maybe you were, too." I winced as Ilianna's cream began to sting, then added, "He wants these keys found as much as anyone else. Only he wants *me* to find them."

"Why?" Tao said. "That's what I don't get. Why you, and why now?"

"Because the keys can only be found and destroyed by someone of *his* blood, and because his flesh form was ripped from him by the other Raziq, he can no longer interact with this world."

"It takes powerful magic to rip the flesh being from an Aedh," Azriel commented. "If they are capable of that, we had better move. *Now.*"

There was a note of urgency in his voice that hit the rest of us like a storm. I glanced at Tao, but he was already up. "I'll grab Stane," he said. "You want some shoes or will your feet be too sore?"

"Grab me a pair of boots and some fresh clothes." I wasn't about to run around barefoot and half naked as well. I gulped down the rest of the burger. Ilianna was finishing up on my feet. "What do you think our chances of being invited into the Brindle are?"

Ilianna said, "Scant to none. But we can try, all the same."

"Then we'll contact your mom on the way over there. If not, we'll have to think of somewhere else."

Though I doubted anywhere else would be safe from the Aedh. It would just take them a little longer to find us.

Tao came out of my room carrying a backpack and, a heartbeat later, Stane appeared out of the spare room. He looked rumpled and unwashed, his face haggard and the shadow of a beard decorating his chin. But there was a victorious light in his eyes.

"God," I said, "don't tell me you cracked it?"

He shoved his overnight bag on the table but kept hold of his laptop. "We now have the names behind the consortium," he said, and his sudden grin was infectious. "James Trilby, Garvin Appleby, and John Nadler. But the even bigger news is, one of them has a sister who's a witch."

"It couldn't be that easy," Ilianna said.

"But it is," Stane said. "The sister is one Margaret Trilby, and three years ago she was banished from the Brindle all-witch society because she was practicing blood magic."

"Margaret Trilby is the name of the witch who raised the soul stealer?" Azriel asked.

"Yes," Stane said, looking over his shoulder. "You know, it's somewhat disturbing to see my uncle standing so calmly in the middle of the room. Especially given I know it's not my uncle, but a reaper."

"I cannot help what you see," Azriel said with a slight shrug. "It is your subconscious that dictates my form, not anything I actively do."

Stane grunted. "Now that we have the names, what are we going to do with them?"

"The logical step," Tao said before I could open my mouth, "would be to give the information to Rhoan."

"He's not equipped to deal with black magic—"

"No," Ilianna agreed, "but the Directorate is. They have some very powerful witches in their employ, and I know for a fact they've dealt with blood witches before. It *is* the best option."

I tossed my phone into the pack Tao handed me. "But it means I'm not a part of the resolution."

And I wanted that. *Needed* that. For little Hanna's sake—and for mine.

Ilianna wrapped a hand around my arm and squeezed gently. "I know. But as you said, right now we've got bigger problems."

I blew out a frustrated breath, then nodded slowly. "Okay, let's get out of here. Tao, you drive. I'll ring Aunt Riley—" I stopped and frowned. "How come she's not here? Does she even know I went missing?"

Hell, Mom would have sensed something had happened to me, and the first—and only—person she would have rung was Riley.

Tao grimaced. "Both she and Rhoan were here. Madder than hell and ready to tear up the world to find you. Azriel convinced them to let him do the finding."

That raised my eyebrows. "Really?" I said, looking at him. "How in the hell did you conduct that miracle?"

"I can be persuasive when I want to be."

"Riley basically considers me one of her own. There's no way in hell she'd be convinced to let someone else do the hunting."

He shrugged. Matter closed, obviously. "Please, we must be going. We have delayed here too long."

Again, his words held an edge that motivated. I

grabbed my Coke and gulped it down so quickly the gas rose back up my throat. I smothered the burp, then stood. Pain slipped up my legs and I grabbed at the table, swearing softly. I hadn't felt a damn thing when I was on the run in the tunnel, but maybe fear had killed all other sensations. Now, though, normal programming had resumed. And in this case, that meant feeling all the aches and pains—not just my feet, but the dull ache somewhere deep inside where the Aedh had bludgeoned and ripped.

Tao wrapped an arm around my waist and half supported me as we headed for the door. Ilianna had disappeared, but reappeared moments later with a bag. If the bits hanging out were anything to go by, it was stuffed more with an assortment of magical detritus than clothing. We locked up, ensuring all the sensors and cameras were active, just in case anyone other than the Aedh tried to get in, then walked—or in my case, hobbled—down the stairs.

Ilianna's Jeep was closer than my SUV, so we piled into her car and headed out. Azriel wasn't with us in flesh form, but the heat caressing the back of my neck suggested he was still very much present.

Once we were on the road and there was no indication that we were being followed, I grabbed my phone and called my mom.

"Risa," she said, voice heavy with relief. "Are you okay? The vibes I'm getting suggest you're hurt."

"I tore my feet up on some glass. Nothing to worry about." I hesitated, waiting for her to denounce the lie. When she didn't, I added, "How are you? Did you sort out whatever was troubling you?"

"Ris, you've got far bigger things to worry about right now than me."

"You're my *mom*," I retorted testily. "There *is* nothing—and no one—else that matters more to me."

"And, my darling girl, I feel exactly the same. Which is why you need to get to the Brindle as quickly as possible. They're out to get you."

Fear snaked through me. "Who?"

She hesitated. "I'm not sure. But it's dark and it's dangerous. Get to the Brindle, Ris. All of you."

"We could swing by the house and pick—"

"No!" she said, and the alarm in her voice had my apprehension rising. "Don't. There's no time—and no need. There are some things you can run from, Ris, and some things you can't. Yours is the former, and mine the latter. I accepted mine a long time ago, but I need to know you're safe—"

"Oh fuck. Mom, I'm coming—"

"Don't! You have one chance—one slight, slim chance—to reach the Brindle and safety. Take it, because it just might mean the difference between life and death for one of your friends. I can't see who, but someone's life really *does* hang in the balance. Promise me you will go there, Ris, not here."

"Not if it means abandoning you—"

"Coming for me would be a waste. I won't even be here when you arrive."

"Mom—"

"You're overdramatizing my problem," she cut in gently. "I assure you, compared with what's headed at you right now, my predicament is practically a picnic."

I didn't believe her. I *couldn't* believe her. Fear for her safety was a deadweight in the pit of my stomach, and right on top of it sat the sick sensation that something bad was about to happen. To her—and to us. Yet I couldn't deny the urgency of her warning and the growing need to get to the Brindle. I didn't *want* any of my friends hurt, but she was my mom. If I had choose one or the other, then my mom was going to win every time.

And yet, if I tried to go to her, she *would* go elsewhere. And whatever was about to happen to her would still happen no matter where she was.

Fuck, fuck, *fuck*!

I closed my eyes and rubbed them wearily. None of this was helping the ache in my brain. "Maybe you *should* leave home. At least if you're out, you have the Fravardin to protect you."

"This is not something they can help with."

Meaning either that it wasn't a personal threat—and therefore didn't require the interference of the Fravardin—or that it was beyond the ability of the Fravardin to protect her. After all, they weren't infallible. Mom's brother had died despite their protection.

"Promise to be careful, all right?" I said wearily. "I'll call when I get to the Brindle."

"Good," she said. "Just tell Tao to put his foot down."

"Heard that, and obeying," Tao murmured, and a second later the Jeep surged forward.

"I'll talk to you later," I said, and hoped like hell that I could. "Love you lots."

"And I'll love you forever," she replied softly.

The ache in my heart and the fear in my gut grew worse as I hung up.

"Trouble?" Ilianna said, her expression worried as she faced me.

"Probably. But she won't tell me what."

"Then get Riley on it."

"Oh, I'm about to. You'd better call your mom and warn her we're coming in fast and could have trouble on our heels."

"She hasn't even said we're welcome—"

"My mom said get there, so get there we will."

Ilianna looked dubious, but she nevertheless dialed her mom. I called Aunt Riley.

The first words out of her mouth were, "Fuck, Risa, I'm going to kill you for scaring me like that."

I laughed, although the sound had an edge that almost sounded like hysteria. "It's not like I actually planned to get kidnapped or anything."

"But going to a meeting without backup? That was stupid."

Yeah, it was, and I'd do it again if it meant getting answers—not that I'd ever admit that to her. She'd lock me up and throw away the key. "It was my father, he had answers, and if I didn't go alone, he wouldn't have appeared. You would have done exactly the same thing."

"*That* is not the point."

It *was* the point, and we both knew it. "The name of the witch raising the soul stealers is Margaret Trilby. Her brother is one of the men behind the consortium threatening the shop owners, then buying up their property."

"Stane got this for you?" she said, surprise in her voice. "If so, maybe he needs to work for the Directorate. They can always use a decent hacker."

Stane snorted softly. "Yeah, like I'm ever going to work for someone like the Directorate when I've spent half my life hacking places like that."

"I'll pretend I didn't hear that," Riley said, half smiling. "Where are you now? Not going after that consortium or the witch, I hope."

"We're running for the Brindle. It seems the safest place right now given we're not sure if the Aedh are going to come after me again."

"What's the Brindle?"

I blinked. Aunt Riley always seemed to know *everything,* so it was a surprise that she didn't know about the Brindle. "It's the witch repository, and the most magically protected place in Melbourne."

"Then running there sounds like a good plan," she said. "It's better to leave cleaning up this mess to Rhoan. And maybe Quinn can sort out something to help with the Aedh."

I hoped he could, but I wasn't about to hold my breath waiting. "Look, I'm still worried about Mom. I don't suppose you could go visit her tonight, and keep her company until I can sort out something else?"

"Sure," she said, "but she was pretty strong with her assurances that nothing untoward was about to happen."

"She's lying. She mentioned having accepted this a long time ago. That sounds ominous to me."

"Oh," she said. Then, *"Oh!"*

Again, alarm rose. "What?"

"Nothing," she said, and this time *she* was lying. "I'll head over there now."

"Please be careful. I have a really bad feeling about this."

"Just what I need," she muttered. "You and your mother could scare half a lifetime out of a person with your bad feelings."

I smiled, as she'd no doubt intended. "Well, according to Uncle Quinn, you've got plenty of lifetime left in you, so that's not going to be a problem."

She snorted softly. "He's another one who seems intent on scaring me half to death. Did you know he's taken up skydiving? What the hell is that all about?"

This time I laughed. "He wants to know what it's like to fly."

"He owns planes and spaceships and he's half Aedh. He flies all the time."

"It's not the same."

She grunted, and the amusement faded from her face. "Send Rhoan the information on the names you found ASAP, and let me know when you get to the Brindle. I'd hate to have to raid them for no reason."

"I will. And thanks."

She gave me a smile then hit the DISCONNECT button. I took a deep breath and blew it out slowly. The sick fear twisting my stomach hadn't eased any. In fact, it had probably gotten worse. By asking Riley to go over to Mom's, I'd put her in the path of whatever was about to hit Mom.

But she'd cope. She was the one person in this

world—besides my mom—whom I had complete and utter faith in. She was a guardian, and a whole lot more. If there was anyone who had any hope of saving my mom—and herself—then it was Riley.

"Feeling better?" Tao said, his gaze meeting mine in the rearview mirror.

I grimaced. "I'll feel a whole lot better when morning comes and everyone is fit, healthy, and in one piece."

"Amen to that," Ilianna said as she hung up the phone. "Mom said there's no official approval for us taking sanctuary at the Brindle, but if we happen to turn up on the doorstep, the Brindle's perimeter magic will at least give us some protection until we get a yea or a nay."

And that was better than nothing. I pulled up Uncle Rhoan's number, then glanced at Stane. "Could you send all the information you have about the consortium and Margaret Trilby to this number?"

Stane said, "You're going to be sensible and let the Directorate handle it? Color me surprised."

I elbowed him. "It's the safest thing to do."

"It is, which is why I'm surprised. I had the distinct feeling that you wanted a finger or two in that particular pie."

"She does," Tao said before I could. "Which is why you and I will be keeping a close eye on her until the Directorate *has* cleaned up the mess."

Exasperation ran through me. "I'm not going—"

"I can taste how much you want to be a part of the resolution, Ris, and I'm more than a little acquainted with your determination." His gaze met mine in the mirror again. "But even if the Aedh weren't out there hunting you, you're not trained for that sort of work."

"Nor would you really want to witness it," Ilianna murmured. "Death is never a pleasant sight, and execution even less so."

I stared at her for a minute, then said, "You've seen someone executed?" God, we were closer than sisters, and yet this was something she'd never, ever even hinted at.

She shrugged, like it was nothing, but the flash of horror in her gaze gave the game away. "It's the reason I walked away from the Brindle, but this isn't really the time to get into it."

Wow, I thought, surprised. Who'd have thought the Brindle would have such a bloody skeleton in its closet—especially given the witch creed and threefold rule?

"Okay," Stane said, "Information sent—"

The rest of his words were lost under the sudden squeal of tires. The Jeep slewed sideways, skidding on the wet roads as Tao battled for control. We half spun, then came to a rest hard up against the side of the truck that had rocketed out of a side street.

"Fucking idiot!" Tao yelled, hanging out the window. "Watch where you're going next time."

The man in the truck gave us a one-finger salute. Tao flung open the door and was half out by the time I lurched forward and grabbed his arm.

"Don't," I said, voice urgent with the fear that was growing inside. "It doesn't matter. We need to keep moving."

"But that idiot could have killed us!" He ripped his

arm free from my grip, but nevertheless climbed back into the car. "Get his license plate. The least I can do is report his stupid driving."

"I will. Just get mov—"

The rest of the sentence died in my throat as I stared through the windshield. There were things coming at us. Half-human, half-animal things.

"Oh fuck," Ilianna said. "Tao, move!"

He didn't answer, simply threw the Jeep into reverse and planted his foot on the accelerator. The wheels spun slightly on the wet roads, then gripped, and the Jeep lurched backward. We were fast, but those things were faster.

"Stane, get down," I said as I leaned over the front seat and shoved Ilianna down into the front foot well.

"I can fight," he said. "I won't cower behind a seat while you and Tao make a stand."

I opened my mouth to argue, but I simply didn't have the time. Despite our speed, those things were on us. Two of them landed on the roof, denting it alarmingly as their half-claw hands scrabbled for the doors.

Stane and I moved as one, slamming the door locks down. Tao spun the wheel and the car swung sideways, riding up on two wheels briefly before dropping and lurching forward. One of the shifters on top of the car tumbled backward, hitting the roadside hard but scrambling to his feet almost immediately. A heartbeat later he was back on top of the Jeep, his claws tearing into the metal and barely missing Stane's head.

A third shifter hit the front of the car, its fist smashing into the windshield, cracking the glass. Tao swore and braked hard. The creature grabbed the wipers, trying to hold on, but the abruptness of the halt sent him flying, the wiper going with him.

Again, Tao planted his foot, cutting across a traffic island then hurtling down the wrong way of the road. Ahead, horns blew and cars swerved out of the way. But the things on top of the Jeep clung like glue.

The creature's claws tore deeper, peeling back the car's roof. Stane swore and twisted around, kicking upward at the talons. The creature snarled and lashed out, his claws raking Stane's leg. The metallic tang of blood tainted the air.

Tao swore and stomped on the brakes. As the Jeep slid to a halt, he threw the car into neutral and twisted around. Flames leapt from his fingers into the hole created by the creature, and there was a *whoosh* of sound followed by a gargled scream.

Then the driver's door was wrenched open and Tao was hauled from the car.

"No!" I flung off my seat belt and scrambled across the seat after him. Tao was aflame, his whole body burning with fire—flames that would not hurt him but should have consumed the creature holding him.

Only they didn't.

Instead the fire swirled inches from the creature's skin, not touching him even though the maelstrom of energy heated the air around us and blasted my skin.

As Tao struggled to free himself from the creature's massive arms, I launched myself at the two of them. Tao saw me in time and doused the flames but, in that instant, there was a bright flash of light, accompanied by a surge of power that echoed with evil and wrongness. In the space that the two of them had occupied, there was nothing.

I hit the ground, rolled to my feet, and twisted around, frantically looking for the pair of them.

But both Tao and the creatures had disappeared.

Chapter Thirteen

I jumped into the Jeep and threw the gears into drive, slamming my foot on the accelerator.

"What are you doing?" Ilianna said, fear in her voice. "Tao is out there—"

"He's gone," I said grimly, not looking at her as I concentrated on getting us on the right side of the road. "I don't actually know where he is, but it's not out there."

"They went after him," Stane said. "Not you, not me, but him."

"Yes." I swerved around a too-slow motorist and gunned the Jeep through an amber light. "Which suggests the consortium is behind this attack, not the Aedh."

"But why take him when they simply killed the others to get the signatures they needed?"

"I don't know." But I knew that killing was still an option. Knew that maybe they'd just taken him elsewhere to do the deed.

I swung onto Lansdowne Street then right into Treasury Place. The repository was situated in the white, four-story building that had once been a part of the Old Treasury complex. The minute we neared the building, I felt the veil of its power—a tingling caress of energy that seemed to burn.

I stopped and flung open the door. Stane and Ilianna were right behind me, Ilianna taking the lead as we ran—or in my case, limped—for the main entrance.

They were waiting for us. Three witches, their hands clasped in front of their tunic-clad bodies and their faces serene.

"You cannot enter here," the oldest of the three said. An almost unearthly halo of blue seemed to shimmer around her—meaning she was a teacher, a nurturer, a caretaker.

So why was she turning us away?

"Kiandra," Ilianna said, her face emotionless as she stopped and bowed slightly. "We are in dire need of your help. One of our party has been taken, and—"

"I know what you need," the older woman said, "and you will not find it here. To provide you with protection will endanger the lives of all those within."

"And yet by turning us away," I said softly, "do you not break one of the very basic rules of your order?"

Her gaze swept to me. The sheer level of power evident behind her gray eyes had the instinctive part of me shivering. "We are not turning you away. We are simply saying you cannot enter this building. This is a center of learning and a safe place for historical documents. What chases you could jeopardize all that we hold within."

"But you have no objection to us staying within the halo of the Brindle's outer ring of protection?" Ilianna asked.

Kiandra's gaze briefly left mine, and I couldn't help feeling a slight sense of relief. It was short-lived.

"You may stay," she said, her gaze back on mine. "And if the dark witch attacks, you will be protected. However, the halo was never designed to protect you from what now hunts Risa."

"So the Brindle couldn't protect us from the Aedh even if we were allowed inside?" The answer was pretty obvious from what she'd already said, but it never hurt to get clarification.

"No, it cannot."

I nodded and glanced at Ilianna. "Then we'll make camp here until we get Tao back and the consortium is dealt with, then we'll leave."

She frowned. "But that could take a few days—"

"I doubt it," I cut in. "In fact, I'm betting that Stane's phone will ring any moment now."

And right on cue, it did. "Shit," he said, digging his phone out of his pocket. "Sometimes you're *very* scary."

"No, she's just her mother's daughter." As Stane walked away to answer the phone, Ilianna glanced back at the three women and bowed again. "Thank you for your time, Kiandra. We shall endeavor not to inconvenience the workings of the Brindle."

Kiandra smiled, but it held very little warmth. "Your friends will not be here long enough to be a burden. And you, Ilianna, are welcome within anytime you wish."

Ilianna's smile was ghostly, but just as cold. "You know my answer to that."

"I do. But there will come a time when that answer will change. We shall be waiting."

Ilianna didn't answer, and the three women turned and walked into the scented shadows of the Brindle. I blew out a relieved breath and glanced at Stane. He wasn't saying much, just listening, but his cheeks were stained red and his free hand was clenched.

After several more seconds, he said, "All right," then hung up and turned around. "They want a trade."

"Well, I guess that means Tao is still alive."

"He is. I talked to him. The witch has bound his fire somehow, and he's chained with silver."

Silver was deadly to a wolf. Silver shackles might not provide death as quickly as a bullet, but they would irritate and burn his skin, and the longer they were left on, the more the metal would eat away at him, destroying his flesh and poisoning his system. "What time did they want to meet?"

"Midday."

I glanced at my watch. It was nearing eleven now, so we had just over an hour. "Okay, let's contact Rhoan—"

"No!" Stane said, voice holding an edge of panic. He took a deep breath, then added, "They said if we involve the police or the Directorate in any way, shape, or form, Tao will die."

"Stane," I said, holding fiercely on to the fear and trying to ignore the twisted sense that everything that could go wrong surely would. "Unless we get this right, he's *going* to die. This consortium has played hardball up to now. I doubt that's going to change."

"I know, I know." He grimaced and half shrugged. "Tao's not going to be at the meeting. I'm going to meet one of them there, and then be taken to him. If I sign the papers, they'll let us both go."

"And you believe that?"

"Honestly? No. But signing the sale agreement doesn't give them the property, because the law states there has to be a cooling-off period before the transfer of land documents are signed. That can't—or won't—happen if either of us is dead."

"That won't stop them from holding on to you or Tao."

"No, it won't. But are you willing to put Tao's life on the line by calling in the Directorate? Because I'm not, Risa. And if you call Rhoan, God help me, I'll flatten you."

He wouldn't. He *couldn't*. He might be a full-blooded werewolf, but I was something a whole lot more. But as we stood there staring at each other, I knew it didn't matter. He would do whatever it took to protect his cousin and I would help him, no matter how inestimably stupid that might be. This is what Mom had warned me about. This is what she'd seen. Tao's life hung in the balance, and I wouldn't risk losing him.

"You can't be serious," Ilianna said, looking from me to Stane and back again. "Risa, you *can't*! Not against these people. Call Rhoan. Let him—"

"Tao is my cousin," Stane said softly. "This is my choice to make, not Risa's."

"But these people have a Charna at their beck and call," Ilianna said, voice rising. "And I haven't a hope in hell of defeating her!"

"You won't have to," I said, then glanced behind

me, to the space near the trees that was filled with an unearthly heat. "Azriel?"

He appeared in an instant, his arms crossed and the sword at his back running with an ethereal blue fire. "I will take care of the dark witch, and anything she may raise to stop you. I cannot, however, help you with those she works with."

"Why? I mean, I wasn't asking you to, but why can you deal with the Charna and not the men?"

"Because the men hold flesh."

I frowned. "So does the Charna."

He nodded. "But by working her magic and calling forth the demons, she has flirted with the edges of the gray fields. The protection that flesh and life offer her no longer applies."

"But you killed the Razan who were chasing me in the tunnel, and they haven't messed with the gray fields."

"No, but they work for the beings who wish to undo the fabric of life as we know it."

"And the Aedh themselves?"

He said, "The Aedh are not flesh beings. Like us, they can take the form, but it is not who they are."

"So because of what they're doing, you can kill them?"

"If they are not more powerful than me, then yes."

Good to know. Although knowing he could kill the Aedh and actually doing it were two entirely different things. And I had a feeling that when it came to my safety, he would only step in to keep me alive if it suited his purpose.

I glanced back at Ilianna. "What we need now is Tao's location."

"I can do a location spell, but what good will that do us?" She frowned and glanced at her watch. "We have less than an hour. That's not enough time to find and free Tao before Stane has to meet them."

"Agreed. So we deal with whoever—whatever—is guarding Tao, and then wait for Stane and his guards to arrive."

"And if it's *that* easy, I'll eat my hat." Stane thrust a hand through his already disheveled hair. "But right now, it's the most sensible plan we've got."

"If you think that's sensible, then you've both got rocks for brains." Ilianna took a deep breath and blew it out slowly. "First things first. Protection circle, then a locating spell."

She spun and walked to the car, rummaging through her bag and returning with her athame. She glanced at me. "Step back. And don't say anything."

I nodded and limped over to the trees. Azriel's warmth burned into my back and I suddenly wondered what those within the Brindle would think of having a sword-carrying reaper standing in their front yard.

Ilianna raised the athame, holding it forward and slightly to the right of shoulder height. Facing east, she drew a pentacle in the air, then said, "Masters of the Watchtowers of the East, Masters of the Air; I wake and summon you to witness my works and to guard the Circle."

She turned to the south, then west and north, repeating the pentacles and beseeching the masters of fire, water, and earth for their protection. A light wind sprang up, teasing the ends of her hair and tugging lightly at her clothes. Then it died, replaced by a sense of watchfulness.

She sat cross-legged on the ground and began the finding incantation. I glanced at Azriel. "Where will the soul of the Charna go when you kill her? Hell?"

He glanced at me. "Why would you think she would go to hell?"

I shrugged. "Because she's played with evil and will now pay the price?"

He shook his head. "She didn't play with evil. She summoned it. There is no purgatory for her, no moving on after paying penance. She will simply end."

"So no chance of redemption?"

"No."

"Good." I crossed my arms and watched Ilianna. But I could feel the weight of his gaze on me.

"You would make a good Mijai," he said, after a few moments.

I snorted softly. "Why? Because I feel no remorse for the bitch when the thing she raised stole a little girl's soul?"

He half smiled, but it was oddly sad. Something inside me wanted to weep—not for him, but for me. I rubbed my arms and tried to ignore the sensation of fate staring out at me from the blue of his eyes.

"Because you do not quibble with what needs to be done. You simply do it."

I snorted softly. "Yeah, that's me all over. Decisive and proactive."

"You have the heart of a warrior, Risa, even if the outer shell dabbles with weakness."

The sound of my name on his lips was somehow ominous. I met his gaze again. "I decided several years ago I didn't want to be a warrior, Azriel. That hasn't changed. I just want to keep running our restaurant and have a normal life."

His gaze moved from me, and yet that sense of fate bearing down on me didn't ease. "Sometimes we must do things we do not want to."

"Like you having to follow me around?"

A smile flirted with the corner of his mouth. "Yes."

"Why is that? And why, if you've been following me around incessantly, did you not step in and stop the Aedh from kidnapping me?"

His gaze met mine again. His face was still impassive, but there was an odd sense of impatience rolling off him. "You have already guessed why I did not step in to rescue you—having heard what your father said, I wanted to see how the Aedh would react. But once they took energy form, I was unable to track them or rescue you."

And the truth is, he probably wouldn't have done the latter anyway—at least, not until he'd gotten every scrap of information possible. "That's the second part of the question answered. What about the first?"

"As I have already said, I am a Mijai." He shrugged, a casual gesture that oddly seemed filled with tension. "I should not be following you but rather fighting those that come through the portals."

"But that's not why you don't want to be here, Azriel."

"And why would you think that?"

I half smiled. "Because I am sometimes my mother's daughter, and I can sense the avoidance in your words."

"There is no avoidance." He looked away again. "There is no other truth. I do what I must."

Yeah, he did. And his disquiet about being here had *nothing* to do with his wish to be hunting, but rather his proximity to me. Of that, I was sure.

Ilianna pushed to her feet and walked across to us.

"Anything?" I asked.

She nodded. "He's at an old warehouse on Ramsay Street, Spotswood. I couldn't see much more than that—I think the witch has spelled the building. There was thick resistance when I tried to get inside and see his exact location."

"You didn't push?"

She shook her head. "I don't know what type of spell she used, so it's safer not to. At the very least, it might have tipped her off that we'd found him." She hesitated, her expression a mix of fear and determination. "If there's magic, you'll need me along."

"That's too danger—"

"Yeah," she cut in, "for *you* if you blunder blindly through whatever spell she's set up. I have a good chance of unraveling it if I'm close enough to examine it."

I wanted to argue, but I could also see her point. We wouldn't save Tao if we couldn't even get into the building. "What if it's dark magic?"

"It didn't feel dark. It felt like a simple guarding spell, but I'll know for sure when I'm there."

I nodded and looked past her to Stane. "Are you going to be all right alone?"

He snorted softly. "It's not like I have any choice in the matter. Besides, as I said, they need me alive to sign the papers. Just make sure you're there to rescue us once I do."

"Then we'd better get going—"

"Wait!" Ilianna turned and bolted for the car. She rummaged through her bag for several seconds, then came back carrying a can of drink in one hand and something clenched in the other.

"Here," she said, offering what looked like an old copper coin to Stane. "Swallow this."

His look was one of disbelief. "Swallow it? Why in God's name would I want to do that?"

"It's a talisman of protection. The Charna won't be able to spell you."

"And I can't wear it because . . . ?"

"Because whoever is meeting you might know enough about magic to rip it from your throat. If you swallow it, they can't."

"But they *can* gut me." He picked up the coin somewhat gingerly. "It feels heavy."

"It's neither heavy nor large," Ilianna said impatiently. "And it'll pass through your system within a day or so. Don't be such a baby. Swallow it."

He gave her a somewhat dark look, but put the coin in his mouth. She offered him the can. He took a long drink, then shuddered. "God, I can feel the thing sliding all the way down to my gullet."

"Bullshit." Her voice wasn't in the least sympathetic. She glanced at me. "Shall we go?"

I nodded, glanced at Stane, then headed for the car. Ilianna climbed into the front passenger seat, but Azriel was nowhere to be seen. And this time, I couldn't feel the heat of him. Maybe he'd decided to keep a little more distance between us, just in case I decided to ask any more pesky questions.

The thought brought a smile to my lips, but it died just as quickly. I had a friend to rescue, and it was time to start concentrating on that rather than a reaper who held far too many secrets.

Tao was being held in a long red-brick building that had obviously been a warehouse at some stage in its past. There were old metal roller doors at regular intervals along its length, and the windows that dotted the front façade were small, solid, and barred with rusting metal grids.

"There's no way I'm going to get my ass through those," I commented. "Even if I *could* get the grids off without making a racket."

We'd parked in the building site just down from the warehouse and on the opposite side of the road. There were other cars parked here, so we wouldn't look too conspicuous, even though the site itself had no construction work currently ongoing. I crossed my arms and leaned back against the Jeep, my gaze sweeping the roofline. It was a single-story building, so getting up there wouldn't be a problem. But the metal roof looked as solid as the brick walls, and breaking in would create way too much noise. Hopefully, there was a back entrance that would provide a more viable option.

I glanced at Ilianna. "You got anything yet?"

She held up a hand to silence me, her expression intent. I leashed my impatience and called Azriel instead. He appeared beside me, his arms crossed as he studied the building. The sword at his back was dark. Whatever magic set it off was currently silent.

"I can feel life forces inside," he said. "Three of them. None is the dark witch."

"Would the protection spell placed on the building restrict you from entering or set off the alarms?"

"Human-cast spells are usually aimed at flesh or spirit. I'm energy. That"—he nodded toward the building—"would not stop me."

"Which means it probably wouldn't stop me, either." But I'd have to regain flesh if I wanted to free Tao, and I couldn't risk that setting off the magic.

He studied me for a moment. "Meaning you wish me to go inside and locate your friend?"

I wished he'd stop reading my fucking thoughts. "If it wouldn't be too much of an inconvenience."

Sarcasm edged my tone, but again, he seemed to miss it. Or perhaps he merely chose to ignore it. I was beginning to suspect my reaper was a whole lot more knowledgeable about this world and human emotions than he was making out.

He disappeared again, and I returned my gaze to the building. I couldn't see any indication of a spell protecting the building—there was no faint, kaleidoscope shimmer as there had been in the underground cell—but I wasn't about to question Ilianna's word. She knew her magic, even if most of the time she played around with minor potions and spells.

And her mom *was* the keeper of the secrets—the guardian of the Brindle's massive library. You didn't get that position without having some serious magical mojo. In fact, I'd heard whispers that Ilianna had been in line to take over her mom's position before she'd walked away from the Brindle and everything it represented. Whether it was true or not I couldn't say, because Ilianna refused to confirm or deny the possibility.

Azriel winked back into existence. "He is being held in a room at the west end of the building. I believe there is some sort of spell binding him."

"Probably something that restricts his use of flame," Ilianna commented. Her gaze met mine. "I've integrated you into the spell's properties. You'll be able to walk through without the Charna knowing about it."

"Good." I glanced at the west end of the building, studying the windows and the roller door. There was definitely no entrance that way. "Once I deal with the men guarding Tao, you'll have to come in and despell him."

She frowned. "I can't weave my presence through the magic, because she'll sense the insertion of another magic user. And if I walk through it, it will notify her."

"Precisely. And hopefully, she'll come out of hiding."

"Or go so deep undercover that we won't find her."

"If she does that, then she's the Directorate's problem."

"No," Azriel said calmly. "She is mine."

I glanced at him. "Only if she appears before us, because you're restricted to following me."

Annoyance flashed briefly in his eyes. "She won't disappear. There is an arrogance in most of the dark ones that makes them believe they can best any situation. She will send her forces against us, and I will be able to locate her through them."

"Great, but I hope you'll understand me hoping like hell she *doesn't* send something against us. I really, *really* do not want to be confronting a soul stealer today."

Or any other day, for that matter.

"If I kill the Charna, then her creature should also die."

"It's the bits in between—you know, the part where it attacks me *before* you kill its master—that worries me."

"You will not die," he said, amusement flirting with his lips. "After all, if you do, how will I get my answers?"

"There is that," I muttered, glancing at Ilianna. She was smiling at Azriel—but then, she hadn't seen what a soul stealer could do, or felt the agony it caused. "When I've dealt with the guards, I'll give you a call. Come in fast. I wouldn't want the Charna's creatures to find you alone."

She nodded and rubbed her arms. "Don't be long. I hate standing in godforsaken places like this alone."

I resisted the urge to point out that we were only one block away from Scienceworks—which was no doubt packed with visitors exploring all that the museum had to offer—not to mention the fact that one block in the other direction was not only a major housing development, but a church and a small shopping district. Mares were herd animals, and they tended to get very spooked when left alone in strange areas.

"Stay in the car and keep out of sight." I squeezed

her arm lightly to comfort her, then headed across the lot and jumped the fence that separated it from the next property. After walking across the road, I jumped into the scrap-metal yard next to the old warehouse.

Only to be confronted by two rottweilers.

They came running at me, teeth bared and growls low in their throats. I swore softly, but stopped and faced them—not meeting their gazes but keeping an eye on them all the same—then held out my hand. Both dogs slowed, noses in the air and snarls still low in their throats—undoubtedly because they sensed the wolf in me.

Azriel appeared beside me, his sword unsheathed and glowing blue in the brightness of the day. Once again the blade hummed, but this time the sound was oddly calming.

The dogs lowered their heads and backed away.

I glanced at him. "Dogs can see you?"

"Of course." He sheathed his sword and stepped to one side, motioning me to continue with a sweep of his hand. "They are extremely sensitive to those who traverse the gray fields."

I knew animals—especially cats and dogs—were sensitive to the spirit world, but I had no idea that sensitivity also extended to the reapers. Meaning I wasn't so special after all, I thought wryly. "So why did they back away?"

"Because they have no more wish to die than you do."

I frowned as I grabbed the top of the fence and hauled my butt over it—and winced as I hit the ground a little too hard on the other side. I'd forgotten about my battered feet. "But you said before you could not attack flesh. Dogs are flesh."

"Yes, but dogs are generally more sensible than humans. They do not throw themselves into situations where they know the danger is greater than their ability to cope."

I snorted softly. "You need to talk more to Aunt Riley, because she's one wolf who will blow that theory out of the water."

He smiled. "She holds human form, and I fear there is something about the shape that infects common sense."

"I think you could be right." After all, it wasn't exactly sane for Ilianna and me to be here right now. Sanity would have involved Uncle Rhoan and the Directorate. "Although I will note that you're also holding human shape."

"Which is no doubt why I am here, helping you, when in theory I should be observing."

"No one is stopping you, you know."

"I know." He motioned me forward with an elegant wave of the hand. "Proceed."

I did. The driveway curved around to the rear of the building, revealing several more roller doors and shuttered windows. But right in the middle of the brickwork wall were a concrete landing and a regular door.

"Can you sense anyone near that door?" I asked, flaring my nostrils. The air was rich with the warmth radiating off Azriel, but underneath it ran the lingering wetness of last night's rain and wisps of rust and rubber emanating from the scrap yard behind us.

"No," he said. "They remain at the far end of the building."

"Thanks."

I ran forward, jumped onto the platform, and headed for the door. It was padlocked, and both the chain and lock looked brand new. But breaking either might just alert the guards to my presence, and I had no idea just how good their hearing was.

"Well, fuck," I muttered, then stepped back and studied the windows to either side.

The one on the left had a broken pane. I'd been hoping to avoid using my Aedh form, simply because it would sap my strength and I really wasn't sure just how much I had left after the Aedh's questioning. There was still an ache deep inside my head and a sick sensation in my stomach, and though my limbs weren't shaky, I had a suspicion it wouldn't take much effort to make them so.

"The lock is a problem?" Azriel asked.

I glanced at him. He expression was noncommittal, though I suspected there was amusement lurking underneath. "You could say that."

"Then I shall remove it for you." He drew his sword, hooked the end of the blade through one of the metal links, and said something in that musical language of his. The sword flared briefly; then the link simply melted away. I caught the chain before it could hit the ground. The metal was red-hot, and it was all I could do to place it down quietly rather than drop it.

"That's a handy trick."

"Valdis is a very handy sword."

I turned the handle and carefully pushed the door open. "You speak about her as if she's alive."

"She is."

I glanced back at him. He returned my gaze evenly. He *wasn't* kidding. I shivered, not wanting to think about a sword that had a spirit and a life of its own, and stepped into the shadows of the warehouse.

Shadows crowded the interior, and the air was thick with the scent of dust, age, and disuse. I closed the door then stopped, my gaze sweeping the immediate area. I was in some sort of loading bay. The platform I was on ran the width of the building, stretching from the roller door nearest me to the one on the other side of the building. Several offices led off from the platform on the other side of the bay, but on my side there were just the two doors.

I walked across to the nearest one and grasped the handle, but didn't open the door. I couldn't smell anything or anyone on the other side, but apprehension was building in my stomach. Or maybe that was just nerves. After all, as everyone kept pointing out, I wasn't really trained for this sort of stuff.

I licked my lips and pulled the handle. The door was heavy, but opened quietly. It turned out to be an old refrigerator. I swore softly and walked down to the next door. This one led into a wide hallway.

There were several doors leading off it, and one at the very end. I checked each one as I went, but they were little more than dust-strewn offices. The end one led into another loading bay.

"Your friend is being held in the rooms beyond the door to the right," Azriel said softly.

"And the men?"

"One is near the door, the other outside the room that contains Tao."

Which had to mean they were human—any nonhuman would have sensed my presence by now. "And are they armed?"

"They have guns, yes."

Which meant there was no way of getting through that door without alerting the man guarding Tao. And I had no idea what his orders might be if there were intruders.

I could slip past them in Aedh form, but that still left them conscious and dangerous. Both men needed to be out of action before I attempted to free Tao, but how did I bring the first man down without alerting the second?

I glanced at the roller door. "Can Valdis melt that lock as easily as she melted the chain?"

"Of course. Why?"

"Because they have guns, so charging straight at them isn't a viable option."

He studied me for a moment, then nodded and jumped down to the loading bay floor. I followed, watching the ripple of muscle across his back as he moved. Real or not, it was mighty damn fine.

He placed Valdis against the lock, and a second later it was little more than metal puddles on the concrete. "You'd better do that disappearing thing you do," I said, as I reached for the shape-shifting magic.

He did as I asked. I fixed the image of a dark-haired, green-eyed woman in my mind and reached for the shifting magic. Its rise was almost reluctant, slithering through my body rather than surging, so that it took longer than normal to alter my features. When the magic finally faded, I grabbed at the nearest wall for support and briefly wondered how the hell I was going to get through the rest of the day. I took several deep breaths that seemed to chase weakness away—at least for the moment—then tied the ends of my shirt up under my breasts, exposing a whole lot of stomach. Then I grabbed the roller door and opened it up.

"Hello?" I called out. "Anyone here?"

For a moment there was no response, then, "What the hell do you want, lady?"

My gaze swept the still-closed doorway. I couldn't see him through the small glass porthole but I had no doubt he could see me. My senses crawled with the awareness of his proximity. "My car broke down and for some stupid reason I can't get phone reception. Have you got a cell I can borrow?"

There was no immediate answer, but, after a moment, the door opened and a big, tattooed man appeared. As I suspected, he was human, but he was also all muscle, and he moved like a fighter—light on his feet.

His gaze swept me, resting briefly on my exposed stomach before flicking back to my face. "There's a phone booth down the road."

"Yeah, I've already tried that, but it's been vandalized."

"So why come here?" Though his pose was casual, he had one hand slightly behind his back, and I had no doubt it held a gun. "How did you even know we were in here?"

It was just my luck to strike a guard who was neither a fool nor sidetracked by the flash of flesh. "How do you *think* I knew? I'm a werewolf. I *smelled* you."

He raised his eyebrows. "Really?"

"Really," I said, the irritation in my voice not in the

least bit faked. "Look, if you don't want to help, fine. Just tell me where another phone booth is, and I'll be on my way."

"There are some houses one street over, or Science-works is a block away to the right."

"Thanks for nothing, bud," I muttered and turned away. So much for doing things the easy way.

"Wait," he said, just as I ducked under the door.

I turned, bending back under the door and, in the process, flashing a good bit of breast. It might not help, but it couldn't hurt, either. "What?"

He reached into his pocket and withdrew a cell phone. "Use this," he said, "but make it quick. I'm expecting a call."

"You're a doll." I flashed him a big smile and sauntered over, throwing in plenty of saucy hip action. His gaze slipped down, and though the scent of desire touched the air, a sense of watchfulness remained. Not one to be easily distracted by a wanton woman, obviously.

He offered me the cell, and I took it without attempting to catch his hand. I stepped away, dialed home, and asked a nonexistent boyfriend to come rescue me. Then I hung up and flashed the guard another smile.

"Thanks for that."

I held out the phone. As he reached for it, I dropped it, then wrapped my hand around his and yanked him forward. *Hard.* But even unbalanced, he reacted, his free hand moving so fast it was almost a blur as he raised the gun. I clenched my fist and punched him in the neck. The gunshot zinged past my earlobe, and warmth spurted down my neck. I cursed silently and grabbed his leg, yanking his feet out from underneath him. He landed with a thump on his butt, his face at eye level and perfectly positioned for a punch.

I hit him again, feeling skin mash and bone shatter under the force of the blow. As he went down, I grabbed the gun, leapt up onto the platform, and ran into the hall. Over my shoulder, I said, "Azriel, hide the body in one of the rooms."

I didn't wait to see if he would do as I asked. The other guard would have heard the shot, but he hadn't come running. Which meant he was either taking care of Tao or lying low. If it was the former then I had to get there fast. And if it was the latter . . .

I didn't want to think about the latter. Not when there was already blood running down the side of my neck.

The end of the hall came into sight. It was a T-intersection, and shadows haunted both the left and right corridors. I slowed and flared my nostrils, searching through the scents in the air in an attempt to pinpoint the guard's location. I couldn't smell him, but Tao was located to the right, which meant the guard probably would be as well.

If I was wrong, I'd get a bullet in the back.

I closed my eyes briefly, gathered my courage, then ducked low and stepped out, keeping as close to the walls and the thicker shadows as I could.

At the far end of the corridor, a door was open. Inside, two men were struggling. The one on the bottom of the pile—and taking one hell of a beating— was Tao.

I slid to a stop and pointed the weapon. I might not have fired a gun at a human target before, but I did have weapons training—though I'm sure Mom would have had a fit if she'd known just how extensive Riley's fight training had been.

Mom. My gut clenched at the mere thought of her. I thrust the fear aside and said, "Hey!"

The guard whipped around and reached for his weapon. He was fast, I'll give him that, and had the weapon in his hand between one heartbeat and another. But I didn't give him a chance to fire. My shot took him in the shoulder and flung him back against the wall. As his gun dropped to the ground, Tao twisted around and kicked it to the other side of the room.

"About fucking time you got here," he said, his hostile tone negated by the relief evident even through the swelling almost encasing his eyes. "I was beginning to think I'd actually have to free myself."

He'd obviously recognized my scent rather than my face. I grinned. "Have I ever let you down before?"

Amusement teased the corners of his lips. "Never, my sweet."

"So there was no need for impatience now, was there?" I squatted down beside the guard and pressed two fingers against his neck. His pulse was rapid but strong. He might be out right now, but I doubted it would last all that long. I removed his shirt, tore it into strips, then tied his hands and feet together. I used the remainder to stanch the shoulder wound. I didn't want him bleeding to death before Rhoan got here.

"Um, I could use a little attention myself," Tao commented.

I squatted beside him. His hands had been chained

tightly behind his back, and his wrists were raw and bloody. The silver was eating into his skin.

"Azriel," I called softly.

Tao jumped when the reaper appeared next to him. "Damn," he muttered, "I wish you'd give some warning before you do that. You could send a less sturdy heart into failure."

"Given your heart *is* sturdy, I don't see the problem." Azriel glanced at me. "You wish me to melt the chain?"

"Please."

He released Valdis and the sword began to hiss and spit fire. Azriel frowned. "There is magic attached to that silver."

"Ilianna said that Tao had been spelled to prevent him using his fire—could the chain be the source?"

"Possibly." He passed the tip of Valdis over the links, not quite touching them. The hissing grew more intense. "The spell is twofold. One is containment, the other is notification."

I paused. "You can tell this by just passing the sword over the links?"

"I can't. But Valdis can."

"Hang on," Tao said, craning his neck around to see what Azriel was doing. "Who the hell is Valdis?"

"The sword," Azriel and I answered together. I added, "So the Charna will be warned when you melt the links?"

"Something will." His gaze met mine. "It may not necessarily be the witch."

"I don't care what comes after us," Tao said. "Just get the fucking things off."

"I wouldn't advise—"

"Do it," I cut in. "Silver is poison to wolves, and it's already eating into his wrists."

He stared at me for a moment, then said, "If I melt the cuffs, the Charna *will* know Tao is free. Which may endanger Stane's life."

"Stane?" Tao said. "Why the hell would he be in danger?"

"Long story." I rubbed my eyes wearily. "Azriel's right. We can't risk it until Stane and the others—"

I cut the sentence off at the sound of footsteps and moved swiftly to the door. I flared my nostrils, sifting through the flavors in the air, recognizing Stane's scent mixed with the spice of a stranger. Another human, which was good. He wouldn't scent either us or the blood.

"Hank, Terry, where the hell are you two?"

The voice was coming from the loading bay end of the hallway. I crept forward.

"Fuck it," the stranger said. "If you two are goofing off again, there's going to be hell to pay."

I lowered myself to the ground and carefully inched forward on my belly. The shadows were thicker near the floor, and while I doubted the guard would actually see me, I took every precaution and moved as quietly as I could. One wrong move could get Stane killed.

I risked a look around the corner. Stane was walking in front of the guard and didn't appear restrained in any way, though his expression was tight and his shoulders tense. His nostrils flared as he breathed deep, then his gaze flicked down. I held up three fingers, keeping the movements small so as to not attract the attention of the man behind him, and nodded toward the left. He smiled grimly in acknowledgment.

I counted down my fingers. As the last one dropped, he threw himself sideways. I raised the weapon and fired, again aiming for the shoulder. The guard grunted and dropped. Stane ensured he was out with a quick fist to the face, then glanced back at me. "Tao?"

"Alive and well. Was there only one guard?"

Stane nodded as he flipped the man around and pulled his jacket halfway down his arms, effectively pinning them. Then he pulled the man's belt free and strapped his legs together. "What about the witch and the men in charge?"

"None of them is here."

"Obviously. But can we trace them?"

"Maybe."

I turned and walked back to the cell. He followed, and his anger surged, tainting the air, when he saw Tao.

Tao grinned and said, "Hey, you should see the other guy."

"I can. And I'm barely resisting the urge to kick him repeatedly when he's down."

I squeezed Stane's shoulder and glanced at Azriel. "You want to release Tao now?"

"Do you think that wise when Stane is in the room? You and I can protect ourselves from whatever might be bound to the restraints, but Stane has little except his own strength."

"Hey, I have Ilianna's charm and I *can* fight—"

Azriel's glance barely even flicked his way. "The

charm protects you against being spelled, not magic of this sort."

"But—"

I touched his arm lightly, stopping him. "He's right. Ilianna's in the parking lot across the road. Go keep her safe, just in case the Charna doesn't send only magic against us."

He grunted unhappily, but spun on his heel and headed out. I waited until the sound of his steps had faded away, then glanced at Tao. "You ready?"

"If you don't do it soon, I'm not going to have any fucking wrists left."

Azriel touched Valdis's tip to the links. The hissing ramped up, becoming fever-pitched, then the links simply exploded. Shrapnel spun through the darkness, embedding itself into the walls but somehow avoiding skin.

"The notification spell was in fact a minor demon," Azriel said. "It has left to warn the Charna. I can trace its path."

I blinked. "There was a demon spelled to the cuffs?"

"Yes. It is a messenger, nothing more."

"Glad no one told me," Tao muttered, gingerly pulling his shirt away from his torn and bloody wrists. "I think I would have freaked out."

"So once warned, won't the Charna attack? That's what we want, right?" I asked.

Azriel didn't answer immediately, his expression intent and his head cocked to one side, as if he were listening to something.

Unease raced through me, and I glanced nervously over my shoulder. The corridor beyond remained shadowed and quiet, and I had no sense that there was anyone or anything in the warehouse but us.

And yet . . .

I shivered, and resisted the temptation to rub my arms. The silence suddenly seemed charged. Threatening.

Tao climbed carefully to his feet. Flame danced briefly across his fingertips, and his smile was cold when his gaze met mine. "I hope she *does* attack. I'll enjoy watching her burn."

"It is not the Charna that is coming," Azriel said. Valdis, still clenched in his hand, was running with angry blue flames.

That cold, hard lump tightened in my gut, and for a moment I couldn't even speak. "Then what is?" I managed eventually.

"Hounds," he said softly. "Hellhounds."

Chapter Fourteen

"HELLHOUNDS?" TAO SAID, HIS VOICE INCREDU-lous. "As in rabid black dogs straight from the bow-els of hell?"

Azriel glanced at him. "Yes. I can feel the force of them."

So could I. That electric sensation in the air was get-ting stronger, and the air around us was beginning to stir. It was almost as if the hounds were preceded by a wind of evil. "Can you stop them?

"Yes." He glanced at me. "But it will mean letting the Charna go free. Even now, the messenger's trail is fading."

"Then why are you standing here?" Tao said, with all the determination of a man who had never heard Aunt Riley's stories about the hounds and just what they were capable of. "The sooner you trace and stop the Charna, the sooner those hounds will be sent back to the hell they came from, right?"

"Right." Azriel's gaze didn't move from mine. Waiting. Judging.

If he was looking for bravery, he wasn't going to find it. I was terrified—so terrified that my legs were barely supporting me, my gut was churning, and I thought I might puke. But if the Charna was to be stopped, I couldn't let fear sway my decisions.

I clenched my fist and said, "Do it. But hurry."

He bowed, ever so slightly. For a heartbeat, I swear there was a glimmer of respect in his eyes. But maybe that was a trick of the firelight gleaming off Tao's hands. "Do not attempt to use your Aedh gifts to reach into their flesh and rip them apart. It will destroy you."

Tao glanced from me to Azriel and back again. "What the hell is he talking about?"

"If I take Aedh form, I can seep into flesh and tear it apart," I said absently. Tao swore, but my gaze stayed on Azriel as I added, "Why not?"

"Because they are not flesh, nor are they energy. They are spirits—essences of evil, if you like. They cannot be pulled apart like flesh beings."

"Okay, *that's* a gruesome skill," Tao muttered.

Azriel added, "Do what you must to keep alive, Risa Jones. I shall return as quickly as I am able."

With that, he disappeared.

I briefly closed my eyes and swallowed back the bitter taste of bile.

A taste that got worse when the howling began.

I ran for the door and slammed it shut. The hounds might be demons, but they held flesh when on earth, and as flesh beings, a locked door would delay them—if only for a moment. But every moment we delayed them was a moment for Azriel to track down the dark bitch.

The howling grew closer. I stripped off my shirt, tearing it in half, then wrapping the remnants around my hands. Once my skin was protected, I pulled two of the bigger pieces of silver from the walls. The largest shard was barely two inches long, but it was curved and jagged, and was a better weapon than just hands.

I backed away and joined Tao near the rear wall. The flames still burned across his hands, filling the room with an eerie, yellow-white radiance.

"Do you think fire is actually going to hurt them?" he said, his gaze on the door.

The howling was getting closer, and the smell of death, decay, and ash was beginning to ride the air. Riley had never mentioned the smell, but maybe she'd never come across this type. There was more than just the one kind of hound.

"As Azriel said, the hounds are demons, not true flesh and blood. Their outer skin might burn, but they will probably just form more."

"Comforting thought," he muttered.

The scent was becoming thick and cloying, filling my nose and catching low in my throat, making it difficult to breathe.

They were close. So close.

Then the howling stopped. The hairs on the back of my neck stood on end.

Tao doused the flames on one hand, then repeated my earlier actions, tearing off a shirtsleeve and wrapping it around his bloodied hand before he grabbed a silver shard from the floor. "You know, I'm not feeling too comforted by this little bit of—"

He cut the words off as something hit the door. The wood shuddered and splintered. There was a brief pause, then the door shuddered again. The wood fractured further, and the lock pulled away from the frame, hanging on by little more than two rusting screws. Through the gap I could see two dark, sinewy shapes.

With the third blow, it gave way, and the door crashed back against the wall. Tao released his flames, filling the doorway with fire. The creatures stepped through it, their heads low, their red eyes glowing brightly against the inferno surrounding them. Thick yellow teeth gleamed eerily as the pair of them snarled.

Then they leapt, their bodies aflame. I dove to one side and slashed upward with the shard. The silver sliced through the creature's burning flesh, melting it like butter. Thick, black blood splattered across my body, stinging like acid where it touched bare flesh. The amulet at my neck burned even brighter.

The creature hit the wall, twisted, and leapt again. I rolled away from it, but its teeth slashed, scoring my thigh. Pain rolled through me, thick and hot. Or maybe that was the blood pulsing down my leg. I didn't know. I didn't have the time to find out. I pushed to my feet, saw the thing leap again, and lashed out wildly with the shards. Again they met burning flesh. More black blood sprayed, but the silver wasn't stopping it. These shards—and the two of us—were never going to be enough to stop the creature.

We had to get out of here if we wanted to survive.

And I could see only one way of achieving that—by doing what Azriel had done when he'd rescued me from the tunnel.

The thought *terrified* me. God, I hadn't even known it was possible to extend the Aedh shift to another person until Azriel had done it. How the hell could I ever hope to pull off the same trick and not shred Tao like a cheap bra?

I'd kill him. I'd kill me.

But what other choice did we have? Staying here was a death sentence. At least if I attempted the shift, we had a chance—albeit a very small one.

I ducked another leap, then twisted and ran for Tao, calling to the Aedh within me as I leapt straight at him. I could feel the hound behind me, feel the wash of its fetid breath against my neck. I knew it was going to be close. I hit Tao hard, heard his grunt in surprise as I wrapped myself around him. Saw the gleam of yellowed teeth as the creatures leapt at us . . .

Power surged through me, around me, a fear-fueled storm that shattered both our forms, tearing us apart swiftly and brutally, until there was nothing left but two streams of tremulous smoke, separated and yet together.

In that state, I fled the cell.

It was hard—harder than I'd ever imagined it could be. Every particle ached, as if carrying Tao was a physical weight even in this ethereal form.

I wouldn't—couldn't—go far. But the minute we re-formed, those hounds would come after us. They had our scent. Had the taste for our flesh.

We needed to find somewhere safe. Somewhere as far away from Ilianna and Stane as we could get.

I could think of only one place.

I didn't really believe in heaven or God as such, but if ever there was a sanctuary from hellhounds, then surely a church would be it. After all, holy water and blessed knives could destroy them, so there *had* to be some form of protection offered by churches themselves.

If I was wrong, we were dead meat. I wasn't going to be much use fighting-wise after this flight. Tao—who'd been caught so unaware by this move—wouldn't be, either.

Hell, he probably wouldn't even be coherent.

Tao's weight forced me low to the ground as I fled the building. I whisked along the street, feeling the grime of the concrete seeping through my pores, feeling the terror of what we were fleeing pulse through every aching part of me.

The streets were quiet still, but I could hear the howling of the hounds. They were hunting for us. If I could have shivered, I would have.

I rolled on, heading for the small brick building I'd seen on the way down here. It was only a couple of blocks away, but it might as well have been several miles. By the time I whisked underneath the old wooden doors, I was barely holding it together.

I stopped near the pulpit and reached for the Aedh magic once more, carefully piecing together our two separate entities, until flesh was fully formed and we became ourselves once again.

I landed with a splat on the old wooden flooring, and even though I wanted to do nothing more than collapse, I twisted around, ignoring the red-hot needles that jabbed into my brain as I looked for Tao.

He was lying several feet away, his clothes shredded but his flesh whole. And he was breathing.

I hadn't killed him.

The relief that swept me was so great that for several seconds I could barely even breathe. It had worked. Against all the odds, we were out of the cell, we were alive, and for the moment, we were safe.

But shifting with another person in tow was something I *never* wanted to attempt again.

I closed my eyes and waited until the shaking and the sweeping bouts of dizzy nausea eased, and I became aware of groaning. Not mine. Tao's.

"You okay?" I asked, my voice sounding as wretched as I felt.

"What the *fuck*," he said, his voice whispery and filled with pain, "did you just do?"

"I saved our asses."

But for how long? The second we'd regained flesh the howls had intensified, and even now I could feel the ill wind of their approach. If the church didn't stop them, I didn't know what would. There would be silver somewhere in this church, but I really doubted we'd have the time to find it.

I forced myself to roll over onto my stomach, then closed my eyes again, breathing deep and trying to ease the quivering. When it finally began to ease, I looked around.

The church was small and sparse, with old wooden benches for seating and little in the way of decoration other than the beautiful, stained-glass windows. The fading sunlight filtered through the glass, filling the barren interior with rainbows and warmth. The place was still, with nothing to break the silence other than our uneven breathing. This church might still be in use, but there was no priest here at the moment. I wondered whether it would make a difference to the hellhounds or not.

I guess we'd find out soon enough.

I gathered my strength and forced myself upright. If death was my fate, then I'd damn well meet it on two feet, not four.

Tao stared up at me from his prone position. His face was ashen, his clothes little more than a mess of barely-held-together threads, and the bits of flesh that were exposed were covered in a cobwebby sheen of fiber.

"Don't ever do that again," he said. "Not even to save my life."

Despite the growing symphony of the hounds' cries and the ever-growing certainty that we might yet meet our death here, I smiled and held out a hand. He lurched up and clasped it, his fingers so warm compared with mine. Which meant his flames still burned deep inside him and of that, I was glad—if only because it suggested I'd put him back together right.

He climbed slowly to his feet—using me as a stabilizer more than anything else—then looked around. "Do you think the church keeps holy water close by?"

"Most churches do." I saw the simple basin and pedestal sitting near the entrance. "That's probably it."

He followed the line of my finger and nodded, but didn't walk over, moving behind the plain wooden pulpit instead. "Nothing much in the way of cups behind here."

I smiled and forced my feet forward. The scent of death and sulfur was once more beginning to stain the air, and my fingers twitched, wanting a weapon they didn't have.

"I think you'll find the church is canny enough to lock away its valuables in an area like this."

"I meant the paper kind of cup, not the sacred chalice type."

I glanced at him briefly. "What, you thought the priest might have been secretly sucking on a Coke during Sunday service?"

"Well, these days you never know." Amusement laced his tones as he followed me down the aisle, yet I could feel the tension in him, smell the fear. They were as sharp as my own. "Will the church offer any more protection than the cell?"

"I don't know." I hoped so, but I really didn't know enough about the supernatural to say.

The smell of sulfur suddenly intensified, catching in my throat and making both of us cough. The howls of the creatures swirled around us—a force that sent goose bumps fleeing across my skin and caused the temperature in the old church to suddenly plummet. The wooden doors shook, even though nothing had physically hit them.

I gripped one side of the basin and hoped like hell the water had been properly sanctified. It might be our only chance.

Tao gripped the other side, his expression resolute as we stared at the age-stained doors. The hounds stood on the other side. I could feel the heat of them. Smell their anger.

Again, the doors shook. I licked my lips, but I couldn't do much about the dryness in my throat or the trembling in my limbs.

Another crash, then the doors were wrenched open, revealing the two hounds. The smell of their blood mingled with their scent of death and hell and evil, swirling around the inside of the church, somehow darkening it.

But the creatures didn't move.

Neither did Tao or I.

Seconds ticked by. Sweat began trickling down my back and my hands grew clammy inside their wet bandages. The creatures growled low in their throats, the sound rumbling through the building—a sound of such power that dust and bits of masonry began to fall from the ceiling.

"Fuck," Tao said. "They could bring the whole place down on top of us."

"But this is still sacred ground. We might be buried, but at least we won't be torn apart."

"I'm not convinced it's a better option," he said, glancing nervously upward.

One of the hounds stepped forward. His paw hit the threshold and something flared—something bright and wholesome and somehow clean. The creature leapt back as if stung and their low growling intensified, until the air hummed with fury and the whole building shook under its assault.

"Well, at least that proves the theory that churches are sacred ground," Tao commented. "Now we've just got to hope it doesn't fall down around our ears."

As he said it, a huge chunk of plaster crashed onto the bench behind us. Dust flew upward in a cloud, briefly smothering the rainbow streams of sunshine and creating an even darker atmosphere.

And yet there was a strength here, too.

I could feel it, feel the heat of it . . .

Joy leapt through me. It wasn't the church, it was Azriel.

He appeared behind the hellhounds, Valdis held high above his head, the blade screaming in fury and dripping flame.

The hellhounds twisted around, then, as one, leapt. Azriel stepped to one side, and Valdis swept down, her scream almost ear shattering. She cut one creature in half, but it simply reformed and leapt again. Again the blade flew, separating flesh but not killing. The hounds were fast, not giving him the chance of a kill.

He needed help.

We threw the water on their backs. It hit the nearest hellhound full-force and splashed across the back of the other. Their flesh began to bubble and steam, and the first creature twisted and howled as his body disintegrated, the flesh dropping from his bones in chunks and the water like acid on his bones. Soon even they fell away, until all that remained was a writhing, boiling mass. Valdis hit the middle of it, and her blue fire exploded, sweeping away the shadowy smoke.

The second creature leapt. A warning surged up my throat, only to get stuck as Azriel swung around, his bright blade a smoking blur. It took the creature in the neck, severing its head from its torso. They fell to the ground in separate pieces that were consumed by the sword's dripping blue flames.

Azriel waited, holding Valdis over the remnants of the creatures until her screaming died and her flames muted. Only then did he turn around. His gaze swept the two of us and a small smile touched the corners of his lips. It said something about my exhaustion that I couldn't muster any sort of reaction.

"It was a very shrewd move to come to this church."

"It wasn't like we had much choice." I wiped a shaky hand across my forehead. It came away sweaty and bloody. I hadn't even realized I'd wounded my head. "Is the witch dead?"

"Yes." He hesitated, then added, "There were two men with her. I did not harm them, but I *did* restrain them."

"Then you need to give me the address so I can send it to Uncle Rhoan." *He* could uncover who the two men with Margaret were—and if they *weren't* two of the three men behind the consortium, he could take over the task of tracking them down, too. Right now, I'd done more than my fair share.

I stared at Azriel for a moment, unable to believe it was all over, then added, "I know they'll pay for their crimes with their lives, but somehow that just doesn't seem enough given what they did to little Hanna and the others."

Tao's hand grasped mine, squeezing lightly, but it was Azriel's small, cold smile that brought me the most comfort.

"Never fear, they will have an eternity to regret what they have done," he said softly. "The dark path has a special kind of purgatory for those who would destroy children."

"Good." I took a deep breath, but it didn't do a lot to ease the sick tension still roiling around inside me.

Which was odd, because the hellhounds were gone and we were safe . . .

And then I realized just what that sick tension was. *Mom.*

Something had happened to her.

For a moment the fear was so great I couldn't think and I couldn't breathe. Tao's grip on my arm tightened, and though I knew he was speaking, I had no idea what he said. There seemed to be a veil between me and the two of them—a veil that held the chill of death.

Oh God, oh God, *no!*

I wrenched free of Tao's grip and called once again to the Aedh. Heat and pain exploded through my brain, and an odd sort of redness blurred my vision.

Too much, something inside me whispered, *you've done too much.*

I didn't care, simply held on fiercely to the power, forcing it to sweep me from flesh to energy form. Then I spun out of the church and raced for Toorak and home.

Mom's home. The one place she felt safe. The one place she *didn't* have the protection of her Fravardin guards.

Except I'd sent Riley there . . .

No, please, no . . .

Everything was a blur. The landscape, my thoughts. Nothing connected, nothing meant anything, all that mattered was getting home, seeing Mom, making sure she was safe.

She *had* to be safe. Damn it, she'd promised she'd be safe! She was all I had, all the family I had. I might have grown up with Riley, Rhoan, Quinn, and Liander, but they weren't flesh and blood, no matter how much I might love them.

I couldn't lose my mom. I just *couldn't*.

Familiar landmarks began appearing through the blur of movement. I reached for greater speed, felt agony shimmer through every particle, and knew I would pay when I re-formed.

But I didn't care.

Nothing mattered, nothing except getting home and Mom being safe.

She's safe. She has to be.

It was a sentence that looped through my mind. A hope I knew deep down to be false.

There were vehicles outside our house. Black vehicles. Directorate vehicles.

No, no, no, NO!

I raced down the driveway and past the two men collecting evidence near the front door. It was whole and untouched, showing no sign of forced entry, and yet the fear in me increased.

I flowed into the entrance hall. There were voices deep in the house. Familiar voices. Riley and Rhoan, and one other. One I *didn't* expect.

Director Hunter.

Why was she here? What the hell did she have to do with my mother?

They were in the kitchen, at the rear of the house. I rushed on, the fear in me so heavy it was beginning to weigh me down.

There was blood on the marble tiles just outside the kitchen doorway.

And more blood on the door itself.

And smears of something else—something that almost resembled flesh—on the wall inside.

Please don't let it be Mom. Please don't . . .

I swept into the room. Saw Riley. Rhoan. Hunter. Saw them hunkered near the center island.

Moved to the right so that they no longer blocked my view.

Saw the hair. The face. The head.

Just the head.

Mom.

Everything seemed to explode. My brain, my heart, my strength.

My body re-formed and I dropped to the floor, as bloody as the tiles that surrounded me. There were gasps, movement, hands on my skin, questions.

But I couldn't move, couldn't think, couldn't see.

All I could do was scream.

Chapter Fifteen

THE DAYS PASSED IN A BLUR.

A never-ending, agony-filled blur.

Because of Mom's death, because of the way she'd died—and because I'd pushed my body to extremes and had all but broken it.

And the worst of it was, I didn't care.

Not about anything or anyone.

Especially not myself.

I'd failed the most important person in my life, and there was no escaping that knowledge. No escaping the guilt of it.

Riley took me home. Not to my home, but hers, keeping me safe, keeping me away from anywhere and anything that might remind me of Mom, of the way she'd been tortured and then dismembered.

I was never alone. Someone was with me twenty-four/seven. I was aware of them on a peripheral level, knew that they kept me alive and functioning, and updated on what was happening.

But nothing really registered on a conscious level. I didn't *care* what they said. Every inch of me was raw—and it was a rawness that was both physical *and* emotional.

My body was battered and bruised, and my sight,

like my hearing and my voice, had been damaged. It would recover, because I was half wolf and self-healing was a part of my heritage, but it would take time.

It could have taken an eternity and I doubted it would matter. Nothing mattered. Nothing *could* matter. Not when I failed to save my own mother.

Part of me wanted to die, to just walk away from the heartache and the pain that burned through every fiber.

It would be easy enough to do. I could slip away to the gray fields, let my body waste away and maybe find a peace in death that would not be possible in life.

It was tempting.

But if I did that, then I would never know who killed her, or why.

And I would never taste the sweetness of revenge.

It was that need, more than anything, that eventually dragged me back to the realm of full awareness.

Which didn't mean the days that followed became any clearer or that the pain eased. My body might have started healing itself, but my heart was broken, and no amount of consoling from my second family or my friends could ever heal that.

Mom was gone.

End of story—at least in this life, this time, and with me.

I could only hope that we'd meet again, somewhere down the track in another lifetime—because we at least still had that. Azriel had assured me that her soul had moved on, and that she could be reborn. Unlike little Hanna, who was gone forever. But at least I'd given her vengeance.

Mine would come.

I held on to that knowledge fiercely, feeling it wrap around me like a security blanket, letting it warm me and give me strength as we sorted through the mess that was the investigation—an investigation that got nowhere fast—and then finally the funeral arrangements once the remnants of her body had been released.

But Mom was a media star, and her funeral was a circus. I went through the motions, constantly flanked by someone who cared—Riley and Quinn, Liander and Rhoan, or Tao and Ilianna, Liana, Ronan, and Darci—smiling vacantly and answering by rote when confronted by reporters or her many clients.

Even Lucian was there, keeping his distance but nevertheless letting me know that he was close if I needed him.

We held her *real* service a few days later. It was small and intimate, just Riley, Quinn, Rhoan, Liander, and all their children, as well as what remained of my family—Tao and Ilianna. Mike was also there, and though he showed no outward sign of grief, he seemed even more remote than usual. We shared her favorite champagne and stories of her life as a wolf chaplain blessed her body while she passed through to cremation.

Which had led me here, standing alone in a clearing in the middle of this vast, wooded stretch of land situated near Harrietville, high in the Victorian Alps region.

She'd owned this place for ten years, and had planned to retire and raise lots of grandchildren here.

Plans that were so much dust on the wind.

As her body soon would be.

Tears stung my eyes. I closed them, then raised my face to the sky, letting the fading sunlight warm my skin and dry the tears on my cheeks.

I'd shed more than my fair share over these last few weeks. But the time had come to move on—however reluctant I might be, and however hard that would be.

Life went on. Or at least, my life went on.

And Mom would have been the first one to tell me to get on with it.

I smiled and looked down at the small box in my hands. It was a simple wooden box, nothing ornate. She'd asked for that, just as she'd asked for this. A simple good-bye, just me and her, high up in the hills that she'd loved.

The wind swirled around us, crisp and fresh, filled with the scent of eucalyptus and the musk of the kangaroos that grazed nearby. I waited, watching the colorful fingers of sunset creep across the sky, until the blue had become a kaleidoscope of red, orange, and yellow.

Time, something within me whispered.

With fingers that trembled ever so slightly, I opened the little latch and raised the box above my head.

"May your ashes fill this place with the peace and beauty that was yours, and may you find that same peace and beauty in whatever path is now yours."

I tipped the box, letting her ashes loose on the wind, watching her scatter through the trees.

"Good-bye, Mom," I whispered, my voice broken with the tears that were flowing down my cheeks. "I love you."

And I will find your killer. No matter how long it took or what I had to do. I had a lot of leads to follow—the human shifters, the men from the consortium, Handberry and whatever the bug had picked up in his office, to name just a few—and behind one of them, I would find her killer.

There was no answer to either my words or my unspoken vow. There could never again be an answer. Yet just for a moment, I thought I heard the joyful sound of her laughter.

Then it faded, as the sunlight faded, and I was left standing alone in the middle of the shadowed clearing.

I swiped at the tears, then dropped to my knees and picked up the small shovel I'd carried up here with me. I dug a hole in the soft soil, then kissed the box and buried it.

Then, with a final smile at the forest that was her final resting place, I turned and made my way back down to my car.

To find I was no longer alone.

Director Hunter was leaning against my SUV, her arms crossed and her demeanor reminding me somewhat of a snake about to strike.

I stopped and stared at her. Eye-to-eye contact. The worst thing you could do when faced with a vampire as old and as powerful as her.

I should have been scared. I wasn't. Far from it, in fact. This moment was *mine*. Mine and Mom's. She should *never* have intruded.

Anger surged and I had to clench my fists against the sudden urge to do something stupid—like attack her.

"It's an extremely wise decision to restrain yourself," she said softly, "because any such attempt would only end badly. For yourself, at any rate."

My smile was thin and cold. "Keep out of my head, or I *will* annihilate you."

She arched a thin eyebrow. "You truly think you're capable of such a feat? Because many people have tried over the years and, as you can see, none has succeeded."

"Have you ever seen an Aedh reach into someone's body and tear out their heart, Director?"

"No, but I've seen more than my fair share of vampires and various other creatures do it."

"Ah," I said softly, as I called to the Aedh within. Her power flowed through me gently—carefully—and I concentrated it on my hand, letting my fingers become little more than transparent wisps. The embers of pain stirred enough to warn me not to try for more—not yet, not until I'd fully recovered—but I had no intention of doing so. This was a demonstration, nothing more. "The difference is, with an Aedh, you don't see them coming. Nor can you smell them, or hear the beat of life through their veins. They don't exist on any known plane, and are invisible right up until the moment they destroy you."

Her green eyes glittered despite the shadows that hid much of her features. A hunter with a prey in its sight. It really *should* have scared me. Maybe that part of me was still too numb from my loss to react sensibly.

"Now that we have the pissing contest out of the way, let's get down to business, shall we?"

I released the energy and re-formed my hand. The veil of tiredness ran through me. It was going to be a while yet before I could claim that part of me more fully. "You came to me, Hunter, so why don't you tell me what the hell you want?"

"I want to help you."

I snorted loudly. "Yeah, right. Believing that." The only thing Hunter was interested in furthering was her own agenda.

She arched that eyebrow again. "You do not believe that I want to catch your mother's killer?"

"Oh, I believe you will place the full might of the Directorate behind it. I just don't believe that's what you actually came all the way up here to tell me."

"And you'd be right."

She uncrossed her arms, then pushed away from the car and walked toward me, every movement economical and yet powerful. Dangerous. She stopped several feet away, her scent teasing the air. It was pleasant enough—until you saw what lay underneath it.

There was no warmth in her, no lingering vestige of humanity. She was a vampire in thought and deed, and that was all she cared about.

She might have started the Directorate, but it hadn't been for humanity's sake. Rather, it had been little more than a PR exercise for the vampire council.

If ruthlessness and cunning had a smell, then it would be this woman.

"You are your mother's daughter, aren't you?" she commented. "But you are right, of course. It benefited the council to have humanity protected by a body perceived as separate from the council."

Part of me wondered what Rhoan would say to something like that, and whether Jack actually knew he was running a front for the council. But the truth was, it didn't really matter. Not to me. And I very much suspected it wouldn't matter to humanity, either, simply because the Directorate *did* protect them.

"Director, either tell me why you're here, or leave."

She gave me one of those cool vampire smiles. "I want you to work for me."

For me. Not the directorate. *Her.* "Why?"

"I believe we could be useful to each other."

I paused. "Why would you think I'd in any way want to help the vampire council?"

"Because you want to find your mother's killer."

"The Directorate has that investigation well under control." And even if there were very little in the way of leads, I had faith in Uncle Rhoan. If anyone could catch whoever had done this, he could.

"The Directorate, as efficient as it has proven itself to be at hunting and killing those foolish enough to transgress against humans, has neither the proficiency nor the potency of the high council. Trust me when I say it is like comparing a breeze to a cyclone."

"To quote an old, somewhat clichéd saying . . . I wouldn't trust you as far as I could throw you."

Humor flirted with her lips. I wondered if emotion ever did.

"Which is most definitely wise. However, I am serious. I want your help, and in return you will have the full services of the council and its Cazadors to hunt down this killer."

"Why the hell would I want the help of the Cazadors? They're little more than leashed murderers, aren't they?" A fact I knew because Uncle Quinn had once been one. He'd survived the experience, which apparently was rare in that line of work.

"The Cazadors are the most dangerous and deadly hunters ever created. Once they are unleashed, they will not stop until they bring down and destroy their target. If anyone can find the person or persons behind your mother's slaughter, it will be them." She hesitated, and that cold, cool smile twitched her lips again. "They do not have the legal restrictions that the Directorate has."

I stared at her for a moment, trying to ignore the chill creeping across my skin, the knot of fear deep inside that suggested even standing here listening to this was a very dangerous thing to do.

"I can't give you my father. He doesn't exist on this plane anymore. His recourse to flesh has been stripped from him."

"So you have had contact with him?"

"Briefly. He didn't really tell me anything I didn't already know."

If she sensed the lie, she didn't react to it. "Which means there is the possibility he might contact you in the future."

"Maybe." I shrugged. "So is that all you want me to do? Inform you when my absent parent contacts me?"

"In part, yes."

"And the rest of it?"

She tilted her head sideways and studied me for a minute. "You are aware, of course, that all three of the dark path's gates were recently opened?"

I nodded, then crossed my arms and waited for the rest of it. And tried to ignore the thick knot of apprehension growing in my stomach.

"Were you also aware that, in the brief time they were open, things came back through?"

I stared at her, then licked my suddenly dry lips and said, "Things? What sort of things?"

She shrugged. "Creatures who can gain flesh and walk in this world, and others who maintain spectral form and who can only be seen by those with certain talents."

Like mine.

"I am not a hunter or a killer, nor do I wish to be." But Azriel was. And if things had come back through the gates, why hadn't he mentioned it?

Then again, why would he?

I was not part of his world. I was just a chore—someone he had to follow against his own wishes and desires.

Although if things *had* come through, then it explained why the Mijai were apparently so busy—and why he was so pissed off about having to tag around after me.

"We would not expect you to kill. We have Cazadors more than capable of doing that."

I frowned. "Then what do you want me to do?"

"Hunt."

"No." It came out automatically. Walking the gray fields to talk to a soul lost or confused was one thing.

Hunting an escapee from the bowels of hell was another matter altogether.

"But what if one of those creatures was responsible for your mother's death?"

"It wasn't." Again, the response was automatic. And yet, it *was* a possibility—it was just one I didn't *want* to consider. Mom had spent half her life conversing with spirits. I didn't want to believe one of them had killed her.

Hunter merely smiled. It was a cold, inhuman thing. "The crime scene was clean. Completely and utterly. There was no DNA, no prints, no evidence of any kind that anyone other than your mother, the housekeeper, and the occasional guest—all of whom have been vetted and cleared—has ever been in that kitchen. The place was not wiped down in any way. There is simply nothing there to indicate who or what might have done this."

I didn't say anything. I couldn't say anything. Not when she was giving me facts that could only ever lead to a conclusion I didn't want to believe.

"The Directorate will never find this killer if it is a spirit, but we can," Hunter said. "Trust me on that."

I stared at her, digesting not so much the words as the unspoken threat behind them. "You would ensure that?"

She looked surprised that I would even ask such a question. "Of course."

"But *why*?"

"Because I have always done what must be done to keep my people safe. And these spirits—as well as the people who opened the gates and released them—threaten that."

Her people. Not humanity. Not the rest of us. "But you've already said you have Cazadors who can hunt spirits, so why do you need me?"

"We have Cazadors who astral-travel, true, but if we had someone who could walk the fields at will and track down the location of our targets, it would make their job easier."

There was a ring of truth to her words, but that didn't mean I believed them. There was more to this. There were the gates, and the keys, and her desire to control them for the high council's benefit.

But to achieve any of that, she needed me on her team.

"The one thing you have to ask yourself, Risa," she said softly, "is just how desperately you want to find your mother's killer."

I didn't answer, simply because it was a pointless question. We both already knew the answer.

"Become an adviser to the council, and I will throw every available resource we have at tracking down those responsible." She paused, and that cold, cruel smile touched her lips again. "Refuse, and not only will the killer go free, but you will bear some responsibility for whatever destruction hell's escapees wreak."

That wasn't fair, and we both knew it. But she hadn't come up here to play fair. She'd come up here to get what she wanted.

And what she wanted was me.

It would be madness to accept. Sheer and utter madness. I knew it, but I did it anyway.

"You betray me, you play me or try to control me in any way, and I will destroy you, Hunter. Whether you believe I can or not."

"I will play as fair with you as you play with me."
She held out her hand. "Deal?"

"Deal," I said, and clasped her hand. Her flesh was
cool against mine, her grip like iron.

And I knew in that instant I'd made a deal with the
devil herself.

But I didn't fucking care.

I had a vow to keep, and a killer to hunt down.

Vengeance *would* be mine.

If you loved

Darkness Unbound

be sure not to miss

the next thrilling installment of Risa's story in

Darkness Rising

by

Keri Arthur

Coming soon from Piatkus

THE HOUSE STILL SMELLED OF DEATH.

Two months had passed since Mom's murder, but the air still echoed with her agony and I knew if I breathed deep enough, I'd catch the hint of old blood.

But at least there were no visible reminders. The Directorate's cleanup team had done a good job of removing the evidence.

Bile rose up my throat, and I briefly closed my eyes. I'd seen her—had seen what had been done to her—and it haunted me every night in my dreams. But in many ways, those dreams were also responsible for me finally being able to walk through the front door today.

I'd done enough remembering, and shed enough tears. Now I wanted revenge, and that wasn't going to happen if I waited for others to hunt down the killers. No, I needed to be a part of it. I needed to do something to help ease the ferocity of the dreams—

dreams that came from the guilty knowledge that I should have been there for her. That if I had, I might have been able to prevent this.

I drew in a deep breath that did little to steady the almost automatic wash of fury, and discovered something else. Her scent still lingered.

And not just her scent. Everything she'd been, and everything she'd done—all her love and energy and compassion—filled this place with a warmth that still radiated from the very walls.

For the first time since I'd scattered her ashes in the hills that she'd loved, I smiled.

She would never entirely be gone from this world. She'd done too much, and helped too many people, for her memory to be erased completely.

And that was one hell of a legacy.

Still, despite the echoes of the warmth and love that had once filled these rooms, I had no intention of keeping the house. Not when all I had to do was step into the kitchen to be reminded of everything that had happened.

I walked along the hallway, my boots echoing on the polished marble floor. Aside from the few items of furniture placed to give prospective buyers an idea of each room's size and purpose, the house was empty. Mike—who'd been Mom's financial adviser and was still mine—had made all the arrangements, talking to the real estate people on my behalf and shifting most of the furniture into storage so I could deal with it later. Only the items in the two safes remained untouched, and that was a task only I could handle—although it was the one thing I'd been avoiding until now.

I drew in a shuddery breath, then slowly climbed the carpeted stairs. Once I reached the landing, I headed for Mom's bedroom down at the far end of the hall. The air had a disused smell. Maybe the people employed to keep the house spotless until it sold hadn't been as generous with the deodorizer up here.

But the soft hint of oranges and sunshine teased my nostrils as I walked into Mom's bedroom, and just for a moment it felt like she was standing beside me.

Which was silly, because she'd long since moved on, but my fingers still twitched with the urge to reach for her.

I walked across the thick carpet and opened the double doors to her wardrobe. Her clothes had already been donated to charity, but somehow seeing this emptiness hit me in a way that the emptiness of the other rooms had not. I'd often played in here as a kid, dressing up in her silkiest gowns and smearing my face—and no doubt said gowns—with her makeup.

She'd never once been angry. She'd always laughed and joined the fun, even letting me do *her* face.

I swiped at the tear that appeared on my cheek and resolutely walked into the bathroom. Most people wouldn't think of looking for a safe in an en suite, which is exactly why Mom had installed her second one here. This was where she'd stored her most precious jewelry.

I opened the double doors under the basin and ducked down. The safe was embedded in the wall and visible only because all of Mom's makeup had been cleared away.

After typing in the code, I pressed my hand against the reader. Red light flickered across my fingertips; then there was a soft click as the safe opened.

I took a deep breath, then sat and pulled the door all the way open. Inside were all her favorite items, including the chunky jade bracelet she'd bought the last time she was in New Zealand, only a few weeks before her death. There was also a stack of microdrive photo disks and, finally, an envelope.

There was nothing written on the front of the envelope, but faint wisps of orange teased my nostrils as I flipped it over and slid a nail along the edge to open it. Inside was a folded piece of paper that smelled of Mom. I took another, somewhat shaky breath and opened it.

I'm sorry that I had to leave you in the dark, my darling daughter, it said, and I could almost imagine her saying the words as I read them. Could almost feel her warm breath stirring the hair near my cheek. *But I was given little other choice. Besides, I saw my death long ago and knew it was the price I had to pay for having you. I never regretted my choice—not then, and most certainly not now, when that death is at my doorstep. Don't ever think I accepted my fate placidly. I didn't. But the cosmos could show me no way out that didn't also involve your death or Riley's. Or worse, both of you. In the end, it just had to be.*

Live long, love well, and I will see you in the next life. I love you always. Mom.

I closed my eyes against the sting of tears. Damn it, I wouldn't cry again. I *wouldn't*.

But my tear ducts weren't taking any notice.

I swiped at the moisture, then sat back on my heels. Oddly enough, I almost felt better. At least now I knew why she'd refused to tell me what was going on. She'd seen my death—and Riley's—if we'd intervened. And I would have intervened. I mean, she was my *mother*.

And as a result, I'd have died.

Her death still hurt—would always hurt—but a tiny weight seemed to have lifted from my soul.

I glanced down at the letter in my hand, smiling slightly as her scent spun around me, then folded it up again and tucked it into my pocket. That one piece of paper was worth more than anything else in her safe.

I scooped up the remainder of the jewels, but as I rose, awareness washed over me. Someone—or something—was in the house.

I was half werewolf, and my senses were keen. Though I hadn't actually locked the front door, I doubted any humans could have entered without me hearing. Humans tended to walk heavily, even when they were trying to sneak, and with the house almost empty the sound would have echoed. But this invader was as silent as a ghost. And it wasn't nonhuman, either, because in the midst of awareness came a wash of heat—not body heat, but rather the heat of a powerful presence.

An Aedh.

And he was in spirit form rather than physical.

My pulse skipped, then raced. The last time I'd felt something like this, I'd been in the presence of my father.

The sensation of power coming up from the floor

below was growing stronger. Whoever it was, they were closing in fast. I needed help, and I needed it *now*. And the only person I could call on so quickly was the one person I was trying to avoid. Azriel—the reaper who was linked to my Chi. I hadn't heard or seen him since Mom's death, and part of me had been hoping to keep it that way.

I should have known fate would have other ideas.

Of course, Azriel wasn't just a reaper. He was a Mijai, a dark angel who hunted and killed the things that returned from the depths of hell—or the dark path, as the reapers preferred to call it—to steal from this world.

But what he hunted now wasn't a soul stealer or even my soul.

He—like everyone else—was looking for my father.

Azriel, I thought silently, not wanting to alert whoever was approaching that I was calling for help. I knew from past experience that Azriel could hear thoughts as well as spoken words. *If you're out there, come fast. There's an Aedh in the house and it could be my father.*

He didn't answer; nor did the heat of his presence sting the air. Either he *had* given up following me or something else was going on.

Which was typical. There was never a fucking reaper around when you wanted one. I took a deep breath that did little to calm the sudden flare of nerves, and said, "Whoever you are, reveal yourself."

"That, as I have said before, is impossible, as I can no longer attain flesh." The reply was measured, cultured, and very familiar.

Because it sounded like me. A male version of me.

My father.

"The last time you and I met, the Raziq came running. And that was your fault, by the way, not mine." I crossed my arms and leaned back against the wall. The pose might appear casual, but every muscle quivered, ready to launch into action should the need arise. Not that I'd have any hope against a full Aedh—I knew *that* from experience.

"I have taken precautions this time." His cultured tones reverberated around the small room, and his presence—or rather the energy of it—was almost smothering. "They will not sense me in this house just yet."

"Why not? What have you done this time that's any different?"

He paused, as if considering his reply. "Because I was once a priest, I emit a certain type of energy. If I remain stationary for too long, they can trace me."

Facts I knew, thanks to Azriel. "That doesn't answer my question."

"Wards have been set. They not only give misinformation as to my whereabouts, but they will prevent any beings such as myself from entering."

Hence Azriel's failure to appear. Reapers were energy beings, the same as the Aedh.

I didn't bother asking how'd he'd actually set the wards when he couldn't interact with this world, simply because he'd undoubtedly had his slaves do it. Or rather, his Razan, as the Aedh tended to call them. "And are you sure these wards will work?"

"Yes. I have no wish for you to be captured a second time."

So he knew about that—and it meant he was

keeping a closer eye on me than I'd assumed. "So why are you here? What do you want?"

"I want what I have always wanted—for you to find the keys."

"And destroy them?"

"That goes without saying."

Did it? I really wasn't so sure. "You haven't yet told me what will happen when the keys are destroyed, and I'd prefer to know that before I do anything rash." Like endanger the very fabric of my world.

The heat of him drew closer. It spun around me—an almost threatening presence that made my skin crawl. And it wasn't just the sheer sense of power he was exuding, but the lack of any sense of humanity. This was a being who'd worn flesh rarely even when he was capable of it, and who had no love or understanding for those of us who did.

Which made his desire to find and destroy the keys even more puzzling. Why would he care what would happen to this world if the keys were used? He *wouldn't*. Which meant something else was going on. Something he wasn't telling me.

Although I wasn't surprised that he was keeping secrets. That seemed to be par for the course for everyone searching for these damn keys.

"I am sure that when the keys are destroyed, everything will remain as it currently is."

"But aren't the keys now tuned to the power of the gates?"

"They are," my father said. "Destroying them should sever the link, and the gates should remain intact."

It was those *shoulds* that were worrying me. "You

know," I said slowly, "it seems that it would be a whole lot safer for everyone if these keys were to remain as they are—indefinitely hidden."

Energy surged, making the hairs along my arms and the back of my neck rise. "Do you honestly think the Raziq will let matters lie?"

"Honestly? No. But they can't kill me if they need me to find the keys."

"Then what about your friends? Such a move could place them in peril."

"Not if I let the Raziq grab me. Once they realize I can't help them, I'm guessing they'll forget me and start concentrating on you again." After all, he might not know where the keys actually were, but he had some general knowledge of where they'd been sent, and he knew what they'd been disguised as.

Although admittedly, handing myself over to the Raziq wasn't at the top of my list. I'd barely survived their interrogation the last time.

The threat in the air was growing stronger. My father's energy was so sharp and strong that it hit with almost physical force. Part of me wanted to cower, but the more stubborn part refused to give in.

"You forget it is not just the Raziq who want the keys."

"The reapers aren't going to—"

"I am not talking about the reapers." His cultured tones had become soft, deadly. "I am talking about *me*."

The words were barely out of his nonexistent mouth when he hit me. Though he didn't have a flesh form, and though he'd told me he couldn't interact with things of this world, his energy wrapped around my body, thrusting me upward, squeezing so tightly it felt like every bone in my body would break. Then he flung me back to the floor, all but smothering me with the fierce, blanketing heat of his presence.

"How the hell did you—"

"You are my blood," he cut in, his voice a mere whisper that reverberated through my entire being. "It is the reason you can find the keys, and it is the reason I can do to you what I cannot to others."

Meaning he *couldn't* do this to Ilianna and Tao. But even as relief surged, he added, "But do not think your friends are any safer. I have Razan to do my bidding."

"If you touch them, you'll get nothing from me."

Amusement seemed to touch the fierce energy surrounding me. "Do you really think you have the strength and will to resist me? You might hold out for a little while, but in the end you *will* do what I want."

Not if I'm dead, I thought. And therein lay the crux of the matter. I didn't want to die. Not until I'd at least found Mom's killers.

"You *will* find those keys for me," he added.

"Go fuck—"

But I didn't get the rest of the sentence out, because he flung me violently across the room. I hit the shower doors sideways, tearing them off their hinges, and fell in a tangled heap of shattered glass, twisted metal, and bruised limbs.

"You will get those keys for me," he said, "or what I do to you today I will have done to your friends tomorrow. Only my Razan will ensure they do not survive the experience."

Bastard, I wanted to say, but the words stuck somewhere in my throat, caught up in the desperate struggle to breathe.

"The information you need to find the first key is in the Dušan's book," he continued as his essence continued to bear down on me. My lungs were beginning to burn and panic surged, making it even harder to breathe. "Only one of my blood can read it, and only from the gray fields while the book lies here. But it must be retrieved from the Raziq first. They have it concealed. And again, only one of my blood will be able to find or see it."

"Why—" the words came out croaky, barely audible thanks to my lack of air. I licked my lips and tried again. "Why not simply tell me everything you know?"

"Because if I only feed you small pieces of the puzzle, you are still almost useless to the Raziq if they capture you."

I guess that made sense, even if the rest of it didn't.

"You still have the locker key," he continued. "Go there today at one PM, and you will find further instructions."

"Why not just give them to me now?"

"Because my Razan foolishly set the wards for a brief window, and I am out of time." The smothering energy evaporated, and suddenly I could breathe again. "And the less I am close to you, the less likely the Raziq are to use you to come after me."

Yeah, right. There was more to these fucking games of his than just a need to keep his distance.

"And what happens once I get the book?" I asked instead.

He didn't answer immediately, and his retreating energy became more distant.

"I must go."

"Wait!"

But he didn't. I drew a shaky breath and slowly picked myself up from the shattered remains of the shower doors.

"Are you all right?"

The words emerged from the silence even as the heat of Azriel's presence washed over me. Reapers, like the Aedh, were creatures of light and shadows, with an energy so fierce their mere presence burned the very air around them. And while they weren't true flesh-and-blood beings, they could attain that form if they wished.

Which is how I'd come about. My father had spent one night in flesh form with my mother and, in the process, created me—a half-breed mix of werewolf and Aedh who was lucky enough to mostly get the best bits of both and few of the downsides.

"Do I look all right?" I said, trying to extract myself from the remains of the shower door.

Azriel appeared in front of me, taking my arm and holding me steady as my foot caught on an edge and I stumbled. His fingers were warm against my skin—warm and disturbing.

While reapers were basically shapeshifters, able to take on any form that would comfort the dying on their final journey, they did possess one "true" shape. And while the combination of my Aedh blood and my psychic skills usually allowed me to see whatever form they used to claim their soul, for some weird reason I saw Azriel's real form rather than whatever shape he decided to take on. And that shape was compellingly attractive.

His face was chiseled, almost classical in its beauty, and yet possessing a hard edge that spoke of a man who'd won more than his fair share of battles. He was shirtless, his skin a warm, suntanned brown, and his abs well defined. The leather strap that held his sword in place seemed to emphasize the width of his shoulders, and faded jeans clung to his legs, accentuating their lean strength. A stylized black tatt that resembled the left half of a wing swept around his ribs from underneath his arm, the tips brushing across the left side of his neck.

Only it wasn't a tatt. It was a Dušan—a darker, more stylized brother to the one that had crawled onto my left arm and now resided within my flesh. They were designed to protect us when we walked the gray fields. We'd been sent them by person or persons unknown, although Azriel suspected it was probably my father's doing. He was one of the few left in this world—or the next—who had the power to make them.

Azriel's gaze met mine, his blue eyes—one as vivid and bright as a sapphire, the other almost navy, and as dark as a storm-driven sea—giving little away.

"I have seen you in worse condition," he commented. His voice was mellow and rich, and on any other man it would have been sexy. But this *wasn't* a man. He merely held that form. And if I reminded myself of that enough, then maybe that tiny, insane part of me that was attracted to this reaper would move on. "What happened?"

"My fucking father." I pulled my arm from his

grip and tried to ignore the warmth lingering on my skin as I thrust a hand through my sweaty hair. "And his spell prevented you from answering my call, didn't it?"

He nodded, and I leaned a shoulder against the nearest wall. My legs were still as shaky as hell, and my stomach was still doing unsteady flip-flops.

"What did your father want?"

"Aside from beating me up and threatening to kill my friends, you mean? He wants me to find the keys, and he got rather irked when I suggested that the damn things would probably be better where they are."

He frowned. "Why would you want to leave them as they are?"

"Because if no one can find them, then they can't endanger the fabric of my world."

"But that is foolishness. If they are out there, they will eventually be found. The Raziq will never give up looking."

"And my father won't let me give it up, either." I sighed again and walked unsteadily across the room to scoop up the scattered jewelry and photo disks. "He's directed me back to the locker at the railway station. Apparently, he's had further instructions left there."

"If he was here, why did he not simply tell you?"

"He claimed he was out of time," I said irritably. "But who knows? It's not like anyone is actually confiding in me."

Azriel studied me for a moment, expression neutral even if a faint hint of annoyance flickered through the heated energy of his presence. "I tell you what I can."

"No, you tell me what you think I need to know. There is a difference."

He didn't dispute it. No surprise there, given it was the truth.

"The last time you followed your father's instructions, you ended up being captured by the Raziq."

"My father won't be anywhere near me this time, so he claims it shouldn't be a problem. Besides, if the Raziq wanted me, they could have come after me anytime they wished."

"I doubt it. The wards that Ilianna has set around your apartment are as strong as those at the Brindle. They would make it difficult for the Raziq to enter."

The Brindle was the witch depository, and few outside the covens even knew of its existence. "We were told that the magic surrounding the Brindle wouldn't keep the Aedh out, so it's unlikely to keep them out of our apartment."

"Granted, but they also now know that I guard you, and they could not be certain whether there would be one or more Mijai waiting for them if they *did* attempt it. The Raziq are single-minded when it comes to their goals, but they are not stupid."

"So why haven't they snatched me outside the apartment? And why don't the wards make it difficult for you?"

"I am attuned to your Chi, so any magic that allows you to pass should also allow me."

"And yet the wards my father set up *did* stop you?"

"Because those particular wards were designed to reject energy forms. Human wards are not, so even the strongest will not prevent the Raziq—or a reaper—from getting through."

"If the Raziq did come after me a second time," I asked, suddenly curious, "would you actually stop them?"

He raised an eyebrow. "Do you think I wouldn't?"

"To be honest, I have no idea what you'll do in *any* situation." Especially given how many times in the past he'd stated that he would not interfere in the daily events of my life. And in fact, he hadn't— not when I'd been attacked by humans who could somehow attain half-animal form, and not when the Raziq had captured me. Although he had, at least, saved me and Tao—one of my best friends—from the hellhounds.

But once again he changed the subject. "You are fortunate the Aedh can only form a permanent telepathic connection through sex. Otherwise, your trip to the railway station would now be compromised."

Did that mean that Lucian—the fallen Aedh who'd become my lover—had formed a telepathic connection with me? Or was that one of the skills that had been stripped from him when they'd ripped the wings from his flesh? I didn't know, but I suspected it might be wise to find out—even if I was positive Lucian was on no one's side but his own. Still, given what the priests had done to him, I had no doubt he'd kill them given the slightest opportunity. His punishment might have happened many centuries ago, but the anger still burned in him.

I frowned at Azriel. "The priests rifled through my thoughts when they held me captive, and they certainly *didn't* do that via sex."

He nodded. "Aedh—like reapers—can read thoughts when in the same room as a person, but unlike human telepaths we are incapable of doing so from any great distance."

Thank God for small mercies. Although I did wish my rebellious hormones would remember more often that, when I was in his presence, he knew exactly what I was thinking. "Then you'd better be vigilant. If the Raziq get their hands on me, any information we get from the locker will be theirs."

Because I certainly wouldn't be able to resist them. I might be psychic, but my skills were on a more ethereal level. And as I'd already discovered, me fighting the Raziq was like a leaf fighting a gale.

"When it comes to you, I have learned to be *very* vigilant."

"And just what is *that* supposed to mean?"

"Nothing more than it says." But a glint in his eyes belied his words.

Desire calls. Danger lurks. But . . .

DESTINY KILLS

'She's got a dangerous secret – and powers far beyond human . . .'

When Destiny McCree wakes up beside a dead man on
an Oregon beach, she knows only this: she has to keep moving,
keep searching and keep one step ahead of the forces that have
been pursuing her from the heart of Scotland to this isolated spot.
Why? The death of her lover has left her alone, with little memory
of her past. A glimmering serpent-shaped ring is the one clue
she has – and a bargaining chip in a most dangerous game.

Enter Trae Wilson, a master thief with a sexy, knowing grin
and a secret agenda of his own. Destiny and Trae both have
powers far beyond human – and both are running for their lives.
Together they're riding a tide of danger, magic and lust . . . but
with killers stalking their every move, they must use any means
necessary, even each other, to survive – until the shocking secret
of one woman's destiny finally unravels.

978-0-7499-5302-7

Do you love fiction with a supernatural twist?

Want the chance to hear news about your favourite authors (and the chance to win free books)?

Keri Arthur
S. G. Browne
P.C. Cast
Christine Feehan
Jacquelyn Frank
Larissa Ione
Sherrilyn Kenyon
Jackie Kessler
Jayne Ann Krentz and Jayne Castle
Martin Millar
Kat Richardson
J.R. Ward
David Wellington

Then visit the Piatkus website and blog
www.piatkus.co.uk | www.piatkusbooks.net

And follow us on Facebook and Twitter
www.facebook.com/piatkusfiction | www.twitter.com/piatkusbooks

piatkus